Eyes of the Beholder

Eyes of the Beholder

Barbara Robinson

Published by,
BeuMar Publishing Company
The BeuMar Building,
12 W. Montgomery Street
Suite 100
Baltimore, Maryland 21230

This is a work of fiction. The characters have been invented by the author. Any resemblance to actual persons, living or dead, is purely coincidental.

FIRST EDITION – June 2002

Printed in the United States of America

Barbara A. Robinson
The BeuMar Building
12 West Montgomery Street
Baltimore, MD 21230
410-727-1558
barbara@selfpride.com

Library of Congress Catalog Card Number: 2002092476

Robinson, Barbara A.
Eyes of the Beholder

ISBN: 0-9720851-0-6

10 9 8 7 6 5 4 3 2 1

USA $18.00
Canada $23.50

"Sometimes a heart waits a long time for happiness. Sometimes it gets lost along the way. But almost always it finds its way to the one it really loves."

ACKNOWLEDGMENTS

There are so many people I need to thank for making this book become a reality. I wanted to get a male's perspective of its contents so I contacted my friend Victor Holiday. He read the manuscript and gave me feedback. Thank you Victor for your support. I can't forget Jericka's friend, Tammy Lancaster, an avid reader. Tammy read the manuscript through several edits to ensure that it would become a book that she would find interesting. Thanks, Tammy. Thanks to Danita Boonchaisri, who edited this work so many times she probably dreamed about it. Danita not only edited the work, she added valuable suggestions for changes. And to my daughter, Jericka, what can I say except, "Thank you for your encouragement and your persistence for me to finish the manuscript; *Eyes of the Beholder* is your baby." Since Jericka was in elementary school she claimed the title following a story I wrote for her. Well, Jericka, here it is, enjoy!

PROLOGUE

When Jericka, my oldest daughter, was in high-school and I worked at the District Court of Maryland, she had to write a story for school and asked that I help her with the story. I made up a story about a woman whose face was scarred and her daughter was ashamed of her. Since then that plot belonged to Jericka. She immediately took over ownership. It didn't matter that the cliche' is "Beauty is in the Eye of the Beholder," Jericka was holding fast to the title, "Eyes of the Beholder."

It also didn't matter that I wanted to work on another manuscript, she kept pushing me to finish this book. Although it's a work of fiction the characters may depict real scenarios. The names of the characters are fictitious and any similarity is strictly coincidental.

ALSO BY BARBARA ROBINSON

And Still I Cry
Yes You Can

TABLE OF CONTENTS

Chapter		Page

INTRODUCTION

Eyes of the Beholder is about a woman named Rebekah, who saw her mother as an ugly disfigured woman, until she learned the circumstances of her mother's disfigurement. Rebekah goes on a self-destruction trip in the abyss of life that lasted over twenty years.

She and nine other women, who have also gone through many trials, experienced many obstacles and overcame many hurdles in life, founded an organization to help other women. *Eyes of The Beholder* discusses some of the women they helped and the men in the lives of the women.

The book is also about a man loving a woman so much that he's willing to wait a lifetime for her.

For Beulah, Rebekah's mother, life had seemed to lay nothing but pain and torment at her doorstep. But the shining light of her existence was her daughter, Rebekah.

However, as Rebekah got older, she managed to find things to blame her mother for and she became increasingly embarrassed of Beulah. This embarrassment created a wall of silence between Rebekah and Beulah. This great divide caused a deep and quiet suffering within the heart of Beulah that day-by-day tore her apart.

The truth was that Beulah was protecting Rebekah by withholding a secret. Rebekah learned of the secret after her mother died. Now, faced with the guilt of understanding what happened to her mother and reflecting on how she had treated her, caused Rebekah to sink into a long destructive period of depression.

This is a heart-wrenching, yet beautiful story of how Rebekah, and the nine women fought to rebuild and reclaim their lives after falling into the darkness of life created by circumstances sometimes beyond their control. Often hanging by a thread, each of these women had to find something — anything — to help them to once again believe in life. Rebekah had to look the hardest and the deepest to find that core within herself that allowed her to rise up and find her life, and her love. *Eyes of the Beholder* is Barbara Robinson's third book, her first novel, and what a book it is!

CHAPTER ONE
Heartbreak

What happens to a dream deferred?   Today becomes the tomorrow you worried about yesterday and if you don't follow your dreams they will never become goals.   That was a lesson Rebekah learned after years of self-destructive behavior and self-defeating attitudes.

My eyes beheld beauty and didn't recognize it.   My heart beheld love and didn't understand it.   My spirit beheld joy and then destroyed it.   That was another lesson Rebekah learned from life — her life.   *Eyes of the Beholder* tells you how she learned those lessons.

****

Rebekah was born in 1938 in Mobile, Alabama.   Her mother was Black, her father was white and Rebekah had always been confused about her identity.   She felt that she was too dark for the white race, too light for the Black race, and an outsider of both races.

Rebekah was growing into a beautiful, intelligent woman. "That's my refined, little lady," Beulah would say when she bragged about her daughter, Rebekah.   She was always bragging about Rebekah.   Beulah worked hard trying to give Rebekah the best that she could afford.

However, Rebekah wasn't as "refined" as Beulah thought.   In the mornings, Beulah prepared Rebekah's breakfast then left for work. Rebekah would leave home, going to school wearing clothes that Beulah had approved for her to wear.   She would borrow clothes from her girlfriends — the type of provocative clothes of which she knew Beulah wouldn't approve.   She hid the clothes in her book bag until she got to school.   Then she would go into the girls' restroom and change clothes, becoming the sexy Rebekah as she was known in high school.

Sometimes when she thought her skirt wasn't short enough to show her legs, she'd roll it at the waist to make it shorter. When leaving home, she didn't wear makeup but when she arrived at school, she applied it generously. She wore brown and white saddle oxfords and bobby socks when she left home, but when she arrived at school, she put on stockings and high-heeled shoes.

Her clothes were just conservative enough to keep the teachers from calling her mother, but sexy enough to be thrilling. She thought the clothes Beulah chose for her were prudish, too conservative, and too old-fashioned. She liked to show off her body as much as the school would permit.

Rebekah was a slim, tan-skinned, green-eyed, beauty with shoulder-length reddish-brown hair. She was the majorette leader with the school band and could she step! She wore a majorette uniform with a short skirt and marched up the main boulevard leading the majorettes and the school band. When she marched in the homecoming parade, onlookers stood on the sidelines and cheered. They loved to see her prance and turn corners.

When she marched, her skirt would fly up and she'd do a dip, prance a few steps, do a little dance, and kept marching in step with the music, never missing a beat. Beulah was always working and didn't have the opportunity to see Rebekah march but she sure was proud when she heard people talking about the parade and the talented majorette leader.

"She's a great stepper. She's gonna be a dancer one day, mark my word," Beulah heard someone say about Rebekah.

One day when Rebekah was in the twelfth grade, she was in the restroom at school and overheard a conversation between four of her schoolmates, Thomasine, Ruby Jean, Gloria, and Tyra. They were talking about Rebekah's mother.

"Did you see her?" Tyra asked her friends. "I mean she was so ugly, I could hardly keep from throwing up. She was all bent over and them scars on her arms and face, I would be afraid to touch her. Imagine, a baby having to look at that face! I bet Rebekah must have woke up crying every night, dreaming about her ugly mama."

They all laughed.

"Or maybe Rebekah didn't cry at night 'cause her ugly mama would come to see what was the matter," said Ruby Jean.

They laughed again.

"Or maybe Rebekah only called her mama when she got the hiccups, so her ugly mama could smile and scare the shit out of her," Thomasine said.

Gloria was the only one not laughing and not talking about Rebekah.

"Why do y'all talk about her mama like that? Y'all don't know what happened and why her mama has those scars. How would you like it if someone talked about your mama?" said Gloria.

"Oh, Little Miss Goody-Two-Shoes," Tyra said. "You're always taking up for Rebekah. Why don't you hang out with her instead of hanging with us if you like her so damn much?"

Tyra was one of the most popular girls in high school and Gloria didn't want to ruin their friendship. Because she hung around Tyra and her buddies, Gloria was also popular. Still, she liked Rebekah and she didn't think it was right for them to talk about her mama like that. Besides, Gloria felt that Tyra was hateful toward Rebekah because of Eugene Broadnax; everyone called him Gene.

Gene was captain of the football team and he also played basketball. He and Tyra dated a few times and she was crazy about him. He really liked Rebekah, but Beulah wouldn't allow Rebekah to hang out late and go to parties like Tyra and her crowd. Rebekah had to read a book each week and do homework every night. Tyra's crowd called Rebekah a "square." Nevertheless, Tyra envied Rebekah and always tried to find ways to torment her.

"If I ever catch her up in my man's face, I'll kick her yellow ass," Tyra said.

Gloria shrugged her shoulders, caught between right and wrong. "I'm not taking up for her. But she's a nice-looking girl. She's smart and friendly. I just think that if she heard you talking about her mama like that, she could cause trouble by telling the principal. But, it ain't no skin off my back," she said.

Thomasine was as vicious as Tyra, and said to Gloria, "Listen, girl, either you're with us or you're against us. You can't have your cake and eat it, too. So what's it gonna be? Maybe you think she's nice-looking 'cause she's half-white. Maybe she thinks she's too good for us 'cause she's a high-yellow bitch."

"I ain't got nothing more to say," said Gloria. "But if y'all get in trouble, I'm gonna be the first to say, 'I told you so.'" She sashayed out of the restroom.

As Gloria walked out, Thomasine started to say something else to her, but Ruby Jean lightly touched Thomasine's shoulder to stop her. "Aw, leave her be, she's one of us," said Ruby Jean.

The three girls walked out giggling and chatting. After they left, Rebekah came out of the stall where she was hiding. Until that day, she had always seen her mother as a friendly, kind person with a soft voice, gentle eyes, gentle hands, a heart of gold and lots of patience.

The brick fireplace in Beulah's house was built into the wall and a wooden shelf went the length of the fireplace. Beulah always kept an old black iron kettle filled with water sitting in the fireplace. During the winter months she cooked sweet potatoes in the hot ashes, rubbing the potatoes in lard so the skins wouldn't burn, then she and Rebekah ate them with freshly churned butter and drank hot tea sweetened with honey.

They enjoyed a special mother-daughter bond. Rebekah had overlooked Beulah's disfigurement because she saw so much love in Beulah. But after she heard her classmates talking, Rebekah's feelings toward her mother started to change.

Sometimes white folks brought their clothes to Beulah late in the evening, wanting them washed, ironed, and ready to be picked up by the following morning. Beulah stayed up all night doing other people's laundry. It angered her when she passed some of those same people in the streets and they turned their heads to keep from speaking to her.

The only time Rebekah saw Beulah angry was when she was disrespected by white folks because of her skin color. One afternoon when Rebekah was about five or six years old, she and Beulah were walking past the train station when Rebekah had to use the restroom. The door to the restroom in the Colored section of the train station was broken and leaning against the wall.

On the opposite side of the station was a clean waiting room with a "White Only" sign over the entrance. Hotdogs, hamburgers, french fries, sodas, and chips could be purchased at the snack shop in the white section. The colored section was dirty, there was no snack shop and no place for passengers to sit and wait for trains. Colored passengers had to wait on the platform outside where the trains came in. Even during winter months, colored passengers couldn't wait inside the small station.

"Come on," Beulah said to Rebekah. "Today we be white, 'cause we ain't gonna use no toilet where they don't think we're human enough to deserve a door for privacy."

Beulah, holding Rebekah by the hand, marched into the "white only" waiting room, past the horrified gasps and stares of white passengers and ignoring the protests of the station employees. They marched straight to the door that had a "White Women Only," sign on it. Beulah told Rebekah to go inside, use the toilet, not to sit on the seat, and to wash her hands with soap and warm water when she finished.

"Don't be afraid. I'll be standing right here guarding this door. If anybody bothers you, they got to come through me first," Beulah said.

Beulah stood in front of the restroom door with her arms folded across her chest. The station attendant walked to where she was standing and tried to make her leave.

"When my child finishes using the toilet we'll leave, and not one minute before," she adamantly said. "If you call the police, we'll be gone by the time they get here. If you touch me or my child, I'll call my boss, Pete Waldon, and tomorrow you'll be looking for another job."

Beulah was furious. The station attendant didn't want to lose his job. He knew that Beulah was right. In a town as small as Mobile, especially the little area of the city called Asheville where Beulah and Rebekah lived, everyone knew about the friendship between the Waldon family and the Mosley family. Everyone also knew of Beulah Mosley's friendship with Amy Waldon.

"When that gal finishes, I want both of you to get out and don't come back," the attendant said angrily, then walked away.

Beulah smiled and ignored him and the angry stares and comments from white passengers. When Rebekah came out of the restroom, Beulah asked her if she had washed her hands. Rebekah said she did, and they left the station. Rebekah had heard the conversation between Beulah and the station attendant and she tried hard to keep from laughing.

She looked up at her mother and proudly said, "I guess we showed them, huh, Mama?"

"We sure did, baby," Beulah said, and they both laughed.

****

The years flew by. Rebekah was popular in high-school but the color of her skin always caused her trouble. She had to be tough to survive. Some of her high school peers called her, "half-breed."

Amy Waldon had watched Rebekah grow into a beautiful young woman and had seen the sacrifices that Beulah made to give Rebekah the best of everything, things that Beulah never had. Sometimes Beulah really couldn't afford them, but she got them for Rebekah anyway.

Amy warned Beulah to stop lavishing an expensive lifestyle on Rebekah; but Beulah said that she wanted to make up for Rebekah not having a "normal family."

"A child needs a mother and a father, so since I'm the only family she has, I have to take the place of both parents," Beulah told Amy.

****

One of Alabama's nicknames, the "Yellowhammer State," originated during the Civil War. According to stories told by the old folks, one day, a company of Alabama troops paraded in uniforms trimmed with bits of bright yellow cloth. The soldiers reminded people of the birds called yellowhammers, which have yellow patches under their wings. After that, Alabama soldiers were known as "yellowhammers."

Beulah, however, had her own story as to why Alabama was called the "Yellowhammer State." She said it was because of the yellow daisies that covered the hillsides of Mobile like yellow blankets. She was intrigued with the hills of yellow daisies where she and Rebekah walked and lay, looking up at the sky and daydreaming.

Mobile was a city that kept the attractiveness of a small community in spite of its rapid growth. Huge oak trees arched over wide boulevards.

There were many Sunday afternoons during the summer months when Beulah and Rebekah sat under the oak tree that stood in their backyard, with Rebekah listening to Beulah make up stories about Rebekah's future of being a fine, educated career woman.

Stately old homes added to the charm and dignity of the city. The Waldons lived in such a house with huge pillars supporting the front porch. Their house was reminiscent of the plantation houses that existed during the 1700s and 1800s. When looking at Pete and Amy Waldon's house, one almost expected to see a horse-drawn carriage in the circular driveway and Negro slaves standing on each side of the driveway greeting finely dressed white men and women.

Baptists and Methodists were the largest religious groups in Alabama. Beulah was a Baptist, as was her family before her. The Waldons were also Baptists, although they worshiped at a different church than Beulah.

Like most southern states, Alabama had separate schools for white and Negro children. In 1963, Alabama began to desegregate some schools. However, by that time, Rebekah had finished high school and left mobile.

Alabama faced serious racial problems in the fifties and sixties. In 1955 and 1956, Dr. Martin Luther King, Jr. directed the Montgomery bus boycott. Many Negroes refused to ride public buses in Montgomery because the law required them to sit in the rear. Mobile was affected by that boycott and Beulah refused to ride buses. She and Rebekah walked wherever they went. When the distance was too far to walk, they rode in one of the private cars driven by Negroes.

It was during that time that Rebekah graduated from high school and headed for college.

When Rebekah graduated from high school, she knew she was going to college. It wasn't an option. Beulah had talked of college ever since Rebekah could remember. Beulah tried to convince Rebekah to go to a college closer to Mobile, but Rebekah wanted to leave the South for a life away from Beulah and the teasing she received from her highschool schoolmates.

Many days she ran home crying because someone had been mean to her and called her names. Beulah tried to shield her from the pains of cruelty but Rebekah couldn't or wouldn't understand. She just felt she had to get away.

Amy asked Beulah why she allowed Rebekah to go to a college so far from home. Beulah felt that Amy, being a white woman, didn't understand Rebekah's concerns and issues about race and skin color.

Besides working as a housekeeper and cook for Pete and Amy Waldon, Beulah also took in washing to help pay Rebekah's college tuition and personal expenses.

CHAPTER TWO
Never a Greater Love

Tamara and Rebekah met during their freshman year at Morgan State College in Baltimore, Maryland. They were roommates, became good friends, and remained roommates throughout college. Rebekah was intrigued with Tamara's street savvy, since she came from a small southern town, Rebekah wasn't familiar with big city ways.

Tamara was a year older than her brother Donnie. She had graduated from high school a year before he did, but she chose not to go to college at the time, deciding instead to work in her family's business. She said that she was trying to get herself together.

Tamara and her father had been very close. His sudden death during her senior year in high school had deeply affected her, and left her with little ambition to go to college — that is, until Donnie graduated and announced that he wanted to become a doctor. She and Donnie had always been close, and he talked her into enrolling at Morgan State College with him.

"It's a historically Negro college and we can learn about our heritage. Besides, you owe it to yourself and to Dad to get a degree. You know how he was about our education. Remember the time he threatened to quit his job and walk me to school everyday to keep me from joining a gang?" he said to Tamara as he laughed at the thought.

"It worked, too," said Tamara laughing with him. "But years later Daddy told us he was bluffing, 'cause he couldn't afford to quit his job. But we believed him at the time. You must have been in the eighth grade."

"I was scared to death. I'm glad he kept me out of that gang," said Donnie.

Sadie, Tamara's and Donnie's mother, was proud that her children were going to college, yet she was concerned about Tamara's ambivalence toward her education. Nevertheless, Sadie packed her van with clothes, two radios, two record players, two televisions, and headed for Baltimore, Maryland with her children.

When they arrived on Morgan's campus four hours after leaving New York, there were signs posted directing people to Holmes Hall, the building where registration was being conducted.

Sadie parked her car, they got out and walked to Holmes Hall. Once inside, Donnie and Tamara saw students registering for classes and felt the excitement of the beginning of college life.

Donnie was checking out the good-looking young women when he spotted Rebekah walking up the hallway, laughing and talking with two other young women, and his heart started pounding. He fell for her the moment he laid eyes on her. It was as if an arrow was pointing him to her. She was beautiful and laughed easily. Her green eyes danced in a sea of white snow, so clear. Her hair was worn loose like a young stallion's mane. Her skin was tan like milk with just a hint of chocolate. He thought she was the prettiest girl he had ever seen.

He stood staring at her, mesmerized by her beauty. Tamara looked at Donnie and then looked in the direction in which he was staring and realized that he was looking at two women standing nearby. She nudged him in his side to break his stare.

"Wha' huh.., oh yeah," he said pretending that he didn't know why she had nudged him, and they both laughed.

Tamara and Donnie finished their registration and were assigned dormitory rooms. When they started toward the van, Tamara told Sadie about the incredibly beautiful girl who had just blown Donnie's mind.

"Tam, you talk too much," he said teasingly.

"Gawd, Donnie, you haven't found out where your dorm is or who your roommate will be and you're cruising women already?" teased Sadie.

"'Cruising? Uh oh, Ma's trying to use slang on me." he joked. "I just said she was beautiful," he grinned.

"I hope between parties and looking at pretty women you can find time to study. Don't forget that I'm footin' the bills," warned Sadie, pretending to scold him.

They drove across campus to the women's dorm and unloaded Tamara's clothes and personal belongings from the van. They then drove to the other side of the campus where the male dormitories were located and unloaded Donnie's stuff. After Sadie was satisfied that her children were safe and registration completed, she left for home, returning to New York.

Tamara was unpacking her things when Rebekah — her new roommate — walked into the room. Tamara recognized Rebekah as one of the young women at whom Donnie had been staring during registration. They introduced themselves.

On the dresser in their room was an announcement about a get-acquainted get-together dance that was being held in the gymnasium the following evening. Donnie called Tamara's room to ask if she was going to the dance and Rebekah answered the telephone. Donnie asked to speak to Tamara.

When she came to the telephone he said, "Your roommate sounds nice. How does she look? Is she pretty?"

"Oh, you'd love her. But you've already been smitten by someone you saw during registration. You won't like this girl as much as the young lady we saw at registration," teased Tamara.

"I'm just looking and weighing my options. I don't have a ring on my finger," joked Donnie. "Are you both going to the get-together dance tomorrow?"

"Yeah, I think so. We haven't had time to discuss it. But if we do go, you can meet my roommate then," she said.

Rebekah and Tamara talked and got to know each other. Rebekah made up lies about her family, trying to be someone she wasn't. She told Tamara that her parents were dead. Rebekah continued the lie by saying that she didn't have any living relatives.

The following evening, they went to the dance. As soon as Donnie and his roommate, Lawrence, walked into the gymnasium that had been converted into a dance hall, he saw Rebekah. He was excited to see her with Tamara. Could this possibly be Tamara's roommate? Could he be so fortunate? he wondered.

"Be still my heart. I see the woman who's about to become my lady," Donnie said to Lawrence. Donnie was smiling, looking at

Rebekah and rubbing his chin. "I'm about to introduce her to her future husband. I've made up my mind; I'm going to marry her one day. I love a woman with green eyes."

"Aw, man. You ain't even met the chick yet. How do you know whether or not she already has a man? And how do you know her eyes are green? You can't see her eyes from here," said Lawrence.

"I saw her during registration but she didn't see me," said Donnie. "But it don't matter if she does have a man. Don't make me no difference at all. If she's got somebody, he'll just have to go. I don't like to hurt another brother, but I see something I want and that's just the way it is."

"Oh, just like that, huh Bruh?" teased Lawrence.

"Yeah, just like that," said Donnie. "But the truth is, I think she's my sister's roommate. That's the beauty of having a sister attending the same college with me. I'll talk to you later, Bro. I'm going to join the women. Buh-bye, now!" he walked away laughing and pointing at Lawrence. "See ya lata, Bro," he waved goodbye.

Lawrence just laughed, shook his head and waved Donnie off.

Donnie walked over to where Tamara and Rebekah were standing, talking and looking at couples dancing. "Hello, beautiful ladies," he said. "Having this get-acquainted dance the second night of orientation was a terrific idea. We fellows get to see pretty women who'll be attending classes with us," said Donnie, smiling, flashing even white teeth and deep dimples in each cheek.

"Rebekah, this is my brother, Mister Funny Man," teased Tamara.

Donnie pretended to be insulted, with his hands on his chest he said, "I am humbly crushed." He blushed and pretended to be embarrassed.

Rebekah and Tamara laughed.

"Hello, 'Mister Funny Man,' my name is Rebekah."

"Hello, Rebekah. My name is Donnie."

"Tamara, I didn't know you had such a cute brother," said Rebekah.

"Don't tell him that. His head is already too big," teased

Tamara.

"Let me buy you a glass of punch," said Donnie, as he looked into the greenest eyes he had ever seen.

He and Rebekah started walking toward the refreshment table.

"Oh sure, just leave the little wall flower all alone by herself," shouted Tamara. "It's okay. I know when I'm in the way," she teased.

Rebekah turned around to go back and stay with her. Donnie gently put his hands on Rebekah's shoulder guiding her back toward the refreshment table. "She'll be all right. She's just trying to play the part of a big sister," laughed Donnie.

"I have a confession to make," Donnie said to Rebekah. "I saw you in Holmes Hall when you were registering. I told my sister and mother that I had seen this incredibly beautiful woman. My sister saw how I was looking at you. When I called her room, she told me that she had a beautiful roommate but she didn't tell me it was you. She kept that as a surprise, a pleasant surprise, I might add. Me and my roommate came to the dance together and when I saw you standing with my sister I said a silent thank-you prayer."

"So, you were stalking me," teased Rebekah.

"If that's what you want to call it," he joked.

The record, "I Only Have Eyes For You," by the Flamingos was playing on the record player that sat on a table next to the refreshments. A senior student was acting as a disc jockey, playing records.

"May I have this dance, My Lady?" he teased, bowing from the waist.

"Yes, you may, Sir Knight," she teased and held out her hand for him to take.

They whirled onto the dance floor. She danced as if on clouds floating across the floor.

"I told my roommate that you were going to become my lady and he said you might already be taken. Are you taken?" Donnie asked.

"No, I'm not taken. But don't I have anything to say about becoming your 'lady?'" Rebekah asked.

"No, the only thing you have to say is, 'Yes, Donnie. I'll be your lady.'"

They both laughed and that was the beginning of their romance.

Rebekah and Donnie were both freshmen when they first had sex. It was just after spring break when they returned to college. They had been dating a little over eight months and the smell of spring was in the air. Donnie had gotten a part-time job in the community health clinic that was operated by Dr. Klein, the college's medical director. Donnie wanted to become a doctor someday, so whenever he had the opportunity, he volunteered to work with Dr. Klein.

One Saturday afternoon, Donnie was working alone in the clinic. Dr. Klein had gone out of town on business, and Donnie was left to mind the office. He called Rebekah's room and Tamara said that Rebekah was downstairs in the basement laundry room washing clothes.

"When she comes upstairs, tell her to call me at the clinic," said Donnie.

Rebekah came in with a basket of clothes in her hands. "Donnie said to call him at the clinic. He sounded lonely," teased Tamara.

Rebekah called him; he asked her to come to the clinic and keep him company.

"How am I supposed to get there?" she asked.

"Take a taxi and I'll pay the fare," he said. "I'll be watching for you. When the taxi gets here, come inside and get the money to pay the driver." He was excited about her coming but she was apprehensive.

"Are you sure it'll be all right? asked Rebekah.

"Sure, I'm here alone. Who will know that you're here other than you and I?" said Donnie.

Rebekah called a taxi and went to the clinic to join Donnie. He was watching for her from the clinic window and when the taxi stopped in front of the clinic, his eyes got brighter. The back door on the passenger side opened, and Rebekah got out. He grinned.

Donnie watched her long, slim legs unfold as she exited the

taxi. First she stuck out her right leg, aware of the effect she was having on Donnie, then she put the other leg out, stood up and adjusted her halter. She smiled and waved at Donnie. Her white teeth flashed against her tan skin. She wore white shoes and her size thirty-six breasts were squeezed into a halter top one size too small.

She ran inside to get the taxi fare from Donnie. He was standing in the clinic door, waiting for her with a $5 bill in his hands to pay the taxi fare.

"You're beautiful," he said, as he handed her the money.

"I bet you say that to all the girls," she teased.

She took the money from his hand and ran back down the steps to the waiting taxi. She paid the driver and he drove off. She went back inside the clinic, gave Donnie the change and he laid it on the table. As she walked through the door, Donnie grabbed her arm, pulled her to him and passionately kissed her. She whirled and stepped away from him, smiling teasingly.

"So, this is where you spend your time," she said.

"Come on, let me show you around. Dr. Klein really does have a nice setup here." He took her hand and led her into another room. "This is the doctor's lounge," he said.

"Ooh, it's nice," she said, pretending to be interested. The room smelled of fresh pine oil. "I can see that the doctor keeps everything nice and clean."

"Well, give me a little credit," laughed Donnie. "I do help keep the place clean too, you know."

"Okay, I'll give you credit too," she teased. "You both keep things nice and clean."

Donnie put his hands on her shoulder, a little apprehensively at first. He didn't know how she would respond. He gently turned her to face him. She looked into his eyes; they were misty.

"I love you, Rebekah. I love you so much. For the first time in my life, I'm in love," he whispered.

"I love you, too, Donnie," she said. "I've never felt about anyone the way I feel about you."

He gently kissed her on her neck, then he kissed each cheek, he kissed her nose, and finally her lips. Her body melted into his. She was nervous and so was he. It was their first time. They had talked about going all the way in their lovemaking, but they hadn't.

He kissed her again. Beads of sweat formed on his brow. She started to unbutton his shirt, got nervous and stopped. She walked to the window and looked out. He walked to where she stood and put his arms around her waist.

"What's the matter?" he asked.

"Suppose someone comes in here and sees us," she said nervously. "Our reputation will be ruined."

"I told you, no one will come in here," said Donnie. "I'm always here alone when the doctor is out of town. He's not expected back for two more days. I wouldn't have asked you to come here if it wasn't safe."

Rebekah relaxed and folded her arms to embrace his. He kissed her on her neck again. She leaned back to rest her body against his. She felt the bulge in his pants. He slid his hands around to massage her buttocks, and he slowly began to explore her body. He slowly moved his hands from her buttocks to her thighs. He gently rubbed her thighs, then his hands moved slowly to her breasts, back to her stomach and then slid slowly down to the area of her vagina. She put her hands over her head reaching back to caress his face and the back of his neck. She turned to face him and felt his penis. It seemed to be struggling to break out of the zippered cloth cage. It was so hard, it was throbbing and Donnie had started breathing heavily.

Rebekah massaged the bulge in Donnie's pants. He softly moaned. She continued unbuttoning his shirt and kissed him on his chest and naval as she unbuckled his belt and unzipped his pants. She gently sent a trail of kisses down his body as she stooped to pull off his trousers and undershorts.

Rebekah turned for him to unbutton her halter. She slipped her arms out and let the halter fall to the floor. He unbuttoned and unzipped her shorts. She stepped out of them and he saw that she wasn't wearing any under-panties. Donnie moaned again.

Rebekah was surprised at how knowledgeable she was about lovemaking. She had read plenty of romance magazines, saw movies and listened to her friends talking about sex, but she didn't have any experience. It just came naturally. She just knew that her body wanted to get as close to Donnie's as possible.

They moved toward a big leather sofa that stood against the wall on one side of the room, both moving as if glued to each other. They lay down and Donnie mounted Rebekah like a young stallion mounting a filly. She spread her legs as an invitation for him to enter her. Donnie slightly raised his body just enough to guide his penis into her waiting vagina. It found its target as if being pulled by a magnet. His penis was so hard he didn't need to use his hand to guide it; when he raised his body, it was as if it had a mind of its own. For the first time in her life, Rebekah was a woman experiencing sex.

They made love many times during the next three and a-half years. Rebekah had experienced the thrill of lovemaking and she and Donnie took every opportunity to engage in the act. Like the time they were leaving the homecoming football game at the stadium.

Donnie was co-captain of the football team. His buddy, Lawrence, was the captain. Both young men were popular on the college campus. Rebekah was proud when her classmates teased her about dating one of the most popular men on campus. This night, Morgan had won the game and everybody was in high spirits. Rebekah waited for Donnie by the dugout entrance. After he had showered, he came out and met her. It had just started to rain.

"I'm glad the rain waited until the game was over," said Donnie.

"Me, too. You looked so handsome in your uniform. I know some of the other girls get jealous when they see this hunk and know that you're off limits to them," she teased.

"Yeah, 'cause I belong to the prettiest girl on campus," he said as he hugged her while walking to the car he had purchased from his family's dealership. They got into the car and headed out of the parking lot.

"Are you going to the homecoming party at the ballroom?" Skeeter, another football player, called from his car.

"That depends on what my lady wants to do," said Donnie.

"Does that mean that you won't be dancin' 'til dawn?" teased Lawrence.

"I don't want to go to the party. It's raining and I don't feel like being around a lot of people tonight. I just want to be alone with you," said Rebekah.

"No, I won't be dancin' 'til dawn. I've got more important things to do," Donnie shouted to Lawrence.

"I hear ya partnah. Wish I was in ya shoes," called Lawrence.

"I have this fantasy about making love while rain is falling in my face. I saw that in a movie once and I've wanted to try it ever since," said Rebekah as she lay her head on Donnie's shoulder and moved closer to him.

"Well, let's see if we can fulfill that fantasy tonight," Donnie grinned.

Donnie put his right arm around Rebekah and steered the car with his left. She was sitting so close to him it appeared as if she was sitting in his lap.

When they had driven about five miles, they came to a dark dirt road with tall trees on both sides. Donnie turned onto the road and parked. He turned off the motor and turned to face Rebekah. He took her face in his hands, looked into her eyes, and gently kissed her.

"Your lips are so soft," he whispered. "I think the reason we won the game tonight was 'cause I was in a hurry to get to you."

"Yeah, and I ordered the rain just for this occasion," she laughed.

"It's so cramped in the front seat. Let's get in the back so we can have more room," whispered Donnie.

Rebekah didn't answer, she just climbed over the front seat and laid down on the back. Donnie got on top of her, all the while kissing her and whispering words of endearment.

"Roll down the window so I can feel the rain," she whispered.

He rolled the window down just enough for the rain to come in. As she lay on the seat, the cool, fresh, raindrops gently splashed in her face and she and Donnie experienced the colors of the rainbow created by their lovemaking.

It appeared that each time Donnie and Rebekah were together, they couldn't keep their hands off each other. They were at

Lawrence's birthday party at his parents' house just outside of Washington, D.C. and Rebekah and Donnie went outside on the porch. It was a wooden house with a front porch that went the length of the house. There was a wooden swing on the left side of the porch hanging from the ceiling by a rusty chain that squeaked when the swing moved. The right side of the porch was enclosed in screen wire and was used as a sunroom.

Donnie sat on the banister; Rebekah stood between his legs and leaned against him. He put his arm around her waist and nestled his face in her hair. He teased her about the way she talked, her southern drawl. They had just gotten back together after Easter holidays. Donnie had gone to New York and Rebekah had gone to Mobile for Easter. It was one of those times when she felt the need to go home. She told Tamara and Donnie that following the death of her parents, she went to live with a friend of her parents.

"I missed you," he whispered.

"I missed you, too," she said.

The sky was clear. The moon was so bright it looked like a giant spotlight shining down on diamonds in the earth. Donnie pulled her to him.

"Gee, you smell good," he said. "You always smell good."

The breeze was just enough to cool off the muggy night. It was unseasonably warm for a spring night. He unbuttoned her blouse to expose a black lace bra.

"Suppose someone comes out here and sees us," said Rebekah.

"If they do, they'll just see a guy hugging his girl," said Donnie as he looked at Rebekah, smiling, showing white teeth and deep dimples. "Besides, why would anyone come out here? They're probably in their own groove, scarey cat."

They made love many times. Although she was concerned about getting pregnant, she still engaged in unprotected sex.

Donnie and Rebekah planned to get married on Christmas Day their senior year. The wedding had been planned for months. Donnie and his family asked Rebekah if anyone from her family would attend the wedding and she said, "No." She kept up the lie that her parents were deceased and that she didn't have any living relatives. She had told so many lies about her family. Donnie asked her if the family friend with whom she had lived was coming to the wedding. Rebekah said she was invited but had declined to attend.

Rebekah loved to spend the summer with Donnie and Tamara's family. Sadie was a pleasant lady and a savvy business woman. Tamara's father had died and left his family a prosperous car dealership. Sadie expanded it into a profitable enterprise, adding limousine services, truck rentals, and car leasing. She purchased several pieces of property, added parking spaces and rented them out weekly and monthly. She opened parking garages in various sections of New York and had begun working on franchising her business.

When Rebekah worked for Sadie during the summer, she pretended that Sadie was her mother. "This is my family," she pretended, speaking softly to herself. "We're rich and famous," she giggled. "Someday I'm going to be rich, buy pretty clothes, drive fancy cars, and live in a mansion." She always dreamed like that when she was around Donnie and his family.

CHAPTER THREE
Beulah Goes to New York

During her freshman and sophomore years, Rebekah went home for Thanksgiving, Christmas, Easter, and Mother's Day. During summer breaks, she went to New York to stay with her college roommate, Tamara, and worked in Tamara's family's car dealership as a saleswoman and switchboard operator.

During her junior year, Rebekah spent more time in New York than she did in Mobile, Alabama. Beulah asked Rebekah why she didn't come home more often. Rebekah said that she went to New York each summer to find better employment. Beulah wanted something better for Rebekah so she didn't object to her going to New York to find work.

Rebekah had graduated from high school in June 1957, and entered Morgan State College in Baltimore, Maryland, in September 1957. It was November 1960, the first semester of Rebekah's senior year. She would graduate in June 1961. Beulah had already started paying on a new outfit to wear to Rebekah's graduation.

Beulah had said to her friend Williemae, "I'm gonna be one proud woman come June, when I watch my chil', my pride and joy, receive her Bachelor of Science degree in Political Science from Morgan State College. Yes-suh-ree-bob, I'm gon' be the proudest woman there. That's gonna be the biggest day of my life."

Beulah danced around the room, prancing around in her cotton dress, waving her apron with glee. Williemae danced and laughed with her.

It was near the Christmas holidays, Rebekah called Beulah and said she was bringing a college friend home with her for Christmas. Beulah was elated that Rebekah was coming home for Christmas. Several times when Rebekah had said she was coming home, Beulah had prepared a big meal, and decorated the house with balloons, but Rebekah hadn't come. There was something that always came up at the last minute.

Yet, each time, Beulah said to herself, "Maybe this time she'll come." Beulah wanted to believe Rebekah's excuses for not coming home. She kept saying to herself, "Maybe it's because Rebekah knows that money is scarce, and she's trying to help me save." This time would be different, Beulah thought.

So just as before, Beulah decorated the house and planned a special meal for Rebekah and her college friend. Beulah was so full of pride and joy, if someone stuck her with a pin she would burst.

But three days before Christmas, three days before Beulah was to meet the train bringing Rebekah home, Rebekah called Beulah to say she was sorry but she couldn't come home for Christmas.

"My roommate's parents were killed in a car accident and I'm going to New York to be with her and try to console her in whatever way I can," Rebekah lied.

"Of course, you must go," Beulah replied, trying to conceal her disappointment. "Such a tragedy, especially during this time of year when everyone is in the Christmas spirit. I'm so sorry. Were they young people?"

"Yes, they were in their early forties and on their way home from work. It was a head-on collision with a drunk driver. They were killed instantly. The driver of the other car was only slightly injured." Rebekah was amazed at how well she could lie.

"Of course I understand," Beulah said again.

Beulah remembered the tragedy of an accident over twenty years ago when her twin sister, Beatrice, her brother-in-law, Gary, and her parents, Clarence and Julia Mosley, were killed. Beulah almost lost her life trying to save them. She did manage to save Rebekah from being burned to death but Beulah was disfigured in her efforts. Beulah would carry those scars to her grave, and for the rest of her life, suffer the ridicule of people looking at her burned, disfigured, scarred face and making unkind comments about it.

She shook her head as if trying to erase the memory of that tragic day. The pain was still as fresh and as sharp in her mind as if the accident had occurred yesterday. Her heart ached for the family of Rebekah's friend. She thought they would now have to experience the unbearable pain of losing a loved one, the same pain that she had experienced so many years ago. Rebekah talked on the telephone with Beulah a while longer, and found herself telling lie after lie to cover up the first lie. Rebekah hung up the telephone and began to pack her suitcase to go to fun-filled New York and join Donnie. She hummed a song and danced around the room, giving no thought to Beulah's disappointment and the lies she had just told.

When Beulah hung up the telephone, she wept for the family in New York. She wept for the heartache they would face. She remembered the caring neighbors who had been her support when she lost her family. She thought about her family, now gone.

"Will Rebekah be coming home for the Christmas holidays?" Amy asked Beulah.

"No," said Beulah. "She won't be able to make it this year. There was a terrible accident and her roommate's parents were killed."

"How horrible," said Amy. The expression on her face reflected sympathy for the grieving family. "So close to Christmas. That makes the loss more tragic."

"Yes," replied Beulah. "I feel so helpless. The family must really be in agony." Beulah walked out of the living room where she and Amy were standing and headed toward the kitchen, trying to conceal her disappointment.

But when Amy saw the anguish in Beulah's face, she immediately knew what her Christmas present to Beulah would be that year. Amy called Pete, her husband, at his office and told him about Beulah's problem and he agreed with Amy's idea. After she finished her conversation with Pete, Amy walked into her sparkling clean kitchen, where Beulah was washing vegetables for their dinner. Amy saw her friend and housekeeper silently weeping. When Beulah heard Amy approaching, she hurriedly wiped the tears from her eyes and tried to fake a smile.

"Don't worry, old friend," Amy said as she put her arms around Beulah's shoulders. "You'll spend Christmas with your daughter. As your Christmas present this year, Pete and I are giving you a week's vacation in New York. You can spend Christmas with

Rebekah and visit with her roommate's family."

Beulah couldn't believe her ears. She jumped for joy as she hugged Amy. Beulah went home and tried to call Rebekah at school to tell her the good news, but Rebekah had already left for New York.

"I'll surprise her," Beulah said. "I ain't never been nowhere but right here working, but this old Colored gal is gonna be steppin' high in New York City this Christmas!"

Beulah danced around the room, laughing. She hummed "Jingle Bells" and started to pack for her trip to New York. She called her friend Williemae to tell her the news.

Amy Waldon made hotel and plane reservations for Beulah. When Beulah arrived in New York, all she would have to do is take a taxi from the airport to the hotel. Amy wrote the hotel and flight information on a piece of paper and gave it to Beulah, who was both excited and scared. She had never been in an airplane before, but the thought of being with Rebekah overshadowed her fear of flying.

Amy was determined that her friend would travel in style. She had purchased first-class plane tickets, made reservations at the Waldorf Astoria, one of the finest hotels in New York, and let Beulah use her expensive luggage. Beulah felt like a high society woman and laughed at the thought.

Beulah felt blessed for having a good friend like Amy. Both women knew what Southern white people thought about white folks befriending Negroes, especially if the Negro folks were employees of the white folks. But Amy didn't care what people thought about her friendship with Beulah. Beulah was the kindest woman Amy had ever met.

Amy drove Beulah to the airport almost two hours before her plane was to leave. She knew that Beulah had never flown before and she wanted Beulah to have time to get accustomed to the idea of flying. They sat in the airport and talked about the good time Beulah would have in New York, shopping with Rebekah, going to Broadway plays, seeing all the sights that Beulah had only read and heard about.

When the 102-story Empire State Building was dedicated in 1931, Beulah had read about the dedication but she never dreamed that one day she would go to New York and actually see the building.

Lena Horne was appearing in the Broadway play, "Jamaica." Beulah thought that she and Rebekah could go to see it. Still, Beulah couldn't help but feel a tinge of guilt. There she was, feeling as gleeful as a schoolgirl, going on her first date, while all the time she knew that her trip would lead her to a tragic situation of attending the funeral of two people cut down in the prime of their life, or so she thought.

When Beulah's plane finally arrived and boarding announcements were made, she tried to pretend that she was no longer afraid, but Amy saw through her pretense. "All right, Miss I'm-Not-Afraid, I know your knees are knocking. I can hear them above the roar of the plane," Amy teased.

The two women laughed and hugged each other.

"Are you sure you don't want me to go with you?" asked Amy.

"No," said Beulah, as she brushed away the thought with a wave of her hand. "I'll be fine, honest. I'll be all right. As old as I am, I need to get away and see that there's another world outside of Mobile, Alabama."

"You promise to call me as soon as you get there?" Amy insisted.

"Yes, yes, I promise to call said Beulah," glad that her friend cared about her well-being. Beulah went aboard the plane and settled into her seat. The captain illuminated the "fasten seat belt" sign. One flight attendant demonstrated how to use the oxygen mask in the "unlikely event of an emergency landing," while another gave verbal instructions. The pilot's voice came over the public address system, welcoming passengers onboard, explaining the cruising altitude, aircraft speed, and estimated time of arrival. As soon as the plane began to ascend, Beulah's ears felt like they were closing and her hearing was muffled. She called the flight attendant and told her about her ears. The attendant smiled and asked Beulah if this was her first flight. Beulah said it was. The attendant instructed her to yawn so her ears would clear up. She yawned, and sure enough, her ears seemed to open. Beulah felt foolish for asking about her ears but the flight attendant assured her it was all right.

"You are not alone. It happens all the time," the attendant said.

Beulah thought about her friendship with Amy. She closed her eyes and silently thanked God for putting Amy in her life. She couldn't have afforded the trip to New York without Amy's help. In fact, there were a lot of things she wouldn't have been able to afford without Amy's financial help.

Beulah looked out the window of the plane at the floating white clouds resembling puffs of smoke and white cotton balls. She was so excited she forgot about her fear of flying. She thought about the times when she and Rebekah walked through fields of yellow daisies and made up stories about the different shapes of the clouds. "Now here I am above the clouds like an angel," she thought. She settled back and enjoyed the flight, refusing to allow the stares and whispers of the passengers to spoil her joy. Beulah was accustomed to such looks from strangers and even from some people who professed to be her friends.

When the plane landed at Kennedy Airport in New York, Beulah asked the attendant where to retrieve her luggage. She was instructed to follow the signs leading to the baggage claim area on the lower level of the airport.

As she walked through the airport, she was aware of strangers turning their heads to look at her. But Beulah was too excited about seeing her daughter. She ignored their stares as she went to retrieve her luggage.

A skycap asked her if she needed assistance with her luggage. She told him that she did. He put her luggage onto a cart and headed outside to get one of the taxicabs parked at the curb. The sky cap put her luggage into the taxi. Beulah gave him a fifty cent tip and got into the taxi. Amy had instructed her to get help with her luggage and to tip the person who helped her. Beulah told the driver to take her to the Waldorf Astoria Hotel.

As they drove, she noticed the driver looking at her in the rearview mirror. When she caught him staring at her, he quickly looked away.

Beulah was born in February 1910, one of the coldest months of the year. But she learned that cold weather in Mobile, Alabama, was nothing compared to the harsh cold weather in New York.

She was in awe of the vastness of New York City. She had read about New York in magazines and newspapers, and had seen movies about the bright lights, night clubs, and rich people, but she never expected there to be *so many* people. The ride to the hotel was awesome — so many sights to see, tall buildings, bright lights, and strange-looking people.

It intrigued Beulah that people walked the streets dressed as they were. In Alabama, when women wore long dresses, they were usually going to a ball or to a formal affair, but in New York, women wore long dresses with high-top tennis shoes as leisure attire. Beulah felt out of place dressed in a stylish business suit. Compared to how some people in New York were dressed, her conservative shoes seemed to be a carryover from the "olden days." The taxi pulled in front of the hotel and the bellhop in his fancy uniform came to assist Beulah with her luggage. She couldn't believe her eyes. She had never imagined such grandness. She had never seen such beautiful furnishings, carpeting, and drapery. Not even in the most expensive hotel in Mobile, where she worked as a part-time cleaning woman, had she seen such luxury.

I hope this isn't a mistake, she thought, as she looked wide-eyed at the magnificent furnishings and felt the plush carpet under her feet. She tried to walk like she imagined a grand lady would walk, as if she belonged in such luxury, as if she were accustomed to all the richness by which she was surrounded. She didn't mind the stares from people passing her in the hotel.

When she inquired about her reservations, she thought she would burst into laughter when the front desk clerk said to the concierge, "Please see that Madame's luggage is taken to the penthouse suite."

The concierge signaled for the bellhop to escort Beulah and her luggage to the penthouse. They got on the elevator and the bellhop pushed the button for the penthouse. The soft music playing in the mirrored, carpeted elevator added to Beulah's feelings of royalty.

When the elevator door opened into the living room of the penthouse, she could only gasp.

"It's almost as large as my whole house back home in Mobile!" she exclaimed.

She put her hands over her mouth, trying to take back the words that sounded like they were spoken by a "back woods" dummy. She looked shyly at the bellhop and giggled. "You must think I'm a ninny because I ain't never seen such fine furnishings," she said.

"No, ma'am," he said, "I like to see people enjoy themselves. Is this your first trip to New York?"

"Yes it is. I came to surprise my daughter, but I also came under sad times. I came to attend a funeral," said Beulah.

"I'm sorry to hear that. If there's anything the hotel can do, please let us know," he said.

Amy had told her that she was supposed to give the bellhop a tip for carrying her luggage, but when she tried to give him a fifty cent tip, he refused it. She thought his refusal was because the fifty cents was too meager.

"What's the matter, you mean it should be more?" she asked.

"No, ma'am. The tip was already taken care of by the person who reserved the room. We were instructed that everything was taken care of," he said.

"Amy, you did it again," Beulah whispered.

When the bellhop closed the door behind him, Beulah jumped on the bed, got up and jumped on it again. Then she twirled around the room mimicking the words of the hotel clerk.

"Please see that Madam's luggage is taken to the penthouse suite," the clerk had said.

Beulah couldn't stop laughing.

After she unpacked her suitcase, she decided to freshen up before going to surprise Rebekah. There was no way that she could sleep; she was too excited.

When she walked into the bathroom and saw the sunken bathtub, and double sinks with brass fixtures, she was speechless. She thought the king-sized bed was fantastic, but the bathroom was as large as her living room at home; it took her breath away. She had to pinch herself to see if she was dreaming. She knew that she would remember this Christmas for the rest of her life.

She couldn't resist getting into the bathtub. She turned on the water, equally mixing hot water with cold, then she dipped her finger into the water to gauge the temperature. She saw a bottle of scented bubble bath oil on the bathroom shelf — compliments of the hotel — and poured some into her bath water. She undressed and got into the tub of hot, sudsy, sweet-smelling water, gave a sigh of pleasure, laid her head back, closed her eyes, enjoyed the bath, and pretended that a bubble bath was an everyday occurrence for her.

After she had bathed and changed clothes, she got on the elevator and went downstairs. She asked the desk clerk for directions to the car dealership where Rebekah worked. The clerk wrote the directions on a piece of paper and instructed the bellhop to get a taxi for Beulah. She tucked the piece of paper with the directions into her pocket and followed the bellhop outside where a taxi was parked at the curb.

The bellhop held the taxi door open for Beulah to enter and closed it behind her. She sat back in the seat, smiling to herself at the service she was getting.

Rebekah had written to Beulah one summer while she was working in New York and the car dealership's address was on the stationary. Beulah realized that she didn't know where the funeral would be held. She thought there might be a notice posted at the dealership informing customers why it was closed.

"Perhaps there's a telephone number where I can call and get more information," she thought to herself.

She was still in awe of the tall buildings. It boggled her mind to see people living in cardboard boxes, sleeping on the streets, sleeping over grates with steam rising from them, trying to keep warm in the cold, December weather. Coming from a small town in Alabama, Beulah didn't see many homeless people, and certainly she didn't see them living in the conditions in which they lived on the streets of New York. Her eyes filled with tears as she thought of their plight.

Beulah was fascinated with the many shops they passed. The

taxi driver pointed out sights to her and gave her a history of some of the buildings. She felt as if she were in another world. She laughed, thinking of the fun she would have when she returned to Mobile and bragged to her friend Williemae about her adventures in the, "city that never sleeps." She had heard some movie star call it that.

"Williemae will be green with envy when I tell her about my trip up North and the sights I've seen. I can't wait to see the expression on her face," she laughed.

"Did you say something, ma'am?" the driver asked.

"No, I'm just enjoying the ride, and praying for a family I know that's hurting," she answered.

The taxi stopped in front of the dealership that was sandwiched between two buildings also owned by Sadie Crawford, Donnie and Tamara's mother.

"Please wait a few moments," said Beulah. "I'm just stopping here for an address."

The driver agreed to wait.

The dealership was almost deserted except for a salesman who was, "holding down the fort," he laughingly said.

Beulah asked him for the Crawford's address.

"I can't give you that, ma'am. But they probably ain't home no way. Everybody's at the wedding rehearsal," said the salesman.

Beulah thought the poor family was probably at the church making last-minute funeral arrangements, or receiving guests who had come to pay their respects, and the dumb salesman didn't even know about it. He thought it was a wedding.

"I guess good help is hard to find, even in New York," she mumbled.

Her heart went out to the family.

The salesman gave Beulah directions to the church. Still, she thought it was strange that he didn't say anything about the accident and had called the funeral a wedding. She also thought it was strange that the dealership was open for business when the owners had been killed. She put those thoughts out of her mind, thinking that must be the way people up North did things.

In the South when there's death in a family, neighbors bring food to the grieving family to help feed the people who come to pay their respects. But Beulah thought people seemed more impersonal in New York. Since the salesman didn't mention the accident, neither did she.

She was glad the taxi had waited. The church was on the other side of the city. During the ride to the church, Beulah was anxious. Her hands were sweaty and she dreaded the thought of a family's pain of losing a loved one.

When the taxi stopped in front of the big cathedral, Beulah thought it was the most beautiful church she had ever seen. It seemed that the little Baptist church in Alabama where she worshiped each Sunday could fit into one corner of the beautiful cathedral.

"Here you are, ma'am. That'll be two dollars," the driver said as he turned off the meter.

"Two dollars!" exclaimed Beulah. "Do you know how long I have to work to earn two dollars?"

"I gave you a break and turned off the meter while I waited for you at the car dealership," said the driver. "But I drove you from one side of the city to the other."

Beulah paid the driver, mumbling under her breath about how much it costs to ride a taxi in New York, compared to taxi fare in Mobile. "Just highway robbery," she grumbled.

The taxi drove away and Beulah walked up the steps to the church. When she walked inside she saw a group of people at the altar. As she walked closer, she saw Rebekah standing in the middle of the group and a man dressed like a priest was giving instructions.

Trying to control her joy at the sight of Rebekah, Beulah walked closer to where the people were standing. She imagined the happy surprise Rebekah would get when she turned around and saw her. Beulah covered her mouth with her hands to stifle the giggle. She had an urge to laugh out loud but she didn't want to spoil the surprise.

As Beulah walked closer toward the altar, she realized that there wasn't a casket. Instead of being in mourning and grief-stricken, the people gathered seemed to be laughing and in happy spirits. The longer she watched the group, the more apparent it became that they *were* rehearsing a wedding.

The minister instructed everyone to take their places. She heard him say something about a ring bearer, a best man, and the maid of honor. She listened to the laughter and conversation and discovered that they were, indeed, discussing Rebekah's wedding to Donnie. Beulah knew that Rebekah and Donnie were dating, but she had never met him. Beulah had no idea their relationship had gotten as serious as marriage.

Beulah stood there and listened, confused. The minister saw her standing in the background.

"Excuse me, ma'am, are you a part of this rehearsal?" he asked.

Rebekah and her friends turned and saw Beulah standing there looking bewildered. Beulah and Rebekah looked each other in the eyes, each waiting for the other to be the first to speak. Beulah was smiling, anxiously waiting for that happy scream of surprise from Rebekah, but it never came.

Instead a look of shock, fear, shame, and then disgust came over Rebekah's face. Beulah recognized that look all too well. She had seen it hundreds of times on the faces of strangers as they looked at her burned, disfigured face and badly deformed body. Then they looked away in horror.

That look from strangers no longer hurt Beulah; she had grown accustomed to it over the years. But when she saw that same expression on Rebekah's face, something inside of Beulah died.

Rebekah had lied so many times about her family, she didn't want Donnie's family to discover her lies.

After she regained her composure, Rebekah said to the minister, "No, she's not a part of this rehearsal. I don't know her. Please ask her to leave. She's disrupting my wedding rehearsal."

Rebekah turned her back to Beulah and resumed talking with her friends.

Beulah's eyes filled with tears, and her heart broke as she became aware of her hand-me-down clothes that she had received from Amy. For the first time in over twenty years, Beulah wished that she were dead.

"No, I'm not a part of this rehearsal," she said to the minister. "I'll leave."

Beulah backed toward the door with tears running down her cheeks. She didn't want to take her eyes off Rebekah, trying to relish every minute of looking at her face.

"Please, forgive me. I didn't mean to intrude on such a happy occasion. I thought I saw my daughter in here, but I was mistaken. I must be in the wrong church. My daughter is attending her roommate's parents' funeral. You don't have to escort me to the door. I'll not cause any trouble. I'll leave quietly. Good luck to the happy couple."

Beulah turned to leave, tears blinding her vision.

Rebekah turned and watched Beulah stumble out of the church. "Ma...," Rebekah said, then hesitated without completing the word "Mama."

She turned back to her friends with tears in her eyes, and hurriedly wiped her eyes before her friends noticed that she was upset.

As Beulah walked out of the church, she heard one man say, "Did you get a look at her face? Wow, I'd hate to see her on a dark night."

Everyone except Rebekah, laughed.

"She must be drunk, not knowing where the funeral is being held," said Sadie.

Rebekah's heart felt like a knife was twisting inside. She realized that she had hurt her mother. As Beulah left the church, Rebekah started to call her back. But she had lied so many times, she was ashamed to tell Donnie's family the truth. Rebekah was quiet during the ride back to Donnie's mother's house.

"What's wrong, sweetheart?" Donnie asked concerned about her silence. "Did that old woman at the church upset you that much? You've been acting strangely ever since then."

That was Rebekah's chance to tell Donnie the truth, but she didn't.

"I'm okay. I'm just tired," she lied. She was actually thinking about Beulah and how she used to enjoy being with her.

"When did I begin to feel ashamed of the way my mother looked?" Rebekah wondered. "Was it when I was about to graduate from high school?"

She dismissed those thoughts from her mind.

Beulah walked out of the church into the cold December air, but she didn't feel the cold. She walked and she cried. She walked so long in the cold that she had to feel her arms and legs to see if they were still there. Her whole body was numb. Her thin coat and gloveless hands were no match for New York's cold December night. Her body wasn't accustomed to such temperature; she was a Southern girl.

As Beulah walked, she thought about Rebekah. Each step took her farther away from the church where Rebekah's wedding rehearsal was being held and farther into the dark, cold night. With each impact her feet made on the cold concrete sidewalk, a piece of Beulah's heart broke.

Warm tears rolled down her cold cheeks, as the night wind blew them dry and left tear tracks on her face. Beulah walked blindly into the night, tears clouding her vision. She was confused and hurt, and suddenly unnerved by the bright lights of the nightclubs and the homeless people. All the sights with which she was in awe when she first arrived in New York had become frightening.

What had started out as a beautiful trip for Beulah had turned into one of misery. New York and its bright lights suddenly seemed drab and grey. The Christmas season seemed more like a dream. Beulah felt as if she were sleepwalking through a funhouse in an amusement park where nothing was real, just ornaments intended to frighten ticket holders.

Beulah's whole world was shattered by just one sentence from Rebekah.

At the wedding rehearsal, Rebekah had said, "I don't know her; please ask her to leave, she's disrupting my wedding."

Beulah couldn't get those words out of her mind. Yes, there was a death after all; Beulah's heart had died.

"I wonder how long Rebekah has been ashamed of me, embarrassed by my deformity, repulsed by my disfigured face. No, I really don't want to know. I just want to get as far away from this church and the people in it as I can," she said to herself as she walked in the cold weather.

She was in luck, a taxi stopped and the driver went into a restaurant to get a cup of coffee. When he came out, Beulah asked him to take her to the Waldorf Astoria Hotel. When they arrived at the hotel, Beulah went inside and took the elevator to her suite. She tried to shield her eyes from the people she passed and the people on the elevator. She didn't want them to see her crying.

She lay across the bed, trying to decide what to do. She decided that she didn't want to go back to Mobile. She didn't want to go back to a life in a small neighborhood where she would forever feel the pain of Rebekah's embarrassment.

She decided to stay in New York, find a job, and get lost in the city of thousands of different cultures. She didn't know anyone in New York and she felt alone. "What should I do? Where should I go? If I don't return to Mobile, how long will it take me to get a job in New York? Will my deformity keep me from getting a job? I don't know what type of work to seek. I know I'm a good servant; I can always find a job as a maid in some white folk's house, or as a cleaning woman at one of these hotels," she said sarcastically. "Lord, I just can't go back and have to answer questions about my trip."

She knew she wouldn't be able to keep a lie going forever and she was too embarrassed and too hurt to tell the truth. What would she say to Williemae? Should she make up a lie and say that she and Rebekah went to see a Broadway play? No, that wasn't her character to lie.

CHAPTER FOUR
Friendship

Although Amy was a white woman, she was the closest thing to family that Beulah had, other than Rebekah. Beulah decided to write Amy and tell her about her decision to remain in New York. After she wrote the letter and sealed it, she called Amy.

She was hesitant about making the telephone call; Amy had already paid for her trip to New York. Beulah didn't want to impose on their friendship by charging a telephone call, too. But Beulah felt that she had no choice. She had to speak to Amy.

When the operator asked Amy if she would accept the charges for the telephone call from Beulah, without hesitation Amy said, "Yes."

"Hello, Amy," Beulah said, trying to sound cheerful, not wanting Amy to know how much she was hurting emotionally. But she couldn't fool her old friend.

"Are you all right, Bea?" Amy asked, using the nickname she had used since they were children.

"Yes, I'm fine," Beulah lied. "I saw Rebekah a few minutes ago and everything is fine. She's with the family."

Beulah fought back sobs. She reasoned that she wasn't really lying. Rebekah was with the family, it just wasn't a bereaved family.

"Amy, I'm calling to let you know that I won't be returning to Mobile. I'm going to stay here in New York. I'm mailing a letter to you. I'll send your luggage when I get a chance. I called you because I needed to hear the voice of a friend. I want to thank you for being my friend and thank you for always being there for me all these years. No one knows my pain better than you. I know there were times when your social crowd couldn't understand why a rich white woman like you befriended a poor, old, ugly, Negro woman like me. I just wanted to tell you how much I love you. You've been like a sister to me. I never wanted Rebekah to be ashamed of me."

Beulah started to say more but she couldn't stop her voice from quivering. She hung up.

"Bea! Bea!" Amy called, until she heard the dial tone and realized that Beulah had hung up the phone.

Beulah went downstairs to get a stamp to mail the letter. She got one from the desk clerk and dropped the letter into the mailbox just outside the hotel. She was confused about where to go and what to do with the rest of her life. She wanted to be near water, as she had been so many times when she needed to make an important decision. She asked the doorman if there was a river near by.

"What river?" the doorman asked. "There are several rivers in New York. It depends on how far you want to go."

"Any river," Beulah said. "I just want to see a body of water."

"The East River is about a ten-minute walk from here in that direction," he said and pointed East.

She thanked the doorman and walked in the direction he pointed. She thought about that awful day that she could never forget, the day that haunted her memory and had robbed her of countless nights of sleep for over twenty years.

****

As Beulah walked toward the river and thought about her past, she knew that her life would never be the same again. When she wanted to think through a situation, she always sat by the water in the bay down the road from her house in Mobile. The sound of the water was soothing and relaxing to her. She felt she could think better in that quiet solitude listening to the sounds of the waves beating against the shore.

That was her plan that night in New York. She wanted to think things out. She knew that she didn't want to go back to Mobile, and she also knew that she never wanted to see the look of shame on Rebekah's face again.

"My daughter," Beulah laughed sarcastically. "I don't have a daughter, just someone I helped a long time ago."

She hoped the blackness of the night and the sound of the waves would console her. No one could see her ugliness in the dark. She could get lost in New York City among all those strangely dressed and strange-looking people, and with all the soup kitchens and homeless shelters the taxi driver told her about, she thought she could survive until she found employment.

She didn't see the truck as it came around the curve, nor did she hear the horn. She was engrossed in her own thoughts and her own pain. When she did see the truck, it was too late. Her crippled legs couldn't move fast enough to get her out of harm's way and the driver couldn't stop in time. He tried to put on brakes but it was too late, he was already upon her.

The squeal of the brakes could be heard in the night and finally the awful sound as the truck crashed into Beulah. The truck knocked her to the ground, then the back tires rolled over her body, crushing her. She felt a thud, a sharp pain, then blackness as she slipped into unconsciousness.

Beulah saw a bright light shining in the distance. Her spirit left her body and floated toward the beautiful, soothing light. As Beulah's spirit hovered above, she took one last look at the frail human body that had been her home for many years. The crumpled form lay in the street under the headlights of the truck and cars, where people had stopped to look at the accident. Then Beulah's spirit floated away to join her sister, mother, father, and brother-in-law.

After Beulah's telephone call, Amy was frantic. She called the telephone number Rebekah had left for her mother to use for emergencies. In her heart Amy knew something was wrong. She left a message with Sadie to tell Rebekah to return her call the minute she arrived.

"I'll tell her as soon as she comes in," the Sadie said. "She and my son are getting married tomorrow. We're just getting in from the rehearsal. I'm sorry that no one from her family could come to the wedding."

Amy didn't know how to respond. She knew that Beulah hadn't known about a wedding before leaving Mobile. Amy wondered how her friend felt all alone in a strange place like New York.

Rebekah walked into the room while Sadie was talking to Amy. She handed Rebekah the telephone. "It's an important message for you, Rebekah. Someone named Amy. Sounds like an emergency," said Sadie.

Rebekah took the telephone from Sadie's hand.

"Miss Amy, what's wrong?" Rebekah asked, trying to calm her mounting fear. She had felt guilty ever since she ignored her mother at the wedding rehearsal. She couldn't forget the look on Beulah's face. Amy told Rebekah about Beulah's telephone call and that contributed to Rebekah's fear. Amy told Rebekah the name of the hotel where Beulah was staying. Rebekah hung up the telephone and hurried for the door.

"I have to find my mama. She needs me. I treated her badly. I have to find her and ask her to forgive me. Beg her to forgive me," Rebekah said.

Sadie looked puzzled and said, "Your mama? You said you didn't have any living relatives."

"Yes, my mama. She's here in New York and I hurt her; now I have to find her. I'll explain later. I don't have time right now." Rebekah rushed out the door and into the night.

"Wait, I'll go with you," Donnie shouted and ran after her.

They ran outside and jumped into Donnie's car.

"I thought you said your parents were deceased," Donnie said.

"I lied as I've been doing all along. I was ashamed of my mother and now I've hurt her. Lord, please let my mama be safe. She doesn't know anything about being alone in New York. Please don't let anything happen to her," Rebekah prayed.

Donnie realized that Rebekah was hurting and scared. He didn't question her anymore. He thought there would be another time when he could learn the truth about Rebekah's family.

They went to the Waldorf Astoria Hotel but Beulah wasn't there. They asked the desk clerk if Beulah had said anything before she left. The clerk told Rebekah that she had seen Beulah talking to the doorman. They asked the doorman about Beulah and he told them that she had asked about the closest river.

Rebekah remembered how Beulah liked to sit by the water and think. They drove in the direction the doorman said Beulah had gone. As Donnie drove, Rebekah wanted to stop and ask people if they had seen Beulah. But with so many people on the streets of New York and most of them minding their own business, she knew that no one would remember seeing Beulah. Because New York City was so big, Rebekah feared that she would never find Beulah.

They searched the area between the Waldorf Astoria Hotel and the church where the wedding rehearsal took place, but they couldn't find any trace of Beulah.

Then they heard on the car radio that an unidentified woman had been hit by a truck just a few blocks from the river near the hotel. Donnie and Rebekah were not far from where the radio announcer said the accident had happened. Rebekah recalled the look in her mother's eyes when she rejected her at the wedding rehearsal. Somehow she knew that the unidentified woman was her mother but she prayed that she was wrong.

"Lord, please let me find my mama and please let her be all right," Rebekah prayed.

She urged Donnie to drive faster. When they arrived at the scene of the accident, she didn't wait for him to bring the car to a complete stop. She was off running as soon as the car began to slow down.

She pushed her way through the crowd, still praying. An ambulance and police cars were on the scene and Rebekah's worst fear was confirmed. The body in the street was Beulah. Rebekah ran to where Beulah's body lay in the street, so still, so peaceful. Even in death, behind the disfigurement of her face, Rebekah saw a smile. The glow of the headlights from cars and trucks reflected on the still face of Rebekah's mother.

The smile on Beulah's face seemed to widen the moment Rebekah's tears fell on it. Beulah was always smiling, even when people recoiled from her disfigured face, she smiled, comfortable knowing that she was loved by God and Rebekah. When people touted her, she smiled. When little children pointed at her and called her ugly, she smiled. When people whispered about her, thinking that she didn't hear the names they called her, she smiled. But when she saw shame in her daughter's eyes, she did not smile.

Rebekah knelt by her mother's body, cradled her in her arms, and screamed with such horrified sounds, that seemed to be coming from someone else. Donnie tried to console her but guilt and grief were attacking her, ripping out her soul, tearing open her heart. The sound coming from her throat was the sound of her anguish, the sound of her guilt, the sound of a heart dying. Rebekah was so distraught, her legs would no longer support her body. When she tried to stand, she collapsed. Donnie had to physically pick her up and carry her to the car.

The ambulance took away Beulah's body, and Rebekah and Donnie followed in his car. People in the crowd that had gathered were shaking their heads and whispering to one another.

"She just started across the street and couldn't make it. Poor woman, she never had a chance. It was like she didn't hear the horn," someone said.

Rebekah made arrangements for Beulah's body to be shipped back to Mobile. Donnie made plans to accompany her. Sadie wanted to go too, but said she had to stay with her business.

"If you need anything, feel free to call me," Sadie said.

Rebekah told Donnie and Sadie the truth, how she had lied to her mother, lied about her mother, rejected her mother, and how she was ashamed of her mother's burned face and disfigured body. She was sure God was punishing her for lying about the phony car accident.

She felt that she had been cursed because the lie about the accident came true, but her mother was the victim. Rebekah didn't care anymore about what people thought. She had lost the woman who loved her more than life. Rebekah knew that she would never again find a love like her mother's love.

After Rebekah told Sadie the truth about her family, she felt that Sadie's attitude changed toward her. Rebekah couldn't think about that now. She had to prepare to take the last trip with her mother. How ironic, Rebekah thought, her mother's first trip to New York was the last trip of her life.

CHAPTER FIVE
Mama's Party

The train ride to Mobile seemed to take forever. The sound of the train whistle reminded Rebekah of a funeral song. She, Donnie, and Beulah's body arrived in Mobile about six o'clock in the morning, the day after Christmas.

Dawn was just breaking, the settled people of Mobile were just waking up and the folks living the "fast life" were just going to bed. Rebekah had never known Mobile to be so deserted, so quiet, and so lonesome.

Amy and Pete met the train. Amy's eyes were red and swollen from crying, she couldn't stop crying. She kept telling Pete that the train's whistle sounded as if it were crying, too. As Rebekah walked from the train, Amy embraced her. Rebekah introduced Donnie to Pete and Amy.

Rebekah's eyes were also red and swollen from crying.

Donnie was glad that he had made the trip with her; she had cried all the way from New York. They had changed trains in Atlanta, Georgia, and Rebekah was so distraught and engrossed in her sorrow that they almost missed their connecting train. Had they missed it, Beulah's body would have arrived in Mobile before Rebekah and Donnie.

After finalizing the transportation arrangements for Beulah's body to go to the funeral home, Donnie and Rebekah went home with Amy and Pete. Amy told Rebekah that she had already made funeral arrangements.

"I knew you wouldn't feel up to doing it. When you have rested and eaten, we can talk. We have plenty of space at our house. I know you don't want to stay in your mother's house. It holds too many memories. Besides, Pete and I would love the company of city folks, especially folks from New York," she said. Amy tried being witty to lessen Rebekah's pain, but to no avail.

Although it was December, it was a warm, sunny day — and a sad day, for tomorrow Rebekah would bury her mother. Rebekah couldn't forget the look on Beulah's face when she rejected her at the wedding rehearsal. She wondered if she had contributed to her mother's death.

After she had rested a while, Amy said to her, "Let's walk outside in the yard and chat. We'll leave the menfolk to talk about menfolk's stuff and we'll talk women talk."

She smiled, still trying to cheer Rebekah.

As they walked in the yard, Amy pulled Beulah's letter from her jacket pocket.

"I have something from your mother that I think you should read. She mailed it to me from New York," said Amy.

She handed Rebekah the letter. They stopped and sat on the steps leading into the fruit orchard. The moonlight from the December moon seemed to cast a spotlight on the two women. A flood light hung over the steps, Rebekah stood under the light, took the letter from the envelope and silently began to read it.

"Dear Amy,

"It's time that Rebekah and you know the truth. Amy, please take care of Rebekah; you're her stepmother. Your husband, Pete, is her father but he never knew it. I know I made a mess of things but I thought it was best that I kept this secret.

My friend, you never let my race nor my disfigurement get in the way of our friendship. You'll never know how much I appreciate you being there for me through the years.

I'm sorry to have to hurt you with this secret. Rebekah belonged to us both, to my sister Beatrice, who was her biological mother, and to me, her aunt. But to me she was never my niece. She was my daughter. I devoted my life to making her happy.

I pulled Rebekah from her burning crib when she was three months old. I was engulfed in flames in the effort. I risked my life to save hers and she grew up and became ashamed of me. Jesse, my tall, handsome husband-to-be, was waiting for me at the altar. When I was finally released from the hospital, he couldn't bear to look at my burned face.

"When Rebekah was a little girl, about two or three years old, before she learned society's definition of what's pretty and what's ugly, when she looked at me I saw love in her eyes. She hugged me and kissed me goodnight every night before she went to bed. She used to say to me 'I love you, Mommy' every night before she understood what those words meant.

But as she grew older, I noticed a change in the way she looked at me. She stopped bringing her friends home and she stopped telling me about functions at her school, although her classmates' parents attended those functions.

I always learned about such things through my neighbors when they asked me why I hadn't attended. She grew ashamed of me and I couldn't bear that look from her. The neighbors used to tell me how Rebekah could really step when she was the majorette leader. But I never got a chance to see her march; I was always working.

"I gave up all hope of ever getting married. Who would want me? I was an ugly, poor, colored woman, and I knew you were paying me more than the going rate for housework. Amy, I don't know what we would have done without your help. The insurance that Gary and Beatrice had was gone a long time ago.

There was only one reason why I stayed in Mobile, because one day I wanted Rebekah to know that Pete Waldon is her father. I wanted her to know that her father is a man of means, one of Mobile's most prominent attorneys. I'm going to stay in New York where no one will be ashamed of me. Don't worry about me. I'll be all right, I'm a survivor.

Goodbye, Amy.

I love you and Rebekah"

"After I read Beulah's letter, I wanted to know more about the tragic fire that claimed her family and, I must admit, I wanted to know more about her relationship with Pete. I talked with Beulah's longtime friend, Williemae, and I learned that she was with Beulah the day your family's tragedy occurred. Williemae was going to be one of Beulah's bridesmaid," said Amy.

The following is what Amy learned from Williemae:

****

Beulah and Beatrice were like two peas in a pod, exactly alike in every way. They walked alike, talked alike, and enjoyed dressing alike. They were inseparable, identical twin daughters of Clarence and Julia Mosley. Both Clarence and Julia worked for the Waldons. Julia was their cook and housekeeper; Clarence was the gardener, handyman, and chauffeur. Julia's parents and Clarence's parents had also worked as servants for rich white families in Mobile.

Clarence and Julia wanted their twin daughters to be more than servants for rich white families. They wanted their daughters to be educated, professional women. Clarence and Julia made sure that Beatrice and Beulah went to school everyday. After leaving the Waldon's house in the evenings, tired and weary, Julia went home, cooked supper for her family, prepared clothes for Beatrice and Beulah to wear to school the following day and helped them with their homework as best she could. They were hard times but they were the best of times; they were a loving family.

Pete Waldon, Jr., Beulah, and Beatrice grew up together. When they were babies, Julia had to go to the Waldon's house to take care of Pete, Jr. While she took care of him, she also took care of her twin daughters. All three children played together and even ate at the same table while Julia cooked for Judge Pete Waldon, Sr., his wife Hettie, and Pete, Jr.

Pete, Jr. went to an all-white high school, while Beulah and Rebekah went to Spencer High School, an all Negro school. The twins grew into beautiful young women and Pete grew into a handsome young man. When they graduated from highschool, Pete went away to college and Beatrice and Beulah got jobs in the local mill. They were going to work and save money to go to college, one day.

During one of his visits home from college, Pete saw Beatrice differently. She was now a beautiful, desirable woman and one night under a full Alabama moon, they made love, the first of many times to come. Soon, they were secretly meeting every time Pete came home from college and a romantic relationship developed.

Three years passed after they graduated from highschool. Beulah and Beatrice were now twenty-two years old. Pete would soon start his last year of college. Judge Waldon, Sr. had already started the process of registering young Pete for law school, when he overheard Pete's friends teasing him about liking dark meat.

When another friend asked why they teased Pete that way, the friend said, "'cause he's got a colored girlfriend."

Judge Waldon, Sr. had suspected that Pete, Jr. had a secret lover, but Judge Waldon had no idea it was their servant's daughter, and a Negro at that. He immediately took Pete out of college and sent him to a private school where a friend, a former law partner, was the President.

Meanwhile, Beatrice discovered that she was pregnant with Pete's baby. She wrote to Pete but her letters were returned unopened. Pete's mail was censored at the request of Judge Waldon, a powerful, political figure in Mobile and a fraternity brother of the Dean of the private school where Pete, Jr. had transferred. Pete was afraid to write to Beatrice at her home, her family might discover their secret affair. Beatrice didn't know that Pete's mail was being censored. She interpreted her returned letters as rejections. She had always felt uncomfortable being Pete's secret lover. She knew there would be serious racial repercussions if they were found out.

Beatrice didn't want to bring disgrace on her family by being an unwed mother and felt abandoned by Pete. She felt that if he had really loved her and wanted to be with her for the rest of his life, he could have found a way to see her in spite of his father's objections and in spite of his father's efforts to keep them apart.

She thought their racial difference was the reason he hadn't answered her letters. Beulah and Beatrice cried together and discussed what to do to keep their parents from finding out about the pregnancy. Beatrice couldn't work and take care of an infant. Her parents would be disgraced, she couldn't afford to provide for a baby, and an abortion was unthinkable.

Gary, a supervisor at the mill, was ten years older than Beatrice and crazy about her. Gary was a tall, light-complexioned man, with a neatly trimmed mustache and wavy hair that he wore combed back off his face. He had been working at the mill eight years before he met Beatrice and Beulah. Gary had already saved a little money for "a rainy day" as he said when his friends asked him why he always put most of his paycheck into a savings account or investment opportunities. Beatrice dated Gary a few times but her heart was with Pete.

It was on their third date that they had sex initiated by Beatrice. Gary felt he had disrespected her and he said he was sorry things had "gotten out of hand." A month later Beatrice told Gary she was pregnant with his child. Gary was elated and insisted that they get married before the baby was born.

Beatrice and Gary were married and moved into a small house. Clarence and Julia were thrilled that they would soon be grandparents. Beulah was ecstatic at the prospect of becoming an aunt.

Beatrice was happy with her pregnancy because her family was happy about it, yet she was apprehensive, she feared Gary would one day discover that he was not the real father. She hoped she could pull off the deception.

Gary bought baby clothes and transformed one of the bedrooms into a nursery. He hung new wallpaper with little hearts on it and made a rocking chair out of an old wooden beer keg. Gary was beaming with pride the entire nine months Beatrice was pregnant. Soon Rebekah was born, as pretty as a picture. Since Beatrice and Gary were both light-complected, it was easy to believe that Gary was Rebekah's natural father.

Rebekah was three months old when her aunt Beulah was preparing to marry Jesse Torrance, her highschool sweetheart. After graduating from highschool, Jesse joined the Army. He had recently returned to Mobile, Alabama and he and Beulah started "courtin.'" A few months later, he proposed and she accepted.

Julia, a seamstress, was excited about making Beulah's wedding dress. Because Beatrice and Gary had married in a hurry, Julia didn't have the opportunity to make Beatrice's wedding grown. Julia, Clarence, and the wedding party were at Gary's and Beatrice's house the night before Beulah's wedding, adding last minute touches to her gown and enjoying cookies and fruit, drinking sodas, laughing at Gary's jokes and "Ooohing" and "Ahhing"at how cute baby Rebekah was.

"We'll save the gown for Rebekah to wear when she gets married. Then she can really have something old," Julia joked.

"It's a masterpiece, Mom," Beulah said as she admired her slender body and beautiful green eyes in Beatrice's full length mirror. The satin gown with handmade lace was indeed exquisite.

It was late when members of the wedding party left for home. Beulah had planned to leave for her wedding from her twin sister's house. Clarence and Julia also chose to stay over to be with their daughters. The wedding was to be a big event. Beatrice would style Beulah's hair before the wedding and place the halo and veil on her head.

After the wedding, there was to be a barbecue and reception in Beatrice and Gary's backyard. Julia, Beatrice, and Beulah had done all the cooking and Gary was going to mesmerize everyone with his famous barbecue sauce.

The following morning when they got up, everyone was too excited to eat breakfast; they were all focusing on the wedding. Gary was to be the best man and Beatrice was the maid of honor. Beulah was as happy as a school girl; she was finally going to marry her love. She dressed in her beautiful gown and modeled it so her mother and sister could see it. Beatrice and her mother were proud of the way Beulah's wedding gown had turned out. Julia beamed with pride and lovingly touched her daughter's face.

Clarence hugged his daughter.

"You're as pretty as a picture," he said. "You look just like your mama did when she married me."

Beulah wiped her tears.

It was a beautiful day in May. The birds were singing and Beulah was in love. The limousine had arrived to carry the wedding party, the bride, and her parents to the church. Beulah and the wedding party had gone outside, and were talking to the driver and preparing to get into the limousine, she expected the others to follow her outside as they were all dressed and ready to leave.

Julia and Clarence were going out the front door and Beatrice was gathering the baby, the baby's bag, diapers, and extra bottles of milk and apple juice. Gary gave a last minute check on the food for the barbecue. All of a sudden, the house shook and Beulah heard a loud boom that sounded like thunder. Immediately, the house was engulfed in flames as if someone had set a torch to it. Beulah's family was in that house, and she struggled to go back inside, but the intense heat wouldn't permit her. The limousine driver, her friend Williemae, and other members of the wedding party tried to restrain Beulah, but to no avail. She had to try to save her family.

The windows of the house blew out. The fire was so intense, the metal around the door frame melted. Beulah screamed for her family.

"Beatrice! Mama! Lord, what happened to my family? Daddy! Gary!"

She screamed as she ran toward the burning house. She was wearing a long, white wedding gown and veil. Neighbors and members of the wedding party tried to put out the fire, but it was too intense. Beulah ran to the back door, tried to open it, and the hot door handle burned her hands. Her wedding veil was just long enough to be a fire hazard.

Beulah heard Rebekah, the baby, crying and coughing. But her cries were getting weaker. She knew that Rebekah was still alive, but the firemen couldn't reach her because of the smoke and heat. Beulah went into the house through a window off the back porch. She wasn't going to let her niece burn to death. She got down on her hands and knees and crawled through the thick smoke, calling for her family but she got no answer. She heard the faint whimper of the baby and crawled in the direction of her weak cries.

When Beulah the baby's crib, a burning ceiling beam directly above the crib broke and began to fall. Beulah covered Rebekah's body with hers to protect Rebekah from the falling beam. The beam struck Beulah on her head and back and knocked her down, almost unconscious, but she couldn't lose consciousness, she had to save the baby. She fought back the dizziness and the blackness that attempted to overcome her.

The smell of burning flesh permeated the air, a smell Beulah would never forget. Her sister's once beautiful home was now ashes and her best friend and parents were gone. Her hands, face, and hair, were burned. The hem of her long gown had caught fire and burned up to the waist. Engulfed in flames, Beulah still managed to save her little three-month-old niece. People pulled off their shirts, and jackets and threw them on her, trying to put out the fire. She remembered the pain that seemed to go right to her bones.

Three days later she awakened in the hospital in excruciating pain and covered in bandages from her head to her feet. She asked about her family. The doctor told her that the baby was all right and Beulah slipped into blackness, peaceful, soothing blackness. Blackness that shielded her from the terrible, intense pain. She floated slowly toward a soft light and the sound of sweet music that seemed to take away the pain.

She heard her sister's voice. "Beulah," the voice said, "take care of my baby. She needs you. It's not your time yet."

"Not my time? Beatrice, don't leave me. We're twins. We were born together. We're supposed to stay together," Beulah said. "Where's Mama and Daddy?" Beulah asked. "I want to come with y'all."

"No, not yet. We'll be together again, but Rebekah needs you. You must go back," the voice said.

Beulah tried to protest and follow her sister's voice as the nurse restrained her in bed.

"She keeps asking for her parents and her sister. We told her the baby is okay but we didn't tell her that her entire family perished in that fire. It was just awful. Her twin sister, mother, father, and brother-in-law, all gone. It's a miracle that anyone made it out alive," said the nurse to the doctor.

The pain returned and Beulah became aware of people standing around her bed. She heard the nurse's conversation with the doctor, and vowed that she would become Rebekah's mother and raise her as if she were her own child.

No one knew what caused the explosion. Some people speculated that someone left the gas stove on and when they tried to light it, too much gas had filled the room and then ignited. Others theorized that the house was built on a site where a dairy once stood and a gas pipe in the ground burst and the built up gas exploded. Whatever the reason for the explosion, houses in that section of development outside Mobile's city limits stopped selling. They were soon torn down and that section was turned into a wooded area of trees, bushes, and tall grass.

Beulah was in the hospital for eight months initially but over the following years, she would return several times for skin grafts and other operations to regain her body functions and to attempt to make her deformity less repulsive to other people.

The doctors informed her that the tissues of her face were burned too badly to be reconstructed. The burning beam that fell on her injured her spine and left her body permanently disfigured. Her shoulders were stooped and she walked with a limp. Her hair was burned off, there were only holes where her nostrils should have been. Her lips were curved at the side, her ears were burned off and only holes were left where the ears had been. Her skin was mottled dark and light brown and resembled the hide of a lizard.

Jesse, her beloved, who had promised to love her forever, couldn't bear to look at her disfigured body and burned face. He still would have married her. She knew he would have; that was the type of person he was. But each time he looked at her, when she saw the look of disgust on the face of the man she loved, she would have died a little every day. She remembered the look of relief on his face when she suggested canceling the wedding.

Beulah had Rebekah to live for, her little orphaned niece. She had promised to be Rebekah's mother and father and she would keep that promise.

Beatrice and Gary, Clarence and Julia were smart enough to have life insurance policies and wills. Beulah and Beatrice were beneficiaries of their parents' wills and insurance policies. Rebekah was the beneficiary of Beatrice and Gary's wills and insurance policies, and Beulah was Rebekah's guardian.

Beulah used some of the insurance money and her inheritance to move back to Asheville, the section of Mobile where she and Beatrice were born. She bought a little cottage for her and Rebekah, not far from the bay where she loved to walk along the shore. She filed papers to legally adopt Rebekah.

Beulah also used some of the insurance money to pay hospital bills for operations to help her walk, regain use of her arms and hands, and reconstruct her facial muscles so that she could open and close her mouth. She also had a wig custom-made to cover her head where hair would no longer grow.

Because she was handicapped and ugly, she had to take any job she could get. Her circumstances forced her to take a servant's job with the Waldons. She worked for Judge Waldon, Sr. until he and his wife died. When Pete, Jr. and Amy married, Beulah went to work for them.

Beulah also scrubbed floors downtown at the Panmora Ritz Hotel when the regular cleaning woman was out. Beulah was good enough to scrub their floors, but when she wanted to rent a room to give Rebekah a surprise pajama party for her sixteenth birthday, the hotel manager told her they didn't allow Negroes as guests in the hotel. "Besides, y'all probably will like the Rex Hotel better," the manager had said.

The Rex Hotel was a little rundown building in the colored section of Mobile, called Needmo. Beulah decided to give Rebekah a birthday party at home. She decorated the house with balloons and games. She had planned to serve Rebekah's guests hotdogs, hamburgers, ice cream, cookies, and potato chips.

"Everybody serve that at their parties. I want you to serve hotdogs and hamburgers too, but I also want you to cook some fried chicken, make your famous 'tata salad. That'll be part of my birthday present. Please Mama," Rebekah pleaded.

Beulah never could resist Rebekah. She prepared the food for Rebekah's party and for weeks Rebekah's school friends talked about what a good time they had at her birthday party.

Beulah used to say, "I make 'tater salad. Don't be callin' my taters po," then she'd laugh.

****

Rebekah never knew the details of her mother's disfigurement. She knew about the fire but she never knew all the details until Beulah's death. Beulah always explained her disability as the result of a horrible accident that happened a long time ago. Beulah felt if she told Rebekah all the details of the accident, it might cause Rebekah emotional pain, and Beulah wanted to shield her from that. She didn't want Rebekah to have horrible dreams of almost being burned alive, and losing her parents and grandparents at the same time in a horrible fire.

Rebekah cried. All those years, when her aunt took the place of her mother, raised her as her own daughter, loved her more than life, she tried to spare Rebekah pain by not telling Rebekah about the horrible experience of the fire. And even after Beulah lost her chance to marry, she was never bitter.

Beulah didn't have to assume the responsibilities of a single parent. She didn't have to be disfigured. Rebekah wasn't her biological child. Beulah didn't have to risk her life to save Rebekah. Beulah could have been happily married, but she had done all this out of love for her twin sister, Beatrice, and her niece, Rebekah.

That awful fire had claimed the lives of Rebekah's mother, grandparents, and stepfather. With that knowledge, Rebekah's grief was almost overwhelming. She thought about suicide. She put the letter in her pocket, rested her head on Amy's shoulder, and they both wept.

"She was my aunt but she loved me like I was her daughter," Rebekah sobbed.

"This is a small town and I used to hear gossip about Beatrice and Pete," said Amy. "I've always loved Pete, and I knew that whatever happened in his life before we married, I would either have to accept the past or move on. I chose to accept.

Beulah was the most beautiful person I ever met. I didn't care what other people thought about our friendship. Nor did I care about how she looked. She was such a warm, caring person. There's an old saying, 'Beauty is in the eye of the beholder,' and when my eyes looked upon her, I saw great beauty.

I loved her because she was nice to me, to my family, and to everyone who knew her. She didn't look at people she helped as being colored or white, she just saw them as people needing her help, and she happily gave it. Mobile will never be the same without her. We were blessed to have known her."

Rebekah cried. She hugged Amy, put the letter into her pocket and ran inside.

Amy let her go.

****

It was December 27, 1960, a rainy Thursday afternoon when Beulah's funeral was held. She was killed two months before her fiftieth birthday. If all Rebekah's plans had gone as scheduled, she would have been married to Donnie for two days. But as she reflected on the way she handled things, she wondered if a marriage built on lies and deceit could have lasted.

On each side of the white hearse that carried Beulah's body – and on each side of the white limousine in which Donnie, Rebekah, Amy and Pete rode — were signs that read, "Beulah Margaret Mosley's Home-Going Party, all are invited." On the side of the other cars in the procession were signs that read, "Guests of Beulah Margaret Mosley."

When cars filled with Beulah's neighbors and friends showed up at Pete and Amy's house as part of the funeral procession, they said, "We're all her family."

The sky was grey and dreary and Rebekah was saying goodbye to the woman she had called "Mama." She couldn't breathe. She felt as if her heart was about to burst.

When the funeral procession came to a stop in front of Bethel Baptist Church, Donnie had to help Rebekah out of the limousine. Her legs were so weak, she could barely stand.

She used to love to worship in the little church where members of the congregation were like her family. When she was growing up in Mobile, she knew everybody at Bethel Baptist Church and they knew her. She loved to hear the choir sing and Reverend Ashford, the senior pastor, was her favorite preacher. She had been blessed by listening to him preach about God from the time she was born, but this day was the hardest she had ever known.

This day, she didn't want to enter the doors of Bethel Baptist Church. This day, it appeared that each face she looked upon mirrored the dark, dreary sky. This day, she would remember forever, because this day was the last day on this side of Glory that she would look upon the face of her best friend, the woman who had been her mother.

The walk from the limousine into the church, down the aisle to behold her mother's face and take a seat on the front row, was the longest walk Rebekah had ever taken. Beulah's body lay in a yellow and white casket surrounded by flowers and draped in a blanket of yellow roses. Rebekah looked at Beulah's face for the last time.

It was strange, but Rebekah didn't see the disfigured, scarred face she had known. Instead she saw the face of an angel. She never realized how beautiful her mother really was until that moment. Instead of looking at her mother through the eyes of the world, Rebekah was looking at her mother through the eyes of love, admiration, and respect.

The funeral procession drove slowly through the streets of Mobile, Alabama. Amy sat in the limousine as part of Beulah's "family," and began remembering the good times she had shared talking with her dear friend, Beulah. One day when they were sitting and talking, Beulah had said that when she died she didn't want a black hearse carrying her body.

She had said to Amy, "When it's time for my going-home party, I want to be taken in a white limousine. I don't want no black hearse at my party. I've lived a good life and I want to wear white, like the angels. And I don't want you to call my party a 'funeral,' call it a 'celebration.'

"You might not be able to see me, but ol' Beulah will be dancin' around Heaven, singin' praises to God for givin' me such a fine life. I'll be laughin' 'cause I won't have to get up early and scrub no more floors in places where folks don't want to be around me 'cause my skin is dark. And don't call the folks who take time off from their busy lives to come to my celebration, 'mourners.' Them be my 'guests.' They're guests at my party."

When Beulah talked to Amy about death, Amy shushed her, saying, "Bea, you're going to outlive us all. I don't want to hear nothing about you dying."

"I'm serious," Beulah had said. "If I go first, I want you to see to it that I have a party. I don't want my daughter to grieve for me. I want her to understand that death is just a temporary condition. I'll see her in Heaven."

Amy and Beulah had made a vow that they would see that each other's funeral wishes were honored. Amy had kept her promise.

"Although," Beulah had said laughing, "I don't see them rich white folks takin' no heed to what a poor colored woman like me got to say about your funeral."

"Now you never mind," Amy had said laughingly. "I'm going to leave instructions that you're in charge of my funeral arrangements, and if my instructions ain't honored, I'll come back and scare the hell outta everybody."

They both had laughed.

****

Rebekah was overwhelmed at the number of people who knew and loved her mother. She never knew how many lives Beulah had touched. There were people in Beulah's church who called her "Mama Beulah." There were young people whom Beulah helped to enter this world; she was the midwife who delivered them when their mothers couldn't afford a doctor.

There were white and Black people with whom Beulah had sat up all night when they were sick. She had cleaned their houses, fed their children and sent their children to school when the parents were too weak to get out of bed. Then she would hurry home to make sure Rebekah had a hot breakfast before she left for school. Rebekah couldn't remember ever leaving home without first eating a hot home-cooked meal.

There were neighbors who had eaten Beulah's cooking over the years. She used to pretend that she had cooked too much food and needed to give some away before it spoiled. But the truth was, she knew some of her neighbors were struggling to pay bills and put food on the table. She said as long as she had food, her neighbors had food, too. Beulah was also struggling to survive but she was better off than some of her neighbors.

Bethel Baptist Church was a small church and on this day it was filled to capacity with family and friends who had come to say goodbye to Beulah. The mourners, both Negro and white, spoke of the love Beulah had for everyone. Reverend Ashford talked about how Beulah attended church every Sunday, rain or shine, and praised her God.

He talked about how much she loved Rebekah, and how hard she worked, scrubbing floors, washing clothes for other folks, and cleaning other folks' houses, just to be able to give Rebekah the best of everything; trying to make life better for her. He talked about how at night, after working all day in the homes of white folks, tired yet determined, she went to scrub floors on her hands and knees.

"Sister Beulah, you're at rest now. The evils of this wicked old world can't touch you anymore. Sleep, my sister. This is your going-home celebration. When we march through the streets to the cemetery, that's your parade. When you're laid to rest, I know you won't be in that cold ground. I know you're in Heaven, dancing with the angels.

"The skies are grey today because the world mourns our loss, but I see light in the Heavens; the angels are rejoicing because their sister is home at last. No more crying, no more cruel words from insensitive people, no more finger pointing and talking about your earthly vessel, your body. Your work on earth is finished and God called you home."

People in the church wept as they shouted, "Amen," and rocked side to side in their pain.

Rebekah swayed back and forth, crying. Her mind drifted back to the days when her mother was alive.

She could hear Beulah saying, "Come and give me a big hug. My, but you're the prettiest little girl I've ever seen. I'm going to start carrying a baseball bat to keep the little boys away. You're going to be a heartbreaker when you grow up. You're going to break a lot of fellows' hearts, 'cause you're going to be so popular, you'll have many suitors. You're going to be a beautiful queen 'cause you're a beautiful princess.

"Now come here and give Mama a great big teddy-bear hug, then run and jump into bed. Don't forget to say your prayers and ask the angels to watch over you while you sleep."

Rebekah remembered waking up in the middle of the night, seeing Beulah prostrate on the floor, praying.

The yellow and white casket stood in front of the altar. The organist softly played, "Nearer My God To Thee."

"Mama, I'm sorry," Rebekah cried. "Mama, don't leave me!"

Donnie tried to console Rebekah, but the agony of losing her mother and learning of the tragic death of her family was too much for Rebekah to handle at once.

The seat where Beulah had sat for over twenty years was empty. There was a sign on the bench where she had sat that read, "This seat belongs to Sister Beulah Margaret Mosley. She's gone Home, but she's with us today in spirit and love."

Beulah's favorite song had been, "Precious Lord." She loved to hear Sister Vickie sing it, and when she heard it, Beulah would shout. This time, as Sister Vickie sang the song, there was no shouting, only soft sobbing. Beulah was now shouting in heaven. Rebekah wanted to join her mother in her everlasting sleep.

Sister Johnson read the Scripture from I Corinthians 15:51-58:

Behold, I shew you a mystery; We shall not all sleep, but we shall all be changed. In a moment, in the twinkling of an eye, at the last trump; for the trumpet shall sound, and the dead shall be raised incorruptible, and we shall be changed.

For this corruptible must put on incorruption, and this mortal must put on immortality. So when this corruptible shall have put on incorruption, and this mortal shall have put on immortality, then shall be brought to pass the saying that is written, Death is swallowed up in victory. O death, where is thy sting? O grave, where is thy victory?

The sting of death is sin; and the strength of sin is the law.

But thanks be to God, which giveth us the victory through our Lord Jesus Christ. Therefore, my beloved brethren, be ye steadfast, unmovable, always abounding in the work of the Lord, forasmuch as ye know that your labour is not in vain in the Lord.

Rebekah found comfort in those words, but she didn't find peace. She was still consumed with grief and guilt. At the cemetery, she cried for her mother's forgiveness. She fell to her knees in the wet cold dirt, buried her face in her hands and wept for the times when she could have gone home to spend time with Beulah but didn't. She wept for the memory of happy times.

Rebekah had no idea what she was going to do now that her mother was gone. Rebekah wasn't ready to face life without her. Beulah had always been no more than a telephone call away from Rebekah. Rebekah finally realized how much she had taken for granted that Beulah would always be there for her. Reality set in now that it was too late.

Donnie wanted to tell Rebekah that he was there for her, but he kept silent. He tried to understand what she was feeling and to comfort her however he could.

Meanwhile, Amy had no idea how she would explain Rebekah and Pete's relationship to her friends and family. She couldn't help but feel a little jealous that her husband had fathered another woman's child, especially since she herself was barren. Both Amy and Pete were respected professionals in Mobile and the Waldon name was one of the oldest in Asheville. Amy could have anything she wanted except the one thing she wanted the most, a baby.

Amy shrugged the thought out of her mind, feeling guilty that she had just buried her friend and was feeling jealous over something that happened before she and Pete married.

CHAPTER SIX
A Guilt Trip

Rebekah returned from the funeral with Amy, Pete, Donnie and friends she hadn't seen since high school. She was comforted to see so many of her friends. She hoped the expression on her face mirrored her appreciation. However, she didn't want to be with the crowd; she wanted to be alone. She went upstairs to one of the Waldon's guest rooms and stayed there.

The next morning, Rebekah awakened to the smell of bacon, cheese, eggs, grits, hot biscuits, and fried chicken. Miss Williemae had taken Beulah's place working for the Waldons, and was in the kitchen cooking. When Rebekah was a little girl, she knew Miss Williemae. Many days, Williemae and Beulah sat at Beulah's kitchen table, discussed the Bible and talked about old times.

Williemae was a robust woman in her fifties. She always had a big smile that showed beautiful white teeth. She wore her mixed grey hair pulled back into a bun on the back of her neck with a hairnet covering the bun.

Rebekah was surprised to see that Williemae's hair was long enough to wear in a bun. She remembered it being so short that she used to burn her fingers trying to straighten and curl it, using an electric hot plate to heat the curling iron and straightening comb. Sometimes she heated the curling iron and straightening comb in the hot ashes in the fireplace, or on top of the wood-burning stove.

Williemae and her husband, Tanner, lived two doors from Beulah and Rebekah. Williemae caught Tanner having sex with her cousin, so Williemae and Tanner separated when Rebekah was a little girl.

"If I ever get my hands on some money, the first thing I'm gonna do is start an organization to help women like Williemae," Beulah had said to Rebekah one day when they were daydreaming under the evening sky, laying in a field of morning glories and yellow

daisies. "I see a lot of women being hurt and ain't got no place to go and nobody to help'em. Maybe one day when you grow up and finish college, you can find a way to
help."

Rebekah was glad to see that Williemae was the person who had taken Beulah's place working for the Waldons.

"Now you go in there and sit yourself down at the table. You need a good hot breakfast. I knowed yo' mama fo' mo' years than you've been in this world. We're family. If you ever need me, call me. I sure did call on yo' mama when I needed her, and she was always there fo' me and fo' a heap mo' folks in this city too. Now you go on in there and join the men at the table," Williemae said to Rebekah.

Rebekah walked into the dining room where Donnie and Pete were just sitting down to eat. But Rebekah wasn't in the mood for breakfast. She walked into the dining room, said, "Good morning" to Pete and Donnie, drank a glass of orange juice, and made conversation about the sunny, cold day.

"The weather can fool you this time of year," said Pete. "It looks warm, but it's cold. Here, put on this sweater if you're going outside." He handed Rebekah a sweater that had been hanging behind the door.

"Needless to say Beulah's letter came as quite a shock to us all. I had no idea that you were my daughter. Amy and I stayed up most of the night talking about the letter, the situation, and how we're going to handle it. I want you know that I'm proud of you, it'll be difficult, but we'll work things out," Pete said to Rebekah.

"'Situation' and 'Work things out?' Work things out for whom and how? I guess I'm supposed to be a 'situation' now," she said. She took the sweater from Pete and headed for the front door. As she passed the hall mirror, she glanced at herself and became aware of her white ancestry with her green eyes and naturally curly reddish hair.

She walked outside, and pulled the sweater tightly around her shoulders. She walked around the yard looking at the tall trees standing like giants with arms stretched upward to the sky. She thought about what she was going to do with the rest of her life.

She thought about Donnie and Pete. She thought about Beulah and the tragic fire that killed her family, and she thought about college. She sat on the bench in the backyard a few moments and thought some more.

After forty-five minutes had passed, she walked back into the house and into the dining room where the two men were still sitting at the table talking.

"I've been doing some thinking about my life and I've made up my mind. I'm leaving tomorrow." Rebekah said.

Pete and Donnie looked startled.

"I thought you would stay a few days. Mobile is your home. My home is your home. Now that I have a daughter, I'd like to get to know you better," said Pete.

"No, I need to get away," said Rebekah. "I don't want it to be necessary for you to 'work things out' for me. And I certainly don't want to be a 'situation' to you."

Realizing what he had said, Pete tried to explain his meaning. "That's not how I meant that. I just meant that I didn't know I had a daughter, but now that I do know, it means that I'll have to readjust my life. I'm glad that I have a daughter. I'm glad that you're my daughter," Pete said.

Rebekah was still adamant about leaving.

"Where will you go?" asked Donnie. "College is still closed for the Christmas holidays. Why don't you wait a few days before you make up your mind? I realize you're under a lot of stress right now."

Rebekah was a beautiful, intelligent, young woman, but because of his family's name and his position in Mobile, Pete was a little apprehensive about the public knowing that he had fathered a Negro child. He wanted to take care of her financially, but publicly acknowledging that she was his daughter would take some thought. Rebekah sensed his reluctance to let people know that he was her father, and she wouldn't accept his offer of financial assistance.

Pete continued to try to convince Rebekah to stay in Mobile.

"I'll help you can locate a college closer to home than Maryland. Let's work on this together," Pete said.

But Rebekah was dying inside, partially because she had lost the only mother she had ever known, but mostly because she had mistreated her mother and didn't have the opportunity to say she was sorry.

"If I could just let her know that I really did love her and if I could just ask her forgiveness, I'd feel better," Rebekah said to Pete. "But Mama is gone and nothing that I can do will bring her back. I just can't stay here where everything reminds me of her. I have to get away."

Rebekah tried to explain to Donnie that she needed time to reflect and deal with her life. She would always remember the Christmas of 1960 that was almost her wedding day. But she would also remember the Christmas of pain and deceit, and feel that she had caused it all.

Donnie still wanted to marry her, but he couldn't persuade her to go through with the wedding plans. She was too embarrassed to face his family. He tried in vain to convince her that she wasn't marrying his family, she was marrying him. But still, Rebekah remembered how she had pretended that Sadie was her mother, not wanting to accept Beulah, the woman who had been both mother and father to her.

Donnie was heartbroken. He wanted to be there for Rebekah. He could sympathize with her grief but he couldn't convince her to marry him.

"What am I supposed to do, Rebie?" Donnie asked. "What am I supposed to do about our life together? Why can't we go through these troubles together? Isn't that what marriage is about, sharing troubled times as well as good times?"

Of course he was right; but still Rebekah refused to marry him. She decided that she was not fit to be a wife, especially to the man whom she was going to marry without inviting her mother to the wedding.

She informed Pete and Donnie that she wouldn't return to college. She said that she couldn't bear to graduate without her mother sitting in the audience.

Amy walked into the dining room in time to hear Rebekah's

announcement about not returning to college.

"That's nonsense," Amy said. "Beulah would want you to finish college. She worked so hard to see that you had the opportunity to go to college. Besides, you can't leave Mobile yet, there are legal matters to be resolved, such as Beulah's insurance policies and her will. You are her sole beneficiary."

"I don't want the insurance money. If I took it I would feel like I was profiting from my mother's death. I feel responsible for her death. I don't want any of my family's money. And about the will, the only assets my mother had were her house and furniture. I could never live in that house again; there are too many memories there. But I do want to go over there and look inside one last time. I want to get some personal items, like Mama's photo albums and other pictures of friends and family," said Rebekah.

"We'll invest the insurance money and the money from the sale of Beulah's house. You might not want it now, but you don't know what life has in store for you. We'll let the money grow until you need it," said Amy.

Rebekah went for one last visit to the house where she grew up. There were pictures of her all over the house, when she was one-year-old, two-years-old, and each year on her birthday until she went away to college. There were also pictures of Peggy, her dog that was killed when hit by a limb that fell from a tree during a thunderstorm. Most of the pictures of Beulah and Beatrice were destroyed in the fire that took the lives of Gary, Beatrice and her grandparents.

It would soon be New Year's Eve. Classes wouldn't start for almost another week, so Donnie decided to go back home. He kissed Rebekah goodbye and Pete drove him to the train station. Amy continued trying to convince Rebekah to stay in Mobile but Rebekah was so filled with self-loathing and was indecisive about her future, she refused to stay one day longer than was necessary.

Amy said, "You're Beulah's only living relative. You need to stay a few days to complete her business affairs."

After much pleading from Amy, Rebekah reluctantly agreed to stay until after New Year's then return to college.

****

After Christmas break was over, Rebekah went back to Morgan to finish her last semester of college. Donnie also went back to college but things were different between them. Rebekah appeared to lose all interest in school and in Donnie. Although she was once a good student, now she didn't study at all. She started skipping classes and flunking exams which she would have easily passed under normal circumstances.

There was a time when Rebekah wouldn't have touched drugs or alcohol, or hung around with a crowd that used either. But, after her mother's death, she started smoking marijuana, popping pills, and drinking liquor just to be able to sleep at night. She also started snorting heroin and cocaine, smoking marijuana mixed with angel dust and hash, smoking cocaine mixed with tobacco, and drinking Robitussin AC cough syrup with codeine.

Rebekah would try anything if she thought it would make her high. Someone once told her that she could get high smoking dried banana skins and she was dumb enough to try that. She put the skins into an oven and when they were dry, she crushed them up and tried to smoke them.

The codeine in the Robitussin cough syrup made her sleepy and caused her to itch. After drinking it, she would nod and scratch like a junkie. Sometimes the sweetness in the syrup made her vomit. But when she did manage to keep from vomiting, it was a nice high, especially when she chased it with beer or wine.

She started hanging with a crowd of students and ex-students who lived off campus. Some of them lived in Baltimore City, a few lived in Turner Station, some lived in Cherry Hill, some lived in East Baltimore, and some had dropped out of college. They were a crowd of young people who liked to get high and party every weekend. At one party she met Nicole, a tall brown-skinned woman, of husky-build, who wore her hair cropped in a masculine cut. Nicole had been a student at Morgan but dropped out in her sophomore year. She shared an apartment in East Baltimore, with three women, one had a regular job and was also a booster — stole items of clothing and sold them — two were boosters and hustlers, and they all got high on weekends.

After that night at the party, Nicole contacted Rebekah and they started hanging together in night-spots where such as, Twin Pines, Bill Dotson's Lounge, and The Forest — places outside of Baltimore City that didn't require identification to get in.

Rebekah's grades and conduct got so bad that Mrs. Harper, the Dean of Women, called her into her office hoping to help her stay in school.   "What's your problem, Miss Mosley?" Mrs. Harper asked Rebekah. "Why are your grades so poor, and what is this I hear about you skipping classes? We can't tolerate that kind of conduct from our young women. Morgan girls are cultured girls. I can't let you ruin the good name of this school with your bad reputation. I know you're going through difficult times right now after losing your mother, but you must understand that life goes on and I'm sure your mother would be very disappointed with your present behavior."

But Rebekah wasn't listening to anything that Mrs. Harper was saying. She just wanted to get away, wallow in her own guilt and continue with her self-imposed pity parties. She felt that if she hadn't been embarrassed or ashamed of who she was, her mother would still be alive. Rebekah felt that her mother wouldn't have been in New York in the first place if she hadn't lied about the fake accident.

"I need some time away from everyone, Mrs. Harper," Rebekah said. "I need to get away. I don't know where I'm going. I can't go back home. There's nothing for me there. I can't go to New York, there's nothing for me there, either. Wherever I stop, I'll call it home. I'll be moving out of the dormitory in the morning."

"How will you live?" asked Ms. Harper with concern in her voice.

"I'll be fine. I can stay with a friend until I get on my feet," said Rebekah.

"But you're throwing your life away. You're throwing your youth away."

Mrs. Harper continued to try to talk Rebekah out of leaving school but it was no use. Rebekah had already made up her mind. She thought that the best thing for her was to get lost in the world like

Beulah had planned to do.

Tamara also tried to talk Rebekah into staying in school and so did Mamie. Mamie was one of the young women with whom Rebekah was talking during registration when Donnie first saw her. Mamie, Tamara and Rebekah became friends over the years.

"You don't understand," said Rebekah. "My family is dead. The lie I told about my family being dead came true. How am I supposed to pay college tuition? I'm certainly not going to take any money from my white daddy. I can't believe he didn't know I was his daughter. And where do I go during vacation and holidays, to his house in Mobile and live with my white step-mama? I don't think so! My life is so fucked up, I don't know whether I'm going or coming."

"That's why you need to be with people who love you like me and Donnie. You know you're always welcome at our house. Besides, this is February. Your birthday is next week and it's only three months before graduation. You can do three months standing on your head. Come on Rebie. Don't be a quitter. Stick it out. What about you becoming my sister-in-law? That's out, too, huh?" asked Tamara.

"Tamara, you're the sister I never had, and as much as I love you, I can't take handouts and that's the way I would feel if I went home with you and stayed with your family. Three months seem like three years to me right now. It's not only my birthday next week, but the following week is my mother's birthday.

I can't stay here knowing that Mama is gone. We used to plan how we would celebrate my graduation. Now, two months before my twenty-third birthday, she's dead. And as for me being your sister-in-law, I'm not fit to be a wife right now. I don't even know who I am," said Rebekah.

"You're making a big mistake," Tamara and Mamie pleaded.

But Rebekah had already made up her mind. The following morning while Tamara was at breakfast, Rebekah started packing her suitcases with her radio and other personal belongings. She had made arrangements with Nicole to come and get her. Rebekah withdrew from the college credit union the little money that she had managed to save from her monthly allowance and from the small salary she received from working in the college library.

Had she continued the way she was going, she would eventually have been expelled from college for cutting classes, not doing homework, and sleeping in class. She thought she would beat the college to the punch and leave on her own without completing her last semester.

Nicole had borrowed a friend's car to help Rebekah move. While Rebekah was packing her belongings into Nicole's car, Donnie walked up. Tamara had told him about Rebekah leaving. Tamara had seen Nicole parking the car and figured that she had come to help Rebekah. When Tamara saw Donnie in the cafeteria she told him to try and talk some sense into Rebekah.

"So, it's true. You are leaving college. When were you going to tell me?" asked Donnie.

Rebekah stopped packing the car to talk with him.

"Donnie, my life is a mess. I would only ruin your life if I stayed. I wish things could go back to the way they were, but we know that's impossible. I know I'll never find another love like the love you offered me. But again, maybe that's my punishment," said Rebekah. "I lied to you, to your family, to my mother, and to myself. I denied knowing the woman who risked her life for me, she gave me nothing but love and I couldn't even give her respect," she said in anger at herself.

"You're hurting and you seem to be enjoying hurting all by yourself. Why are you shutting me out of your life? I told you before, I'm in love for the first time in my life and I don't want to lose you. But I can't live not knowing where you are," he said.

"I have to leave, Donnie. I can't face you or your family. I'm too ashamed."

Donnie was visibly upset. He had tears in his eyes and he tried unsuccessfully to keep them from rolling down his cheeks. He put one hand on her shoulder, held her chin with his other hand, and looked deep into her eyes.

"You are not marrying my family. You're marrying me, Rebekah," he said. But she still refused to listen and continued packing the car.

"No matter where you go, who you're with, and whether or not I'll ever see you again, you'll always be my girl. I believe that we were meant for each other, and if that's true, I'll see you somewhere in life. You'll come back to me someday. So, go on, baby, find yourself, and when you do, bring her to me. We almost made it, didn't we, baby?"

Having said that, he turned and walked away from her so she wouldn't see the tears that he could no longer hide. She watched him until he was out of her sight, tears running down her cheeks.

After she moved off campus, Nicole and Rebekah found a place together. The women with whom Nicole was staying was only temporary until she could afford a place of her own. When Rebekah moved with her, Nicole saw her opportunity to save money to move back home to Boston, Massachusetts, her home.

CHAPTER SEVEN
Forbidden Fruit

After Rebekah left college, she didn't change her mailing address right away, but remained in contact with Tamara. Tamara called Rebekah and told her that she had mail at the dorm. But Rebekah was too embarrassed to go to get her mail. She didn't want to face her former college buddies. She asked Nicole to stop by the campus to get her mail from Tamara.

There was a letter from Amy about a $20,000 insurance policy Beulah had left Rebekah and $7,000 from the sale of Beulah's house and furnishings. Rebekah called Amy and told her again that she wouldn't profit from her mother's death. Amy told Rebekah that she and Pete had invested the money.

"We'll maintain financial records until you're ready for the money. You're still young and you don't know what the future will bring," Amy had said. "Your money will be available when you want it. We'll reinvest the interest so it can grow for you."

Rebekah packed Amy's letter away with her other personal papers.

After moving off campus, Rebekah started looking for a job. It wasn't long before she was hired at a meat packing plant in East Baltimore. She soon learned where to purchase drugs, and she started lying to herself that she only used drugs for recreational purposes.

She was also hiding from her college friends, ashamed to face them. She felt they were all pointing their fingers at her, judging her. She felt that she didn't fit in with them anymore. They knew the directions their lives were taking them; they had goals. Rebekah didn't know what she was going to do from one day to the next. She didn't have goals anymore. All she had was a drug habit and bad dreams.

Rebekah and Nicole both worked for six months, and after paying their drug bills and living expenses, they managed to save a little money. When they finally accumulated enough money for bus fare to Boston and a few dollars to hold them until they found employment, they packed what little belongings they had in their furnished apartment and bought one-way bus tickets to Boston.

Nicole's family lived in Boston and they promised to help Nicole if she moved back home. Rebekah had no such promise of help. Nicole's family helped her and Rebekah find a two-bedroom, furnished apartment on Dudley Street in Roxbury, a section of Boston that was beginning to deteriorate.

It was 1961, property values were plummeting and the banks had stopped lending money to homeowners in Roxbury for renovations. The only way some people could recoup the money they spent in renovations to their homes was through fire insurance. So, one by one, they torched their houses to collect the insurance.

The apartment where Nicole and Rebekah moved was over a bar where drug addicts and other unsavory characters hung out. Pimps, prostitutes, and hustlers hung in the stairway that led to Nicole and Rebekah's apartment.

Rebekah made friends with Marie, their next-door neighbor. Marie had two children and a live-in, unemployed boyfriend who drank beer all day while Marie worked in the local shoe factory. Marie was a short, stocky woman with long black hair, olive-skin, and a wide smile.

When Nicole visited her family, her parents gave her money to help with her living expenses, but Rebekah was almost broke. She had been in Boston for one month and hadn't found a job. She and Nicole ate potatoes for every meal and often made mayonnaise sandwiches. One day Marie told Rebekah that they were hiring at the shoe factory where she worked. Rebekah went to the factory, filled out an application and waited to hear from them. Two days later they called her to come in for an interview, she was hired to work the assembly line on the 4:00 p.m. to 12:00 a.m. shift.

Almost immediately after she began working in the factory, Rebekah met Amanda, a co-worker. Although Rebekah couldn't understand why, there was something about Amanda that fascinated her.

One night when they worked late, Amanda invited Rebekah to go to a party with her after work. Rebekah agreed. "It's awfully late. Do you think the party is still going on? It's after one o'clock in the morning," said Rebekah.

"Are you kidding? The party is just getting started and will last all night. I can see you ain't used to going to real parties," teased Amanda.

Rebekah stopped asking questions. She didn't want Amanda to know that she was as inexperienced as she really was. Rebekah and Amanda rode the bus to the other side of town to the party. When they arrived, Rebekah began looking for something to drink. Any type of alcohol would do; she just wanted to get drunk and drown her memories.

She noticed there weren't any men at the party, only women. She also noticed that some of the women were dressed in masculine clothes. At first Rebekah didn't think anything about the way the women were dressed. Nicole also had a close haircut and wore pants most of the time, but Nicole didn't appear to be gay. She had never made a pass at Rebekah.

But when some of the women slow danced with other women, and held the women as men would do and gyrated their bodies against each other, Rebekah soon realized that it was a gay party, and everyone at the party was either a lesbian or bisexual. But instead of being apprehensive about being at a party in the company of lesbians, Rebekah was excited.

She had been curious about the gay life ever since she heard two college friends in the dorm next to hers and Tamara's, making love. They were moaning, making throaty sounds of pleasure, and Rebekah was aroused. She never mentioned her feelings to Tamara; she was too embarrassed.

Rebekah watched as more women arrived at the party. The way lesbians walked fascinated her; they were cool. She thought they walked with an attitude, as if they knew they were in control. A few of the women had on nurse's uniforms when they first arrived, then they went into a back room and changed into slacks and shirts. Some arrived in business suits and changed into either sweat suits or pants and shirts. Rebekah just watched, fascinated by it all.

She was surprised at how much all this excited her. Someone asked her to dance and she did. Her dancing partner introduced herself as Marty. Rebekah felt her heart flutter as Marty pressed her soft body against hers and she smelled Marty's cologne.

"Are you Amanda's lady?" Marty asked Rebekah.

"No, we just work together," said Rebekah.

"Then whose lady are you?"

"I'm my own lady," said Rebekah nervously.

"Suppose I want you to be my lady; what would your reaction be?" Marty asked.

"I don't know you," said Rebekah.

Marty was amused that Rebekah was nervous and encouraged because Rebekah hadn't said, "No."

"But you do know me. I just told you that my name is 'Marty,'" Marty said, smiling at Rebekah. "I've been watching you ever since you and Amanda got here. I was just checking you out. I noticed the other studs watching you, too. I figured I'd better make my move before someone beats me to it. Amanda may have brought you to the party, but I want to take you home. Is that all right with you?"

Rebekah didn't answer. Secretly, she was glad, eager, and excited that Marty wanted to take her home. She was excited that other women were looking at her in a desirable way. She wanted to be with Marty; Rebekah had been watching Marty too. There was something about Marty that turned Rebekah on. Marty's take-charge attitude fascinated her.

Rebekah had never made love with another woman and the expectation of it was almost more than she could handle. She rested her head on Marty's shoulder as they danced. That was Marty's answer. She knew she would be going home with Rebekah when the party ended. She pulled Rebekah's body closer to hers.

When the record ended, Rebekah looked for Amanda but couldn't find her. The last time she caught a glimpse of her, Amanda was standing by the bedroom door, kissing a woman who was wearing only a pair of panties.

Marty was a tall, thin, fair-skinned woman in her late twenties. She had deep dimples in both cheeks and wore her curly hair cut close. Ringlets of short curls cradled her face. She wore slacks and an open shirt, with a tee-shirt underneath and loafers.

Rebekah couldn't see the imprint of Marty's breasts. Her chest looked as flat as a man's. Rebekah thought Marty must have awfully small breasts.

About four o'clock in the morning, couples began leaving. Rebekah noticed that some couples had gone into other rooms and hadn't come out. Marty asked Rebekah if she was ready to leave. Rebekah said that she was. As Marty helped Rebekah with her coat, she kissed Rebekah on her neck. Rebekah couldn't deny the thrill she felt from that kiss. She knew that Marty and she would make love that night, and the anticipated thrill almost left her breathless.

They left the party. Marty took Rebekah's hand and put it through her arm and they walked up the street arm-in-arm, as a man and a woman would do. Rebekah felt embarrassed as they passed strangers in the street. She wasn't accustomed to walking with a woman in such an intimate way.

Rebekah was impressed with the way Marty knew all the things that pleased her, like opening doors for her, taking her hand as they crossed the streets, touching for no reason other than for the sake of human contact.

Marty whistled for a taxi; one stopped and they got in.

"Where to?" asked the driver.

"What's your address?" Marty asked Rebekah.

"248 Dudley Street," said Rebekah.

Rebekah noticed the driver watching them in the rearview mirror. Marty gently tilted Rebekah's head back and kissed her on her lips. Rebekah was surprised at how the kiss aroused her. Marty's lips were as soft as cotton and the warmth of her body combined with the smell of her cologne made Rebekah dizzy with passion.

"I have a roommate," said Rebekah. "We moved to Boston together from Baltimore. I don't know where she is tonight. She might be home."

"I thought you said you were your own woman," said Marty.

"I am. She's not that kind of roommate," said Rebekah. "We moved together to share expenses. We're just friends and nothing more. In fact, I don't know how I'm going to explain you to her."

They both laughed.

The driver stopped in front of Rebekah's apartment building.

"Do you want me to keep the taxi?" Marty asked Rebekah.

"No," Rebekah replied. "I want you to spend the night with me." She was amazed at her own boldness.

Marty didn't say another word. She had a smile on her face like a person who had just won a prize. She paid the taxi driver and followed Rebekah into the apartment building. They walked into the tiny kitchen and a note from Nicole was stuck on the refrigerator door with scotch tape. Rebekah read the note, gave a sigh of relief, and handed the note to Marty.

"This was my roommate," said Rebekah. "This note says that she's moving back home with her parents. Looks like I'll need to recruit another roommate."

"Will I do?" asked Marty.

"You mean you'd like to move in with me?" asked Rebekah.

"Why do you sound so surprised?" asked Marty.

"Because we just met tonight. How do you know that we can get along?" asked Rebekah.

"We'll work through whatever happens. As fine as you are, I don't think we'll have any problems getting along," said Marty.

"But this is so quick. We haven't been together yet," said Rebekah.

"'Been together yet,'" teased Marty. "You're so green and refreshing. We'll talk about it later," she laughed.

Marty took the initiative. "Let's lie down," she said.

They walked into the bedroom. Marty slowly undressed Rebekah.

Rebekah started undressing Marty. Then she discovered why the imprint of Marty's breasts didn't show through her shirt. Marty had gauze wrapped around her breasts to give the appearance of a flat chest. Rebekah was shocked to learn that Marty's breasts were larger than hers.

When they both were completely naked, Marty gently nudged Rebekah to lie on her back on the bed. Marty got on top of her, gently nibbling each breast until the nipples stood at attention like ripe blackberries. She kissed Rebekah's stomach and the muscles contracted with desire. Rebekah hadn't imagined that a woman's touch could feel so good.

Marty caressed Rebekah's body, planting warm, wet kisses as she slowly slid down to where soft dark pubic hairs grew. When she reached Rebekah's vagina, she gently spread Rebekah's legs and opened the lips of her vagina. The exposed clitoris was waiting to be caressed. Marty's warm, tongue gave the clitoris what it was waiting for, a gentle massage.

Rebekah moaned.

Marty knew just what to do and how long to do it. She knew just how to please. She knew the exact places to touch. She continued to gently nibble Rebekah's clitoris with her lips and tongue, being careful not to let her teeth touch the sensitive area, and when she heard Rebekah cry with passion, she knew she had done her job well.

When they had finished their lovemaking dance, Rebekah said, "You'll do just fine as my roommate."

"Then look no farther," Marty said smilingly.

They made love all through the night, and Marty stayed with Rebekah the entire weekend. They didn't leave the apartment the entire time. They spent the hours discovering and rediscovering each other and learning what pleased each other.

It never occurred to Rebekah that Marty might already be committed to and involved with another woman. Rebekah was lost in the pleasure of enjoying her newly discovered forbidden fruit.

Amanda called Rebekah the day following the party and learned that Marty was still at Rebekah's apartment. Amanda was upset with Marty. She accused Marty of stealing her woman. Although Amanda and Rebekah were only friends and co-workers, Amanda had hopes of making Rebekah her "piece," as Amanda called her women.

Amanda's skin was as dark as Marty's was fair. Amanda

thought that Marty was sought after by other women because of her complexion, and Amanda resented Marty for that. She planned to get even with Marty – to pay her back for stealing Rebekah from her.

Tanya and Marty had lived together for two years. When Marty hadn't come home over the weekend, Tanya called Amanda looking for Marty. Amanda was eager to tell Tanya about Marty and Rebekah. Tanya called Rebekah's apartment and Rebekah answered the telephone.

"Hello, this is Tanya, I want to speak to my husband," she demanded.

"Excuse me?" Rebekah said.

"Bitch, you heard what the fuck I said. I want to speak to my damn husband and you know exactly who the hell I'm talking about. I know she's there. You tell that bitch that if she don't come to this damn phone, I'll come over there and kick her ass and yours too. I know where you live. Now tell Marty her wife said come to the fucking phone!"

Rebekah put the telephone down and went into the bedroom where Marty was lying across the bed watching television. She told Marty what Tanya said. Marty swore under her breath.

"Nobody knew where I was but that damn bitch, Amanda. I'm going to put my foot up her ass when I see her."

Marty picked up the telephone.

"Hello, Tanya. Why are you calling here?" asked Marty. "I'm not coming back there. That's not home to me anymore. I've finally found someone I can really love. This breakup didn't just happen. You knew it was coming sooner or later. Why do you want to pretend that you're so hurt? Why do you want to start trouble? You don't want me, but you don't want nobody else to have me. Why don't you just go on and do your thing like you've been doing? It's over between us and you might as well face it."

"You just met that bitch, and now you say you're in love with her? She must be a good piece of ass, 'cause you're thinking with your pussy. You'll be back. Mark my words. You won't forget me that easily," said Tanya.

After they argued for a while, Marty hung up the telephone

and turned to Rebekah who was sitting on the bed.

"I think that big bitch is going to try and make trouble, baby. She thinks I left her for you. She's not accustomed to losing. But truthfully, you didn't take me from her. This breakup has been coming a long time. Meeting you just helped me make my decision faster," said Marty.

"Why didn't you tell me that you already had someone when I first met you?" Rebekah asked.

"Would you have let me stay with you that first night if you had known that I was living with another woman?" Marty asked.

"Probably not," Rebekah said. "But I'm not in the mood for any problems. I've had enough in my life. I don't need this shit."

"And there won't be any problems for you," Marty promised. "I can handle Tanya. I fell for you the minute you walked through the door with Amanda. I knew you were new to the crowd. I made up my mind that whatever it took to get you, I was willing to chance it. After you and I talked, I realized that you were an intelligent woman. I knew that I wanted you to be my lady."

Rebekah was curious, and a bit jealous that Marty had been involved with another woman. She asked Marty how she and Tanya met.

"Aw, baby. Why do you want to go into that shit?" Marty protested.

"I just want to know. Now tell me," said Rebekah.

"I met Tanya at a bar called Dee Joint. She was sitting on the bar stool with her legs crossed, wearing a short skirt. She had beautiful legs. She had been a strip-tease dancer in her younger days," Marty said.

As Marty talked, she noticed the expression on Rebekah's face. "Are you sure you want me to talk about this? See, you're getting angry. I don't want to talk about Tanya no more. Let's talk about us, you and me."

"No, I'm not getting angry. Go on, how did you meet the woman with the 'beautiful legs,'" Rebekah said.

"See, I told you that you were getting mad. No, I don't remember nothing else," Marty lied.

"I was only teasing. Honestly, I'm not mad. How did y'all meet?" Rebekah asked.

"I asked to buy her a drink," Marty said. "But she said 'No, I'll buy you one.' I sat on the stool next to her and started a conversation. When I put my hand on her leg, she didn't move my hand, nor did she move her leg. When I ran my hand up her dress, she slightly spread her legs so nobody else at the bar would notice, and I touched her vagina. She wasn't wearing any panties. I got jealous and pushed her legs closed and she laughed. I had just met her and I was jealous.

"That was five years ago. I went home with her that night and never left. We broke up several times and went back together. We've been living together for two years this time, but I wanted out of the relationship. I couldn't see us getting anywhere. Gay people want the same things out of life that so-called straight people want. I hate it when people look at me as if I'm some kind of freak."

"How will you get your clothes and things from Tanya?" Rebekah asked.

"My clothes? Does that mean you want me as much as I want you?" Marty asked, smiling. "Does that mean I'm your new roommate?"

Rebekah laughed. She hadn't experienced sex like she had with Marty. "Yes, I want you to move in with me. I'm taking you at your word when you said, 'Look no further for a roommate,'" said Rebekah.

Marty laughed. "I was hoping you'd say that 'cause I'm dead serious. I'll get my things tomorrow, but I want to concentrate on you right now."

They spent all day Sunday in bed listening to the radio, watching television, talking, and making love.

Monday morning when Tanya went to work, Marty went to the apartment they had shared and got her clothes. Marty left her door keys on the kitchen table with a note to Tanya that read, "Good luck."

After that, Marty and Rebekah were inseparable. They settled into a new life together and set "family" rules, as they called them. Whoever got home from work first started dinner.

When Rebekah arrived home from work one evening, water was running in the bathtub, which was filled with sweet-smelling bath oil. The apartment was spotless, the linoleum floors were shiny clean and the smell of fried chicken filled the air.

"Hi, Rebie," Marty said, as she kissed Rebekah and hurried off into the bathroom to turn off the water that had been running for Rebekah's bath. Rebekah walked into the kitchen and saw fried chicken wings, fried cabbage, with green peppers on the stove, and she smelled the aroma of corn bread, baking in the oven. She hugged Marty.

"Uhmmmmm, baby, I smell something good," Rebekah said.

"Yeah, our dinner is almost ready and so is your bath water," said Marty.

"I think I'll take a hot bath now. I want to wash today's problems away and step into a calmer atmosphere," Rebekah joked.

"Well, you've come to the right place, baby," said Marty laughingly.

Rebekah went into the bathroom and got into the tub of warm sudsy, sweet-smelling water. It smelled of baby powder and wild flowers.

Marty went into the bathroom while Rebekah was in the tub. She knelt by the tub and put her hands into the warm water searching for the soap and wash cloth. She found them, put soap on the wash cloth and began to gently wash Rebekah's body.

"I could get accustomed to this," Rebekah said.

"I hope you do," laughed Marty.

Rebekah laid back in the tub and rested her head on the back of the tub. "I just might fall asleep," said Rebekah.

"No you won't," said Marty, "Not before you eat the dinner that I slaved over the hot stove to cook for you," she teased and pretended to scold Rebekah.

Marty went into the kitchen to attend to their dinner.

Rebekah stayed in the water a few minutes longer and then stepped out of the tub into a pair of terry cloth house shoes and a housecoat laying on the sink. She went into the kitchen where Marty had already prepared a plate of food for her. While they ate they discussed their day.

Marty was a security guard in a place that made paint. Because she worked in security, she carried a set of warehouse keys. Sometimes she slipped back into the warehouse late at night, stole paint, and sold it. Marty was "hard-looking," as they called it. She wore men's clothes, and she walked and acted like a man. At a party one night, she tried to smoke a cigar like a man and got sick.

After they finished dinner and cleaned the kitchen, they went into the bedroom and prepared for bed. They both got into bed naked. Marty kissed Rebekah's body and massaged her breasts. She explored Rebekah's body.

"Your body is so hot," whispered Marty.

"Keep it up and you're going to be in big trouble," Rebekah said, as she closed her eyes and enjoyed Marty's gentle foreplay. Marty placed warm kisses on Rebekah's body, kissing each breast, and gently nibbling the nipples. Marty slid her body down Rebekah's stomach to her navel, planting warm kisses as she slid.

Marty's caresses felt good. Rebekah slowly opened her legs and gave a moan of pleasure when Marty touched her vagina with her fingers. Marty spread Rebekah's vagina open and gently let her finger massage Rebekah's clitoris.

"Oh, baby, that feels so good," Rebekah moaned.

Marty reached for a pillow.

"Raise your body, baby," she whispered.

Rebekah raised her body and Marty put the pillow under Rebekah's butt, elevating her hips.

"I want you to watch me make love to you," Marty said.

She kissed Rebekah on her thighs, legs, around her vagina, then tenderly kissed her vagina.

Rebekah moaned with pleasure.

Rebekah watched Marty's mouth make contact with her vagina. She could feel her warm breath and tongue on her clitoris. Rebekah's body started gyrating, responding to Marty's tongue massage.

Rebekah felt as if she were floating. Her body was tingling all over. It was as if her entire being was concentrated on one spot, that one feeling. Rebekah saw noiseless firecrackers exploding. She felt electric waves slowly moving through her body. She experienced utopia.

When Marty was satisfied that Rebekah had reached her climax, she slowly began her kisses from the navel up to her breast. Marty got on top of Rebekah, put one leg between Rebekah's leg and put one of Rebekah's thighs through hers, which made Rebekah's vagina rub against Marty's thigh and Marty's vagina rub against Rebekah's thigh. They masturbated each other like this until they climaxed together, and collapsed, exhausted, in each other's arms.

****

Rebekah and Marty always went to parties together. It seemed that every weekend the gay community had a party. One weekend there was a party at Bertie's house. Bertie was a stud, who lived with Cheyenne for over a year. Cheyenne always wore African style clothes. She wore her hair natural before the style was fashionable, and she always smelled of incense. She was tall, thin, light-brown skinned and she wore no makeup. She reminded one of a gypsy fortune teller. Rebekah and Cheyenne smoked reefer together and snorted cocaine and heroin, called doogie.

One night Helen and her sister Cleo were at Bertie's party. Cleo was a fat dike who, always tried to play hard and tried to act, walk, and dress like a man. Cleo was a nice-looking woman but she weighed over three-hundred pounds. She was always bragging about how good she was in bed, and how she could get any woman she wanted. But she was so fat, no one wanted her. They went to her house for her parties because she always had plenty of food and liquor.

Helen was a medium-built, brown-skinned woman in her late twenties and acted as if she was a little slow mentally. She worked every day as an office clerk. Her clothes looked as if they belonged to a much older person. They appeared to be too old-looking for her and too large. Helen wore her hair turned under at the ends and combed back from her face.

It was after midnight on a Sunday night at Bertie's and they had smoked all the reefer except the nickle bag Rebekah had. She had poured the reefer on an album cover so she could clean out the seeds before rolling joints. She used a matchbook cover to scrape the reefer so the seeds would roll out.

Rebekah was sitting on the side of the bed grooving to the music, sipping a glass of wine. She was feeling the effects of the two amphetamines called "big reds," that she had taken earlier, as she rolled joints from the reefer on the album cover in her lap.

Helen leaned over Rebekah's shoulder to read the album cover. Rebekah had rolled a joint and was licking it to seal the roll.

"Hey, that's Aretha Franklin's latest album," Helen said. "I've been looking for that album."

She snatched the album cover from Rebekah's lap, oblivious to the reefer that was on it. She turned the cover over to read the back.

"You dizzy bitch," Rebekah shouted, "You just knocked over my fucking reefer."

"Ohmygaw! I'm sorry," said Helen. "I was just reading the album cover. I didn't see your reefer."

"Bitch, I know you ain't waste my shit," said Rebekah. "I went to get that shit and used my last five dollars to pay for it. Ain't no place I know of where I can get no more reefer this time of night. I feel like kicking your ass. Get your ass down on the floor and pick up my shit."

The reefer had fallen on the carpet and it was almost impossible to salvage any of it. But Helen got down on her hands and knees anyway and tried to scoop up as much as she could.

"I'm sorry. I'm sorry," whined Helen. "It was an accident. I didn't mean it. Shhhh, don't tell Cleo, she'll kill me."

Helen put her finger to her lips signaling Rebekah and Bertie not to talk so loud. Cleo might hear them. Cleo would cuss Helen out and make her go home. Everyone said that Helen was operating on half a brain. "Her elevator doesn't go all the way up," Bertie said.

"It goes all the way up, but the doors don't open," said Cheyenne, and they all laughed.

Everybody started fussing and cussing at Helen, and each person in the bedroom took turns trying to get a hit off the last bit of reefer. Helen managed to scrape up enough for two joints. Cleo heard the commotion and came to see what was going on.

"Oh, shit," said Helen. "I'm in big trouble now!"

When Cleo learned what had happened, she cursed Helen and told her if she didn't sit her dumb ass down, she would knock her down. Cleo didn't mean it; she was just playing the big sister role. She had never hit Helen but she sure didn't hesitate to cuss her out.

After the party, Rebekah and Marty went home.

"I don't know if I like this gay life. I'm miserable all the time. In the straight life I know who to trust, but in the gay life, I don't trust men or women. I see men looking at you 'cause you're a good-looking woman and they're attracted to you, and I see women looking at you, 'cause they know you're gay and some of them want you," Rebekah said to Marty that night.

"But you don't seem to understand that I want only you," Marty said.

"I guess I'm just afraid that you'll leave me and go back to Tanya," Rebekah said.

"Stop worrying about past shit. That's over. You're my present and my future," Marty said as she hugged Rebekah for reassurance.

But Tanya wasn't about to let Rebekah have Marty in peace. Tanya felt that she had invested too much time in her and Marty's relationship to give up so easily. Tanya called Rebekah one night when Marty wasn't at home.

"Where is my husband, bitch?" demanded Tanya.

"She's not at home. Why don't you just leave us alone, Tanya? Marty doesn't want you anymore, she wants me. Can't you get that through your thick head? You seem to be the bitch and a dumb one at that!" said Rebekah angrily.

"How do you enjoy having sex with my baby?" Tanya asked obviously amused at Rebekah's anger.

"I think she's terrific," Rebekah said, feeling proud of herself.

"You're right; she is. I taught her everything she knows. I'm sorry, but I've got to have her back. I can't let you keep her," Tanya said.

"And just how do you suppose you're going to get her back?" Rebekah asked, almost gloating.

"You'll see," Tanya threatened. "I'll make your life miserable. Besides, Marty hasn't forgotten me. Do you think she can just walk away from a five-year relationship? I bet I can get her to make love to me. Do you want to make a bet?"

Rebekah didn't answer. Secretly, she was afraid of that very thing. She wondered if Marty had really gotten over Tanya. Tanya had referred to herself as Marty's wife and five years is a long time to be in a relationship, even in the straight life.

One night, after Marty and Rebekah had been together for almost six months, Dino, one of Marty's friends, gave a party. Rebekah didn't want to go to the party but Marty did. Lately, every time they went to parties, Amanda was there and tried to start an argument with Marty. Marty and Rebekah usually ended up leaving the party angry and Marty always took her anger out on Rebekah, accusing her of wanting to be with Amanda.

Once, in a fit of anger, Marty slapped Rebekah, but she promised it would never happen again.

Rebekah pleaded with Marty not to go to Dino's party. She suggested that they stay home and enjoy each other, put on some records and sip wine. But Marty wanted to go to the party to show off the new outfit she had just gotten out of lay-away. Marty had been paying on the expensive black and gold outfit for several months. She worked out at the gym three times a week, and she wanted to show off the results of her efforts. She was proud of the way it hugged her body. Marty was a sharp dresser and the crowd sometimes complimented her on her clothes. She convinced Rebekah to go to the party and promised they wouldn't stay long.

When they arrived at Dino's apartment, Tanya and the old crowd were already there. They were Tanya's friends; Rebekah was considered the outsider. During the months that Marty lived with Rebekah, their friends constantly encouraged Marty and Tanya to get back together.

Dino lived in a duplex apartment. The front porch was divided by a partition. One side belonged to Dino and the other side belonged to another tenant.

It was a hot, muggy night in June. Not much air was stirring. The apartment where Dino lived was partially hidden from the street by thick shrubbery. The windows were practically blocked by the greenery and not much air entered into the apartment. The electric fan in the window hummed, but it was just making noise, not making the room any cooler.

Because it was so hot, almost everyone in the crowd was wearing only panties — no brassieres. Next to Cleo, Tanya was the second heaviest woman at the party. She hadn't worn any panties to the party so she borrowed a pair of Dino's, and Dino was two sizes smaller than Tanya.

Rebekah noticed that the more Marty drank that night, the more she became possessive and protective of Tanya. The lesbians who played the role of the males and who were more aggressive were called "studs;" the more feminine partners were called "fems." Rebekah was a fem and Marty was a stud.

A slow record was playing and one of the studs asked Tanya to dance. Marty walked over to where Tanya stood, pushed the stud away and said, "Naw, man, she don't want to dance."

Rebekah was standing against the wall sipping a glass of rum and coke, smoking a joint, and watching Marty. She had an uneasy feeling in her stomach, like something bad was about to happen. Marty had given Tanya the encouragement she needed.

Tanya looked at Rebekah with a smirk on her face as if to say, "I told you so," and strutted her big ass over to the table where the liquor was and poured another drink.

To make Marty jealous, Tanya began to do one of the dance routines that she did when she was a strip-tease dancer. She danced around Marty, shaking her hips and caressing the nipples on her breasts. Using her tongue, she moistened her lips while coyly looking at Marty.

Marty looked at Tanya and begin to rub her crotch as a man does his penis when he's aroused.

"Damn, my thing is getting hard," Marty murmured half to herself and half to Dino, standing nearby. "That woman can still fuck up my mind."

Tanya was pleased with herself. She had gotten the desired response from Marty. Rebekah was furious and Amanda was enjoying it all. Amanda decided that she would just sit back and watch the action.

Tanya was a heavy-set, light-skinned woman with grey eyes. She had clearly been an attractive woman in her younger days, but the weight she had gained made her look older than her thirty-eight years. She was thirteen years older than Marty. Tanya was once married and had two children, a boy and a girl who lived with her parents.

Around one o'clock in the morning, when everybody was drunk or high and had paired off, Rebekah noticed that Tanya was missing from the room. When she looked for Marty, she noticed that she too was gone.

Amanda walked over to where Rebekah was standing and leaned against the wall.

"If you're looking for your woman, she's in bed with her wife. Now, if you had been my woman, you wouldn't be standing here looking like a damn fool with everybody but you knowing what's going on," said Amanda.

"You're a liar," Rebekah said adamantly, trying to show in her voice that she didn't believe what her heart knew was true.

"If you don't believe me, go upstairs and look in the first bedroom on the right," said Amanda. "But I warn you, your feelings are going to be hurt if you do."

Rebekah had to know. She started up the stairs. Everyone got quiet, watched her ascend the stairs, and waited to see what would happen when she found Marty. Rebekah knew what she would find but she hoped she was wrong.

With each step she took up the carpeted stairs she felt like turning around and running out the door, but she restrained herself. She had to know about Marty and Tanya. She reached the top of the stairs, turned and saw everyone's eyes on her. As she opened the bedroom door she heard Marty's voice.

"I miss you, baby, damn, I miss you. I miss the taste of this good pussy," Marty said.

Rebekah opened the door wider. The room was dark and, the light from the hallway was just bright enough for Rebekah to see Marty's head between Tanya's legs. Marty never looked up.

"Whoever the hell you are, shut the damn door. This room is occupied," Marty shouted.

Without saying a word, with tears in her eyes, Rebekah closed the door, walked down the stairs, past the staring eyes and the smirks on the faces of Tanya's friends, past Amanda, and out the door. She heard them laughing as she walked out.

"Hey, pretty lady," Amanda called to Rebekah. "You want me to take you home?"

"No, thank you. That's what got me in this shit in the first place, someone taking me home. I can find my way home alone. Tell your friend when she finishes making love to her 'wife,' to come and get her shit out of the apartment," Rebekah shouted over her shoulder as she walked out the door.

Rebekah went back to the apartment, crying all the way. She wasn't going to let Marty treat her the way she had treated Tanya by moving out while she was at work. Rebekah didn't know what she was going to do. Marty didn't come home that night. Rebekah cried herself to sleep, thinking about Tanya and Marty being together. All day Sunday she stayed in bed and cried, waiting for a telephone call that never came.

She thought about a verse she had read somewhere that said, "There are three situations that cause frustration: to try to sleep and sleep not, to try to dream and dream not, and to wait for someone who comes not," and Rebekah had experienced all three situations in one night.

During the six months Rebekah and Marty had lived together, they both shared living expenses, and with Marty selling stolen paint, they managed to save almost two thousand dollars. It wasn't a lot of money, but she and Marty were saving to move into a nicer neighborhood.

When Monday morning came and Marty still hadn't come

home, Rebekah went to the bank and drew out all the money they had saved. The furniture in the apartment belonged to the landlord, with the exception of the television set, the record player, and the radio. Those belonged to Marty. Rebekah called Amanda and told her to tell Marty to come and get her things.

"I'm leaving Boston," said Rebekah. "I won't be back, so tell your friend if she wants her shit, she'd better get it before the landlord sells it."

"Where're you going?" Amanda asked.

"As far away from Marty, you, and the rest of your crowd, as I can. Tell Marty she can move back with her so-called wife. I'm using the money in the bank to help me start over," Rebekah said.

Rebekah packed her clothes, laid her apartment key on the kitchen table, left a note for Marty that read, "Good luck," and walked out. She hailed a taxi and got in. The driver kept looking at her in the rearview mirror. He noticed that she was crying.

"Are you alright, miss?" he asked.

"Yes, I'm alright. I just want to get the hell out of this city and I don't ever want to come back."

"Where're you going?" he asked. "I'm not trying to get fresh with you. I just hate to see a pretty woman cry."

"I'm going back to Baltimore, Maryland" she said. "It can't be as bad there as it is here."

She and the driver talked about how hard things are for colored people. Rebekah didn't tell him that a woman had broken her heart. The driver thought Rebekah was crying over a man. When they arrived at the Greyhound bus station, the driver wished her good luck. She went inside and bought a one-way ticket to Baltimore.

Rebekah had been drinking, smoking marijuana, and snorting cocaine almost every night, but somewhere in her mind she had held on to the idea of finishing college and following her dream.

Rebekah was lost. She couldn't lift herself out of the abyss where she was killing herself with grief and guilt. And Marty and her crowd hadn't helped.

CHAPTER EIGHT
Life's Struggles

It was the fall of 1963, Rebekah was returning to Baltimore, leaving Marty and the heartaches she brought behind. When the bus arrived at the Greyhound Bus Station in Boston, she got on and sat at a window seat. The majority of the passengers on the bus were sharecroppers and migrant workers. They carried shopping bags and boxes tied with rope.

The trip to Baltimore was a long ride on dirt roads through small towns. Rebekah went to sleep and woke up; they were still riding. The driver stopped in a little town and everyone got off the bus, used the restroom, got some water and bought snacks to eat.

Rebekah went back to sleep and when she awakened, the bus driver was calling out, "Next stop, Baltimore, Maryland."

It was early morning; she had been riding all night. Her clothes were wrinkled and her makeup had smeared. She went inside the bus station and asked the lady behind the ticket counter to recommend a place to stay. The lady gave her directions to an apartment building nearby.

Rebekah had two heavy suitcases and she didn't want to walk far carrying them. But the woman had said that the apartment building wasn't far from the station. Rebekah thought she could struggle with them the short distance, so she decided to attempt to walk. She didn't want to spend any more money on taxi cabs; she didn't know how long she would have to stretch her money.

She passed by pimps standing outside the bus station, waiting for young girls to get off the bus. Some of the young girls were running away from home and the pimps would recruit them to become prostitutes. In a lot of situations, a life of prostitution was better than the conditions under which they had lived at home.

A pimp in a beige suit, beige shoes and a beige, wide-brimmed hat approached Rebekah. "Hey, pretty mama," he said. "As fine as you is, why don't you let me take care of you? I guarantee you won't have to worry about living expenses."

"Times ain't that hard for me," Rebekah said. "And if they were, I wouldn't be laying on my back to give my money to a nigga like you."

"You're too damn smart," he said and drew back his hand to slap her.

Rebekah set her luggage down and said, "Hit me if you want to and I'll blow your head off."

She had her hand in her pocketbook as if she were carrying a gun. She had learned that trick hanging around with Marty. The pimp didn't know if Rebekah was lying, but he wasn't taking any chances.

"I got a gun, too, but right now I'm working. I ain't got time for no bullshit with no broke bitch like you," he said and walked away. Rebekah gave a sigh of relief. She was so scared her knees were knocking.

She mumbled to herself, "'...as fine as you is,' you need to take a course in English."

After the encounter with the pimp, Rebekah thought it would be safer to get a taxi. She also decided against the address the lady in the bus station had given her.

Cabs were parked in a line outside the bus station. She went to a Black driver and asked him if he could take her to a place where she could rent a furnished apartment. The driver asked her how much could she afford to pay. When she told him, he said there were some decent apartments on The Avenue. The name was really Pennsylvania Avenue, but everyone called it "The Avenue."

"It's not the best section of Baltimore, but it's about the cheapest. You said you wanted to be where the action is; well, that's where it is. You can get anything you want on The Avenue, even a good ass whuppin'," he laughed.

When they got to Pennsylvania Avenue, the driver let her out at an apartment building with a sign that read, "Apartment for Rent." She went inside and knocked on the door marked, "Landlord." A fat man with an unshaven shaggy beard, wearing a dingy white undershirt and baggy overalls, answered the door. She asked to see the apartment.

"Wait until I get the keys," he said. "Are you alone?"

"Yes, I am," she responded.

"I don't like to rent to single women. Too much trouble. Got too many men running in and out of the apartment and they play the music too loud," the man said.

"Not me. I'm a quiet person. I just arrived in town. In fact, I just got off the Greyhound bus. I sure won't have any men running in and out of my apartment," said Rebekah, too tired to look any further.

The man sighed and acted as if it was a bother for him to show her the apartment. "It's on the third floor, follow me," he said.

They walked up the narrow stairs to the third floor. He didn't ask her if she needed help with her luggage. She struggled with the two suitcases by herself, dragging them up the stairs. She was glad she hadn't tried to walk from the bus station carrying the suitcases.

It was a small efficiency apartment, one large room that served as the kitchen, bedroom and living room. A daybed served as a bed at night and a sofa during the day. The apartment wasn't much, but she could afford it and still have enough money to live on until she found a job.

Rebekah told the landlord that she'd take the apartment and handed him money to cover the first month's rent. It wasn't much of a home, but it would have to do.

Rebekah lived as cheaply as she could, trying to make her money last, but the drugs and alcohol she bought every day took most of it. Finding work wasn't as easy as she thought it would be. She looked for work during the day, got a bottle of liquor and a bag of cocaine every night.

Two doors from the building where Rebekah lived was the Blue Moon Bar. She had stopped in the bar several times and kidded with Mike, the bartender and part owner. She learned that the police had closed the bar several times because of prostitutes hanging in there picking up johns.

Rebekah's money was running out and she still hadn't found a job. She didn't know how she was going to continue paying rent; she was already a week behind. Her landlord was kind enough to let her go without paying rent until she found work. She had explained her situation to him and he understood, but his wife was a different story, she wasn't as understanding. Rebekah had been in Baltimore for over a month and she had stretched her few dollars as long as she could.

One evening she was feeling depressed and she went to the Blue Moon Bar. She had gone to a temporary employment agency the day before and they wanted references from her previous employers. She told the agency about her job in Boston.

"They appeared to be reluctant to hire people with out-of-state references," she told Mike, the bartender. "I've worked in Baltimore before, but the plant where I worked is out of business. That's the first place I tried to contact for a job when I got back here."

"The drug trade is lucrative in Maryland and employers are apprehensive about newcomers if they don't have references. Look, baby, I'd like to stay and talk with you, but I'm going to the Royal Theater to see Ike and Tina Turner tonight and I'm leaving early. Now don't you get a bottle to nurse alone tonight. You're too pretty to be drinking and snorting that shit like you do," he said.

Rebekah laughed and waved him off. She didn't want to tell him how broke she really was. It was Saturday night and she didn't feel like going home alone to an empty apartment. She sat at the bar sipping a drink.

A man walked in and sat on the stool next to her. The bar was empty except for Rebekah and the bartender, but still the man sat next to her. He told her his name was Oscar, he bought her a drink and they started talking.

Oscar was a short, chubby man in his late to middle thirties. He wasn't especially good looking, he had a pot belly and no neck. He offered her fifty dollars to have sex with him. Why not, she thought. The night was dead and nothing was happening. The regular crowd wasn't in the bar; they must have gone to the Royal too, she thought.

After they finished their drinks, Oscar said, "You ready to go?"

"Where're we going?" she asked.

"I know a guy who has a place uptown about two doors up the street from the Lucky Number Club. We can stop at the Lucky

Number, have a couple of drinks, then go to my friend's place," he said.

It sounded good to Rebekah. They walked to the corner and hailed a cab. When they got to the Lucky Number Club, Morris the Music Man was playing the organ and Little Sam Cole was wowing the crowd with his rendition of "Summertime."

Oscar and Rebekah talked for a while and had a few drinks. He told Rebekah that he was in the army and was home on leave. He gave her his telephone number and after a few more drinks, they walked up the street to a rooming house. Oscar rang the doorbell and a short, fat, bald-headed man with no teeth answered the door.

Oscar said to the fat man, "I need a room for a couple of hours."

"That'll be two dollars in advance," the man said.

Rebekah felt cheap. She didn't like the way the bald-headed man smirked at her. When she thought about the fifty dollars Oscar promised her, she soon dismissed her feelings.

Oscar paid the man, and he and Rebekah walked up the narrow, dark stairs to a tiny, dingy room on the second floor. A string hung from the light in the ceiling. The man pulled the string to turn on the light. The bed had an iron headboard; a dresser with a cracked mirror stood in one corner; a table and chair with one leg missing from the chair stood in another corner.

There was no telephone, no television, no radio, the bathroom was on the next floor. The dirty broken linoleum looked as if it hadn't been mopped in weeks, maybe months. The plastic window curtains were torn and dirty and so were the window shades.

Oscar smelled of sweat. He started undressing and Rebekah did everything she could to keep from laughing at the little chubby man with knobby knees, wearing boxer shorts with flowers on them. She undressed and got in the bed with Oscar, where rusty bed springs creaked every time they moved. She giggled at the thought of the fat man downstairs listening to the bed springs squeaking and getting aroused.

They stayed in the room for two hours and most of that time Oscar was trying to get a hard on. When he did get hard, he lasted a hot minute. He started having an orgasm almost as soon as his penis entered her vagina. After they had sex, they dressed and left. Oscar said he had to go around the corner to his sister's house to get the money to pay Rebekah. He hadn't mentioned his sister before, and he certainly didn't say she lived around the corner. Nevertheless, they walked up the street and around the corner where row houses with marble steps lined both sides of the street.

Oscar told Rebekah to wait on the corner while he ran across the street to his sister's house. Like a fool, she stood on the corner and waited for him. He went to one of the row houses, knocked on the door, it opened and he went inside. Rebekah waited for about fifteen minutes and when Oscar didn't return, she walked to the house and knocked on the door.

A woman who looked to be in her late forties wearing an opened, faded pink, terry-cloth bathrobe, a white flannel nightgown, with rollers in her hair, answered the door.

"I'm looking for Oscar," Rebekah said to the woman.

Rebekah realized that she didn't even know his last name. In fact, Rebekah wasn't sure that Oscar was his real name. She hadn't asked for any identification and he hadn't shown her any.

"Oscar who?" the woman asked.

"I don't know his last name," Rebekah said, realizing that she sounded dumb. "He's a little short man, he knocked on this door a few minutes ago and went inside."

"I don't know no 'Oscar, don't nobody live here by that name, and didn't nobody knock on my do'," the woman said.

"I just saw him come into this house. I was waiting for him across the street. He said his sister lives here," protested Rebekah feeling foolish.

"Honey, you just got took, 'cause didn't no man come in my house tonight. I sure hope you wasn't dumb enough to give him no money or nothin' else, 'cause if you did and was waiting for him to come back, you be waiting forever. That's the oldest trick in the book that them old hustlers use on green fish like you. You don't know nothin' 'bout life," the woman said, and slammed the door shut.

Rebekah felt like she had been scolded by her mother. She

had just enough money to get a cab back to the Blue Moon Bar. She walked into the bar, sat on the stool, and tried hard to hold back the tears. She felt like a stupid fool. She had been had.

The next day, Sunday, she woke up with a headache. She took a shower and changed clothes. She didn't have any smack or doogie and she needed a fix bad. She went to the bar and Mike was working.

"You look like shit," he said to her.

"I feel like shit," she said. "My life is so fucked up, I wish I had enough nerve to kill myself."

"Wait a minute. Let's not have that kind of talk," said Mike. "Especially since you haven't given me a chance."

Rebekah looked at him in surprise. She hadn't thought of Mike as a lover. He was a nice guy, but not her type. He was short, chubby and looked to be much older than she was. But what the hell, she thought. I'm already doing bad. I can't do no worse. At least he's got a job.

"I need a job," she said. "Can you help me with that?"

"Have you ever worked as a barmaid?" Mike asked.

"No, but I'm a quick learner," she said.

"You're hired," he grinned.

"Just like that?" she asked, overjoyed at the prospect of earning money.

"Yeah, just like that!" he said.

"When can I start?" she asked.

"How about right now?" he said. "Not many people in here so I can start teaching you the ropes."

So, Rebekah became a barmaid, and she and Mike started dating. She got to know the regular crowd that frequented the bar such as Sassy, Pat, GeeGee, Daisy, Audrey, and the men who dressed as women and the women who dressed as men.

But things changed. Mike used to talk to Rebekah about drinking too much; however, after they started dating, he kept her supplied with liquor and drugs. It seemed like he wanted her to stay high or drunk. She was dating him because he was paying her rent. She knew she was drinking too much, smoking reefer too much, snorting and smoking heroin and cocaine too much, but she couldn't stop. Or maybe she didn't want to stop.

She didn't like having sex with Mike; it was disgusting to her. He reminded her of Oscar, in fact he resembled Oscar. But she needed the money he was giving her.

Audrey, a prostitute, and Rebekah became "hanging-out buddies." Mike didn't like Audrey. He thought she was teaching Rebekah the tricks of the trade of prostitution. Audrey was a feisty, defiant woman. She refused to give her money to a pimp. Rebekah feared that one of the pimps might harm Audrey to teach her a lesson so that other prostitutes would be afraid to be defiant like her.

One night on her night off, Rebekah and Audrey went to the Swan Club, a ritzy night club uptown. Rebekah was enjoying the entertainment and Audrey was looking around the club for possible customers. Audrey often got some high-paying johns from the Swan Club. The waitress came to their table and brought refills of their drinks.

"We didn't order anything else," Audrey said to the waitress.

"They're paid for. That gentleman over there sent them," the waitress said, as she pointed to the singer who had taken a seat at the bar.

Audrey lifted her glass and nodded her head, indicating "thank you."

Rebekah did the same.

The singer nodded his head, indicating "you're welcome." He then took his glass from the bar and walked over to where Rebekah and Audrey were sitting.

"Hello, pretty ladies," he said. "You're too pretty to be alone. Are you waiting for anyone and, if not, may I join you?"

"The answer to your first question is 'no,' and the answer to your second question is 'yes,'" said Audrey.

"My name is Brian," he said as he sat down.

"Hello, Brian, my name is Audrey and this is my friend Rebekah."

"Hello, again," said Brian.

"You have a beautiful voice," said Rebekah.

"Thank you," he smiled, showing even white teeth. "I'm

hoping to get a break soon and do some recording."

"How long have you been singing?" asked Rebekah.

"Since I was four years old. I used to sing for my mother's friends," he laughed. "I saw you two when you first walked in. I told my piano player that I wanted to meet you," he pointed to Rebekah.

"I guess that's my cue to leave," said Audrey.

"No, you're not going to leave me alone," said Rebekah.

"You won't be alone, you'll be with me," said Brian.

"You'll be alright. Besides, I've got things to do," said Audrey. "Looks like I see a customer." She left, promising to call Rebekah later.

A man in a grey suit walked toward the door without taking his eyes off Audrey. It was obvious that he was going outside to meet her, but he tried to act nonchalant and failed miserably.

"I'll see that you get home safely," said Brian. "If you need character references, everybody here knows me. I'm a good boy, well, as good as you want me to be. When I'm good, I'm very good, but when I'm bad I'm better," he teased.

Two middle-aged women were sitting at a table close to the stage where they could almost reach out and touch it. One woman was light-complected and stocky. She wore a purple wool suit, a mink stole around her shoulders that she held as if she were cold, and a pill-box hat with a veil. The other woman, a little smaller, was also wearing a suit and hat. Both women looked as if they were dressed for church.

"That's my landlady," Brian said, pointing to the woman in the purple suit. "That's her girlfriend she's with. My landlady wants my body but she's too old for me. I invite her to the club once in a while to make her feel good, trying to keep peace until I can move out. But tonight I met a flower amongst weeds," he teased.

Brian and Rebekah sat and talked. Meanwhile, the two women at the front table kept staring at her and whispering to each other. He had one more set to do, and he asked Rebekah to wait for him. After his last set, the landlady and her girlfriend talked briefly with him and the two women left. He and Rebekah went to an all-night diner for coffee.

Brian found Rebekah easy to talk to and they talked until dawn. He talked about himself and his dreams of becoming a star. Rebekah didn't tell him about Marty or Mike. She did, however, tell him about her college days and Donnie.

Brian suggested they go to a motel. "I want to get inside of you," he said.

"Some people don't kiss on the first date and here I am about to have sex on the first date," thought Rebekah. "I had sex on the first date with Marty, but that was different," she chuckled to herself.

She wanted to ask Brian why was it necessary for them to go to a motel when he lived alone. She also wondered why his landlady was at the club. Brian was so fine that she dismissed those thoughts. Plus, he had just copped some drugs for them. They got a bottle of wine, some beer, and went to a motel.

After that night, Rebekah started going to the Swan Club every night to meet Brian. They went to motels and to Brian's friends' houses to have sex, but they never went to his apartment.

Two weeks passed, and she wasn't spending much time at the Blue Moon Bar unless she was working. Mike was furious. He blamed Audrey for keeping Rebekah away from the bar and from him. He was waiting on the steps of Rebekah's apartment one night when he saw her get out of Brian's car. When Rebekah saw Mike sitting on the steps, she hesitated. Then she started up the steps, trying to rush past him. She didn't want a confrontation, she tried to avoid him and hurry into the apartment building.

As she passed, Mike grabbed her arm and twisted it. She screamed and told him to leave her alone, that she had found someone else, and she didn't want to see him anymore. She asked if they could still be friends, but he said if she couldn't be his woman, he didn't want any relationship with her.

He threatened to get revenge on Audrey and her. But Rebekah didn't take his threat seriously.

Rebekah and Brian had been dating for almost a month when he said, "I need to be in a place where I can make things happen in my career, so I'm planning to move to California."

She wondered what she would do if Brian moved to

California. She was missing a lot of time from her job at the Blue Moon Bar. Mike had stopped giving her money and she was behind in her rent, again. Brian shared his drugs with her and bought her dinner the nights they were together, but he wasn't giving her money for rent.

After the incident on the steps with Mike, Rebekah spent all of her free time with Brian, but she only saw him when she went to the Swan Club. He didn't make any efforts to get in touch with her and he didn't make it a secret that she wasn't the only woman he was seeing. A month passed and their relationship seemed to cool down. Brian stopped accepting her telephone calls at the club. She hadn't heard from him in over a week. When the weekend came around the second time and she still hadn't heard from him, she went to the Swan Club to see him. He ducked out on her, slipping out the back door, leaving her sitting at the bar. She was hurt and embarrassed and went home crying.

The following night after work, she walked out of the Blue Moon Bar and headed for her apartment. She saw Audrey getting out of a car. Rebekah and Audrey called to each other and Rebekah waited for Audrey to run across the street.

"What you got in that bag?" asked Audrey. "I know you ain't drinking alone again, waiting for that nigga to call you. I told you that you were just a short-term thrill for Mister Crooner. You've got a lot of growing up to do, girl. I ain't got no pimp to rush home and give my money to. I'm going upstairs to your apartment and help you drink your liquor."

Audrey laughed and slipped her arm around Rebekah's shoulder. "That last trick was a trip. He acted like he ain't had none in ten years. My pussy is so sore. Can you imagine having to go home and fuck again? If I had a pimp, that's what I'd have to do if he wanted some. Who wants to go home and fuck after you done fucked nine or ten johns? Not me, that's why I'm still handling my own business."

"Just be careful, Audrey. You know some of these pimps are cold-hearted. They would as soon kill you as they would fuck you."

"Aw, I'll be all right. I just got to keep watching my back,"

Audrey laughed.

Audrey and Rebekah walked into the apartment building, laughing. An eviction notice from Rebekah's landlord was tacked on her apartment door. Rebekah read the note and tossed it in the trash. She wasn't going to let it spoil her time with Audrey. They opened the bottle of rum and poured themselves drinks.

"Tell me about yourself," said Rebekah. "I've told you about myself, but I don't know anything about you."

"Ain't much to tell," said Audrey. "I grew up in Cabrini-Green public housing projects in Chicago, the Windy City. I've never met my daddy. My mama did the best she could to take care of us nine children — five girls and four boys — I'm the oldest girl. Mama worked so hard to take care of us, she died of a heart attack at thirty-six.

I was seventeen, just graduated from high school when Mama died, thinking I knew everything. The younger kids went to live with our grandparents. Me and my older brothers left home to be on our own. The last time I heard from my brothers, one was in the army, one was driving a cab in New York, one was a janitor at a high school, and the other brother was in jail. I don't hear from my sisters.

I got pregnant by this dude I thought was in love with me like I was in love with him. Girl, I loved his last year's drawers! He was so fine, but he wasn't shit!"

"Don't that apply to all men? Ain't none of'em shit," said Rebekah.

"Now ain't that the truth?" said Audrey.

She and Rebekah laughed.

"Anyway," said Audrey, "that nigga flew the coop so fast, he was gone before the baby was born. I vowed to take care of my son and not depend on nobody but myself. But it's hard out here for a colored woman with a child, especially a woman without a skill. And these jobs don't pay nothin'. I kept going to the Department of Social Services to get help and they kept tellin' me that I made too much money. I was barely makin' six thousand dollars a year and taking care of my son, Kevin, and trying to stay off welfare.

Then two years ago when Kevin was five years old, he was hit by a car. He ran into the street after a ball and was killed instantly. I didn't even get a chance to say goodbye and to tell him how much I loved him." Audrey started crying.

Rebekah tried to console Audrey as she too started crying. "I'm sure he knew you loved him. I bet you were a good mother, 'cause you're such a nice person and a good friend. When I met you, I needed a friend. You're the only one who don't want nothing from me except friendship," Rebekah said.

"Now, that all depends on what else you got," Audrey kidded, her mouth twisted to the side. She strutted around the room leaning to one side, holding her crotch like a man. They both laughed and hugged each other.

"How long have you been in the business?" Rebekah asked.

"After my son died and I lost track of my family, I lost everythin' I had 'cause I couldn't work. Girl, I was in a mental institution for a year. I just couldn't cope with life anymore. Every time I closed my eyes I saw my baby lying in the street, blood coming from a deep gash in his head, and him laying so still.

"I've been out of the institution a year now. I couldn't get a job, then I discovered that I still looked good; so I decided to make my looks work for me. I hooked up with Lena's Ladiesland Lounge, and got burned. Miss Lena, the owner, with her big ass and big mouth, ripped me off, charging the johns more than she said she did. We weren't getting the proper percentage so most of the girls left. Some of them went with pimps.

"I just couldn't see myself laying on my back while some big, fat, sweaty mutha-fucka jumps up and down on me. And when he pays me, I got to give my money to another man, who calls himself a pimp, and his only claim to fame is that he'll protect me and fuck me and if I'm a good girl, he'll give me some of my money back. That don't make sense to me. Hell, if I keep my own money, I can protect my damn self, and I get all the fucking I want from them tricks.

"The pimps in Baltimore don't like me. They say I'm a bad influence on the other 'ho's. I tell them 'ho's to manage their own money. Shit, they earned it. They say I'm going to get myself killed for being a maverick, but that's life — live fast, die young, make a good-looking corpse," Audrey laughed.

"I bet you could tell some wild stories about your tricks," said Rebekah.

"Honey, I don't even remember their names. I saw one man at the bar the other night and he got mad when I didn't remember him. He was one of the johns I've had. Hell, after a while, they all look alike," Audrey said.

"I walked past him, he grabbed my arm and said, 'Hello.'

"I said 'hello' and kept walking. He pulled on my arm, and I turned to look at him.

"'You got a problem?'" I asked him.

"Yeah, I got a problem. You're my problem. Do you remember me?" he asked.

"His face looked familiar but I couldn't remember where I knew him from. Then he got sarcastic.

"'Did we fuck?' he sneered.

"Then I realized that he must've been one of those tricks who thought he had it going on but couldn't produce. I forget those real quick. You know, the kind that's always bragging about how they're going to 'put a hurting on that pussy;' or sometimes they say, 'When I get a hold of that thang, I'm gonna wear it out.' Then when they do get it, they can't even get hard; and if they do get hard, it's like instant pudding, it's done before it gets started.

"I looked at him and said, 'Is there a reason for you to be rude and vulgar?'

"Again he said, 'Did we fuck?' By that time I was pissed. I said, 'Obviously we didn't, 'cause if we did, you were the only one at the party.' I started to walk away. He grabbed my arm again. But I wasn't about to let him manhandle me. I said, 'If I remember you correctly, if you put starch on your limp dick, it still couldn't get hard. Or maybe you're the one I remember who had to stoop over to keep from pissing on his shoes.

"Now don't start no shit and there won't be none, 'cause I'll turn this mutha out,' and I jerked my arm away. He called me a bitch and started to walk away.

I shouted at him, 'If I'm a bitch, I must be a damn good one 'cause you remembered me. I don't remember your sorry ass.' He wanted to hit me but he didn't know whether or not I had a pimp in the bar."

Rebekah and Audrey laughed, drank the rum and exchanged stories about encounters with various men in their lives. Audrey took some cocaine from her pocketbook and they snorted it. Rebekah had some marijuana and gungee hash mixed together.

They poured rum into the belly of a bong — an exotic glass water pipe — and put the hash mixture in the bowl of the pipe. When the smoke from the hash mixture circulated through the pipe, it produced a cool exciting high. They laughed and joked until daylight began to peek through the windows.

"Well, good morning, old friend. It was a pleasure talking with you all night," Audrey teased. "I'm a working girl, I got to get some rest if I'm to make any money. I'll see you later."

"Be careful, Audrey. You're the only friend I got," Rebekah said, and hugged her.

"Honey, don't you fret none 'bout me. This ol' gal been takin' care of herself for many years. You get some sleep and I'll see ya when I see ya," Audrey said and walked out the door.

But Rebekah didn't have time to sleep. She had to hurry and get dressed. She was scheduled to work the morning shift at the bar. She showered and rushed to the bar. Mike was working and he was bitter because she had stopped seeing him.

"One of these days, your friend Audrey is going to come up missing. If it wasn't for her, you and me would still be together," Mike said to Rebekah.

"Mike, Audrey had nothing to do with you and me breaking up. You were too possessive. You didn't want me to have any friends, nobody in my life except you. I just can't live like that," Rebekah said, but he wasn't listening.

"You just mark my word," he said. "Tell your friend to watch her back. And, by the way, you're fired."

"Aw shit! I don't give a damn. I'm sick of you anyway. You can take this job and shove it up your ass," she said as she headed out the bar.

"Tell your buddy, Audrey, what I said, and you'd better be careful too," he shouted as she stormed out the door.

Rebekah didn't argue with him. She thought she had learned enough while working at the Blue Moon Bar to get another job as a barmaid. She bought a bottle of rum and went back to her apartment, poured a drink, then lay across the bed and went to sleep, awakening when it got dark. She poured herself another drink, started thinking about Brian, and decided that she wanted to see him.

She poured several more drinks, got dressed and went to the Swan Club. When she entered the club, she saw Brian sitting at a table with a well-dressed, good-looking woman.

Rebekah staggered to the table and said to Brian, "I want to talk to you."

"Look at you," he sneered. "You're nothing but a drunk. Why would I want to waste my time with a lush like you?"

"I'm still the same 'lush' that you been fuckin' for over a month. I see you got a new bitch. Does she know that you ain't shit?" Rebekah slurred.

Rebekah tried to hit Brian and stumbled. The bouncer rushed to the table and restrained her. Rebekah cursed Brian and staggered out the door. She went to the Blue Moon Bar and ordered a drink. Mike was on duty.

"You don't need a drink, bitch, you need a bath 'cause you stink," sneered Mike.

He had never talked that nasty to her before. "Your high-class crooner must don't want you no more, 'cause you come dragging your drunk ass back down here in the ghetto, huh? I don't think so.

"By the way, I hear that your girlfriend, Audrey, has a new address. It's called the morgue. They found her body in an alley, stuffed in a garbage can last night. Her throat was slashed from ear to ear. Poor Audrey, now she can't be ya friend no mo.' I wonder if some pimp finally caught up with her?" He walked away with a smirk on his face.

Rebekah couldn't believe it. She couldn't believe that Audrey was dead. She went outside to get a taxi to go to the morgue and she realized that she didn't have enough money for taxi fare.

"I have a few dollars in the apartment," she said, half talking to herself and wondering out loud. She went to her apartment and the lock had been changed.

The landlord heard her trying to get into the apartment, stuck his head out his door.

"I'm sorry, miss," he said. "I didn't want to do it, but my wife said we've given you enough breaks. I'm going to have to keep ya belongin' 'til you pay ya back rent."

"But what am I supposed to do? I don't have any money. I just learned that a very dear friend was killed last night and I can't even go to see her body. You've got everything that I own in this world. I ain't got nothin' but these two dimes in my pocket." She held her hand out showing him the two dimes.

"I'm sorry" he said again. "My hands are tied."

His wife hollered for him to shut the door. He went back into his apartment, closed the door and left Rebekah standing in the hall. She didn't know where to go. She staggered back to the Blue Moon Bar, deciding to do what she had to do to survive. She didn't have a place to stay, she had lost Audrey, and now she had to look for ways to survive.

That's when she met Teddy.

CHAPTER NINE
A Bitter Lesson

Rebekah was no match for Teddy. He had grown up in the streets. Rebekah was vulnerable and desperate. Teddy was sitting in the bar with his buddies, waiting for the next victim he could mold and train to become his prostitute, when in walked Rebekah.

Rebekah was still attractive, even after doing all those drugs and drinking liquor. Teddy had seen Rebekah in the bar before and he was waiting for the right time to approach her. Her skin color would attract both Black men and white men. He had seen her with Audrey, the troublemaker, as he called her. But now that Audrey was dead, Teddy felt the time was right to recruit Rebekah.

Rebekah sat at the bar and told Daisy, another prostitute, about her landlord locking her out of her apartment and keeping her personal belongings. Teddy overheard the conversation and learned that Rebekah was homeless. He sent one of his men — he called them soldiers — to ask her to join him at his table in the back of the bar.

Teddy always sat at that table in that same chair with his back to the wall where he could have a clear view of the front and side doors. If he walked into the bar and someone was sitting in that seat, they got up so he could sit there. He wouldn't have to say a word. He just looked at the person and they got the message. It was usually a stranger who sat in Teddy's seat; the regulars knew better.

Rebekah went to his table, trying hard not to stagger.

"Hello, pretty lady, looks like you can use a friend," Teddy said. "My name is Theodore but my friends call me Teddy. My very good friends call me Teddy Bear. Are you going to be my friend or my very good friend?"

"We'll see," said Rebekah, trying to act nonchalant.

Teddy was a tall, good-looking man with a diamond-shaped gold tooth in the left side of his mouth and long sideburns. It was evident that he was accustomed to getting what he wanted.

"I can help you find a place to stay," he said. "I can also get your belongings back. The landlord of the apartment building where you live owes me a favor."

"If you do me this favor, what's in it for you?" she asked.

"Gratitude and friendship," he said.

Teddy knew that he would have to go slowly with Rebekah. She was from the South, but she was far from stupid. She could make him big money if he played his cards right. The landlord was a numbers writer for Teddy.

"You shouldn't be struggling like you're doing," said Teddy. "You're sitting on a money-maker. There ain't no reason why you should be broke."

Rebekah had talked to Audrey and Daisy about prostituting. She had that bad experience with Oscar, but she felt she should be getting paid for what she was now giving away.

"How do I get into the business?" she asked Teddy.

"You might need a daddy to protect you and that will be me. I'll be your daddy, but you have to help keep daddy in nice things. That means I take care of you and you take care of me. You treat daddy right and daddy will treat you right. But if you're a bad girl and cross daddy, you'll have to be punished and daddy might hurt you."

Rebekah heard a threat in his voice but she dismissed it. Sassy, a prostitute had just walked in the bar. Teddy called her to the table and told her that he wanted her to take Rebekah under her tutelage and teach her the ropes. He then took Rebekah back to her apartment and knocked on the landlord's door.

"Who the hell is knockin' on my damn do' this time o' night?" the landlord called through the closed door.

"It's me, open up," said Teddy.

The door quickly opened.

"Hello, Mr. Ted," the landlord said. "I didn't know that wuz you. Is anythin' wrong?

"This is my friend," Ted said, as he hugged Rebekah. "She tells me that you won't give her her personal belongings. I told her she must be mistaken 'cause you're not that kind of guy. I told her you were just holding them for her, so we came by to get'em if that's alright with you."

There was authority in Ted's voice.

"Yes sir, Mr. Ted. I'll get them right away," the landlord said. He was so scared, he almost fell running to get Rebekah's belongings. She wanted to laugh but she didn't think that would be a good idea. When he brought Rebekah her belongings, Teddy told the landlord to make a note that her rent was paid.

Teddy put her belongings into the trunk of his Cadillac, and they drove to another apartment building up the street and went inside. It was Teddy's apartment, where he stayed sometimes.

"This is your home for the time being. I want you to get some rest and freshen up 'cause training starts tomorrow," Teddy said.

****

During Rebekah's first time out as a prostitute, she and Sassy walked around the corner from the apartment where Rebekah stayed with Teddy, and over the bridge to a club called The Palace, a place where prostitutes hung out and picked up tricks on a larger scale than at the Blue Moon Bar.

They met two white men, a father and son. The father was fifty-eight years old and the son was twenty-one. It was the son's birthday and the father was treating him to a birthday present — sex with a prostitute. The men were eager to have sex with Rebekah and Sassy, but Rebekah, being new to the trade, chickened out. When they asked her about the price of sex, she shunned them and walked away as if she didn't want to discuss the subject.

"Girlfriend," Sassy said, "you got a lot to learn if you're going to make money in this business. First you say you don't want to be giving your money to no pimp, now you're making me lose money by getting cold feet when we got two tricks lined up. You sound like Audrey and look what happened to her. You're new in this business, so don't get yourself hurt. I like you and all that, but I got to make money. I ain't out here hustling my ass for my health. I got children to feed and rent to pay."

Rebekah understood what Sassy was saying. She said she had

to psyche herself up for the trade. After that first time, she went out with Sassy and other prostitutes several times and learned the business real fast. Soon the johns were saying that she had the best head in the business. Johns were coming to the bar asking specifically for Rebekah.

She was making money, more money than she had ever made, but she had to give it all to Teddy and he gave her a small allowance. She then understood what Audrey meant when she said she wasn't going to sell her ass and give all her money to a pimp.

Some women were pimps too, especially those who were studs in a lesbian relationship. Rebekah was afraid to "buck the system," remembering what happened to Audrey. Teddy had more than one prostitute working for him. He often bragged to Mike that he had several cows in his stable.

One night Mike said to Rebekah, "I see you've advanced, girl. You used to be my woman, now you're a cow in a stable. Good work."

Rebekah lied to herself that Teddy loved her. She was looking for love in all the wrong places. She went shopping in the best stores but she could only purchase what Teddy allowed her to purchase. She wore nice clothes when he took her to nightclubs and to other social affairs, but at those places, he encouraged her to find potential clients. They didn't travel alone; there were always other prostitutes and his body guards with them.

Because of her complexion, Rebekah was called "red-bone" and "half-breed" by some of the crowd and by some of her tricks.

Sometimes when she worked parties, she made as much as two thousand bucks. If she brought home less than two hundred dollars a night during the week, Teddy would send her back out to make more.

Three months passed and one night Rebekah decided to go to the Swan Club to see if Brian was still around and still waiting for his big break. She was supposed to be out working on Baltimore Street, called "The Block." When she worked on The Block, most of her tricks were white men; when she worked The Avenue, her tricks were Black men.

Rebekah walked into the Swan Club dressed in a purple outfit that showed the curves of her body. Teddy had bought the outfit with her money. She sat at the bar in a seat so that Brian could see her from the stage. When his set was over, he came to the bar and hugged her.

"Hello, baby, you look good. You look like a million dollars. Looks like life's been good to you," he said.

"I've been doing what I can to survive. I'm surprised to see that you're still in Baltimore. I thought by now I'd see your face on the big screen or hear your records on the radio," said Rebekah.

"I'm a little down on my luck, but you look like you're doing all right for yourself. I'm sorry about the way things happened between us. Let's spend time together tonight, for old time's sake," he said.

She waited for him to finish his last set. She didn't tell him about her new "business." After he finished for the night, they sat and talked for an hour and had a few drinks. He asked her to go to his apartment with him.

"I got a bag of blow. We can get a bottle and have fun like we used to do," he said.

It was the first time he had invited her to his apartment. She agreed. When they arrived, she wondered why he hadn't brought her there before. It was located in a nice section of the city. But she decided not to spoil the night by questioning him about past behavior.

When they entered the building, he put his finger to his lips signaling her not to make any noise. They crept up the dark stairs to the second floor to his bedroom. He wouldn't turn on the lights.

"Let's enjoy exploring each other in the dark," he whispered. He dared not turn on the light for fear that his landlady would know he was home. He was three months behind in his rent and he had been dodging her for over a month. But he didn't want Rebekah to know that.

He held her hand as he groped around in the dark. The neon lights from the street shone through the shadeless-window and provided light for the room

They sat on the bed and as soon as they started kissing, a booming knock came on the door and a voice shouted through the door.

"I know you're in there, you no good bastard! I'm going to call the police. I've had enough of your shit. Pay me my rent or get the hell outta my house. You been duckin' me for more than a month and I'm gonna have your sorry ass put in jail, Mister, 'I-Think-I-Can-Sing.' If you could sing, you'd be making enough money to pay your rent. If you could sing, you wouldn't be sneaking in and outta here 'cause you ain't got no where else to stay. You're a loser and anybody that's dumb enough to hang around with you is a loser, too. I know you got a bitch in there with you, but did you tell her that you've been fucking me, too every chance you get?"

When Rebekah heard that, she was angry with herself for going back to Brian. Rebekah had suspected that Brian and his landlady had an intimate relationship when she saw the landlady and her girlfriend at the Swan Club.

"Come on, let's go out the window. That woman is crazy. I ought to punch her in her mouth for putting my business in the street. Everybody runs into a streak of bad luck once in a while," he said.

Brian and Rebekah climbed out the window and down the fire escape. The landlady was still shouting angry words at them. They jumped into his car and drove off.

"Please take me home," said Rebekah.

"Why don't we go to your place?" said Brian.

"I was a fool to hook up with you again. Your landlady is right. You are a loser. I'm the fool, but I won't be yours anymore, now take me home," said Rebekah.

Brian got angry. He pulled over to the curb and said, "Get the fuck outta my car, now! I don't need that shit from a bitch like you. You think you got so much going on? You came looking for me; I didn't come looking for you."

"You're right, my mistake. But I won't make it again. I don't give a shit about you putting me outta your car. I can get home. But I bet you won't have this car long. You're still a fuckin' loser," she sneered. She got out of the car and slammed the door. Brian drove off cursing.

Rebekah knew she was in trouble with Teddy 'cause she hadn't made any money. She didn't know what lie she was going to tell him and she was scared, but defiant. She decided to pretend she was sick, couldn't work, and had to return home. After all, it was still early, just a little after midnight. She and Brian had left the club early thinking they would share drugs and make love all night.

When she returned home without money, Teddy told her to go back out and not to return until she had some money.

"I've had cramps all day and I have a headache. I think I might be coming down with a cold or something," she lied. "I don't feel like working tonight, baby."

"Bitch, are you crazy? Tonight's Friday night. You usually make four or five hundred dollars on Friday. You should have already made half of that, as long as you've been out there tonight. Daddy needs a ring for his pinky and you're going to get the money to pay for it." He held up his little finger to show that it was ring-less.

"But I don't feel good. I really do believe that I'm coming down with something," she said again.

"You'll be coming down with something all right. You'll be coming down with my fist up side your head," he said.

He held his fist up and shook it at her.

"Now stop making excuses. Come over here and give Daddy some sugar, and then take your fine ass outta here and make us some money. I'll give you a treat when you come home. Daddy will make love to you real good."

Rebekah started to protest. She wanted to ask him why would she want to have sex with him when she got home, if she already had sex with fifteen or twenty men before she got home. But she decided it was safer if she just kept quiet and suffered peacefully. She went back out but she didn't go to work on the corner as she was ordered to do. Instead, she went to the Blue Moon Bar, sat in a booth and lay her head on the table.

Daisy and Sassy entered the bar and went to the booth where Rebekah was sitting.

"I heard that Brian got busted for selling drugs," said Daisy. I know y'all wuz sweet on each other when you hung out with Audrey. But they say he tried to sell drugs to an undercover cop and got busted a few minutes ago."

"Damn, I just left him," said Rebekah. "Payback is a bitch."

"Why ain't you working tonight?" asked Sassy.

"It's plenty of money out there to be made tonight," said Daisy. They got a stage show at the Royal and it's jammed packed. I started working early so I could make my quota and go to the show. I know I'm gonna be late gettin' there, but I'm on my way. Y'all want to join me?"

"I don't feel like working tonight. I told Teddy I don't feel good, but he put me out anyway. I know we're gonna have a fight when I go in tonight with no money. But I'll just have to take my chances. When me and Teddy started seeing each other things were different. I know we had a business arrangement, but it ain't no business arrangement every time he jumps in my bed and fucks me for free; yet I have to give him the money I make selling my ass to somebody else. What kind of shit is that?

"I've been trying to get out of the prostitution business and go back to school. But every time I talk about quitting, Teddy threatens me," said Rebekah.

"Girl, them damn pimps all think alike. When you're selling your ass to a trick, you're having sex and working. But when you're having sex with your man — or with your pimp who may have several women working for him — you're making love.

"Honey, I thought you knew what was happening when Teddy told me to teach you the ropes," said Sassy. "Did you think he was going to let you just walk away when you felt like it? He had your landlord erase your rent bill. He bought you new clothes. He paid your rent until you turned your first trick. Did you think he did that 'cause he loved you? Bitch, get real. He's got five other 'ho's just like you. What makes you think you're so special? 'Cause you're half white? It don't work like that in this business, sugar."

Before Rebekah could respond to Sassy, Teddy walked into the bar. A hush fell over the bar, everybody got quiet. They seemed to be waiting to see what Teddy was going to do to Rebekah. Sassy saw the look on Teddy's face and stepped out of his way as he headed for Rebekah. Rebekah was scared. She looked at Teddy in fear. His eyes were ablaze with anger.

He marched to where Rebekah sat, stood over her and said in a low, threatening voice, "Bitch, I told you to make me some money! You in here trying to embarrass me? You need to know who's the boss."

Teddy grabbed Rebekah by her arm and slapped her so hard, her lip split and started to bleed. She tried to move out of his way, and he hit her again. Rebekah screamed. He snatched her off the bar stool and shoved her out the door. Still, no one in the bar said anything and no one tried to stop Teddy from beating her.

He drug Rebekah out of the bar and threw her into the backseat of his car. Teddy got in the back seat with Rebekah. One of his soldiers was driving and another was sitting in the passenger's seat.

"Drive around for a while. We're gonna have some fun with this bitch before we dump her," he told his driver.

Teddy took a syringe from a case in his pocket, gave Rebekah a shot of heroin and started beating her with his fists. He then let his boys have sex with her while they drove around.

"You need to learn a lesson like your friend Audrey did," he said menacingly.

She had heard rumors that Teddy had something to do with Audrey's death, but the police didn't have any evidence to prove it. Now she was sure that Teddy killed Audrey, or had her killed. Rebekah wasn't sure of her own fate. She wondered if Teddy had found out that she was with Brian. Sassy had told her that pimps don't like for their whores to be with other men unless they are getting paid.

After they finished with her, Teddy told his men, "Let's dump this garbage. She's beginning to stink."

They dumped Rebekah in an alley. She was bloody, blood was running from her nose and mouth, her eyes were swollen — almost closed — and she smelled of stale alcohol, sweat, and vomit. The alley stunk of urine. The piss-stained walls were filthy with human feces and rotten food.

As she lay in the garbage, she felt a warm wet substance running down her neck. She turned her head to see what it was, and a salty, warm liquid was falling on her. Teddy was standing over her holding his penis in his hand, urinating in her face, while his buddies stood by and laughed. Rebekah put up her hand to shield her face from the urine and turned her head. He continued urinating in her hair and spraying her body with his urine.

When he finished, he shook the drops of urine off his penis, put it back inside his trousers, zipped his pants, and walked away laughing, with his coat swinging over his shoulders. He cursed when he stepped in some human feces.

"Damn nigga shit all over my fuckin' shoes," Teddy growled in anger and disgust. "I paid five-hundred dollars for these mutha-fuckin' shoes. If I could get my hands on the common son-of-a-bitch who shitted here, I'd bust a cap in his ass."

He stepped into his car and left his shoes on the curb.

"This just means that one of my 'ho's got to buy me a new pair of shoes," he said.

He and his henchmen continued to laugh as they drove away.

Rebekah lay in her own vomit, with Teddy's urine running down her face, mixed with her tears and blood. She told herself that she was lucky to still be alive. She also said that she was as low as she could go.

She stood up to see where she was. She was in an alley off Pennsylvania Avenue. She staggered to the corner and saw a bag lady, one of the homeless people, pushing a grocery cart filled with bags and clothes. As Rebekah approached her, the bag lady put her arms around her meager belongings — protecting them from Rebekah, who only wanted to ask where she was. The woman hurried on, eyeing Rebekah suspiciously.

Rebekah staggered around in the streets in the cool October air, afraid to go back to Teddy's apartment to get her belongings. She feared that he would kill her. She thought about what happened to Audrey.

Rebekah felt that the bag ladies she saw in the streets were better off than she was; at least they had personal belongings and controlled their own lives. Rebekah had nothing except the dirty clothes on her back.

She walked into a liquor store and stole a bottle of rum while the clerk waited on another customer. When that was gone, she staggered the streets, looking for food. She passed a store that sold mirrors and saw herself in a full length mirror. Her clothes were tattered and dirty, her face was bloody and swollen, her hands were filthy, and her dirty, matted hair needed to be washed and combed. She couldn't believe how low she had fallen.

She walked the streets crying and praying. She came to a building with a clean stairway leading to the basement. Very seldom did she see a stairway that was unoccupied by homeless people and clean, too. She went down into the stairway, curled into a corner and went to sleep. She awakened to the sound of church bells ringing and a choir singing. She thought she had died and was in heaven.

"Mama, are you here?" she said.

Then she realized that she had fallen asleep in the stairway of a church and had dreamed about her mother. No wonder the stairway was so clean, she thought. It was the Ray of Hope Baptist Church. Rebekah walked inside and sat in the back of the sanctuary. Although she smelled bad and her clothes were torn and dirty, the people in the congregation didn't back away from her. She put her head in her hands.

"What am I going to do?" she whispered. "How will I live?"

She had tried the "fast life," as Beulah called it. Rebekah knew that she was hurting herself by living the way she had been living with Marty, drugs, alcohol, Mike, Brian, and Teddy. She had been brought up in the church. When she was a child, she went to Sunday school every Sunday morning, to church every Sunday afternoon, and again to the six o'clock service every Sunday evening. Her mother was a Christian woman who had loved the Lord.

For almost four years, Rebekah had lived in a sea of blackness, destroying herself. She was now twenty-four-years-old and had nothing to show for those years except heartache, pain, and hopelessness. She knelt where she was. She didn't care if people were looking at her. She felt the need to pray, and she did.

"Lord, please bless my friend Audrey," she prayed. "She talked tough but she was a good person. Please let her meet my mother. Audrey She needs guidance."

As she prayed, tears rolled down her face.

"Lord, You probably aren't listening to me because of the way I've messed up my life. But please, don't give up on me. Please hear my prayer. Please help me get my life back together. I can't do it by myself," she prayed.

After service was over, a woman announced that food was being served in the church's outreach center around the corner. Rebekah was grateful. She hadn't eaten in two days and her stomach growled from hunger. She went to the outreach center. People were standing in line waiting for food; Rebekah stood in line, too. Her stomach was in knots from drug withdrawal. When it was her turn to receive food, she asked one of the ladies serving food about a place to sleep for the night.

The woman looked at Rebekah, handed her a piece of paper and said, "Go to this address and give them this note. They'll let you stay the night. The director knows me. She'll honor this note. They'll also let you take a bath and give you clean clothes to wear."

Rebekah thanked the woman, put the note into her pocket, ate her food and left.

"I must be really stinking badly," she whispered to herself.

She went to the shelter for women. It was only around the corner from the outreach center and, like the center, the shelter was owned and operated by the Ray Of Hope Baptist Church.

The shelter was a large room with thirty single beds with clean sheets and blankets, showers for the women and children, and clean clothes donated by various community organizations. This was home to pregnant women and women with small children. Rebekah fit neither category, but because she had a note from the woman at the outreach center, Rebekah was provided services at the shelter. Rebekah met one woman in the shelter who had just left her abusive husband, who had beaten her so badly that both her eyes were swollen. Rebekah's eyes were also still swollen from Teddy's beating. Rebekah listened to the woman's story and prayed with her. She wished she could do more.

Rebekah knelt and prayed for herself and for the women in the shelter.

CHAPTER TEN
One Day At A Time

That night Rebekah had a strange dream and felt her Mother's dissatisfaction with the way her life was evolving. The following morning, Rebekah got up, took a shower, and prepared to leave the shelter. The church's Food for the Hungry program provided breakfast for the women and children in the shelter.

After Rebekah ate breakfast, wearing donated clothes, she left the shelter, not knowing where she was going. She walked for hours, trying to find work. She didn't go back to the Blue Moon Bar. She didn't want any more of that life. She was still bothered by her dream and the vision of her mother. She was also fighting the demons that kept telling her she needed a fix, a hit, — she needed to get high.

When she couldn't find employment that day, she decided to take each day one at a time. She went back to the shelter and asked the woman behind the desk about substance abuse programs. The woman told her about the one at the outreach center. She stayed at the shelter again that night and the following day she went to a substance abuse meeting at the outreach center. Her craving for drugs was overpowering, but she was determined to get clean.

Rebekah wanted to go to the Blue Moon Bar, but instead, after the meeting, she went to the church and entered the sanctuary. They were just starting the evening services.

"This is where it all began, at a church," she whispered as she walked inside. "A church is where I helped kill my mother."

Grief overcame her and she found herself staying in the sanctuary praying and worshiping God instead of going back to the outreach center for the evening meal. Tears rolled down her cheeks. She sat through the evening service and listened to the preacher, Reverend Wendall Barnes, talk about loving yourself before loving anyone else. He seemed to be talking to her and about her. She couldn't stop crying.

After the service was over, Rebekah went to the outreach center. She was glad they stayed open late on the nights when they had evening services at the church. She ate dinner then read the employment section of the local newspaper to prepare for her job search the next day. After circling possibilities, she walked around the corner to the shelter and prayed that she wasn't too late to get a bed. She was in luck, they had one empty cot left. She was so tired that she lay across the cot and immediately fell asleep.

The following morning when everyone had left the shelter, a kind woman came into the room and saw Rebekah still asleep. The woman woke Rebekah and asked her if she was all right. When the woman learned that Rebekah wasn't ill but only asleep, she asked Rebekah if she had a place to go.

Rebekah began to cry and shook her head, "no."

The woman, feeling sorry for Rebekah, extended her hand and said, "Good morning. My name is Lola Jackson."

"I remember you," said Rebekah. "You're the lady who was kind enough to help me the first night I came to the center. You gave me the note the first night I needed a place to sleep. You don't know how much I appreciated your help. I hate to keep imposing on you but I'm so far down on my luck, I don't know where to turn. Do you know where I can stay until I find a job? I've made a mess of my life." Rebekah continued to cry.

"Have you worked with sick people or elderly people before?" asked Lola.

"I used to go with my mother when she visited sick people and when she took care of people who were disabled," said Rebekah. "And I learn fast. I need a job bad. I'm not going to lie to you. I've lied enough. I need help with a drug problem. I can't kick it by myself."

Rebekah's sobs increased in intensity.

There was something about Rebekah that made Lola believe her.

"Why don't you come home with me," said Lola. "I need assistance with caring for my mother, and I need help with household chores. I'm one of the leaders of this church, everybody here knows me. Would you like that?" asked Lola.

Rebekah was overjoyed. She and Lola worked out an arrangement in which Rebekah would sleep in Lola's spare bedroom and help take care of her mother in exchange for room, board and a small salary. But Rebekah would have to stay in a drug program. That was part of the deal.

Lola was a tall, handsome woman with a smile that lit up a room. Her brown skin was as smooth as velvet and her white teeth against her dark skin reminded Rebekah of pearls laying on a piece of velvet cloth. When she smiled, flashing pearly white teeth, her smile was so infectious it made everyone smile with her. Lola was a member of the Deaconess Board of the Ray of Hope Baptist Church. Her late husband, William Jackson, whom everyone affectionately called "Uncle Bill," was a Deacon in the church for many years before he passed away from a heart attack.

After Bill died, Lola sold their home in the suburbs and moved into a condominium in the city. She and Bill didn't have any children and she couldn't bear living in that house without him.

"In every corner of every room I could see Bill's face and hear his voice, and I always expected him to come walking through the door at any moment. He was the most beautiful man I ever had the pleasure of knowing, and he was my best friend," Lola told Rebekah.

Just about the time Bill died, Lola had received a letter from her aunt — her mother's sister — saying that Lola's mother, who was living in New Jersey, had taken a turn for the worse, and her doctors didn't think that she should be living alone. Lola was an only child, so she went to New Jersey to try to convince her mother to sell her house, return to Baltimore, and live with her.

Lola's mother was an independent woman who had lived alone for years after Lola's father died. She was reluctant to give up her independence. However, Lola managed to convince her mother that after Bill's death, Lola herself, needed help.

"She's a wise old bird," Lola said of her mother. "She's very proud and very independent. She's been my strength all my life. If she thought that I wanted her to live with me because I didn't think she could take care of herself, she never would have moved. So I had to make her believe that I couldn't take care of myself after Bill died. So she feels that she's moving in with me to take care of me."

Lola and Rebekah laughed. Rebekah felt that Lola was blessed, her mother was still alive.

Lola's condominium was located on the fifteenth floor of one of Baltimore's most exclusive apartment buildings, the Hilton Towers. Rebekah felt important living there. The building was only minutes away from Lola's posh office in City Hall where she was chief of the city's law department.

Lola liked Rebekah but she couldn't understand why she was befriending her. Lola had seen many homeless people, men and women, who had sought refuge in the sanctuary of the church, yet she had never been moved to take any of them into her home as she had Rebekah.

At dinner one evening, as they talked about how they met, Rebekah told Lola that she knew someone was going to help her. She said she didn't know if Lola was the one whom God had sent, but she knew that He was going to send someone. She had talked to God while sitting alone in the church, and even the church's name, Ray of Hope, suggested that God would help her.

"When I heard the choir sing, 'What A Friend We Have In Jesus,' I listened to the words for the first time and I knew that God was talking to me," Rebekah told Lola. "I'll never forget those words. We used to sing them in church when I was growing up. But they never meant as much to me as they do now."

Then she began to repeat them:

What a friend we have in Jesus. All our sins and griefs to bear.
What a privilege to carry everything to God in prayer.

Oh, what peace we often forfeit. Oh, what needless pain we bear.
All because we do not carry everything to God in prayer.

Have we trials and temptations? Is there trouble anywhere?

We should never be discouraged, take it to the Lord in prayer.

Can we find a friend so faithful, who will all our sorrows share?
Jesus knows our every weakness, take it to the Lord in prayer.

Are we weak and heavy laden cumbered with a load of care?
Precious Savior, still our refuge, take it to the Lord in prayer.

Do thy friends despise forsake thee? Take it to the Lord in prayer.
In His arms He'll take and shield thee; thou wilt find solace there.

****

Rebekah had been living with Lola for about six months, attending meetings and trying to get clean of drugs, when Lola said, "I'll help you get a job that pays more than I can afford to pay you if you promise to complete your college education. Don't let your mother down. From what you've told me about her, she risked her life for you. Don't let her death have been in vain."

Rebekah accepted Lola's offer. She was struggling, trying to kick her drug addiction, and she didn't think she was ready to go back to school. But after Lola helped her get a better job working as a part-time clerk in the city's law department, Lola would not relent about trying to encourage her to return to college.

Finally, after Rebekah had been working for several months, she took Lola's advice and enrolled at the University of Baltimore. She had dropped out of Morgan in the middle of her last semester, so she thought she only had one semester to complete before she graduated. However, she was required to take more credits than she thought. The University of Baltimore did not accept all of her transfer credits.

Rebekah went to college at night and worked during the day. Law fascinated her and she was impressed with Lola's legal mind. Rebekah thought of Lola as the sister she always wanted. When Rebekah joined the Ray of Hope Baptist Church, Lola was ecstatic.

At the church, Rebekah met Reverend Wendall Barnes and his wife, Sister Berneda, both young, educated, Christian people. Berneda had just completed her Master's degree and was studying for her doctorate in theology. Rebekah joined the Missionary Unit and other organizations in the church which had members around her age.

The months passed quickly. Soon it was graduation time for Rebekah. After she graduated from college with a Bachelor's degree, she surprised Lola by saying that she had registered for the Law School Admissions Test (LSAT), and if she passed, she would enroll in the University of Baltimore's School of Law, the same university from which Lola had graduated. Lola was elated. Being a prominent attorney in Baltimore, Lola was proud that Rebekah wanted to follow in her footsteps.

"I've seen so much hurt and anguish inflicted on women," Rebekah said to Lola one evening. "I don't think there are enough organizations that provide services that women need. That's why I've decided to become an attorney. I want to help women help themselves. I want to organize a club for women. Do you think Reverend Barnes would allow me to do that at the outreach center?"

"I think that's an excellent idea," said Lola. "God knows women sure do need help. Sometimes I volunteer at the center and at the homeless shelter. I've seen the emotional condition some of the women are in when they come for assistance. Go and talk with Reverend Berneda. I'm sure she would agree that it's needed and will do whatever she can to help you get started. She may also talk to Pastor Barnes for you.

"That's one of the reasons I want to organize a program for women. I saw how some of them had to run out of their houses in the middle of the night with small children, half-dressed, running for their lives, chased out by husbands. I've been beaten up and involved in lots of other painful situations so I can identify with many of the issues with which women are confronted.

"Lola, I know that God has a purpose for me. I just don't know what it is, yet. I read in the paper today that Teddy, a man I used to know, was found dead in an alley with his throat cut just like my girlfriend, Audrey. They found her with her throat cut and they never found her killer.

"After I read the article about Teddy, I called the Blue Moon Bar, the place I told you about, and I spoke to Daisy, a friend of mine. She said after the police found Teddy's body, they closed the file on Audrey's case. They stopped looking for her killer. I guess they figured the killer had already been found and justice had already been served. We all suspected that Teddy killed her or had her killed. I'm lucky to be alive. God spared me for a reason. Maybe it was so I can start the organization for women that my mama and I talked about starting," said Rebekah.

Rebekah went to Reverend Berneda and discussed her idea. "I would like to see attorneys, doctors, social workers, and women in other professions joining together to help other women," said Rebekah. "I'm not talking about just helping Black women, I'm talking about helping *all* women."

"We do provide some services for women, but not in the magnitude that you're talking about," Reverend Berneda said. "I love the idea. What do we need to do to get started? You've gotten me excited about the possibilities."

"We'll recruit other women. I know a couple of friends I met at the University of Baltimore, and Mamie, a good friend I met at Morgan State College. I just wanted to get your approval before I said anything to them. I'll start working on it right away," Rebekah said. "I'm excited, too. This has been my dream for a long time. My mama and I used to discuss it a long time ago."

Rebekah learned a lot from Lola. She learned how to be patient. She learned when to fight, and she learned when to concede. That was quite an accomplishment for Rebekah. She had become an aggressive individual who thought the world and everyone in it were against her.

One day when she was confronted with discrimination and sexism from a college professor, she came home boiling mad. She was accustomed to discussing her problems with Lola, who always made time to listen. This time as Rebekah told Lola about the college professor, Lola listened without interrupting.

After Rebekah finished talking, Lola said, "Rebekah, you're right, but you're dead right." Then she paused.

Rebekah sat waiting for Lola to complete her statement.

Lola leaned forwarded. "You are dead right. You're right, but if you fight the system, you're dead. Don't you see that the final decision is not yours? So what if you're right? Does it really matter who's right and who's wrong if being right won't change the situation? Let it go. Don't fight about little things just to prove you're right. Save the fight for when it's really important. Otherwise, you'll get the reputation of being a troublemaker, and when there really is an important issue to fight about, no one will support you in your battle. Don't sweat the small stuff."

Rebekah didn't understand Lola's meaning and her frustration was obvious.

Seeing the puzzled look on Rebekah's face, Lola realized that Rebekah still didn't understand what she was saying.

"Okay," said Lola, "suppose a pedestrian starts to cross the street and the light is red, signaling cars to stop, indicating that the pedestrian has the right-of-way and it's okay to cross. A truck comes around the corner and runs through the red light. The pedestrian starts across the street anyway ignoring the truck, because the pedestrian has the right of way. The truck hits the pedestrian and kills him. The pedestrian was right, the light was in his favor; he did have the right of way but he's also dead. So what does it matter that he was right? He is dead right. Now do you understand?"

Rebekah laughed when she finally understood Lola's message, and she never forgot that lesson.

Although Rebekah was doing well in law school and was glad that Lola was pleased with how she was getting her life together, she was still consumed with guilt and remorse over the way she had treated her mother. After Rebekah started working and going to school, Lola engaged the services of a private duty nurse companion to come and be with her mother during the day. Lola wouldn't accept rent from Rebekah, so Rebekah insisted on helping Lola with the private nurse expenses. Rebekah was emotionally dissatisfied.

The years passed quickly. When Rebekah had been living with Lola for three years, she came home one evening and found Lola lying on the living room sofa, having difficulty breathing. The private duty nurse had left for the day and Lola's mother was asleep. Rebekah called the ambulance and rushed Lola to the hospital.

The nurses made Lola as comfortable as they could, and after the doctor had helped to ease her pain, he informed her that she needed an immediate operation. There was a blockage in her intestines that needed to be removed immediately. Lola adamantly refused to let the doctor operate on her. She said that the Lord would take care of her.

"I'm God's woman," she told the doctor. "I don't need nobody cutting on me. My Father will take care of me. He has all power in His hands. I'm blessed."

The doctor looked at her intensely, and for a moment he was silent. Then he said in a soft voice, "What makes you think that you're the only one who's blessed? God is also my Father. Who are you to insinuate that He doesn't do good work?"

Lola looked puzzled and she said to the doctor, "What do you mean? I haven't said anything against God's work."

"You said that you didn't need anyone cutting on you because God would heal you and you're blessed. I'm blessed, too. My hands are blessed. My eyes are blessed. My mind is blessed. I'm blessed with the power to heal medically, as you're blessed to heal spiritually. God guides my hands so that the scalpel doesn't slip. He guides my mind so that I may mend bodies medically. He gave me keen sight and a keen mind. God is continuing to bless you by sending me to take care of you. He's working through me to save you. He blessed me by making it possible for me to go to medical school. He blessed me by allowing me to graduate from medical school at the top of my class. He blessed me by making me one of this country's top heart surgeons. Are you saying my blessings don't mean anything? Who gave you a monopoly on blessings?"

Lola laughed weakly and shook her head. "When did you say you were going to operate, Doctor? Whatever you say, I'll do. I'll let you do God's will, Doctor. Forget that silly talk from this foolish woman. I'm your patient."

Lola learned a valuable lesson that day. She learned that God is still in charge and still in the blessing business. She recovered from her operation and after a month's stay in the hospital, was sent home and warned by the doctor that she must take it easy and retire from her job. Rebekah helped Lola with her retirement process by getting all her retirement papers together.

After being home for two weeks, Lola was restless. She felt confined being at home all day. She helped with the care of her mother but she also wanted to be involved with business. She helped Rebekah with the legal issues of getting the women's organization started. They hired a young woman from the church to come in once a week to clean the house and Rebekah helped with preparing meals for Lola and her mother.

After six months of recuperating at home, when spring was just waking up the flowers, and the birds had returned to sing in the park across the street from her condominium, Lola made up her mind that she and her mother would move back to Georgia, where life moved at a slower pace and where she and her mother could enjoy the clean air. They didn't want to leave Rebekah alone in Baltimore. Lola tried to convince her to move back to Georgia with them. But Rebekah didn't want to live in Georgia. She wasn't through pursuing her career and felt that the South was no place for a colored woman to succeed professionally.

She wouldn't think of letting Lola and Lola's mother stay in Baltimore for her sake. Rebekah insisted that they move to Georgia as planned. Besides Lola's mother's health was getting worse. Rebekah helped Lola and her mother pack up the furniture and move to Georgia. They left some pieces of furniture for Rebekah. Lola insisted that Rebekah continue to live in the condominium.

"Just in case I decide to return to Baltimore, I'll have a place to stay," Lola said. "But I will return to Baltimore when you graduate from law school. I'll be at your graduation. I want you to go on and start the program for women even if you have to do it alone. It's so much needed."

Rebekah promised she would, and Lola and her mother left Baltimore. Rebekah purchased a few new pieces of furniture and began to settle into life without her friend and mentor.

Rebekah was proud that she could still keep her job even after Lola had retired and moved to Georgia. Keeping her job meant that her employers were pleased with her work and for that, Rebekah was elated. She was also proud because she would graduate from law school in June and she had already been working as a part-time law clerk for over four years. When she did graduate, she wouldn't be an inexperienced law school graduate. She had bonded with other women whom she met at the university and other professional women from the Ray Of Hope Baptist Church. They were providing services for women but not the way Rebekah had envisioned. She wanted the organization to be more structured and provide services on a wider scale.

She remembered her own struggle to get clean of drugs and get her life together. She had struggled with her own battle and fought with a system that seemed indifferent to her pain. She didn't have any children; but she could imagine how women with children must feel when they couldn't get the help they needed. The desire of helping other women preoccupied her thoughts day and night.

A month after Lola and her mother moved away, Rebekah was standing at the corner across the street from City Hall where she still worked as a law clerk. She had run outside to the lunch wagon parked in front of the building to grab a hot dog for lunch, when she saw Anita, a friend she had met at the University of Baltimore. Anita was studying psychology and Rebekah was in law school. Rebekah took a course in psychology as an elective.

When the two friends saw each other, they hugged, glad to see each other. They both bought hot dogs and sodas and started chatting about old times. Rebekah shared her dream of an organization to help women.

"The only people who can help us are us," Rebekah said when she told Anita about her vision. "Only women can understand women's problems. Men may sympathize, but other women can empathize, and there is a difference. Women don't need sympathy, they need help."

Anita agreed with Rebekah. She was excited about Rebekah's vision and wanted to hear more.

As they continued talking they suddenly heard a woman scream, "My baby, my baby. Lord, somebody please help me. Please save my baby!"

Rebekah and Anita looked around and saw a small boy, about two or three years old, running into the street in the path of an oncoming car. Rebekah knew the toddler would never make it across the street without being hit. For an instant, she thought about Audrey and her son, and Beulah's death flashed through her mind.

Without hesitating, she dropped her pocketbook and hot dog and ran toward the small child. She ran across the street, stumbling over newspaper racks in front of the building, and dodging parked cars. She reached the child just in time to push him to safety from an oncoming car. She didn't have time to save herself. The car hit Rebekah, and knocked her to the ground. Her head slammed against the concrete and blood flowed from a gash in her head.

A crowd gathered.

"The baby, is the baby all right?" Rebekah asked as she started losing consciousness.

"Yes, the baby is fine," someone said.

Rebekah heard a voice say, "You're a mighty brave young lady," and then there was blackness, soothing blackness.

Rebekah saw a bright light, felt a warm wind and heard her mother's voice.

"Hello, baby," Beulah said.

"Mama, you've come for me. I'm glad. I'm sorry, Mama. I'm sorry that I let you down. Can you ever forgive me? I want to go with you. I don't want to live without you anymore."

"You didn't let me down, baby, you let yourself down. But I'm so proud of you. You have redeemed yourself. You've made me one happy woman. When you risked your life for that child, the angels sang your praises. But it's not your time to leave yet. Your mission on earth isn't complete. You must use your experience and knowledge to help other women. Remember the conversations we used to have daydreaming and talking about your future? Don't abandon our dream. You'll know what to do when the time comes. When it's time, we, your family, will be waiting to welcome you home, but until then, do God's work."

"But Mama, I'm so tired. It's hard living without you. I'm so alone," Rebekah said.

"I know it's hard, but that's why I'm proud of you, baby. It's not easy, but you have a lot of work yet to do. You won't be able to see me, but I'll be somewhere watching over you. Now you rest and get better so you can do God's work. Now sleep, my beautiful child."

Rebekah slipped into peaceful sleep.

****

Anita rode to the hospital in the ambulance with Rebekah. When they reached the hospital and Rebekah was put in a room, Anita sat by Rebekah's bed praying that she would regain consciousness, but Rebekah wouldn't respond to treatment. The nurses thought they had lost her. Just as they gave up hope and were about to pronounce her dead and pull the sheet over her face, her heart started beating; her breathing improved, and signs of life returned to her body.

"Doctor, doctor," the nurse called. "Come quickly, we haven't lost her!"

The doctor rushed to Rebekah and began life-saving procedures. "Welcome back," he said to Rebekah when she opened her eyes. "We thought we had lost you. You gave us quite a scare."

"No, I still have some time to stay here. Mama said it's not my time yet," Rebekah mumbled. The doctor and nurses had no idea what Rebekah was talking about. They thought she was delirious and were just glad that she was still alive.

Anita thanked God for sparing her friend's life. She sat by Rebekah's bed and cried. She squeezed Rebekah's hand and silently prayed.

Rebekah opened her eyes and smiled at Anita.

"You and I have work to do, " Rebekah whispered. "My mother told me what we need to do."

No one understood what Rebekah meant when she talked about her conversation with her mother, but Rebekah didn't mind if they didn't understand. She turned over and went to sleep with a smile on her face, knowing that Beulah had forgiven her.

The newspapers, radio, and television stations had heard of Rebekah's act of heroism. They were waiting to interview the city's newest celebrity. As it turned out, the little boy was the grandson of Stewart Goldstein, a prominent Jewish businessman and attorney.

The Goldstein family was so grateful to Rebekah for saving the child's life that they paid her hospital bills and offered her monetary compensation. She refused the money, saying she had already been blessed.

After the accident, Rebekah took time off from school to recuperate. Her right leg was broken, several ribs were broken, her arm was broken, and she had severe head injuries. She was to graduate in June but after the accident, she had to go an extra semester. Even then, she couldn't attend college full time. It would take her an extra year to complete her graduation requirements. The Goldsteins hired a nurse to go to Rebekah's house to help her and hired a person to clean her house. Rebekah's insurance paid for her physical therapy. She thought it was amusing that Beulah had worked so hard cleaning floors and other people's houses to send her to college, and now someone was cleaning her house.

Rebekah talked on the telephone to Lola almost every day. Lola wanted to return to Baltimore to be with Rebekah, but her mother's health was rapidly deteriorating and Lola didn't want to leave her. Anita moved in with Rebekah to take care of her until she was able to take care of herself. Anita was the one who oversaw the duties of the visiting nurse and the cleaning woman. Lola depended on Anita to keep her informed of Rebekah's progress.

"I know sometimes she can get stubborn and won't follow instructions, and if she does, you call me. I'll keep her straight," Lola said teasingly.

"I'll handle her," laughed Anita. "She'll just have to

understand that I'm the boss until she gets well."

They both laughed.

"She's upset about missing her last semester but she can use this time to get the women's club organized," Anita had said.

"See if you can convince her to do that, perhaps it will take her mind off her injuries," said Lola. "If you need me, you know how to get in touch with me."

While she was healing, Rebekah organized a group of women to help other women. It was 1968, she was thirty years old. Her mother had been gone eight years, and still she thought about her everyday.

****

Rebekah called her friend Mamie to talk about her vision for a woman's organization. Mamie loved the idea and wanted to be involved with helping to organize it. Rebekah then called Anita and Reverend Berneda and they too wanted to help get it organized and recruit other women to join. The women met at Rebekah's house while she was recuperating from the accident. They agreed their mission would be to fight forces that negatively impact women. The four women discussed a name for the organization. They thought about calling it the "Willing Workers," "Woman to Woman," and many other names.

It was Mamie who said "Women On the Move Against Negativity. We can call it "WOMAN Power."

"Yeah! I can get with that," said the excited Rebekah, nodding her head with approval.

"I like it, too!" said Reverend Berneda. "I like it a lot. We can call it WOMAN Power Club."

"I'm liking this more and more," said Rebekah. "That's what we'll call it."

Everyone liked the name and agreed to adopt it for their organization. So the four women got the organization started and the WOMAN Power Club was born. After they organized WOMAN Power, the four founders and other women they recruited to join the organization, started meeting monthly in the Ray of Hope Baptist

Church's outreach center. The women provided counseling, financial and legal advice, employment training, and professional development seminars to other women. They started an eight-week occupational training program for women, counseling for substance abusers, victims of domestic violence and all other abuses, grief and loss support, parenting classes, widow and grandmother groups and a mentoring program for women. They added a job placement program to help women find jobs. Some women would become entrepreneurs using small loans donated by organizations as start-up capital, repaying the loans with profits from their businesses.

The WOMAN Power Club women worked day and night to get the project started. Each woman donated one thousand dollars to the organization as start-up capital. The Ray of Hope Church donated one thousand dollars and meeting space. With five thousand dollars, four members, and a place to hold meetings, the WOMAN Power Club was in operation. They sent out flyers, developed brochures, and planned fund-raising events to generate additional money. When WOMAN Power advertised its services, the members were overwhelmed by the response. They hadn't realized there were so many women who needed help. With the women who used the services of the outreach center, those who stayed at the homeless shelter around the corner from the church, women in the Ray of Hope Church's congregation, and the neighbors who lived in the vicinity of the Church, there was always an ample supply of clients for WOMAN Power.

The WOMAN Power members were able to get volunteers to help and they started setting track records helping women. They were successful in their mission because they each had lived their own personal hell. They each had their own cross to bear and through their experiences, they could help others.

****

Anita:

After five years of marriage, Anita divorced her first husband,

Chris. She could no longer accept his infidelity and his going back and forth to jail. Anita operated a small business providing personal care to persons with developmental disabilities in group homes that she owned. She trained and hired staff to provide the services. Anita was attending college at night, studying for her Master's degree in psychology.

One night, on her way home from classes at the University, Anita drove past one of her houses and saw Chris's car parked in the driveway. She thought one of the staff had called him about the plumbing problem or some other repair problem. It wasn't unusual for him to get a call in the middle of the night about a leak in the kitchen or bathroom and go to a house to make minor emergency repairs. After all, it was his wife's business, and he considered it his business, too. He was an excellent carpenter and a master plumber. He did most of the renovations to the houses himself, when he wasn't in jail.

Anita was tired that night and she started to go home. But then decided to stop and see what was broken this time. She parked her car in front of the house, used her door key to enter and walked into the dark, quiet, living room. She looked in the clients' bedrooms. They were asleep. She walked into the kitchen; everything seemed to be in place. In the quietness, she could hear water dripping from the faucet in the kitchen sink. She didn't see Chris or any employees. There should have been two employees on duty. She walked to the door leading into the basement and started to turn on the light. She reached for the light switch and hesitated when she heard sounds coming from the basement. She paused to listen and heard a moan. At first she thought someone was sick or hurt.

She reached for the light switch again, then recognized Chris' voice. Her heart started pounding, her hands got sweaty, her throat became dry, and her stomach felt like it was doing flip-flops. She started down the steps and realized the moaning sounds were coming from the staff's sleeping quarters in the basement. Because the clients required 24-hour monitoring, during the winter when the weather prohibited staff from getting to work, employees already on duty took turns resting so they could cover the shifts.

Anita continued down the steps without turning on the light.

She went to the staff's bedroom door and heard Chris say, "Oh, baby, you got some good pussy. I've been thinking about this all day. I could hardly wait to get here."

She heard Seketa's voice. "Ain't nothing like getting a little piece on the job to rest my nerves." Then she giggled. "Especially from the boss."

Anita stood in the dark and listened, tears falling down her cheeks. Her husband was having sex with one of her employees. After she had heard enough, she silently walked back upstairs, out of the house, quietly closed the door behind her, got into her car and drove home, crying all the way.

When Chris came home that night, she pretended to be asleep. He went into the bathroom, took a shower and got into bed. The following day, she didn't feel like going to the office; her eyes were red and her cheeks puffy from crying all night. She got up, fixed a cup of coffee and laid across the bed in the spare bedroom. When Chris awakened and Anita wasn't in bed, he thought she had gone to work.

The telephone rang and she heard him say to the caller, "Hello, baby. I've been waiting on this call. I didn't come by last night 'cause my ol' lady got sick and I had to stay home and take care of things. But I sure did miss you. I thought about you all night. I could hardly wait to talk to you this morning. Guess what I got my hand on and I'll give you some."

Anita could tell it wasn't Seketa on the telephone. She picked up the telephone in the other room without either party realizing it. The woman on the other end said, "You mean you want to give me some of that thing that wouldn't get hard the other night?" Then she laughed.

"All right, all right, don't rub it in," he said, laughing. "I had a little too much to drink, that's all. Stay home from work today. I'll pick you up and we'll go somewhere and spend the day in bed. I betcha it'll get hard today."

Anita had heard enough. "Hello," she said into the receiver. "I want you both to know that you don't have to sneak around and hide your affair anymore, 'cause as of today, Chris will be needing a place to stay."

"Who is that?" the woman on the other end asked.

"Oh, shit," said Chris.

"I'm Chris' wife. There's no need to hang up. You two go ahead and have a good conversation. He's gonna have to bring his clothes to your house 'cause if he doesn't take them out of here today, I'll burn 'em up. By the way girlfriend, he's cheating on both of us. He's also sleeping with one of my employees. He lied to you. I wasn't sick last night and he wasn't at home either. He was in a staff's bedroom with my employee, Seketa Purnell. He didn't know it, but I was standing in the doorway while they were in bed screwing. Now she doesn't have a job and he doesn't have a home. So you can have this two-timing bastard."

"I got a husband," the woman said. "I don't know what he's gonna do but I ain't breaking up my family," the woman said, and quickly hung up the telephone.

Chris hung up, too. Anita walked into the bedroom where he was sitting on the bed, holding his head in his hands.

"I'm sorry, baby," he said. "There's nothing I can say, except I'm sorry. I don't want to break up our marriage. Can't we talk about this? I'll never do anything like this again. Just give me one more chance, please."

"Man, if you don't get out of my face with your lies, the coroner will be picking bullets out of your two-timing ass. What do you take me for? I've had a feeling for a long time that you were unfaithful. But the final straw wasn't that poor bitch who just hung up the telephone, it was you screwing one of my employees on the job. Ever since we've been married, you've been riding my coat tail. The ride is over. I'm leaving out of this house and when I return, I want you and your shit gone.

"I waited for you while you were in jail. I waited while you were sleeping with other women and I was sleeping alone. Now it's my turn. I don't need you in my life. I got where I am not because of you, but in spite of you. I built this business while you were in prison. I tried to have a nice place prepared for us so we could be a family when you were released. But you've been home for almost a year and you haven't worked yet. Telling everybody how you're working in the family business. If you and I were on the same page, we could have done anything together. But you'll never change and even if you do, I'm no longer interested."

Anita walked out the door, got into her car and drove away. She wanted out of the marriage. She had had her fill of Chris and his womanizing ways.

Anita had met Muhammad, a Muslim, at a political function at the University of Baltimore and they quickly became friends, but Anita was still with Chris and she didn't want to complicate things by having an affair. Muhammad was a pre-med junior at the University, and he and Anita were instantly attracted to each other. She discussed her marriage problems with Muhammad and he taught her how to forgive. He taught her how Allah in the holy Koran talks about forgiveness.

After Anita and Chris separated, she began to spend more time with Muhammad. She wouldn't have been able to transform her life in such a beautiful way had it not been for the love of Muhammad. He had loved her almost from the beginning. Their relationship wasn't about sex; he motivated her and respected her as no man had. He encouraged her to continue her college education and to follow her dreams. As time went on, she was so much in love with Muhammad that she could even forgive Chris. She just hoped he had found as much love and happiness with someone else as she had found with Muhammad.

One day when Anita and Rebekah were talking, Anita said, "Boy, I can remember the sleepless nights and the nights when I cried myself to sleep wishing my husband was at home with me. After a while, though, it didn't matter. I didn't worry about who Chris was with or what he was doing."

Anita married Muhammad a year after she divorced Chris. He taught her that Allah gave people a chance to repent and change their ways, but if they didn't, He would take revenge. Muhammad was right. Six months after Anita left Chris, he was arrested for selling drugs.

"Allah is the Great Avenger," Muhammad said. "Allah punishes those who persist in creating disharmony."

Anita was the only member of the WOMAN Power Club who wasn't a member of Reverend Berneda's church. She converted to Islam when she fell in love with Muhammad. Although she worshipped at the mosque, occasionally she and Muhammad visited the Ray of Hope Baptist Church to worship with their friends.

****

Tracy

Rebekah and Tracy met when Rebekah was a law clerk and Tracy was a rehabilitation counselor in a drug program. Rebekah was seeking counseling for one of her clients and someone referred her to Tracy. The court system listed Tracy's services as one of the best substance abuse and prevention programs in the system. Rebekah told Tracy about her dream of forming a support group for women, and Tracy was interested and wanted to be included.

Tracy was a single parent with four children — one daughter, Posie, and three sons, Peanut, Keelog, and Deucy, the oldest. Everyone called him Deucy from the term "acey deucy," because he always dressed in nice clothes with everything matching — his shoes, socks, shirt, suit, and tie. Even the hats that he wore on the side of his head were the color of his suits. He sold drugs and made big money; therefore, he could afford to buy fashionable clothes.

Rebekah was at Tracy's house one evening when the call came that Deucy had been shot. Rebekah had just returned from a business trip and she and Tracy were sitting at the dining room table, talking. It was Posie on the other end of the telephone.

"Ma, it's Deucy," Posie said. "I got a call that he's been shot. I don't know how bad it is. I'm on my way down there now."

"Down where?" asked Tracy, "You're on your way down where? Where was Deucy when he was shot? Where is my son?"

"He was down in the projects where we used to live. Somebody down there shot him. I'll call you back when I know more," Posie said.

Tracy couldn't do anything but hold the telephone and stare at it. She finally said, "Okay, call me. I'll be here." When she hung up the telephone, she said, half out loud and half to herself, "He's dead. I know he's dead. My child is dead. I can feel it."

Rebekah held Tracy's hands. "Don't say that. Don't even think it." Rebekah said. "You've got to believe that he's going to be all right. Let's pray."

As they held hands, Rebekah prayed aloud that Deucy would be all right. Deep in her heart she believed he would be. She never dreamed drugs would take the life of the son of one of her good friends. Not one of Tracy's children had done anything positive with their life, but it wasn't because Tracy didn't try. For Christmas, she always bought her kids a lot of clothes and toys. She took in sewing and worked in factories to support herself and her children.

Rebekah stayed with Tracy, waiting for Posie's call. It finally came. Posie was crying on the other end of the telephone.

"Ma, I think you should come to the hospital," Posie said.

"How is Deucy?" Tracy asked.

"I don't know for sure. The doctor told me to call you," Posie said.

Tracy hurried and dressed, praying the entire time that Deucy would recover.

"I'm going with you," Rebekah said.

They drove to the hospital in silence. The only sound was Tracy's crying. Rebekah fought back the tears, trying to be strong for her friend. When they arrived in the emergency room, Posie met them, she was still crying. "He's gone, Ma. My brother is dead," she said.

Tracy started screaming. Rebekah hugged her, trying to console her. Rebekah and Posie held Tracy and they all wept.

When making funeral arrangements, Tracy made up a story for the obituary of the local newspaper about Deucy being a business owner. Rebekah asked her why she lied about his life and Tracy said she just wanted him to be somebody for once.

Deucy was nineteen when he died. Keelog, who was two years younger, had been in the projects earlier the day that Deucy was shot and had gotten into an argument with some drug dealers about him stealing their drugs. What drugs Keelog didn't use personally, he sold and kept the money. The word on the street was that Keelog was a dead man. Deucy, being a drug dealer himself, had heard that Keelog was in major trouble with the drug gang, and Deucy went into the projects that day to protect Keelog.

No one knew exactly where the shots came from. At least, that was the story the neighbors gave the police. They said they heard a loud explosion and everyone ran for cover. There were two more shots and when the smoke cleared, Deucy was lying on the ground in a pool of blood running slowly from the back of his head and into the gutter.

Rebekah felt sorry for her friend but didn't know how to help her. What do you say to a mother who has just lost one child to drugs, and her other children following the same destructive path?

"It's tearing me up inside that I'm a rehabilitation counselor and can't even help my own children," Tracy said to Rebekah one day when they were discussing Deucy.

"You can't help them if they don't want to be helped. Stop punishing yourself, worrying about something over which you have no control," said Rebekah.

"I know, but it's so hard. These are my children, my flesh and blood. Where did I go wrong?" said Tracy.

"Stop it! You know better than anyone that what they do with their lives is not your fault. They're adults," said Rebekah.

Still, Tracy worried. But she also thought it was time to get her own life together. She was tired of being alone and lonely. After she divorced Ellis for having an affair with a younger woman, she enrolled in college, earned a Bachelor's degree, and a Master's degree in sociology. She started a rehabilitation center to help young people get off addictive substances. That's when she met her second husband, David, a doctor who was starting a new treatment program for substance abusers. David was from East Baltimore, a section of the city known for heavy drug trafficking. After he had completed his residency in Chicago, he returned home, to Baltimore.

CHAPTER ELEVEN
Lies of the Heart

When Rebekah was in law school, she dated Ken, a big man who weighed over 200 pounds, and stood over six feet tall. Ken had wanted to play professional football but he injured his knee in a high school game. He had seen Rebekah several times on campus and looked for an excuse to meet her. One evening after class, he saw her in the library and seized the opportunity to introduce himself to her.

"Hello, pretty lady. My name is Kenneth Harcum but everybody calls me Ken. We have some classes together but I've never had the pleasure of meeting you."

"Hello, Ken. My name's Rebekah Mosley. I've seen you around campus, but to tell you the truth, I thought you were stuck up. You never spoke."

Ken laughed, "Stuck up? Lady, you don't know how I've been trying to get up enough nerve to meet you. I thought you were out of my league."

Rebekah laughed and started getting her books together to leave.

"May I carry your books?" he asked.

Rebekah laughed again. "No one has carried my books since I was in high school."

"That's a shame. As pretty as you are, someone should be carrying your books everyday," he teased.

Ken took her books from the table and walked out of the library with her.

"Are you driving?" she asked.

"No, my car's in the shop. I'm footin' it," he laughed.

"You've been kind enough to help me with my books, the least I can do is give you a ride," she said.

"Well, that's mighty kind of you, ma'am," he joked.

Ken was very pleasant and likeable. Rebekah found him easy

to talk with. He got into her car and she drove him to his apartment. After that initial meeting, Rebekah and Ken started dating.

She told him about her past. She said if knowing about her past made a difference in their relationship he might as well find out in the beginning. Ken said her past didn't matter. He was only interested in their future.

****

Rebekah graduated with honors from the University of Baltimore School of Law in 1969. Anita received a Master's degree in psychology the same day that Rebekah and Ken received their law degrees.

Rebekah could have sworn that she saw Beulah standing in the back of the auditorium, watching her as she walked across the stage to receive her degree. She also thought that she saw Donnie sitting in the audience. But she decided that she must have been mistaken both times. The last time she heard news of Donnie, he was in medical school; after graduation, he planned to practice medicine in Africa. Although years had passed, Tamara, Rebekah and Mamie had remained friends and had stayed in touch. During a telephone conversation, Tamara told Rebekah that Donnie had never married.

"He says he's still waiting for you," Tamara told Rebekah.

She regretted not marrying him. He was the first man with whom she had made love. And judging by her other relationships, it was the only time she had made love. Everything else was just having sex. She hoped Ken would be different.

After graduation, Rebekah was hired as a law clerk with Trukes and Rosenberg, a prominent law firm in Baltimore. She already had experience from her employment at City Hall. When she passed the bar exam, she was promoted to a full-time attorney with the firm. Ken also passed the bar and was hired by the same firm.

Although Lola's mother had passed away two months prior to Rebekah's graduation, Lola didn't tell Rebekah until she returned to Baltimore to attend her graduation.

"I didn't tell you about Mama's death 'cause I knew you

would have tried to come to her funeral," Lola told Rebekah. "You were right in the middle of final examinations, and Mama made me promise not to put any more burdens on you. She said you had enough to bear. But she thought about you to the very end. She couldn't have been more proud of you than if you were her own daughter. And I'm proud of you, too."

Lola visited with Rebekah for a week, sleeping in her old bedroom. They spent hours together talking about old times and future plans. Lola was surprised to learn that Rebekah was still dating Ken. Rebekah said they had discussed marriage. Lola wanted Rebekah to wait a while and get to know Ken a little better before they got married. She felt that Rebekah might be rushing into marriage because of loneliness.

There was something about Ken that disturbed Lola. Maybe it was because they discovered he had lied about owning a car. After Rebekah had dated Ken a couple of times and they used her car for transportation, she asked Ken when would his car be ready. At first he lied and said it would take a few more days to be repaired. Then a week later, he finally told her the truth, that he didn't have a car. When she asked him why he had lied, he said he was too embarrassed to admit that he couldn't afford a car. His lie concerned Rebekah, but she pushed it from her mind. However, when Rebekah voiced her concerns to Lola she wasn't as understanding as Rebekah.

"Why didn't he just tell the truth?" Lola said to Rebekah. "I don't like liars and thieves."

Lola got the feeling that he wasn't all Rebekah thought he was.

When Lola went back to Georgia, Ken moved into the condominium with Rebekah. They lived together for a year, but from the beginning things didn't go well between them. He resented her spending time giving free legal services to women who sought help from WOMAN Power. Ken was giving her more problems instead of supporting her in her efforts. He felt the women she was trying to help were freeloaders, looking for a handout. He thought that he and Rebekah should go in private practice together. Rebekah disagreed and pursued her work with WOMAN Power over his objections.

In the beginning of their relationship, Rebekah thought that she and Ken had a lot in common. They both were from the South. They both specialized in criminal law. They both were paying off school loans. Rebekah felt they both were lonely and could help each other. But the arguments were becoming more frequent and more intense, she soon realized that they had little in common.

The Goldsteins were still so grateful to Rebekah that they offered to help finance her law practice. But Rebekah repeatedly refused any offer of monetary compensation. She said that she didn't save the little boy's life for money. She said it was the human thing to do.

When she told Ken that Stewart Goldstein had contacted her and about the offer he made, Ken said, "I don't know what your damn problem is, lady! You have the chance of a lifetime thrown in your lap, all you got to do is take it. And what do you do? You're too good to take the opportunity!"

"I don't think I'm too good to take the money, but I didn't do it for the money. I told Stewart Goldstein and I'll tell you, it was the human thing to do," protested Rebekah.

"'Human thing' my ass. Don't you know that we could open our own law practice, you and me? How stupid can you be? Woman, you must be crazy. We're struggling to make ends meet, paying off school loans, and you're turning down free money," Ken argued.

"We're not struggling, and we would be doing better than we are if you handled your financial obligations better," Rebekah said.

"So now I don't handle my responsibilities. Is that what you're saying?" Ken demanded.

"All I'm saying is ... Oh, forget it," said Rebekah and she waved him off. Not wanting to start an argument, she walked away.

Ken stormed out of the room.

They also argued about Rebekah's refusal to accept Beulah's insurance money from Amy and Pete. But Rebekah had other concerns. Her dream of helping women meant opening a women's center operated by women. She took her time and planned an organization about which Beulah could be proud. But Ken didn't like the idea. He felt that Rebekah should spend the money on him and on herself. He thought her involvement with the women's group was a waste of time.

Ken changed from the person Rebekah had met in law school. He started coming home later and later. She knew the reasons weren't work-related. She began to suspect him of being unfaithful. One night he came home with lipstick on his collar and the smell of perfume on his clothes. When Rebekah questioned him about the lipstick and perfume, he flew into a rage, accusing her of not trusting him. She didn't want to anger him further, so she let the matter drop.

She called Anita to talk about her problem. Anita advised Rebekah to pray about it and said God would answer her prayers.

Rebekah was a successful and competent attorney, but her personal life was a mess. She was still insecure about her identity, constantly wrestled with being a product of two races. She had spent so much time doing drugs and wallowing in guilt for disrespecting Beulah — the only mother she had known — that she continued to make decisions that caused her grief. Her life of drugs, prostitution and search for love kept ending in despair.

She was really looking for the love she found with Donnie. Every once in a while, she'd think of Donnie and wonder what his life was like. It seemed that she was good at giving advice and helping others, but she wasn't good at fixing the pieces of her own life. Ken sensed her vulnerability and took advantage of it.

One night Ken didn't come home at all. When Rebekah awoke and saw that he wasn't in bed with her, she thought he might have fallen asleep on the couch in the living room. She thought he had worked late and didn't want to disturb her when he came in. She went into the living room but he wasn't there. He had stayed out late before but he always managed to get home before she got up to go to work. She showered, got dressed and went to work, but she couldn't concentrate. She sat in her office, her head in her hands, trying hard not to cry, when her secretary, Rochelle, entered.

"Is anything wrong, Miss Mosley?" Rochelle asked.

Rebekah hadn't heard Rochelle enter and she was startled. Rebekah began moving papers around on her desk, trying to act and look busy.

"No, nothing's wrong. I'm just tired," said Rebekah.

Rochelle didn't believe her. She had seen the tears in Rebekah's eyes.

"Miss Mosley, may I talk to you confidentially?" asked Rochelle.

"Of course, Rochelle. Close the door."

Rochelle closed the office door, walked to the leather chair in front of Rebekah's desk and sat down. Rochelle admired Rebekah and was loyal to her. Rochelle had been on welfare, going nowhere fast, when Rebekah met her. When the Children Protection Services tried to declare Rochelle an unfit mother and take away her only child, a four-year-old son, Rebekah represented her *pro bono.* Rochelle was homeless at the time; her husband had drowned in a boating accident while fishing with his brother, and they didn't have life insurance. She had lost everything. When the Public Defender's office contacted the law office of Trukes and Rosenberg, Rebekah had asked to take the case. Rebekah won the case at trial and had convinced Rochelle to enroll in school.

Rochelle took a course in data processing and administration and Rebekah was impressed with Rochelle's eagerness to become employed and independent. When Rochelle finished the course at the top of her class, Rebekah convinced the law firm's partners to hire her. Rochelle now had a nice apartment, a car, and was planning to enroll in law school at the University of Baltimore. She was indebted to Rebekah for helping her straighten out her life.

"I don't know if I should say anything, but I have so much respect for you and you've been good to me and my son so I feel I owe everything I own to you," said Rochelle.

"It wasn't just me," said Rebekah. "My sisters in WOMAN Power helped you get started."

"Yes, but if it wasn't for you," continued Rochelle, "I wouldn't have met the other women."

Rebekah hadn't allowed Ken's negative attitude about helping people who couldn't pay for her services deter her from her mission. Rebekah could tell that Rochelle had something on her mind, and somehow she got the feeling that it involved her.

"Rochelle, is everything all right in your life? How's your son?" Rebekah asked, showing genuine interest.

"Yes, everything's all right and my son is fine. He's a big boy now. But that's not what I want to talk to you about. It's about Mr. Ken and the gossip that's going on in the office."

Rebekah's heart skipped a beat. She couldn't stop her hands from shaking. "What about Mr. Ken?" Rebekah nervously asked.

"Several of the secretaries said that he's having an affair with Mr. Trukes' wife, Candace. Mr. Trukes' secretary said she heard Mr. and Mrs. Trukes arguing about her going out so much lately. Mildred, who works in the secretarial pool, said she saw Mr. Ken and Mrs. Trukes together at the Berkshire Hotel. Mildred was there with this new fellow she met at the bakery. I thought you should know about the gossip that's going around the office," she said.

"Thank you, Rochelle. I appreciate your concern and loyalty," Rebekah said.

Rochelle smiled and went back to her desk. Rebekah didn't know what to think, so she decided to find out the truth herself. She called Roger Contee, a detective friend who owed her a couple of favors. She met Roger for lunch and asked him to check out Rochelle's story. She gave Roger the picture of Ken that she kept on her desk, and told him she wanted to know if Ken was at the Berkshire with another woman. He was to use the picture to show to the hotel clerk. Ken was Black and Candace Trukes was white, so Rebekah thought the clerk would remember the couple.

About five o'clock that evening, Roger called Rebekah and confirmed her suspicions. In fact, Roger reported, that Ken and Candace were frequent guests at the hotel. On several occasions, Ken and Candace had eaten lunch in the restaurant and then checked into a room.

Rebekah was heartbroken.

"Another wrong person in my life. Why do I keep picking losers?" she said to herself.

She deliberately stayed late at the office, giving Ken a chance to get home before she arrived. He had left the office early that day and she figured he would be late getting home.

When she went home that night, and walked into the house, Ken was on the telephone. As she walked into the room she heard him say, "I'll talk to you later. She just walked in." He hung up the telephone and started up the stairs.

"Where were you last night?" Rebekah asked him.

"Out," he replied sarcastically and kept walking.

"Out where and with whom?" she asked.

He stopped on the stairs, turned to face her, shrugged his shoulders and said, "I don't owe you an explanation about where I go. I'm a man. I can do what I damn well please. I don't have to answer to you."

"But I thought we had a commitment to each other. If I stayed out all night, wouldn't you expect an answer from me?" she said.

"I really don't care what you do," he said and started walking down the stairs toward her. "I've had enough of you trying to save the world. If I *was* out all night, so what? I'm home now, ain't I? Anyway, you should know about staying out all night. That used to be the time you worked best. Once a 'ho, always a 'ho," he said in a nasty, accusing tone.

When she told him about her past in the beginning of their relationship, he had said that it didn't matter. Obviously he had lied about that, too. She didn't care anymore.

"Get out of my house and out of my life," Rebekah shouted. "I'm sick of being used. Get out!"

"And I'm sick of your damn mouth," he said, and slapped her so hard her lip split and started to bleed. "Now I know why my daddy used to whip my mama's ass," he growled. "It was because she had too damn much mouth, just like you."

He hit her again.

In one corner of her living room stood an armoire that once belonged to Lola's mother. When they moved to Georgia, Lola had left it for Rebekah. Because of the crime rate and because it was often necessary for Rebekah to be out at night with her clients, Lola insisted that she keep a gun in one of the drawers of the armoire for protection and Rebekah hadn't told Ken about the gun. Roger had taught her how to use it. When Ken drew back his hand to hit her a third time, she ran to the armoire, pulled open the top drawer and grabbed the gun.

His eyes got wide. The sight of the gun surprised him.

"If you put your damn hands on me again, I'll blow your head off!" she said. "I'm not afraid of you. You ain't your daddy and I ain't your mama! I won't take a beating from you and from no other man anymore. I'm starting an organization to help women who've been abused by jack-asses like you. Do you really think that I'd take an ass whipping from you?

"By the way, you stupid bastard, your boss knows that you've been sleeping with his wife. You're a dumb ass! I didn't want to believe it, but I had a detective friend check out the Berkshire Hotel. You've been busted, Buster. I called your boss today and we had a long conversation. I really don't think you have a job anymore, and I believe your precious Candace will need a place to stay too, 'cause she doesn't have a home anymore, and guess what? Neither do you. I feel sorry for you both. Now get out of my house! You make me sick looking at you."

Ken was shocked and stunned. He realized he had been busted. He went upstairs and packed his clothes. Rebekah was glad that he didn't know about the second gun she kept hidden in her bedroom in the bottom drawer of her night table. Lola had told Rebekah not to tell Ken about the guns.

"I don't know what it is but my gut feeling says he's not to be trusted," Lola had said.

Rebekah was glad she listened to Lola and had taken her advice about the guns.

Ken was scared; he realized he had messed up a good thing. He knew his boss would blackball him from working for any other law firm of substance in the city. He had gotten the job because Rebekah asked Josh Trukes, one of the managing partners, to put in a word for him. Rebekah had established quite a reputation for herself when she was a clerk in the city's law department. Plus, Josh Trukes and Stewart Goldstein were relatives.

Ken went back downstairs where Rebekah was sitting on the

sofa crying. He tried to talk to her, to tell her that he was sorry, but she didn't want to hear it. She had had enough of his lies.

"I'm sorry, baby. Let's not end this way. We've invested a lot of time in each other. I'm sorry for what I said and for what I did. Can't we start over? I promise I'll never hit you again and I'll never be unfaithful again. Please forgive me," he begged.

"I said get out and don't come back! I can do bad by my self. Now, Mister Got-It-All-Together, let me see how well you can piece your life back together. Too bad you tried to think with the head of your dick instead of using your brain. Did you really think that white woman was going to leave her rich white husband for a poor nigga like you? What can you give her that she doesn't already have, except a chocolate dick? She can get from any colored man. You were one of her husband's employees. All she wanted was a plaything for a while; and you were so happy to be getting a piece of white ass, you really thought she wanted you. And to think, I wanted to marry a two-timing jerk like you. I should have known you weren't shit when you lied about owning a car when we were in law school. Now get out and don't come back!" she shouted.

He walked out the door with his luggage, tears in his eyes. He had no idea what he was going to do or where he was going. He went to the telephone booth across the street from Rebekah's condominium and called Candace. She was going through her own problems. After Josh Trukes talked with Rebekah and learned that his wife was sleeping with one of the junior attorneys of his law firm, and a Black man at that, he went home and confronted her. Of course she denied it, but he didn't believe her.

Josh told her what the investigator had found out about Ken and her. She pleaded with her husband not to believe gossip, but Josh wasn't buying that. He told her she had one hour to pack her things and move out. He threatened to divorce her and to fight her in court if necessary. She was scared. She was dirt poor when Josh married her, and she felt that he would use evidence of her infidelity to keep from paying her alimony.

When Candace answered the telephone and heard Ken's voice she said, "Don't call my house anymore. Suppose my husband had answered the telephone? I'm in enough trouble as it is. I don't know what I'm going to do. He knows about us," Candace sobbed. "He has threatened to cut me off without a cent and to file for custody of our son. You can't take care of me. Hell, you can't take care of yourself. Why did I ever get in this mess?"

"But I thought you loved me," said Ken. "What about all those things you said we would do together and all those places we would go? Rebekah kicked me out, and I've been fired from the law firm. What am I supposed to do now? Where am I supposed to go? Are you saying that I just ruined my career for nothing?"

"Oh, you pathetic fool!" snapped Candace. "What the hell do I care where you go? I know you didn't believe all that shit I was saying. I figured we were both lying to each other for the thrill of the moment. Each time I left you, I forgot about all those lies we told to each other. I'm fighting for my own future. You'd better fight for yours 'cause I can't help you. I feel sorry for you but there's nothing I can do to help you. I need my head examined. How did I let this shit happen?" She slammed down the telephone, hanging up on Ken.

At that moment, he realized what a complete fool he had been. He walked back to his car and started to get in. He looked back at the window where Rebekah was closing the blinds and closing the chapter on their relationship. He got into his car and banged his fists on the steering wheel in anger and frustration. He sat in the car and cried, realizing what he had lost. Rebekah was his future. She was the best thing that ever happened to him and he had blown any chances of making their dreams a reality. He turned the key, started the car and drove off.

Rebekah closed the curtains, went upstairs to the bedroom, fell across the bed and sobbed. She had been standing in the window watching Ken in the telephone booth. She figured he was calling Candace.

"It's too late, boy. The party is over," she whispered. "I can't do many things, but one thing I can do is fuck up my life."

The telephone rang. Rebekah tried to dry her tears before she answered it. It was Lola.

"Hi, Rebie," Lola said, "I was looking in the photo album at some old pictures of us and I wanted to hear your voice. How are things going?"

Rebekah was glad to hear from her friend. "I'm glad you called. I wanted to talk to you, but I didn't want to bother you with my problems."

Lola paused.

"Rebie, what's the matter? You don't sound happy. Is everything all right?"

"Sure, everything's fine. I just miss you," Rebekah lied.

"Doesn't sound like everything's fine to me," Lola said. "Is it about Ken? Tell me what's wrong."

Rebekah began to sob. She told Lola that she and Ken had broken up.

Lola sighed. "He wasn't for you anyway, honey. If he was, he'd still be there. Trust in God. You'll meet Mr. Right one day. Pray that God shows you what's best for you. He does answer prayers. You might not get the answer you want, but you'll get the one you need."

"My mama used to say that all the time," said Rebekah.

"Well, it's still true. Ain't nothing changed," said Lola.

Then Lola told Rebekah that she had signed the condominium over to her as a graduation present. Rebekah cried with happiness.

"I love you," Rebekah said. "You've been closer to me than anyone since Mama died. I don't know where I'd be if I hadn't met you."

"You'd be the pretty, intelligent young lady you were when I met you," said Lola. "You were just off track, but God has plans for you. Don't worry about Ken. I'm glad he's out of your life. Now you can concentrate on your own life without him holding you back. I've wanted to say that for a long time but I kept my mouth shut because you loved him. But now that he's gone, it's full steam ahead."

Rebekah laughed.

"That's what I wanted to hear, you laughing," said Lola.

"Well, I guess this is the end of another chapter in my life," said Rebekah.

"And the beginning of something new," said Lola.

CHAPTER TWELVE
Breeze

Two years passed after Rebekah's break up with Ken. She dated occasionally when the WOMAN Power women thought they were doing her a favor by fixing her up with blind dates.

"Don't y'all try to help me. I'm doing just fine by myself. The men I've been meeting have more needs than I do," she said one day at club meeting. "Thanks, but no thanks. I can do bad by myself."

Rebekah became one of the best criminal lawyers in Maryland. She joined the prison ministry at her church to help incarcerated men and women who and were within one to two years of being released. In the meantime, Sister Berneda had become Reverend Berneda. She had earned a Ph.D. in theology, and she helped her husband to pastor the Ray of Hope Baptist Church. She worked with drug addicts, and she, Rebekah, and the WOMAN Power Club members expanded the services of the prison ministry by offering a program to help inmates get job training and education before they were released and followup after being released..

Rebekah remembered how drugs had almost destroyed her life and how God had saved her. The prison ministry from the church began providing a program at the Maryland Correctional Institute in Jessup, Maryland — MCI-J — a medium-security institute right next to the Big House — the maximum-security institute.

It was a beautiful spring day, the kind that made Rebekah glad to be alive. She hoped that she would always remember the beauty of the day, long after it had gone. She wanted to remember how the sun felt on her skin after the long winter. She wanted to remember the sound of birds singing and the smell of freshly cut grass mixed with the fragrance of spring flowers. That fragrance made Rebekah appreciate spring. It was a day that made her glad to have the freedom to go wherever she wanted to go without restrictions or limits.

It was Rebekah's first day of teaching inside a prison. Although she had defended hundreds of criminals, she had never gotten accustomed to being behind prison walls and she still didn't like the sound of the prison gate closing behind her. It was a sound that she hoped she never would have to hear permanently. There was something about the sound of the heavy metal door closing, the sound echoing throughout the building, and the turning of the key in the door that made Rebekah feel uneasy. She imagined how it would be if they couldn't find the key to let her out. It made her uncomfortable to think that her freedom depended on someone unlocking the metal door. She also had never been locked inside a room with thirty male criminals.

Reverend Berneda, Rebekah, and Anita had convinced one of the local colleges to work with the WOMAN Power Club's efforts to go into the prison twice a week to teach English to incarcerated males and females. Rebekah was one of the instructors. She started teaching male inmates as an adjunct professor with the local community college. She contended that one of the main reasons Black men had such a hard time getting and keeping jobs was because of poor written and oral communication skills. Although there were other races of men in her class, the majority of them were Black.

Rebekah was nervous on her first day behind the great walls, but she was looking forward to the experience. She was apprehensive about what to wear, what to say, and when to say it. Her first night teaching inside the prison was exciting and terrifying. She didn't know what to expect from the inmates. To get to her classroom, she had to walk through an area called the Great Hall, among crowds of male inmates who were standing around talking. She didn't know if one would grab her or touch her. When none did either, she was relieved.

After her first night of teaching was over, she sat in her office to assess the day's work.

"Hello," a voice said.

Rebekah looked in the direction of the voice and saw a pleasant-looking woman standing in the office door, smiling.

"My name is Gladys Murray. I heard we were getting a new teacher. Welcome aboard." The woman said, as she extended her hand for a handshake. "

Rebekah extended her hand to shake Gladys' hand.

"Thank you," said Rebekah. "My name is Rebekah Mosley and this is my first night. It wasn't so bad. I'm sitting here reviewing today's activities and trying to see what I can do to improve my skills."

"If I may make a suggestion," said Gladys. "Don't trust anyone in here. Remember, this is a prison. I know you'll hear stories that'll probably bring tears to your eyes. But remember, the majority of the men in here made a living telling lies. They have perfected the art of lying."

"'The art of lying?'" said Rebekah. "When did lying become an art?"

"Honey, you ain't seen nothin' yet," laughed Gladys. "These men have lying down to a science. They can be telling a lie and you know they're lying, but because they're lying so well, you almost believe what they're saying is true."

"Oh, I see what you mean," Rebekah laughingly said.

"Thank you for your suggestions. How long have you been teaching here?" asked Rebekah.

"Five years, and I'm tired. I teach here part-time, but I'm not going to be teaching here much longer. I'm going to resign next month and focus on my high school kids. But before I leave, let's have lunch together."

Gladys was the principal of one of the most troubled schools in East Baltimore. They promised they would get together soon.

After Rebekah had been teaching in the prison for three months, she earned the reputation of being an, "all right" person by the inmates' standards. They learned that she didn't lie to them. If she said she was going to do something, she did it, unless it was beyond her ability to accomplish. The word had gotten around to other inmates that a lady lawyer was a teacher in the prison and that she really knew her stuff.

The fact that Rebekah was willing to listen and tried to understand their problems made the inmates respect her. She didn't go on their turf trying to be a know-it-all. Although she had a law degree, was a prominent attorney, a respected leader in her church, her community, and in her profession, she didn't act as if she was better than the inmates. She realized that she needed the inmates to trust her if she was going to be successful teaching them. She realized that they had to like what they were doing, otherwise they wouldn't participate. She also realized that if the inmates respected her and trusted her, if there was any trouble inside the prison while she was there, they would protect her. After all, she was in their environment. She made a point of getting acquainted with the leader of each group in her class, so that he could assist her in maintaining order in class.

There wasn't enough classroom space inside the prison school for Rebekah to teach her classes. Therefore, she had to conduct classes in the Great Hall, which was nothing more than a large open room that resembled a gymnasium. Partitions divided the room into sections so that several classes could be conducted at the same time.

In addition to teaching English and basic grammar, as a member of WOMAN Power, Rebekah was also a consultant in a program designed to rehabilitate drug addicts. Because the program was funded by the federal government, it wasn't a part of the local college curriculum, as was the English program. The drug program was separate from all other programs and wasn't subject to the same rules.

While teaching class one evening, Rebekah noticed an inmate standing behind a glass wall, staring at her. She later learned that his name was Curtis and he was a student in one of the college courses being taught on the other side of the Great Hall. Without his instructor seeing him, he had slipped out of class to stand and stare at Rebekah.

Every day that Rebekah taught in the prison, Curtis would sneak out of his class to stand and stare at her, afraid to speak to her. His real name was Curtis Jasper Fontain. His nickname was "Cool Breeze." His fellow inmates called him "Breeze," for short. He was tall and good looking. The female correctional officers flirted with him, but he ignored most of them.

Bobo, one of Rebekah's students, told Breeze about Rebekah. Breeze had the reputation of being a ladies' man. He was six feet four inches tall and weighed about two-hundred pounds, with muscles that showed he lifted weights. He had shoulders like a football player, and a creamy chocolate complexion. Most of the time he wore a cap or a bandanna around his head. Sometimes he wore a skull cap. Bobo had a bet that Breeze couldn't get Rebekah romantically interested in him. Rebekah wasn't aware they played games like that in prison. Bobo and Breeze used those same kind of games to get extra favors from female correctional officers, such as extra ice cream and cookies with meals, getting to watch television when they should be locked in their cells, going to the gymnasium to lift weights at times when they weren't scheduled to, and so on.

Some of the female correctional officers also smuggled items into the prison for the inmates, such as drugs, toiletries, clothes, food, and anything else the inmates asked them to bring. The female prison guards traded those items for sexual favors from the male inmates.

The inmates called Rebekah an "uptown woman." The majority of the female prison guards envied her. To them, she was an outsider. They were jealous of her coming into their world, in feminine clothes, while they had to wear uniforms like the male officers. They saw her as competition. Rebekah wore business suits, carried a briefcase, had flawlessly applied makeup, and her hair was always neatly done. Her students told her how some of the female officers pulled down their pants and panties and exposed their pubic hairs to try to entice male inmates to have sex with them. Some female officers staked claims on male inmates and warned other female officers that certain cells and certain inmates were off limits.

After two weeks of standing behind the glass wall watching Rebekah, Breeze started bringing a chair into the area to sit while he watched her. She thought he was taking notes of her lectures, but he was actually sketching her while she taught class.

One day Rebekah was lecturing to her class and one of her students asked her the definition and spelling of a word. Rebekah instructed the student to look up the word in the dictionary. The student told her that he didn't have a dictionary.

"That boy over there got one," another student said as he pointed to Breeze.

She beckoned for him to bring it to her and he did. He walked from behind the glass wall, over to Rebekah, handed her the dictionary and walked away. After she used it, she laid it on her desk. When her class was over, Breeze walked back into her classroom.

"I thought you had forgotten your dictionary," Rebekah said as she handed it to him.

He reached out to receive it and said in a low husky voice, "What are you doing here?"

She ignored his question and asked, "What's your name?"

"My name is Mike. What's your name?" he asked.

"Another damn Mike. Besides, you already know my name. Who're you trying to kid?" she muttered half aloud and half under her breath.

"Excuse me," said Breeze, "I didn't understand what you said.

"I said, I think you already know my name. I've seen you watching me for at least two weeks."

"You're right; I do know your name. I would like to know more about you, such as whether or not you're married, your age, and what you're doing here."

"What am I doing here? I'm teaching a class," she said. "And I don't think my marital status or my age is any concern of yours."

He smiled.

"I'll find out. But, I mean, what're you doing teaching in this type of environment? You should be teaching in a college classroom where your students will appreciate what you're trying to do. These cons don't appreciate you here."

Rebekah was intrigued by his penetrating eyes and the way he looked at her. She realized how little he thought of himself and how the other inmates might be feeling the same way.

"How old are you?" asked Rebekah.

"I'm nineteen," he said.

But Breeze had lied to her about his name and his age. The only truth he told was that he was a Pisces. Based on the lie he told about his age, she thought she was fifteen years older than he was, and she felt the age difference would be a deterrent from any thoughts of an intimate relationship. Besides, she thought, Pisces and Gemini are not compatible signs. As much as she didn't want to admit it, she was attracted to him; and the fact that he stood and stared at her each time she came into the prison was flattering to her.

That evening after her class was over, she began collecting her lecture notes and putting her books and papers into her briefcase. She could feel Breeze's eyes on her. She had been thinking about him all afternoon.

"Here I am thinking about an inmate, a criminal. I really must be desperate for a man," she whispered. Then she dismissed the thought.

Breeze slowly walked to where she stood, taking his time and allowing his eyes to caress her body. He said to her in a slow deliberate drawl, "Who do you belong to and what's your mission here?" That was the second time he had asked her that question.

She didn't know how to answer him. She thought about the similarity between his question and the question Marty had asked her years ago, a lifetime ago.

She answered with indignation. "I belong to myself and my mission here is just what you see me doing."

Breeze asked her where she worked. When she told him the name of the law firm, he said "You mean, you're the man?"

She knew what he meant, but she said, "No, I'm not 'the man.' I'm a woman. Can't you tell?"

Breeze smiled. "If you are the man, I'll find out."

He was amused that she didn't understand his question. She was amused that he thought she was more naive than she actually was.

She slammed her briefcase closed and marched out of the Great Hall without saying another word to Breeze. She muttered under her breath as she left the prison grounds, "How dare that damn inmate question me. What does it matter to him who I am? I don't have to answer to him, a common criminal."

Rebekah taught at the prison two nights a week, Tuesdays and Thursdays, and that was her last night of the week, which meant she would have to wait until the following week to see Breeze again.

When she returned to the prison the following Tuesday night,

Breeze was there waiting for her in his usual place. She had dressed especially carefully. Although she didn't want to admit it to herself, she knew she was dressing for him. After her class was over that day, Breeze walked to where she was standing.

"Well," she said, "am I 'the man'?"

He looked at her amused and said, "No, you're okay." Then he smiled. "You know, I'm going to make you my woman."

Rebekah tried to act insulted, indignant, surprised, disbelieving, angry, anything to hide the excitement that was building inside her. She was trying to stop her heart from racing. She didn't want him to see the expression on her face. It might have revealed how pleased she was at the thought of being his "woman."

"Don't I have anything to say about that?" she asked.

He shrugged his shoulders. "The only thing you have to say is yes, because it's inevitable. I know it and so do you."

After that conversation, Breeze started waiting until Rebekah's class was over to come to her. They talked about anything, just to be holding a conversation. His intelligence surprised her. He soaked up knowledge like a sponge soaks up water. He wanted to read everything he could get his hands on. He begged her to write to him, but she refused.

"In class today, I was reading the newspaper while the instructor was lecturing, and he asked me if I could listen to what he was saying and read the paper too," Breeze said. "'Good question,' I thought. Do you think you could read something and listen to someone else speaking to you? Yes, I believe you can. You read with your eyes and listen with your ears. However, the instructor said something that made me change my mind. He said, 'But you have only one brain to concentrate on either the spoken message or the written word.' That's why I come out of class to watch you. I don't want anything to interfere with my thoughts of you."

Again he asked her if she was married. When she told him that she wasn't, he breathed a sigh of relief.

"I'm glad you're not married, not that it would have mattered. I've already made up my mind that you're gonna belong to me. But if you had a husband, it would have complicated things a little. I don't like to hurt another brother by taking his woman, but I've never met anyone I wanted as much as I want you."

"I can't be your woman, but I will be your friend," Rebekah said. "I'll be someone you can talk to."

Breeze shook his head.

"If you were my woman, I wouldn't want you to be friends with another man. You would only need me and your family. Some of your girlfriends wouldn't even take up your time, if I thought they were talking to you about another man. I'm a jealous and possessive man, and I can tell that if we were lovers, I wouldn't want anyone to touch you but me. You'll be my friend, but you'll also be my woman. It's a done deal."

Rebekah sighed.

"But we're not lovers and never will be. You're too young for me," she said.

"How old are you?" he asked.

Rebekah shook her head. "What does it matter? You're nineteen and that's too young for me."

He looked at her with an intense stare and smiled. "Suppose I lied to you about my age and about my name. Suppose I'm really twenty-five. Would that make a difference?"

Rebekah was thirty-four and she couldn't believe her ears when she said, "Yes, that would make a lot of difference. I wondered how someone so young could have such a great insight about life. Some of our conversations just don't sound as if they're coming from a nineteen-year-old. But I already knew that you lied about your name. One of your buddies told me your real name. I was just waiting to see how long it would take you to tell me the truth. Why did you think it was necessary to lie about your name and age?"

Breeze smiled again. "I wanted to see if I could get away with saying that I was younger than I actually am. And about my name, I had to see if you were the man before I told you the truth. That's what this environment does, it teaches you that lying is acceptable behavior and not to trust anyone. Now that you know I'm not a young hopper, will you write to me?"

"That's the second time you mentioned me being 'the man.'

What makes you think that?" she asked.

"You might be the police, placed here as a plant to spy on inmates."

Rebekah laughed at the lack of trust she found in inmates. They didn't trust each other and no one else. Again, Rebekah told him that she would not write to him. She said that the system didn't permit instructors to communicate with inmates except during class time. "They would certainly frown on an attorney writing to an inmate unless it was business related," she said.

Breeze didn't accept that explanation.

"Who would know that we were writing to each other, except the two of us?" he asked.

"Anyone might find out. I don't trust these officers, especially that Officer Howard," Rebekah said.

Annie Howard, a female correctional officer, was in love with Breeze. Each time Rebekah talked to Breeze, Officer Howard found a reason to break up the conversation. One of Rebekah's students, a friend of Breeze, joked about how Officer Howard told other female officers that Breeze was her man and he was off limits to all other female officers.

Officer Howard had started sending Rebekah messages by other inmates, warning her to keep away from Breeze or there would be trouble. Officer Howard had threatened to make trouble for both Breeze and Rebekah if she caught them alone together, even if they were only talking about lessons. Rebekah wasn't afraid for herself, but she knew that Breeze was helpless against Officer Howard, who had the support of the other prison guards — at least, most of them. Rebekah knew that Officer Howard could get to her through Breeze. Therefore, for his sake, she maintained a low profile.

Nevertheless, Rebekah finally gave him permission to write her at her office address. She assured him that it would be all right and that no one opened her personal mail, not even her secretary. From the beginning, Breeze didn't like the idea of sending mail to her office, but he did so just the same. Rebekah was apprehensive about giving him her home address. She remembered what Gladys had told her the first day she taught inside the prison, about not trusting anyone.

Besides, he had already lied to her twice, about his name and age.

In one of his letters Breeze asked Rebekah to open a savings account for him in her name. He said he wanted to send her money to save for him until he was released from prison. While incarcerated, he worked in the print shop and earned a small salary. It was the first honest job he ever had and it was in confinement. He wanted to send Rebekah his pay checks. He said if he sent them to his mother or to other family members, they would spend them. Rebekah showed the letter to Anita, and asked her what she thought about her opening a bank account for Breeze.

"I think he's becoming too attached to you," Anita told her.

CHAPTER THIRTEEN
Competition In Blue

One night when Rebekah went into the prison to teach, she didn't see Breeze. She dared not ask anyone about him, so she went about teaching her class, expecting him to walk in at any moment.

Rebekah began to look forward to his letters, yet she still wouldn't write to him, even though he kept pleading with her to do so.

Breeze sent Rebekah his mother's address and telephone number. Because of the distance to the prison, his mother didn't visit him often. Therefore, she was grateful for messages from her son.

"Call my mother. Tell her that you see me every week and that I'm doing fine," he said.

After a month of receiving letters and cards from Breeze, he and Rebekah had another conversation about him sending mail to her at her office.

"I don't like it," he said one Tuesday night. "I feel restricted. I would write to you every day, two and three times a day, if I knew you were the only one who reads my letters. Think about it, baby. Suppose someone decided to open one of our letters? Suppose you got sick and I didn't know in time to stop writing to you? I'm not concerned about myself; I'm already in jail. But I am concerned about you. You have your reputation to protect. What would your peers say about the professional attorney, Mosley, receiving love letters from a prisoner?"

Rebekah thought about what he said and she agreed. She also knew that she wanted to start answering his letters. He was a talented artist and made beautiful cards which he sent to her. During each holiday, he asked her to show the cards at some of the professional organizations to which she belonged and try to sell them. But they were so beautiful, she didn't have the heart to sell them. She bought them all herself.

After thinking about the conversation about the letters,

Rebekah went to the post office and rented a post office box. She then wrote to Breeze for the first time and told him about the box.

One night after Rebekah had dismissed her class, Breeze hung around to talk to her. He described his reaction when he received her first letter.

"I returned from lunch," he said. "I walked into my cell and saw the envelope laying on my bunk. It was laying face down so that I couldn't see the name on the front of the envelope. But I knew who it was from. Every fiber of my being knew. I could feel your presence before I touched the envelope. At first I just sat on my bunk and stared at the envelope, afraid to open it, afraid to touch it. I was afraid of what might be written on the pages inside. Suppose she's telling me that I shouldn't write to her anymore; I said to myself. Suppose she's saying that someone opened one of the letters I wrote to her. But again, suppose she's saying that she loves me. I decided that I would save the letter until after dinner. I would make it my dessert. But I couldn't wait. After I sat and stared at it for about ten minutes, I opened it and I felt that you were inside the cell with me. I started talking to you and prayed that the wind would carry my words back to your ears."

After that, Rebekah and Breeze wrote to each other constantly. The post office was six blocks from her office, and she happily walked those blocks while thinking about Breeze. On the days when she went to the post office and found the box empty, she was disappointed. She often wondered if he knew how much his letters had come to mean to her. She wondered if he knew how much *he* had come to mean to her. Rebekah didn't realize herself how much Breeze meant to her. At least, she didn't want to admit it.

Thanksgiving and Christmas came and Breeze complained about not receiving a box from home. He asked Rebekah to call his mother and tell her to send him a pair of gym shoes.

Rebekah called her and his mother said, "What about you? Can't you buy him a pair?"

Rebekah was aggravated by her remarks.

"I can't make a difference between him and any other inmate," Rebekah said. "If I buy shoes for your son, I'll have to buy some for every inmate who asks me. The only reason I called you is because your son asked me to call. I'll just have to tell him what you said."

"Tell him I ain't got no money for no shoes," his mother said in a drowsy voice and hung up the telephone.

When Rebekah saw Breeze the following week and told him what his mother said, he tried to hide his disappointment.

"I love to play basketball," he said, "but I can't play if I don't have gym shoes. Boy, I thought I could depend on my mother, as much money as I gave her. I wonder what she did with the money? I also send her my paychecks. I wonder what she's doing with them?"

Rebekah felt sorry for him. She didn't want him to want for anything. She bought him the gym shoes. She also bought him sardines because he mentioned one day that he missed the taste of them. She bought items in cans that could be opened without a can opener. Cartons of cigarettes were the main things he asked for and she bought him everything but cigarettes. Inside the prison, packets of cigarettes were more valuable than money. Inmates were not allowed to have more than ten dollars on them. There was no limit to the cartons of cigarettes they could keep, so inmates used cigarettes to trade for other items. But because she didn't bring the cigarettes, he complained.

"I'm not going to bring you cigarettes because I don't want you to smoke. You can get lung cancer from smoking," Rebekah said.

But he didn't accept that excuse. He just knew that she hadn't delivered as he had instructed her to do. He was angry, but he didn't show it. He didn't want to kill the goose that was laying the golden eggs. He didn't want to start making too many demands on her.

Rebekah heard him mention that his shorts were ragged so she surprised him with a box filled with silk shorts, a bathrobe, towels, soap, face cream, deodorant, lotion, candy, cookies, shampoo, and a wrap to wear after he took a shower. She said she didn't want anyone but her to see his body.

Since he never mentioned her opening a bank account for him again, she assumed he was depositing his salary into a prison account. She started sending him money orders to deposit into the account so that he could withdraw cash as he needed it. She used a fictitious name on the money orders, but he knew who sent them.

Breeze asked her to take a shower at home, use a towel to dry her body and send the towel to him. "Do you know that I'll still be able to smell your body scent on the towel?" he said.

But Rebekah didn't know who would be opening the boxes, and she was apprehensive about sending the towel. Breeze was disappointed when he didn't receive it.

He told her that he often slept nude because he didn't have any pajamas. He said Officer Howard knew that he slept nude and one morning he awoke to find her standing in his cell, staring at him as he slept. He said he asked her what she wanted and she said that she wanted to borrow a tea bag. The officers knew that he drank a cup of hot tea every morning brewed in a battery-operated teapot in his cell. Breeze told Officer Howard that he didn't have any tea bags, but she didn't believe him. She put her hands under the sheet on his bed and began to feel his body, pretending to look for the tea bags. He pushed her hands away and told her to get out of his cell.

"I guess if I was that bitch up at the school you'd be glad I'm here," Officer Howard snapped.

"You're damn right!" Breeze snapped back at her. "Now get the hell out of here and leave me alone!"

When he told Rebekah about that incident, she sent Breeze three pairs of pajamas.

Although Officer Howard had been having an affair with Officer Arrington for two years and Officer Arrington was the father of Officer Howard's baby, Officer Howard was angry about being rejected by Breeze. To get revenge on him, she told Officer Arrington that she was making a routine inspection of Breeze's cell when Breeze called her a bitch and pushed her out of his cell.

When Officer Arrington heard what Breeze had allegedly done, he gave Breeze a "ticket," and put him in lockup during which time he couldn't have any visitors. Inmates on lockup could only come in contact with the officers assigned to work the lockup area. Officer Howard arranged to be the officer on duty in the lockup area during the entire time Breeze was there. Naturally, since Breeze was on lockup, he couldn't see Rebekah.

Rebekah began to suspect there was a reason for Officer Howard's obsession with Breeze. Although Breeze was good looking and sexy, he wasn't the best looking man inside the prison. One day she asked him if there had ever been anything between him and Officer Howard. He admitted that he had "worked her," like he would do any other female officer.

"When you're in prison," he said, "you use any means necessary to get over. I knew she was attracted to me so I used that to my advantage. I knew that I could sweet talk her into doing what I wanted her to do. I used her to bring me reefer to sell to the inmates and guards. I also used her to do a lot of other favors for me. But when I met you, all of that stopped. I didn't want anyone but you. I knew that if I continued my relationship with her, you would find out about it and I didn't want to lose you. After I met you, she knew that she couldn't do anything else for me. I didn't want any more dealings with her. That's why she hates you the way she does. She knows better than anyone else how I feel about you, but I want you to be careful, 'cause she's treacherous. She said if she ever sees you up town she will hurt you. But if she ever does anything to cause you harm, physically or mentally, I'll seriously hurt her. I don't want anyone or anything to cause you discomfort."

After that conversation, Rebekah dispelled the notion of Breeze being unfaithful to her with Officer Howard or with any other female.

Rebekah searched for every excuse she could find as a reason to go into the prison on days when she wasn't scheduled to be there. She managed to visit the prison at least four or five times a week. She was there so often it was becoming obvious to the regular guards that she was there to see Breeze, so she stopped going except to teach her classes twice a week.

The program in which Rebekah worked lasted ten weeks, then the inmates would "graduate" and a new group of thirty inmates would attend classes for ten weeks and so on. Rebekah had two classes each night with fifteen inmates in each class, and each class lasted two hours.

Rebekah was a member of the Alpha Kappa Alpha Sorority. She had pledged when she was an undergraduate student at Morgan State College. She wasn't active in the Sorority during those years when she was doing drugs. She became financially solid in the Sorority while she was in law school. She asked Breeze to write a poem for her about her Sorority, whose colors are pink and green and whose symbol is the ivy leaf. Breeze used a green writing pen to write a poem for her on pink writing paper, and he drew ivy leaves around the border of the paper. The poem was so beautiful that she framed it and hung it on her bedroom wall.

CAN YOU TELL?

Who are these women who pledge to the pink and green?
Who are these women who pursue their hopes and dreams?

Who are these women who challenge life's many goals
with courage and strength?
Tell me, do you know?

Who are these women, loyal, dedicated and true,
fighting for the rights for me and for you?

Who are these women, please do tell,
who have husbands, children, careers, and handle them all very well?

Who are these women, so beautiful, sweet and kind,
with a style of their own, and each has an intelligent mind?

Well, you can say you can't tell me, I'll have to take a guess.
That can be risky business, you see,
I heard they're the best.

People tell me they're a sorority, and some say they're not,
but the letters they wear, I think, say a lot.

The letters A.K.A., I wonder what they mean.
Who are these women who wear the pink and green?

****

After Rebekah's class was over one evening, one of the inmates handed her an envelope and said, "I was told to personally give this to you."

She opened it and it was a note from Breeze which read, "As I think about you tonight, nothing else means a damn thing. It's Tuesday night. Over the intercom they're calling for the start of educational classes. You're here in this prison. I can smell you in the wind. I can feel your presence and I am frantically pacing in my cell like a wild, caged lion, trying to get to his mate. But I'm caged within a cage and my only crime for the second cage is that I love you. Tonight she set me up. She dropped a twenty dollar bill on the ground behind me and said it was mine. Since inmates aren't permitted to have more than ten dollars on them, having twenty dollars is a violation and an infraction, which warrants a "ticket" and being placed on lockup – a cage within a cage, to be guarded by one officer. And guess who the officer is who's guarding me? And guess who the officer was who set me up?"

Rebekah knew that the answer to both questions was Officer Howard. Breeze was put on lockup five times in two years and each time it was because of Officer Howard. Sometimes when Rebekah went to the prison, Officer Howard was stationed at the front gate in a position to either search Rebekah, or to operate the switch that opened the gate to the main building. Other times she was stationed in the building where Rebekah's class was held. The other officers knew how Office Howard felt about Breeze. Whenever Officer Howard was around, they warned Breeze and he would hide from her.

Rebekah complained to the warden about the noise in the Great Hall and about the lack of privacy while teaching her classes. She said the officers leaned over the partitions that separated the classes and tried to hear what the inmates discussed in class. She felt that the inmates should be able to feel comfortable discussing anything and not fear retaliation from an officer. The warden agreed with her and gave her permission to conduct classes behind the glass wall, where Breeze always stood and watched her. That gave Rebekah's class more privacy and that infuriated Officer Howard.

Rebekah was supposed to end her classes at 9:00 p.m., but when Breeze was around she dismissed her classes early, at 8:30 p.m., so that she and he could spend time together. He had to be in his cell by 9:30 p.m., and depending on which guard was on duty, he could stay with Rebekah until 9:20 p.m. When they talked Breeze sat next to Rebekah, but he wasn't allowed to touch her. One night after classes were over, in an area obscured from the view of the officer on duty, Rebekah and Breeze sat and talked.

"Can I touch you?" he whispered. "I just want to touch your arm. I need to feel the tenderness of a woman."

Rebekah didn't answer. She just looked at him and that look gave consent. He gently touched her arm with one finger, then he ran his finger down the length of her arm.

"God, you're soft, like cotton," he said.

They sat and talked about nothing that was everything and everything about nothing, just being together for a few stolen moments. After they had talked a few moments, the officer on duty shouted at him.

"Hey buddy, I'm going to the main building. I'll be back to get you at 9:20, okay?"

"Thanks, man!" Breeze called out.

"That's Officer Louis. He knows I'm in love with you, but he's cool. I've made some cards for his daughter. Plus, he used to bring me reefer," he said to Rebekah.

They took advantage of being alone and he caressed her arm like a kid experiencing his first Christmas.

One evening Officer Howard was on duty in the Great hall. She allowed Breeze to enter the building where Rebekah's class was held, but she wouldn't permit him to go to Rebekah's classroom. Outside the classroom was a large open space that resembled an auditorium without seats. He was made to wait in that area, sitting on the floor, like a child, next to Officer Howard. So Rebekah went to get him. Officer Howard was furious that Rebekah had the audacity to approach her about Breeze but Rebekah didn't care about her getting angry. Officer Howard could control Breeze but she had no authority over Rebekah.

"I want to speak with this man," said Rebekah in an authoritative voice.

"I ordered him to sit here," Officer Howard said. "Anything you have to say to him, say it while he's sitting here 'cause he'd better not move."

Rebekah was furious. She stormed back to her office, balled her hands into a fist and pounded on her desk top. She waited until she had calmed down before she approached Officer Howard again. Rebekah had taken all she was going to take from that woman.

Rebekah had been using a tape recorder in her English class, taping the inmates giving presentations and playing the tape back so they could hear themselves speaking and correct their own mistakes. She put the recorder into her jacket pocket and stormed back into the room where Officer Howard and Breeze were sitting. Officer Howard was sitting behind an old metal desk, and Breeze was still sitting on the concrete floor beside the desk, his back against the wall. Every time he stood up, she ordered him to sit down.

As Rebekah approached them, she heard Officer Howard mutter to Breeze, "You better not move."

"I know why he's being forced to sit here, and if you think I'll let you get away with it you're dumber than you look. You can throw your weight around with him, but to me you're just a dumb broad trying to entice a man who neither wants you or needs you. I have permission from the warden to be here, and I'll call the warden and tell him one of his female officers is keeping an inmate sitting beside her because she's jealous of me. She thinks I'm trying to take her man. If necessary, I'll get every inmate in my class and all the female officers you've threatened or tried to intimidate to back me up. Don't try to intimidate me, you're out of your league. So, what's it going to be? You want to call my bluff?" said Rebekah threateningly.

Officer Howard was incensed. She jumped up from her chair,

stood and glared at Rebekah, her hands clenched in fists. Then she shouted at Breeze, "You can go, but I'll see you later."

She pointed to Rebekah, her eyes blazing with anger, and shouted to Breeze, "She's not here all the time. When she leaves, your ass is mine!"

"I don't think so," Rebekah said. "As an attorney, I'll fight you in court and I'm good at what I do. I don't think you can afford the legal representation you'll need to fight me, so back off!"

Officer Howard didn't know that Rebekah had a tape recorder in her pocket and had recorded her threat to Breeze. Rebekah took the recorder from her pocket and held it up for her to see. Officer Howard looked shocked and nervous. Breeze was trying hard not to laugh. Officer Howard knew that she would be in trouble if the warden heard the tape of her threatening an inmate, especially without cause.

"If anything happens to this man, I'll see that you lose your job and I'll send a copy of this tape to a friend of mine who's investigating corruption inside the prisons. Sexual harassment claims work for men just as they do for women. You really don't want to mess with me."

Officer Howard stormed out of the building. When she was gone, Breeze and Rebekah winked at each other.

"You carry yourself like you're timid, but you're a terror. I'm glad you're on my side," he laughed.

"There's a lot in my past you don't know. But I can take care of myself," she said.

"You're a mean lady," he joked. "Remind me not to make you angry."

They walked back to her classroom and sat side-by-side in chairs and talked.

"I know I'm going to have trouble with her tonight after you leave," he said. "You made her look like a fool in front of me and she's going to want revenge. But I don't care, it was worth it to see you verbally kick her ass. But that's enough talk about that woman. I want to talk about us, you and me.

"I often visualize you in my mind and masturbate. Men in here do that a lot. A lot of them masturbate after looking at you. They get a photograph of you in their minds, run back to their cells, wave their hand for whoever is in there to leave, their cell mates get the message and leave. Many times I've rushed back to my cell so that I could keep your image in my mind and remember the scent of your body. Like now, I know I'm gonna masturbate tonight. And when you're not here and I can't smell the fragrance of your body, I look at the picture I drew of you and I masturbate."

When he said that, Rebekah felt so helpless. She wanted to touch him, but she dared not. Officer Howard might return. They talked a few minutes longer until it was time for him to return to his cell.

When Rebekah returned to the prison Thursday, she brought Breeze some cookies as payment for making posters for her class. After she dismissed her class, she and Breeze were sitting talking and Officer Howard came into the teachers' classroom office and said, "I want him to leave."

Rebekah sighed. "You're starting this shit again? I thought I made my position clear Tuesday night. The warden gave me permission to talk to this man. He's doing some work for me."

"Do you have a letter from the warden?" Officer Howard asked. It was apparent that she had rehearsed this scene.

Rebekah shook her head. "No, I didn't think I needed one."

"Well, you need one. In the meantime, I want him to leave now." She emphasized the word *now*.

"I think the warden has priority over your jealousy," Rebekah said. "He's not leaving. If you try to force him to leave, I'll tell the warden that the only reason you want him to leave is because you want to screw him and he doesn't want you. He wants a real woman, not some oversexed wanna-be in a uniform."

Officer Howard stormed out of the room and returned with Officer Arrington. Rebekah went through the same conversation about a letter from the warden.

Breeze whispered to Rebekah, "That's okay, let's not get into any more conflicts with her. That's just what she wants. She's trying to ruin your reputation."

Rebekah handed Breeze the cookies and he left the area. So

did Officers Howard and Arrington.

When Rebekah returned to the prison the following week, Breeze told her that Officer Howard took the cookies from him, threw them on the ground and said to him, "I'm your cookie. You don't need nothin' from that bitch."

Rebekah was furious but she let it go.

During the next six months, Rebekah tried to see Breeze alone but Officer Howard kept trying to prevent them from being alone. One day while at home, Rebekah received a telephone call from Delphine, one of the counselors at the prison. Delphine had heard Officer Howard tell another female officer that she suspected Rebekah of smuggling drugs into the prison for Breeze. Delphine contacted Rebekah to warn her to be careful and watch herself around Officer Howard. Delphine said that Officer Howard might try to frame Rebekah by getting another inmate to plant drugs inside her briefcase. As an attorney, Rebekah couldn't afford that type of scandal, especially with her background of drugs and prostitution.

Rebekah was livid. Not only was she incensed because Officer Howard told lies on her, she was thoroughly aggravated because she couldn't do anything about it without attracting suspicion to herself, or perhaps hurting Breeze. Rebekah called Frank, the coordinator of the prisoner's educational program, and told him what Delphine said and asked him for assistance.

Rebekah said to Frank, "I know that I have a lot to lose, but I'm sick and tired of that pig. If she keeps harassing me, I'm going to take it to Kelvin Armstrong, the Secretary of Corrections, the warden's boss. Kelvin is a personal friend of mine. Plus, the WOMAN Power Club has a lot of support in here."

There were rumors that Kelvin was bitter against inmates. He was a handsome man and had a beautiful wife, but he was married for the third time. Both his first and second wives were teachers in various prisons and both had left him for inmates who had been their students. So Rebekah didn't know how much help he would give her. But she used the bluff just the same and it worked. Later, Frank called Rebekah and said that he had talked to Officer Howard and told her to back off, or Rebekah was prepared to make big trouble for her.

Rebekah again questioned Breeze about his relationship with Officer Howard.

"Something more happened between you two that you're not telling me, otherwise, she wouldn't act the way she does toward me. I'm sick of her shit," Rebekah said to Breeze.

Breeze could tell that Rebekah had almost reached her boiling point.

"If I said I don't love you, I would be telling a lie, and right now, I don't feel like lying or going through the motions of pretending that I don't care, when I do," Breeze said. "I don't know why we allow ourselves to go through the bullshit, when happiness requires such a small sacrifice. I thought you were well aware of my feelings for you. Why are you jealous over a damn woman officer? You know her game. She delights in making you sweat."

Rebekah thought about what Breeze said and realized that he might be right. She stopped questioning him about Officer Howard.

Officer Howard was transferred to a new wing in the prison. But they didn't know for how long or if she would return to the area of the school and Breeze's cell. Rebekah still watched her back.

****

Being in the prison was like being in another world. The prison system had its own language, its own rules — not prison rules, inmate rules. It had its own culture, its own way of punishing people and its own way of rewarding and recognizing people.

One night after class, Breeze looked at Rebekah and said, "Yeah, I'm that nigga."

She looked puzzled. "What're you talking about? What nigga?" she asked.

"You know, when something happens or if someone thinks you're involved in a secret love relationship, they say, 'Oh, so you're *that* nigga?' So that's what I'm saying to you. Yeah, I'm *that* nigga."

She laughed because she understood exactly what he was saying. She had heard that phrase used in many situations, but she never thought about what it meant until now. It was kind of like him asking her if she was "the man." This was the prison culture.

Rebekah asked Breeze about the little gay guy who used to attend her class. She hadn't seen him in over two weeks. His absence meant that he was automatically dropped from her class, but still she was curious about why he had stopped coming.

"You mean the blister?" he said.

"Here's another part of the inside language that I don't understand. What does 'blister' mean?" she asked.

"All gay men in here are called blisters. Think about it. Think about two men having sex with each other and you'll understand," he said.

She thought a few moments and then started to laugh. "But that guy was so little and so comical, he couldn't have weighed more than ninety pounds. He said when he was released, he wanted to come and work for me. He talked about walking around my office in a short skirt and high-heeled shoes, and when I pictured him in that outfit the thought was hilarious. I've seen him in shorts; his legs look like toothpicks and his feet look like boats. But I haven't seen him for a while."

"That's because he's in the hospital with a broken back," Breeze said.

"Broken back? What happened to him?"

"There was a 'wedding' last week. These two dudes got 'married.' One inmate was the 'preacher,' one was the 'best man,' and another was the 'maid of honor.' They even had a wedding reception with ice cream, cake, potato chips, and sandwiches. At the 'wedding' when the 'preacher' said, 'If anyone knows a reason why these two should not get married, let them speak now or forever hold their peace,' the little guy you're talking about jumped up and said, 'I know why they shouldn't get married, 'cause the groom slept with me last night, that's why.'

"When he said that, the guy who was the 'wife' grabbed that little dude, raised him over his head, body slammed him to the floor and broke his back. It was terrible. They got to fighting so bad that the entire wedding party was put on lockup."

Rebekah liked the little gay guy, but the thought of him in a short skirt cracked her up. She laughed so hard, she could hardly breathe. Tears rolled down her cheeks. "Did you go to the wedding?" she asked when she could compose herself.

"Yeah, I went. I went to get a good laugh and to eat their ice cream and cake," he laughed and shook his head. "These convicts in here are something else. One of my buddies almost got raped on the same day those dudes were having their so-called wedding. My buddy, Moe, is a young dude. I knew his brother, Big Dan, on the outside. When I got word that Moe was coming in here, I sent word to Big Dan that I'd look out for Moe. I knew Moe was being sent to the joint that day but I didn't know what time he would be coming in, so I was sitting in the recreation room watching television waiting for him. After a while, one of my buddies ran to me and said, 'Man, I heard you been waitin' fo' one of yo' homies to come here today. If you want to save him, you'd better come quick, 'cause I seen Crazy Sam dragging him down in the hole.'

"The 'hole' is a place behind the cells where guards don't usually go. Inmates sneak in the hole to use drugs, drink homemade liquor, to fight, or have sex. The officers know what happens in the hole, but they don't give a damn. They turn their heads the other way. So I jumped up and ran down to the hole and there was Crazy Sam and Big Ditty, two of the biggest and meanest men in this prison, tearing Moe's clothes off him, beating him and daring him to scream. I showed up just in time.

"'Hey motherfuckers, let my bitch go.' I said, "They turned, looked at me and started toward me. I ain't gonna lie. I was scared. Them dudes will really hurt you. They don't like nobody. Then my posse showed up, the men who hang with me. Man, was I glad to see 'em. Most of the inmates think the men in my posse are crazy. So Crazy Sam and Big Ditty didn't want to rumble with me and my boys; they just threw up their hands and said, 'Fuck it.' Boy, was I glad, 'cause them dudes is treacherous."

"I never knew what a hideous place prison was until I started working here. It's a terrible, unnatural place to live. I don't know how you can remain sane, being treated like an animal," said Rebekah.

"I keep my sanity through my writing and through my

drawings," said Breeze. "I keep a journal and I can mentally escape when I write in my journal. But unfortunately, some things I can't write down 'cause I don't want to incriminate myself. The purpose of writing a daily journal is to keep abreast of my changes and the events surrounding those changes while I'm a prisoner. I want you to read about the way I used to be before I met you."

He handed Rebekah his journal to read.

At first she protested, saying that his journal was personal and private. But he said, "Baby, don't you understand, I don't have any secrets from you. I want you to share my personal and private thoughts. I want you to see how much your love has changed me. I don't put dates in my journal. I don't want a reminder of how long I've been in here."

She took the journal and began to read it.

****

Monday

"This morning I woke up as usual in cell 117-A. I washed a few of my things, cleaned out my cell and smoked a joint. a female officer lectured me this morning on the power of kindness. I wish she was kind enough to go into my cell with me and let me get this pressure off my chest and hump out of my back. Then perhaps I could understand the virtues of kindness.

Tuesday

"I'm as high as a kite. I wish I could fly over these years. I was thinking about flying over this fence, but I'd be running from one problem to another and I don't need no more problems. I think I'll blow another joint. I can't see where it will hurt nobody. Since I've been in this prison, I've gotten more drugs than I had in the free world. I'm trying to control my use of drugs. I may mess around and catch a habit. Now wouldn't that be a bitch, becoming addicted to drugs while incarcerated? Oh, well, let me go. I see smoke signals from another cell. I think I'll get high with that brother."

Wednesday

"I was dismissed from the dietary department for running my mouth. I shouldn't have been given such harsh punishment for just talking. I was directing my comments to another inmate, now I'm paying for it."

Thursday

"I got to write my buddy Roots. He's moving too fast and ain't going in any intelligent direction. He's not trying to get any serious money. So he may as well quit fooling himself before he finds his ass behind prison bars for some penny-ante bullshit like me."

****

"You can see, I was talking about doing drugs and messing with these women officers? After I met you my life changed," he said. "I no longer think about getting high and making out with other women. I think about you and our future together."

Rebekah touched his face, told him she loved him and handed him the journal.

Rebekah constantly tried to conceal their affair, but she was only fooling herself. Everyone who knew Breeze knew that he was in love with Rebekah. He told other inmates not to flirt with her, not to use profanity around her and not to engage in any violent behavior in her presence, or they would answer to him. He was popular inside the prison and was known as one of the "king bosses." Those who knew that Rebekah was his lady, envied him for that.

The Brotherhood was an organization inside the prison to which some inmates belonged, and Breeze was one of the top warriors in the organization. Prisoners often found it necessary to align themselves with organizations for protection from other inmates and in some cases, protection from prison guards.

After Breeze met Rebekah, the Brotherhood gave him an ultimatum: he either had to work her for the good of all of the members of the Brotherhood, or leave her alone, or he would be forced out of the Brotherhood. That meant that he had to use Rebekah to do favors that would benefit the entire Brotherhood or he had to stop seeing her. If he did not, they would kick him out.

Breeze tried to make them understand how it was between him and Rebekah. He told them that she was different from the women prison guards that they "worked." He told them that he really cared for her. But the Brotherhood wouldn't listen. Consequently, he quit the organization. Breeze had been the Brotherhood Boss; it had been his decision who would be members and who would be rejected. He felt they would try to retaliate against him if he didn't use Rebekah to do favors for the whole Brotherhood.

But, Breeze was street and jail savvy. He organized his loyal men and told them he was organizing a group called "The Warriors." This was comprised of men whom Breeze had befriended during one of his many visits to the joint. But "Crusher" tried to pit the gangs against each other. He was jealous of Breeze and always found the opportunity to challenge him.

Crusher was a big, muscular man, and wore a headband around his bald head. Crusher was three-hundred pounds of pure muscle, and was as mean as he was big. He wanted the position of King Boss, but he knew he would have to go through Breeze to get it. Crusher had confronted Breeze about Rebekah. He accused Breeze of turning his back on the Brotherhood in favor of a woman. He accused Breeze of being selfish and pointed out how the gang had aided Breeze numerous times during prison fights. Breeze tried to explain that he wasn't turning his back on his brothers, he was just moving to another level in his relationship with his woman.

"Hasn't there ever been a time when you saw a woman you wanted for yourself? What about your wives or the mothers of your children? I know if one of them worked here, you wouldn't share her or insist that she do favors for all these niggas in the Brotherhood, get real," said Breeze.

Most of the gang members agreed with Breeze. They had girlfriends and they knew they would be getting out someday and they could relate to Breeze's feelings for Rebekah. All except Crusher. He sat and rolled his eyes at Breeze, with his lip turned up at the side and a toothpick dangling from his lips.

"If you got that broad's nose opened as wide as you say, my brotha, she'd be a horse fo' us all and brang some shit into dis heah joint so we can re-up our stash. I onwanna heah 'bout yo luv jones," sneered Crusher.

Breeze got angry, "I told ya, it ain't like dat wid her, my brotha! Me and the lady got somethin' goin' and if you can't understand that, understand this, if I hear of any of you niggas steppin' to her in any way, your ass is mine!" said Breeze threateningly.

"Is dat 'pose ta be some kin' o threat, mutha-fucka?" Said Crusher, standing to his feet in a threatening position.

"Naw, man," said Breeze as he used his forefinger to poke Crusher in his chest. "That's a fuckin' promise. The school lady is off limits."

"Who de fuck you think you is puttin' somebody off limits? If I want to tap dat ass when she comes to teach her class, den dat's what I'll do. If I want to walk in her class and sit on the front row, stare at her and masturbate in class, what she gon' do, call the police?"

Some of the members of the Brotherhood laughed. When Breeze menacingly looked at them, they immediately stopped.

"You been wantin' a piece of me a long time and, mutha-fucka, tonight when they open the door for yard-time, meet me in the hole," said Breeze.

The word about the rumble spread throughout the prison like wildfire. All the inmates talked about the rumble going down between Breeze and Crusher. Crusher was bigger than Breeze but Breeze was cunning and swifter on his feet. Breeze was an alley fighter, Crusher was a street fighter, he relied on his imposing size to win his battles, Breeze relied on his agile ways of maneuvering during a fight. Breeze had made a set of brass knuckles in the prison mechanic shop from a pipe one of the guards gave him in exchange for a water-colored portrait of the guard.

At the time of the fight, both men understood that they were fighting for honor and for their lives. They lived each day expecting to get shanked from another prisoner for no reason other than a dirty look or a harsh word. When the fight started, Breeze gave the first punch. He always said the element of surprise is the best defense. When he hit crusher, the bones in his cheek made a sickening cracking sound and Crusher let out a yell in pain. Before he could compose himself, Breeze was on his back with a homemade knife at Crusher's throat.

"It's over mutha-fucka!" Breeze shouted. "It's over! The next time, I'll kill you!"

He let Crusher go and said, "Who's down wid me?"

Over half of the men in the Brotherhood — the most feared men in the prison — went to Breeze's side. "It's done! From now on we'll be known as the "Brotherhood of Warriors," and we'll present our boundaries after count tonight."

He gave them the Brotherhood handshake and they dispersed, impressed with how Crusher got his ass kicked.

CHAPTER FOURTEEN
He Called Her, Ice Cream

One of Rebekah's classes was completing its ten-week cycle and her students were planning a graduation celebration. The warden had given her permission to serve donuts and coffee to the inmates at the celebration, but the staff who worked in the prison's kitchen had forgotten to make provisions for the coffee. Rebekah had brought enough donuts so that each inmate who was graduating could get three, and brought extras for Breeze in case he showed up.

She called the officer on duty in the guard booth and told him that she needed coffee. The guard said that he couldn't leave his post but he would allow her to go into the kitchen and get the coffee if she could find someone to carry the heavy container for her. Breeze was standing nearby and heard the conversation. He volunteered to go with her to get the coffee.

As he and Rebekah walked to the prison's kitchen that spring day, one of his buddies called out, "I see you, Breeze. You're cool, you the man, homey. If I had your hand, I'd turn mine in."

Breeze waved him off, grinning as he proudly walked with Rebekah.

"I can see us up town, strolling in the park like this. Only then, we'd be holding hands. I can hardly wait. These dudes in this place are always panning me," he said.

"Doing what to you?" she asked.

"Panning me. You know, teasing me," he said, grinning at her.

"I could write a book about the unique jargon of the prison's culture," she said.

"You don't know the half of it," he said. "Inside these prison walls is a totally unique community, controlled by inmates, and most of the officers are afraid to do anything about it."

Rebekah listened to Breeze's buddies teasing him, then she

said, "I've wanted to ask you for a long time, why do they call you Breeze?"

He stopped and shook his head, "I didn't want you to know me by that name. That's my street name. You're different from any woman I've ever known. It seems that each woman I've known has been stair steps leading to you. I wanted you to know me in a different way than the way other women have known me, or the way my cronies know me. They call me 'Cool Breeze' 'cause when I was in the streets, I got out of some tricky situations through cunning and deceit. I was nonchalant about my relationships with women. And when I was doing crime, I was always cool. I didn't scare easily. I don't want you to know that part of me. I was reborn when I met you. Can you understand that? Besides, I have a nickname for you, too."

"A nickname for me? What is it?"

"Can I tell you? Promise you won't laugh?"

"I promise I won't laugh. What's my nickname?" Rebekah said, eager to hear the nickname.

"I'm going to call you 'Ice Cream,'" he said.

She looked at him, puzzled, and smiled, "'Ice Cream? Why 'Ice Cream'? That's a strange name to call somebody. What flavor?"

He laughed. "It doesn't matter what flavor," he said. "I tried to think of what I love most in this world and what it is that I can't get enough of, and the answer to both questions is ice cream. Plus, with your Gemini personality, you're always changing up on me. One minute you're so warm and lovable that I could hug you to pieces. The next minute you're cold and distant to me, and it's at those times I get scared and wonder if you'll stop being there for me. Then I tried to imagine what you remind me of, and I decided that I love you whether you're cold or warm, and that's the way I feel about ice cream. Is it okay? Do you mind if I call you Ice Cream?"

"No, I don't mind," she answered as she looked into his eyes.

She wanted to hold him close to her and get lost in the nearness of him. But she realized they dare not even hold hands. If they were found out, Breeze would be punished for fraternizing with the professional staff, and Rebekah's reputation would be ruined. From that day on as she left the prison at night, she could hear

Breeze's voice calling in the night. The sound of his voice reverberating throughout the prison seemed to bounce off every wall. "Ice Cream, I love you. I love you, Ice Cream," he shouted.

When she heard his voice, she cried all the way home.

He often told her how it felt to be locked in a cell with a tiny hole as the only window to the outside world. He had to lay on the floor to see through the hole. He could see only the legs of people entering or leaving the prison as they passed, going to and coming from the main gate. That meant that he could see only Rebekah's legs.

He told her how he would wait for those legs that he had come to recognize and love. When he saw them, he called out, "Ice Cream." Sometimes Rebekah could hear his voice as she drove out of the prison parking lot. She came to love that sound.

Breeze asked Rebekah for the address of one of her girlfriends. He said he wanted to write to someone close to Rebekah. He said that way, he could also feel closer to Rebekah. She gave him Tracy's address and he wrote to her. Tracy didn't understand Breeze's reason for writing to her. Tracy took it to mean that he wanted to develop an intimate romantic relationship with her.

"Your man wrote to me and I think he's trying to get with me," Tracy said to Rebekah.

Tracy let Rebekah read the letter from Breeze and the contents of the letter didn't appear to Rebekah to be anything more than a "Hi, I wanted to get acquainted with you, because we both love the same lady. You love her as a best friend, and I love her as my best lady. Let's get acquainted," type of letter. Nevertheless, Rebekah told Breeze that she didn't want him to write to Tracy any more.

****

The prison guards started hanging around Rebekah, making flirtatious remarks to her while Breeze was present, trying to make him jealous. Rebekah didn't like the way the guards disrespected Breeze, but she dared not show her annoyance at them.

One night as she left the office on the prison grounds, an officer whom she had just recently met walked over to where she stood talking to Breeze. The officer was rubbing his hands together as if trying to warm them. In an authoritative, demanding tone, he said to Breeze, "Okay, buddy, this is where I take over. You're out of your league talking to this lady; move on."

Not wanting to start any trouble, Rebekah told Breeze good night and started walking toward the main gate, heading to her car. The officer walked with her all the time, telling her how much money he earned and what time he got off from work. Rebekah didn't want to show her agitation and risk the possibility of him retaliating against Breeze. She politely told him that she wasn't interested and he walked away looking embarrassed.

A few days later, Rebekah was in her office at the prison sitting at her desk reading the newspaper when Breeze walked in. She looked up at him and smiled.

"You sure look pretty, sitting there so intense. If I asked you to kiss me, what would you say?" he asked.

She sighed and looked away.

"Don't ask me that question because I don't know what I would say," she responded.

"I'm asking you. I want to feel your lips on mine, just once. I'm in love with you and I've never even kissed you," he said.

"No, we can't kiss. Suppose someone saw us?" said Rebekah.

"Are you denying me?" he asked.

"Take it anyway you want to, but the answer is still 'no'," she said.

Breeze was wearing a pair of white shorts, white sneakers, white socks, a white tee-shirt, and a white cap. He was always clean and smelled good. She didn't know how he always managed to look so good in prison. He was standing in front of the desk where she was sitting. As she stood up, the fragrance of his cologne filled her nostrils. She walked in front of the desk, faced him, tilted her head, and stood on tiptoes to receive his kiss. It was just barely a touch when their lips met for the first time, but she felt the sensation all the way to her toes. He got an erection. When they left the office, he carried the newspaper in front of him to hide the bulge in his pants.

After that first kiss, it was hell trying to keep their hands off each other. Occasionally, they were able to touch without being seen, but not often. It appeared that they were watched closer than ever, especially by the female officers. Sometimes Rebekah managed to rub the bulge in his pants when the guards weren't looking. Sometimes he was able to slip his hands inside of her blouse and gently massage her breasts until her nipples got hard. If they were sitting close enough to touch while they talked, Breeze would sometimes let his hand rest on her knee, and slowly, very gently, run his hand up her thighs. She wouldn't move, and she didn't dare breathe. She would slowly open her legs a little wider to give his hand easy access to the hot, needy part of her body. She started wearing low-cut blouses, going without stockings, wearing skirts and dresses instead of slacks, so that he could touch her bare skin.

One night as Rebekah and Breeze left the classroom under a full moon, they walked side-by-side. He was wearing a blue sweat suit and a matching headband. He gently touched her arm and she turned to face him. His tall, muscular frame leaned over her, and he looked into her eyes and said, "I love you, Ice Cream. I love you so much it hurts. If I could hold you just once, maybe the hurt wouldn't be so bad."

Rebekah looked up at him standing tall in the moonlight. He had tears in his eyes.

"Baby, please be strong for both of us. I love you too," she said.

She knew it was true and so did he. She touched his hand, blew him a kiss, and walked toward the parking lot.

"I love you, Ice Cream," he whispered as she walked away. She hurried and wiped the tears from her eyes before an officer saw her crying.

The following week, Rebekah went back to the prison. After she dismissed her class, Breeze told her that the only other woman he ever loved died while he was in prison, and until he met Rebekah, he thought he would never find love again.

Rebekah asked Breeze if anyone visited him while he was incarcerated. He said only his family. He said that he had three daughters by three different women but none of the women visited him, only his daughters.

One night she went to the prison to teach and didn't see Breeze. She learned from another inmate that he was on lockup for trying to escape. She didn't know what to think. She was scared. She never thought that he would be so stupid as to attempt an escape.

When she returned the following week, she saw him and asked about the escape attempt. He told her that his mother died and the warden wouldn't allow him to attend her funeral.

"I started for the gate and just kept walking," he said. "But I'm all right now. I won't do anything that dumb again. I promise."

Rebekah was relieved, but still, she kept talking to him about not adding any more time to his sentence. She wanted him to hurry and get out so that they could be together.

Rebekah met Myron, another counselor inside the prison, and they became friends. Myron had heard gossip about Rebekah and Breeze, and during a conversation one day he told her that he had grown up with Breeze. Rebekah asked Myron for his home telephone number, saying she needed to talk with him away from the prison. Rebekah called Myron and told him that she wanted to come to his house and discuss a problem she was experiencing.

"Is anything wrong?" Myron asked.

"I just have some concerns and I need your advice," she said.

"I'll be home after eight tomorrow evening. Can you stop by then?" Myron asked.

"I'll be there."

After leaving the prison the following night, Rebekah went to Myron's house and talked about Breeze. Myron advised Rebekah not to take Breeze seriously.

"Why not?" Rebekah asked.

"'Cause he hasn't been truthful with you. He's been locked up nine times. He has been in and out of prison since he was fourteen years old. The longest time that he ever stayed free was two years. Since I've been working in that institution, I've tried to help Breeze by getting him a job in my office answering the telephone," said Myron. "I know that he calls you during the day; I sometimes overhear his conversations. But I also know that he calls another woman, too. Sometimes after he calls you, he says to me, 'She loves me,' then he laughs as if you loving him is a joke. I know you care for him and I believe he cares for you. But I don't believe that you're the only woman in his life. Have fun with him and even date him when he gets out of prison, if you want to, but watch your heart. Don't give your all. You'll only be hurt in the end. You only know what he has told you about himself. I've seen him in action in the streets. I grew up with him and his older brother. I changed my lifestyle, but they didn't."

Rebekah didn't know Breeze had an older brother. She was beginning to realize that there were a lot of things about Breeze that she didn't know, but none of that deterred her desire to be with him.

"I've been working in corrections for ten years," said Myron. "I was transferred to this institution a year ago and I was surprised to see Breeze in here. I didn't know he was incarcerated. I'm dating Bonita, a counselor who works in the same office with me at the prison. One day when Breeze came to the office, he met her and took it upon himself to make greeting cards for her. He started writing poems to her and sending letters to her by other inmates. She showed them to me. We read them together and laughed at the thought of him having a crush on her. It was funny but it also pissed me off that he had the audacity to write letters to my woman and send them to my office. He knew we were dating."

Rebekah and Myron talked a while about Breeze and his early life. Myron shared stories with her of pranks they played as children. They laughed and after a couple of hours, Rebekah left, both vowing to keep the conversation to themselves.

When she returned to the prison, she asked Breeze about Bonita and the rumors about him having a crush on her. He said Bonita asked him to make a birthday card for her daughter, and he did. He denied writing letters and poems to her. Rebekah didn't contradict him or call him a liar. She didn't want him to know that she had discussed him with Myron.

Rebekah wanted so much to believe in a fairy tale love affair, but loving Breeze brought both pain and pleasure. No one could send chills up her spine the way he could. Yet, there was a sort of wildness about him. She never felt secure in their relationship. She didn't know whether or not to believe that he loved only her. She felt as insecure in her relationship with Breeze as she had in her relationship with Marty.

CHAPTER FIFTEEN
Looking For Love

Breeze was in his cell sitting on his bunk — the lower one. There were two bunks in the tiny cell he shared with Mouse, another inmate. In one corner of the cell stood a commode and a sink that served as the bathroom. There was no door to close for privacy. In another corner, a milk crate served as a shelf. On the crate sat a radio, and a clock. All of Breeze's personal belongings, such as a comb, toothbrush and tooth paste, pictures, letters and stamps, were kept in a shoe box under the bottom bunk where he slept. When he first arrived at the prison, he had to fight almost every day to let the other inmates know that he wasn't intimidated by them.

It was a Tuesday night and Breeze was getting dressed to go to the Great Hall. He knew he would see Rebekah. As he dressed he thought about her. He looked at his reflection in the plastic compact mirror his mother had sent him. Inmates weren't allowed to have items made of glass or to have any other sharp objects that could be used as weapons. It was taking a long time for the guards to clear the count so that the cell doors could be opened and inmates released to go to various programs. Breeze lay across his cot and thought about Rebekah.

Breeze talked to himself, trying to kill time while waiting for the count to clear. "I'm thinking about you, wanting to see you and this damn countdown is taking forever," he whispered. "I knew these bums wouldn't let me out early tonight 'cause they know as sure as hell that regardless of the consequences, if you're anywhere in this institution, I'll see you. And you are here somewhere inside of these prison walls. I can smell you. I can feel your presence in my very core. I'm like a wild stallion who has smelled his mate."

Rebekah *is* there and she's looking for him, but it's not so that anyone would notice. It's the casual way she looks up whenever she hears the outside door open and she thinks she feels his presence.

Breeze looked out the hole that served as a window. The sun

Breeze looked out the hole that served as a window. The sun was going down; it was getting late and he was getting impatient. He talked in whispers to Rebekah.

"I'll come to you," he whispered, "but it will be when you are totally engrossed in your teachings. I'll come as surely as Romeo came to Juliet, like the wind, I'll come."

He smiled at the thought, "Bottom line, baby, is that if you are here, I'll find you, come hell or high water," he whispered.

Finally, the count cleared and the cell doors opened. Breeze wanted to race to the Hall to see Rebekah, but he restrained himself so the guard wouldn't have an excuse to make him stay in his cell.

"Stay in line!" the guard hollered. "Let's rush it. You're marching like old ladies. Come on, let's keep it moving."

Breeze was only too glad to hurry. He arrived at the Hall as quickly as he could and he went directly to Rebekah's classroom. She was standing in front of her class going over the lessons. Breeze stood in the back of the room watching her as she went through the motions of pretending that she didn't know he was watching her.

She was wearing a black and yellow suit and matching shoes. When Breeze saw her, he leaned against the wall, folded his arms across his chest and grinned. The inmates in class looked at Breeze and back at Rebekah. They smiled and remained silent. Breeze sat in a chair in the back of the room, crossed his legs, stared at her and smiled. She nervously thumbed through papers on her desk, occasionally she looked up, directly into his eyes. She dismissed her class early and when the last person left, Breeze walked to the front of the room and sat in a chair beside her desk.

"Hello, pretty lady," he grinned. "You sure look good in your black and yellow outfit. I hope you wore it especially for me. I've been thinking about you all day. They took forever to get the count straight. It trips me out how these guards mess up the count every night. I can't believe they can't count."

"Maybe they're just trying to keep you from seeing me," Rebekah teased.

"They should know by now that nothing short of death can keep me from you," he grinned. "Did I tell you that sometimes I'm thinking about you so hard that I talk to you?"

"No, you didn't tell me that. But, I believe it, 'cause sometimes I do the same thing," she said.

"Like tonight," Breeze said, "while I was waiting for them to let me out, I imagined that you and I were deep in a conversation. I was actually talking out loud to you. If someone had heard me, they'd swear that I was crazy, talking to myself. It's weird how vivid imaginations are at times."

He looked at her, started to touch her cheek, and quickly drew back his hand before an officer saw him. He moved his chair around to face her, trying to touch her knees with his. He leaned forward speaking softly to her.

He looked into her eyes and said, "Then, one day in prison, I saw a woman of some special means, shifting through papers on her desk. My spirit stirred and cried out to my heart and mind — 'awake, for happiness stands before you, clothed in love and understanding'. I considered it in solitude and wondered if it could be true that I was looking at love. Quickly, my heart threw open its window and my mind moved hesitantly. But my spirit cried — 'Search no more. Behold, your Ice Cream.'"

He threw open his arms as he stood up and said again, "Behold, your Ice Cream."

They both laughed.

Rebekah looked around nervously to see if anyone was watching. When she was satisfied that the officer on duty wasn't paying attention to them, she said, "You're so crazy. You can always make me smile."

"I want to always make you smile," he said. "It was in my wild, ruthless, and reckless search that I found you. With this self same desire, I tried to conquer you. In my efforts to conquer you, it was inevitable that I re-evaluate my own morale, and it was through the process of this self-searching that I finally realized that the greatest luxury of life is love, your love."

Before she could respond, the loud speaker announced that it was time for all inmates to report to their next activity. It was time for Breeze to leave.

"Perhaps I can get one of them officers to let me go to the gym and play basketball," he grinned. "Or, I just might go to my cell and talk to you with my pen and paper. I'll write some poems and send them to you. Before you came into my life, I used to wish that I could find that special love that causes poets to write. Then you were sent to me, and I'm writing poetry to you, trying to get you to understand how much you mean to me."

Rebekah gathered her papers and put them into her briefcase, trying hard to hold back her tears.

"You're beautiful when you do that," Breeze said.

"When I do what?" she asked.

"When you wrinkle your brow in deep thought," he said.

"I was just thinking about how much I miss you and how glad I'll be when we can stop hiding our feelings for each other," she said.

He started to put his arm around her shoulder and jerked it back.

"Damn, I started to hug you," he said. "I must be crazy. Let me get outta here before these officers come and put me back on lockup. I got a hard on and I've got to get past the guards without them noticing the bulge."

Rebekah laughed.

They walked outside together. The night air was cool and crisp.

"Another beautiful autumn night when I'll go to sleep to meet you in my dreams, " he said.

"I forgot to tell you that I'll be here three times this week. I'll be here Thursday, and I'll be back Friday. I made an appointment to meet with Ms. Joyner, the principal of the school program," said Rebekah.

"That means that I'll get a bonus treat," he grinned.

"What do you mean?" she asked.

"I mean seeing you three times in one week is a bonus for me," he said.

She smiled and they continued to walk outside. Their hands barely touched as Breeze hurried off in the opposite direction from the guards' post.

Rebekah walked up the walkway leading to the main gate. She put her briefcase and pocketbook on the counter to be searched. She signed out, and turned in the classroom and file cabinet keys.

When she was outside the prison, heading to her car, she could hear Breeze's voice shouting, "I love you, Ice Cream."

She was sad as she drove up the long, winding road that led from the prison to the highway. All the way home she thought about Breeze.

Walking into an empty house isn't as much fun as it used to be, she thought. She took off her jacket, poured a glass of orange juice, and sat on the sofa, staring at the fireplace. The October air was just cool enough for a fire, but she wasn't in the mood to build one.

She showered, put on a bathrobe, turned on the radio in the kitchen while she made a sandwich, and poured a glass of milk, forgetting that she had already poured a glass of orange juice. They were playing oldies on the radio. She thought about Breeze. She wondered what he was doing at that moment.

The telephone rang. It was Mamie. Rebekah told her the latest about her relationship with Breeze. "I don't know what it is, but I still feel that something is missing in my life. I love Breeze, but I can't explain my feelings of emptiness," she said to Mamie.

"You're a successful woman," said Mamie. "You've accomplished a lot in your life and you're still growing. I don't mean to disrespect Breeze, but have you considered how far advanced you are above him? I mean, he's been locked up a long time and the world has still been evolving. You're above him educationally, economically, socially, and intellectually."

"I've thought about that," Rebekah said, "but he's so refreshing. He's different from other men I've known. It's like I'm discovering the world all over again. He's like a kid."

"Yes," said Mamie, "but you don't need a kid, you need a man. All I'm saying is go slow. You've been hurt before, so lead with your head this time. Besides, he has so many needs. He needs money, he wants you to send him packages, and he needs constant reassurance of your feelings for him. How can he satisfy your needs when he has so many of his own? When is it your turn? Remember Marty, Mike,

Teddy, Brian, and Ken? They all had their own agendas for their relationships with you, and you see who got the 'short end of the stick,' as my mama used to say."

Rebekah knew that Mamie was right, but still she wanted Breeze. She and Mamie talked for a few minutes longer. Rebekah changed the subject and told Mamie that she and Andy, Mamie's husband, were invited to the Christmas party at the law firm where Rebekah worked.

"I saw Carole today," Mamie said. "She and Madge are having a Christmas party, too. She said she'll call you tonight. I'll talk to you before the party. Let's have the next meeting of WOMAN Power at my house. I want y'all to taste my new lemon chicken recipe. It's delicious."

"Sounds good to me. You know how much I enjoy your cooking. I'll tell the others that the next meeting will be at your house." Rebekah said.

"Your voice sounds tired," Rebekah said. "Have you been working harder than usual?"

"Yes, I have," Mamie admitted. "Andy and I are planning to open our own law firm. It takes a lot of work to go out on your own. I've been working late at the office and bringing work home. I'm thinking about joining a fitness class, or maybe I'll start going to the track to jog every morning. I need to do some type of exercise. All this stress in my life and I come home, grab a sandwich and go to bed."

"Why don't you go to the doctor and get a checkup before you start an exercise program?" Rebekah said.

"That's what Andy said. But you know me. When I set my mind to do something, I jump right in and start doing it. Andy plays basketball with some of his buddies. At least he's doing some type of recreational activity, unlike me, just getting fat."

"Well, you can't get sick before I taste your lemon chicken recipe," Rebekah teased.

They both laughed and Mamie promised to call Rebekah later in the week.

****

Restless and unable to sleep, Rebekah poured a glass of wine, walked onto her patio, looked across the freshly cut lawn and stared into the darkness. She drank the wine and went to bed, troubled.

The next morning she was up early. She scrambled an egg, put a slice of bread into the toaster and went outside to get the morning paper. She had planned to go to the bank that day to open an account for the WOMAN Power Club.

The telephone rang. It was Breeze calling from Myron's office at the prison.

"Hello, baby," Breeze said, "I was thinking about you and I wanted to hear your voice. I'm reading one of Myron's books about love and I thought about us."

"This is a great surprise," Rebekah said. "Sitting here in the quiet morning hour, listening to the birds singing their praises, and nature humming with activities, I was thinking of you, too, about how wonderful it will be to share these quiet, beautiful mornings with you. I get goose bumps just contemplating such thoughts."

"Love is such a complicated subject," Breeze said. "I thought I was in love many times, then something happened, and I realized that what I thought I had found in someone else wasn't really there at all. People talk about loving intelligently. I'm not sure I understand what that means. What do you think loving intelligently means? Do you think it's about making intelligent choices in who you love?"

"Loving intelligently shouldn't be confused with education," Rebekah said. "Education isn't necessarily the mark of intelligence. Loving intelligently is loving not for the fleeting, perishable ecstasy of the moment. Intelligent love isn't concerned about age, occupation, or curvaceous hips. Loving intelligently is trying to balance your life harmoniously with that of another. It's being open to change, growth, and challenge. It's building on mutual respect and shared dreams."

"I think you and I are loving intelligently," he said. "And if not, it's too bad 'cause if loving you means that I'm loving unintelligently, then that's the way it has to be."

"Wow, this is a heavy conversation for the early morning," Rebekah teased. "What did you say was the name of that book you're reading?"

"It's a book one of the instructors used in his sociology class," Breeze said. "It was laying on Myron's desk and I just happened to pick it up. It has a chapter on building a lasting love relationship. It says that two people must like each other from the very beginning and that love goes beyond passion. Unfortunately, most people are accustomed to falling in love with the superficial parts of each other, rather than with who they are on the inside, the potential for growth in each other and the natural, simple things that hold people together."

"I understand that," Rebekah said. "But I found in my relationships that when I had tears in my eyes, more often than not, it was because I had given my love to the wrong person for all the wrong reasons. I finally came to understand that rather than trying to change the other person, it was better to take back my gift of love, polish it, cherish it, and only share it with someone who could recognize its value and its significance."

"Building a love that lasts takes understanding, compromise, respect, and trust," Breeze said. "The degree to which two people like each other and want to share their lives together determines how much each will try to know and understand the depth of the other. It determines how much each is willing to compromise. When I think of a love partner, someone to share my life with, I know that I need to be able to groove with her in a cardboard box with no fixings, if need be."

Rebekah said, "I'm only putting my life next to someone who respects and treats my love like the precious gift that it is, with the utmost care. Nothing less will do. I didn't always know what a precious gift love really is. It took many years of heartaches and heartbreaks to realize that I could be happier by myself than I could be subjecting myself to someone's mistreatment. Let's face it, being in love is a delicious feeling. I love to love and to be loved. The most beautiful part is that precious space that love created."

"I like to talk to you, you always seem to understand what I'm saying," Breeze said. "I've found that often when I'm talking to some women, I have to explain my meanings about love. I've searched for happiness for so many years. I had given up the possibility that I would ever find it. I settled for satisfaction, but I never found real happiness. Nor had I found anyone who could make me happy, until I met you.

"I looked for happiness in my world," he said. "I wanted laws changed to make life easier for me in my youth. But the world wouldn't listen and I grew bitter. I searched for happiness in knowledge and found disillusionment. I searched for it in my writing and encountered long and lonely nights. I searched for it in my travels and my feet tired along the way. I searched for it in my daughters and their mothers and found the backhand of despair. I searched for it in crime and drugs and found myself sitting in a prison cell."

"Perhaps all your searching was leading you to me, to our love. I've been hurt before, I hope this time it's for real," said Rebekah.

"I'll never hurt you, Ice Cream. You are the woman I've been searching for all these years."

Rebekah wanted so much to believe him. She put safety aside and concentrated on her wild lover.

CHAPTER SIXTEEN
WOMAN Power At Work

By helping so many women get their lives in order, Rebekah felt that she was finally on the road to her own healing. She felt she was doing what God and her mother wanted her to do. This feeling was especially strong when she helped women like Rosetta. Everyone called her Rose. When Rebekah learned about Rose's life, she felt the best person to help her was Nadine. Nadine could identify with Rose's past; it almost mirrored her own. That was the beauty of the WOMAN Power Club. All the women had baggage in their trunks and used their life's experiences to help other women. When Rebekah contacted Nadine and asked her to counsel Rose, Nadine was eager to help. Rebekah could also understand Rose's grief; she had experienced the same hell.

****

Rose

Rose's white father really did love her Negro mother, though they were as different as night and day. Rose's father was an attorney. He was a tall, blue-eyed, blond-haired handsome man. Her mother's skin was dark and she was beautiful. She looked like an African queen, with every strand of her natural hairstyle always in place. She wore her hair flat on top and cut close on the sides, an inverted triangle. "I was born of that love," said Rose to Rebekah one day. "I'm neither white nor colored. I'm mulatto, and when I was growing up, some of the kids at school called me half-breed."

"I can relate to that and so can one of our members, Nadine. People called her the same thing. Some even called me 'half-breed.' So you're not alone, sister. A lot of us have gone through the same hurts as you have," Rebekah said.

Rose's parents were killed in a boating accident while

vacationing in the Bahamas. They were on the sea when a storm came and they couldn't manage their boat. Three-year-old Rose had been with her paternal grandparents in Washington, D.C. while her parents were on vacation. After her parents' death, Rose lived with her white grandparents until she graduated from high school. Although her white grandparents gave her the best of everything, and her Black grandparents treated her well and sent her presents on her birthday and at Christmas, Rose felt that something was missing in her life. When she was with her white grandparents, that side of her family treated her as a member of the family. However, she noticed that her white relatives didn't invite her to their homes very often.

One summer when Rose finished high school, she was at one of her white relatives' houses attending a backyard barbecue. When Rose went into the kitchen to get some ice, she overheard one of her white cousins trying to defend her to a white school friend.

"I didn't know you had any colored people in your family," the school friend said.

"She's my uncle's daughter," the cousin said. "Mother said we had to be nice to her but she's all right, I guess. I just don't know what to say to her when the family is around. I mean, I don't mind being with her and all, but we don't have nothing in common. She's still colored. I just don't want to spend time with a colored person. I'm embarrassed to be seen with her in public — I feel that everyone stares at us. Look at her. Anyone can tell she's colored. What will my friends say when they find out I got colored blood in my family? Suppose they think I'm colored too and call me a niggra."

"The word is 'nigger,'" said the white friend.

The girls giggled and left the kitchen.

When Rose heard the conversation, she decided to leave the barbecue. She told her grandparents that she didn't feel well and was going home.

"I'll get the bus home," she said.

"No, your grandfather will drive you home. If you don't feel well, you shouldn't be riding the bus," her grandmother said.

"I'll call a taxi," said Rose. She called a taxi and left in it.

When her grandparents returned home, Rose told them she

wanted to go to Boston to live with her aunt Erica, her mother's only sister. Her grandparents tried to talk her out of going. They wanted her to go to college instead. But she wasn't ready for college. She was having difficulty trying to understand who she was.

She went to Boston where she met Alicia, Erica's next door neighbor's oldest daughter. Although Alicia was two years older than Rose, she looked older. Rose and Alicia became fast friends. Rose talked to Alicia about how the prostitutes seemed to live such a fascinating life. She saw the women walking the streets and standing on corners trying to get johns to buy their merchandise. In her young mind that was a cool, exciting, dark, and mysterious lifestyle.

"I bet they earn a lot of money," Rose said to Alicia. "It looks like an easy way to earn money. I might try it."

"Don't make the mistake of thinking that because men want your body, they are approving of you as a person," Alicia said. "You have too much on the ball to waste it in the streets."

"But I couldn't be a prostitute," Rose told Rebekah. "After I talked with my aunt Erica, I started feeling like I would be letting my parents down. They expected so much of me. I came back to Baltimore to live with my white grandparents. I told them how I felt and I was amazed at how much they understood my pain. They were white and I didn't think they could understand what I was going through as a Negro, but I was wrong. They did understand. I just needed to open up and talk to them. When I told my grandmother how I felt about being half-white and half-Black, she assured me that I wasn't half-loved. She loved me all the way. Then she held me in her arms and we cried together."

"'You are my flesh and blood,' my grandmother said. 'My son was your father and he loved your mother. To me, your mother was not a colored woman, she was my daughter-in-law. I know sometimes words hurt, baby. But don't you ever think that you don't have a family. We are your family. I am your family and you are my flesh and blood.'"

It was Rose's grandmother who encouraged her to call the WOMAN Power organization. Rebekah answered the telephone at the outreach center the day Rose called. She told Rose about a seminar

"Releasing the Mess," that she was presenting at the outreach center. Rose attended the seminar and met thirty women who were on the road to healing from many wounds from bad relationships to drug and alcohol abuse. At the seminar, Rose met Nadine.

Rose was grateful that she was blessed with a supporting family who understood her pain. That was what Rose was thinking four years later, as she looked out into the audience and saw the women of WOMAN Power sitting in the same row as her grandparents and the cousin she had overheard in the kitchen years ago. They were all listening to Rose deliver a speech as the president of her graduating class when she accepted her Bachelor's degree in music. How proud they all were. Afterward Rose sang her rendition of "Somewhere Over the Rainbow." She had a beautiful voice and was looking forward to a singing career.

****

Lillian

Lillian was another woman at the seminar whom WOMAN Power helped. One Saturday at the Ray of Hope Baptist Church, ushers and other church members were cleaning the sanctuary, preparing for the evening service. One of the ushers heard a soft voice crying and asking God to forgive her for what she was about to do.

"I just can't take the pain no more," the woman sobbed.

When the usher overheard Lillian, he ran to get Reverend Berneda.

"I think there's a woman in trouble in the sanctuary," said the usher. "I believe she's thinking about hurting herself. Please come and see if you can help her."

Reverend Berneda followed the usher into the sanctuary. The woman was about to leave.

"Sister, may I speak with you a moment, please?" Reverend Berneda called to the woman. The woman turned to face Reverend Berneda and Berneda saw that she was crying.

"Are you talking to me?" the woman asked.

"Yes, I'm Reverend Berneda Barnes. Everybody calls me Reverend Berneda. I guess they call me that so they can tell the difference between me and my husband, who's the senior pastor of this church," Berneda said, trying to bring a smile to the distraught woman. "May I ask your name?"

"My name is Lillian Faulkner," she said. Lillian didn't see the humor in Reverend Berneda's words. She was in too much pain. Lillian dropped to her knees and wept uncontrollably. "I just lost my baby, my only son. I don't want to live anymore."

Berneda knelt beside Lillian and held her in her arms while she cried.

"Why is God punishing me?" cried Lillian. "First, I lost my husband, the only man I've ever loved, and now I've lost my son, my only child. I don't have anything to live for."

"Sis, I know life is hard, but trust in God," said Berneda.

Lillian said to Berneda, "The white policeman said I must not have loved my child because he was in the streets at night when he should have been at home. My son was coming home from the library and was hit by a bullet that was meant for someone else. How could the policeman say I didn't love my child, my flesh and blood? Me, who carried him in my belly for nine months; me, who held him in my arms and nestled him to my breast while he nursed, suckling milk from my body; me, who changed his diapers and wiped his buttocks; me, who watched him being circumcised and cried; me, who wiped milk from his mouth when he had sucked too much and couldn't burp; me, who prayed for him through his bout with pneumonia when he was just a little fellow, so tiny and frail with the fever. God answered my prayers and he was spared. But now he's gone," she started crying again.

Berneda didn't know how to ease Lillian's pain. She felt that Lillian needed to talk, so she simply listened. Berneda learned that Lillian had buried her son that day. And after the funeral, she just started walking and ended up at the Ray of Hope Church.

Lillian sat on the bench, rocking back and forth, holding her arms tightly as she talked.

"Someone at the funeral asked me if I was okay," said Lillian.

"How could she ask me if I was okay? Am I okay with my life being torn apart? Am I okay with my heart laying in front of me in a gold casket? My child, my son, only fourteen years old, barely old enough to know who he is. My son, who everybody said looked just like his daddy. His daddy died a hero, saving a co-worker from drowning when their fishing boat capsized. I don't have anybody now. I'm all alone in the world. I want to join my family, my husband and son."

Berneda touched Lillian's shoulder. "God left you here for a purpose," Berneda said. "But we don't know what that purpose is yet. Why don't you come to my house and spend the night? Things will look better in the morning."

Berneda took Lillian to one of the guest rooms in the parsonage. It was a beautifully decorated room with a private bath. When Berneda and Wendall started their ministry, they took into consideration that they would need a place for people to stay overnight or for a few days. They were thinking of people who might need refuge from a potentially harmful or dangerous situation, such as family violence.

Lillian had a troubled night; she didn't sleep much. She couldn't close her eyes without thinking about her son, seeing his face, hearing his voice. The following morning, she didn't feel like getting out of bed. If I could just go to sleep and not wake up, she thought.

Berneda brought Lillian a hot breakfast to her room. "I know you feel like there's nothing worth getting up for," said Berneda. "But I want you to eat something, take your time, and get dressed when you feel like it. I want you to meet some dynamite women who will understand your hurt. I guarantee you that one of them has experienced your pain."

Berneda had already called Rebekah and Tracy and told them about Lillian. Both of them went to Berneda's home. When Lillian finished eating and took a shower, she went downstairs in the direction of women's voices. Tracy, Berneda, and Rebekah were seated at the kitchen table talking when Lillian walked into the room. Berneda introduced the women. Lillian and Tracy began to talk. After a while, Lillian understood what Berneda meant about being able to share her pain. Berneda knew that Tracy would understand Lillian's pain. She had experienced similar pain when her son, Deucy, was killed. Rebekah, Tracy, and Berneda told Lillian about WOMAN Power's services, and Lillian said she would contact them when she could talk without crying.

"I'll take each day as it comes," Lillian told the women. "And maybe there will come a day when the pain will ease. I know it will never go away. I just hope it will soon ease."

"It will, sister, it will in due time," said Tracy.

****

Cynthia

Cynthia and Montana — both white women — were business partners and owned a clothing boutique. Cynthia was married to Marvin, her second husband, a Black man who was an entrepreneur. Cynthia married Cleve, her first husband — a white man — when she was eighteen and they stayed together for five years. Cleve was a senior partner in an accounting firm he co-founded. Cleve was gay and wouldn't admit it until Cynthia came home early from work one day and found him in bed with Nathaniel, an old family friend. Nat, as they called him, had been the best man at Cynthia and Cleve's wedding. For every barbecue in their backyard, Nat was there with his famous sauce.

When Cynthia caught them in bed together, she just stood there looking at them both. Then she laughed hysterically and ran from the house, which was two blocks from the Ray of Hope Church. She ended up sitting in the sanctuary of the Church. Reverend Berneda was supervising a group of young people preparing for an Easter Sunday program when she heard someone sobbing. She looked into the pews and saw Cynthia. She walked to where Cynthia sat, put her arms around her and never said a word. Reverend Berneda just held Cynthia and let her cry. Cynthia rested her head on Berneda's shoulder and cried out her frustration.

When she finished weeping, she looked at Berneda through tear-stained eyes and said, "Thank you for not asking me 'what's the matter.'"

"It doesn't matter what the matter is. You needed a friend and God sent me. If you want to tell me what the matter is, I'll listen. If you don't want to tell me, I'll still listen. Someone was there for me when it was my time to cry. I'm here for you as long as you need me," said Reverend Berneda.

"But you don't know me," said Cynthia.

"God knows you, and that's enough for me. You're in God's house and there's always plenty of room here."

When Cynthia had cried all she could cry, she told Berneda what she had seen. Berneda's expression never changed. She didn't look disgusted or accusing, she just looked concerned.

"What are you going to do now?" Berneda asked in her soft voice.

"I don't know. I just know that I can't sleep in that house anymore. I feel so betrayed. I'm going home and pack some clothes. I need to get away for awhile."

Cynthia hugged the soft-spoken Reverend Berneda and thanked her for her comfort. She went home to pack her suitcase. Cleve was sitting in the living room in the dark. When she turned on the light, she saw him sitting on the sofa, crying.

"I don't want to discuss anything with you," she said before he could speak. "I just want to pack my clothes and leave. Our attorneys can settle everything. I never want to see your sorry face again as long as I live. For five years I've been true to you. I believed you when you said you didn't want any children until we could afford the kind of life we both wanted. Now I understand that wasn't the reason at all. You didn't want any children because you didn't have enough guts to confront your own sexuality. You disgust me. I'm not disgusted because you're gay. I can understand that. I'm disgusted because you punished me by not having sex with me. All the time, I thought something was wrong with me. You could have told me the truth. You and Nat both betrayed me."

Cleve nodded his head in agreement.

"You're right. There's nothing I can say. I tried to tell you years ago, but I couldn't find the words. I know saying 'I'm sorry' doesn't mean much now, but I *am* sorry. I won't contest the divorce. Whatever settlement you want, it's all right with me. You don't have to move out. I'll leave."

Cynthia shook her head and looked around the room.

"I don't want this house anymore. We'll put it up for sale, or do any damn thing you want to do with it. As far as I'm concerned, you and Nat can live here 'cause I'm outta here."

She packed her suitcases, put them into the trunk of her red convertible and drove off. She had no idea where she was heading, she was just going. She called Montana and told her she was getting away for a few days. "I'll call you when I settle somewhere," Cynthia said.

"Is everything all right?" asked Montana.

"No, everything is not all right. I have to get away to clear my mind. I'll call you in a few days when I feel like talking about it."

Montana could hear the pain in Cynthia's voice so she didn't ask anymore questions. She thought that Cynthia must have found out about Cleve. Cynthia's friends, including Montana, knew that Cleve was gay. Almost everyone knew except Cynthia. She was so much in love with Cleve that she couldn't see what was really happening.

She flew to Nassau and stayed two weeks. When she returned to Baltimore, she checked into a hotel and stayed there until she found a small apartment close to her boutique. Then she had her personal belongings moved to the apartment.

Her first Sunday back, she visited the Ray of Hope Baptist Church. It just happened to be a Sunday when Reverend Berneda was scheduled to preach the sermon. The title of her sermon was, "Through It All, God Is There," she cited Proverbs chapter four, verse seven as her reference text.

"It doesn't matter how educated you are, how many degrees you have, or how much money you make. Understand that God *is* the power of life and *has* the power of life, love and happiness," Berneda preached. She quoted the words of a gospel hymn that helped her when she was in emotional pain. "'Through it all, God was there. Through it all, God did care. Through it all, He still loved me. Through it all, He set me free. There were never times when I did doubt, because through it all, He brought me out.'" Then Reverend Berneda shouted, "I feel my help coming."

The congregation began to applaud. Some shouted; they were in an uproar, filled with the Holy Spirit. Cynthia had never seen such a response to a preacher. They certainly didn't do that at the synagogue where her family worshipped. It sounded as if the message in the songs and the sermon was directed to Cynthia. She didn't feel uncomfortable being in a church with a predominately Black congregation. She felt at home.

When her sermon was finished, Berneda extended her hand to the congregation and said, "The doors of the church are open. Come and give me your hand and give God your heart."

Cynthia didn't know exactly what happened. She just knew that she found herself kneeling at the altar, tears rolling down her cheeks as she praised God for His mercy. After the service, Berneda stood in front of the pulpit as a line of worshipers waited to shake her hand. Cynthia was one of them.

When it was Cynthia's turn to shake Berneda's hand, she asked Berneda, "Do you remember me?"

"Of course, I remember you. You're my sister who needed a shoulder. I see that the Almighty sent you back to where you needed to be. Welcome, sister. Like I told you before, in God's house, there's plenty of room," Reverend Berneda said.

Cynthia started attending church regularly. It was as if she had found a new life filled with hope. She wasn't angry with Cleve anymore. She called him and wished him blessings in his new life.

Cynthia met Marvin at a prayer meeting. They both volunteered to help serve food to the homeless at the Christmas function in the Church's outreach center. They became friends and found they had a lot in common. Marvin was just starting an accounting firm. Cynthia knew a little about accounting. She had helped Cleve start his accounting business. She also had been in business for over eight years, and she shared information with Marvin about how to start a business. Their friendship gradually turned into love. She was from a white Jewish family and he was the son of a Black Baptist preacher. A year after they met, Reverend Berneda officiated at their wedding. They laughingly called themselves "The Odd Couple." That was twenty-four years and two children ago. Cynthia was now forty-eight years old.

"And I love him as much today as I did the day we said 'I do,'" she told everyone when she attended a club meeting and shared her life with the members.

Cynthia joined WOMAN Power because of Reverend Berneda. Cynthia was proud when she was able to help a young woman who was considering suicide. She saw the young woman three years later and learned that she was finishing her junior year at one of the local colleges and considering going into the ministry.

****

Carole

Carole and Madge were two lesbians, who were building a family together and, who had become members of WOMAN Power. Carole and Rebekah met when Carole was in law school and they became fast friends. "I admire you both for coming out of the closet. I know it wasn't easy, so many people condemn you for your sexual preference," said Rebekah. Rebekah was really impressed when Carole revealed her past.

Before she started her educational endeavors, Carole lived in a two-bedroom apartment in the Flag House Court projects in Baltimore with her two daughters, Mona, ten years old, and Hilary, eight years old.

Carole was a fanatically clean person. Every month she took everything out of her kitchen cabinets, all the pots and pans, food, canned goods, dishes, glasses, silverware and trays. Then she scrubbed the inside and outside of the cabinets and washed everything — including the cans of food — before putting it all back. She also scrubbed the walls of every room of her apartment every month.

Mona and Hilary shared a bedroom and slept together in a double bed. The concrete floors in Carole's apartment were spotless, always shining like glass. You could see your reflection in her floors.

Carole washed and ironed clothes every other day, using the Laundromat around the corner. She didn't work outside the home and she received a welfare check each month.

Carole was having an affair with a man she and her friends called "Mr. Jeff," who was seventy years old and she was thirty-five. Mr. Jeff had a wife and family living in Cherry Hill — a predominately Black section of Baltimore. He was a bald-headed, dark- complected man, with a huge flat nose and a slight stoop in his shoulders. Mr. Jeff wasn't attractive; he was a pleasant man and wore thick glasses.

Carole knew about Florence, Mr. Jeff's wife, but Florence wasn't sure who Carole was. Florence knew her husband was having an affair but she didn't know with whom. It didn't bother Florence that her husband was unfaithful to her, as long as he bought the groceries, made her car payments, and paid the other household bills. Florence was also unfaithful to Mr. Jeff. She was having an affair with Mr. Melvin, a widower, and a member of the Men's Senior Usher Board at her church. Mr. Melvin's wife had died three years before he and Florence met.

Every Saturday, Mr. Jeff bought groceries for Carole and her children and for his own household. He carried a week's groceries to his wife and a week's groceries to Carole's apartment. Although Mr. Jeff was an old man, Carole got pregnant and gave birth to a son, Adolphus. Adolphus had a fair complexion like Carole and a large flat nose like Mr. Jeff.

Carole was also having an affair with a younger man she met one night at the bar across the street from the twelve-story project building in which she lived. Carole went to the bar when she knew that Mr. Jeff wasn't coming to visit her.

On one of those nights at the bar, she met Roscoe, a twenty-five-year-old man who worked at the toy store around the corner from the projects. She started seeing Roscoe every time she went to the bar, and pretty soon a relationship developed between them. They started leaving the bar together and went to his apartment several blocks from the projects.

One night Roscoe was at the bar waiting for Carole to join

him. She was dressing to meet him when Mr. Jeff paid her a surprise visit. He had begun to suspect that Carole went out when he wasn't there, but she wasn't a fool. She liked Roscoe — he could satisfy her sexually — but Mr. Jeff paid her bills.

Roscoe helped Carole financially as much as he could, but he wasn't earning as much money as Mr. Jeff, who was receiving money from his retirement pension and his savings. Mr. Jeff had also made some wise investments when he was a young man and they were now paying off. Besides, his living expenses weren't as great as Roscoe's. Mr. Jeff's car, house, boat, and furniture were paid for, and his children were adults living on their own. Plus, Mr. Jeff used his car as a hack — an unlicensed taxi cab service — and made a lot of money on which he didn't pay taxes.

Roscoe stole toys from the store where he worked and gave them to Carole for her children. Between Roscoe and Mr. Jeff, at Christmas time, Carole's children had more toys than other children in the projects. Carole hadn't lied to Roscoe. She told him that Mr. Jeff was her baby's father and that he helped support her other two children. Roscoe said he understood her need for financial support and promised that he wouldn't interfere with her relationship with Mr. Jeff. Carole had no idea where their father was. He had left town with a white woman when they lived in Durham, North Carolina. Carole did domestic work in Durham and had used her last paycheck to move to Baltimore where her parents lived.

Roscoe sat at the bar waiting for Carole that night, and drank several shots of Courvoisier Cognac, his favorite drink. The time ticked by and Carole hadn't come. He figured that Mr. Jeff must have come over, otherwise she would have been at the bar. The alcohol told him that Carole was his woman and that she had no business being with an old man like Mr. Jeff. It didn't matter that Carole had been truthful with Roscoe about Mr. Jeff, the alcohol clouded his judgment.

Three hours passed, Carole still hadn't arrived. Roscoe got angrier and angrier. He gulped down several more drinks, jumped up from the bar stool, ran across the street to Carole's apartment building, took the elevator to her floor, went to her apartment and banged on the door, yelling for her to let him in and professing his love for her.

Mr. Jeff was inside the apartment with Carole and the children. Carole yelled through the closed door for Roscoe to go away.

"Open this damn do' and let me in, woman!" yelled Roscoe. "If you don't open this do', I'm gonna kick it down. I know you got that old nigga in there with you, but you're my woman."

Carole again yelled through the closed door, "I'm gonna call the police if you don't leave. Why do you want to start trouble? Why don't you just go away?"

"Cause I love you and I ain't leaving till you open this do'. Now, open this do', Carole, this minute!" he yelled.

Carole still refused.

"All right," he said, "I'm leavin', just long enough for you to get rid of that old nigga. But I'll be back, and you'd better open this mutha-fuckin' do' or I'm gonna break it down."

He staggered toward the elevator.

Carole didn't have a telephone. She was receiving public assistance — welfare checks — not having any other income, with three children, she couldn't afford the luxury of a telephone. Mr. Jeff wouldn't pay for a telephone for Carole. He thought other men might call her when he wasn't there.

When Roscoe left Carole's door, Mr. Jeff snuck out of her apartment and ran down the back stairs. He could see Roscoe standing down the hall by the elevators. Mr. Jeff ran across the street to the telephone booth outside the bar and called the police.

In the meantime, Roscoe returned to Carole's apartment pounding on the door yelling, "All right, baby, Daddy's back. Now open this fuckin' do'! I gave you enough time to get rid of that nigga."

"You'd better leave! I've called the police and they're gonna lock you up," yelled Carole.

"Fuck the police," yelled Roscoe. "I'm the fuckin' police. If you don't open this do', it's gonna take more than the police to get me off your ass."

Carole had never seen Roscoe so angry. She was afraid of him. She looked out her window and saw Mr. Jeff standing in the telephone booth. "Tell the police to hurry," she yelled down to him. "He's trying to break down the door. He's almost inside, hurry!"

Roscoe kept kicking the door, pounding on it with his fists and ramming it with his shoulders, trying to get inside. A crowd gathered in front of the project building to watch Roscoe. Two police cars pulled in front of the building and two policemen jumped out of each car, one from the driver's seat and one from the passenger's side. Two policemen raced for the elevator, and two ran up the stairs to Carole's fourth floor apartment. Roscoe never wavered; he continued trying to break down Carole's door, oblivious to the policemen's orders to stop. Roscoe seemed to be in a trance. The police rushed him, tackled him, knocked him down and handcuffed his hands behind his back while he lay on the concrete floor. When Carole heard the police at her door, she opened it.

"Are you alright, ma'am?" the policeman asked Carole.

"All I want is for him to leave me alone," said Carole to the policeman.

Roscoe was still professing his love for her.

Mr. Jeff had gotten off the elevator and was walking down the hall, heading to Carole's apartment. He passed the policemen taking the handcuffed Roscoe to the elevator. Roscoe recognized Mr. Jeff as the old man who was supporting Carole and her children.

"There he is!" Roscoe yelled, pointing his head in Jeff's direction, unable to use his handcuffed hands. "See, he's an old man. He's old enough to be her father. What does she want with an old man like that?"

While the police took Roscoe down the hall to the elevator, he still shouted obscenities at Jeff.

"I love you, Carole," he shouted. "That old man will give you worms. He can't do nothin' but make spit babies. You need a young man like me."

"He better hope he lives to be as old me," mumbled Mr. Jeff. "The way he's going, somebody's gonna kill'm before he's thirty. My son, Adolphus, don't look like no 'spit' baby to me."

When the police left with Roscoe, and the crowd had dispersed, Mr. Jeff asked Carole about Roscoe. She lied and said she had gone into the cut-rate store across the street a month ago to buy some beer and she met Roscoe in the store. Mr. Jeff believed her because he wanted to believe her. Where else could he find a nice-looking young woman who would give him a key to her apartment and have him as her lover? Carole thought she could get away with almost anything and Jeff would forgive her.

****

Madge

Madge, her husband Earl, and their three daughters lived on the fifth floor directly above Carole's apartment in the projects. Earl was a tall, handsome man with black straight hair. His Native American ancestry was visible in his physical features. Madge was a short chunky, pigeon-toed woman with long, black hair. It was clear that she, too, was of Native American descent.

The project had a policy against tenants using washing machines in their apartments. Use of the machines caused the water to back up in other apartments and overflow the sinks. Each high-rise project building had coin-operated, commercial washing machines and dryers in the basement. Some residents owned washing machines and stored them in the basement. Those who had new machines had them mounted on wheels so the machines could be pushed onto the elevator and taken to the tenant's apartment for protection from being stolen, damaged, or used by other tenants.

In the commercial machines, a load of clothes could be washed for twenty minutes for a quarter and dried for ten minutes for a dime. But the machines were frequently broken and when they were operating, they didn't wash clothes clean or dry them thoroughly.

Some residents washed their babies' diapers in the machines without first rinsing the feces from the diapers. Because such a small amount of water flowed into the machines during the washing cycle, human waste was often left inside the machines and got on the clothes of the next person using them. The residents complained that the project's management had fixed the machines so that a small amount of water flowed into them in an effort to save on the water bill.

One day Madge was washing clothes in her kitchen using her new washing machine and it overflowed. Water ran down the pipes, between the cracks in the cement, drained into Carole's apartment, and caused her kitchen sink to overflow. She went upstairs to find out where the water was coming from. She knocked on Madge's door. When Madge answered the door, she recognized Carole from seeing her in the projects, but they had never met.

"Hello, my name is Carole and my apartment is under yours. There's water running into my apartment and before I call the maintenance man, I'm trying to find out where it's coming from. Do you know what's going on?"

"Hi, Carole, I'm Madge. I've seen you and your children on the playground. I'm sorry. I didn't realize I was making such a mess. I know I'm not supposed to use the machine in my apartment, but my baby is sick and I needed to wash clothes. I'll come down to your apartment and clean up the mess. If my carelessness has ruined anything, I'll pay for it."

Carole saw that Madge was sincere.

"No, I'll clean it up, you haven't ruined anything. I just wanted to know what's going on. How's your baby now? Is there anything I can do?" Carole asked.

"He's asleep, but thanks for being so kind. Come in and have a cup of coffee," said Madge.

"Thank you, but I have to get back downstairs and start dinner. I'll see you later, but don't worry about the water. I won't call the maintenance man. He'll only complain to management about you breaking the rules. You know how they can get sometimes, and that'll start trouble," said Carole.

She left and they promised to see each other later.

After that first meeting, Madge and Carole became friends. They visited with each other in the evenings after the children were in bed, and they sat outside until the wee hours of the morning talking and enjoying each other's company. Their children played together, went to the same school, and were playmates.

One night, Carole's children were spending the night at her parents' house. Madge's children had gone "down the country" —

meaning South Carolina — to visit their grandparents for the summer. Mr. Jeff hadn't told Carole that he was coming over that night. But Florence had gone out the night before with Mr. Melvin and hadn't come home, so he seized the opportunity to visit Carole. He went to her apartment, put his key into her front door, unlocked it, and walked inside. All the lights were off. Carole was usually at home when he arrived. She hadn't said anything about going out. He hoped she hadn't started seeing Roscoe again.

He walked inside the dark apartment and as he reached for the hallway light switch, he paused and listened. He heard soft, moaning sounds coming from Carole's bedroom. His heart started pounding, his hands got sweaty, and his throat was dry. He didn't know what to expect. He visualized Carole in bed with a younger man; he started to turn around and leave. He didn't want to see who she was with, but he had to know.

Slowly and softly he walked back to the open bedroom door and peeped inside. In the glow of the neon lights from the bar across the street, he saw the silhouettes of two people moving around on the bed. He flicked on the light switch and saw the shocked faces of Carole and Madge.

He stood in the doorway and looked at them both for a long time. Nobody spoke. Madge and Carole were both nude. They pulled the sheet up to cover themselves, shielding their naked bodies from his eyes. He stood there, remembering the years he had provided for Carole and her children, remembering how he had forgiven her for having an affair with Roscoe.

At that moment, he saw her through the eyes of his friends; they had called him an old fool for messing around with a woman half his age. He wanted to hurt Carole as she had hurt him. He thought about killing her. His eyes filled with tears. Finally, without saying a word, he looked at Carole, winked his eye, blew her a kiss, turned the light off, and walked out, quietly closing the door behind him.

Carole never heard from him again. He didn't return for his personal belongings. Adolphus was three years old, and Mr. Jeff never saw him again. Carole didn't know Mr. Jeff's address and she realized that she didn't know anything about him. It was almost as if he didn't exist.

****

"I've always known that I was different from other women," said Madge. "I never liked dolls and frilly girl clothes. When I was growing up I was a tomboy. Boys turned me off, but I had strange feelings for girls. I didn't understand my feelings and I tried to talk to my mother about them. She said they were evil and I'd burn in hell if I told anyone else how I felt. I got married 'cause my mother said that's what I should do."

"I grew up the same way," said Carole. "I always wanted children, but I didn't want to be married to a man. I wanted to adopt children, but my parents expected me to get married and have children."

"When I opened the door and saw you standing there the first day I met you, it was like, 'wow'," said Madge.

"I blew your mind, huh?" teased Carole.

"Yeah, just a tiny bit," laughed Madge.

A few weeks later, Madge and her husband separated. Madge and Carole grew closer. They had similar needs as single mothers rearing children alone and living in the projects. Madge and Carole continued to be lovers. They tried to hide their relationship from their friends and families, feeling they wouldn't understand, and Carole and Madge weren't ready to "come out of the closet." They feared that children would tease their children and it might result in violence. Still, they wanted to be together.

Carole and Madge decided to work toward a better life together. They pooled their money to move into a neighborhood where their children could go to a better school. They found a house in the suburbs of Baltimore County that needed repairs and negotiated with the landlord for a five-year lease opting to renovate the house themselves. Madge and Carole set five-year goals to get jobs and college degrees. They agreed to always help each other with the children and vowed to always think of themselves and the children as a family.

Madge got a night job cleaning offices and went to school part-time during the day. In the evenings, she watched the children and prepared meals. Carole worked during the day at a nursing home and went to school part-time in the evenings. Carole and Madge made sure that one of them was at home when the children returned home from school. They both spent time with their children on Sundays. Sometimes going to church. When it was necessary for both Madge and Carole to be away from home, they hired a friend's daughter to stay with the children, to help with dinner, and to make sure the children completed their homework, took their baths and went to bed on time.

Madge enjoyed remodeling grand old houses and refinishing furniture. "They don't build houses as sturdy as they used to do," Madge said. "I used to help my daddy renovate houses. I always wanted a chance to build things and remodel houses, now I have that chance."

According to the agreement with the landlord, when Madge and Carole were ready to purchase the house and land, all money paid as rent would be converted into a down payment. After two years of paying rent, Madge and Carole began the process of purchasing the house. They had renovated a family room, and converted the basement into a clubroom, complete with a wet bar for adults and a soda and ice cream fountain for the children.

Within five years, both Madge and Carole graduated from college, each taking advantage of the State's efforts to improve the quality of life for welfare recipients and their families by providing college tuition for those who qualified. Madge earned a Bachelor's degree in architectural engineering and Carole earned a Bachelor's degree in political science.

After dinner one evening, Madge and Carole called the children together for a family discussion. Madge and Carole announced that they wanted to continue their education and register for graduate school. The children were very supportive. They remembered how it was in the projects after Mr. Jeff left Carole and Earl left Madge. They remembered having to stand in long welfare lines to receive powdered eggs and milk, peanut butter, government cheese, flour and yellow cornmeal. They also remembered how the children at school whose parents weren't on welfare teased them and called them, "welfare rats." They were proud of their mothers, and seeing Carole and Madge succeed against the odds made the children committed to follow in their mothers' footsteps.

"I knew you wouldn't stop going to college, now," said Mona, now fifteen years old. "It doesn't matter how many years you want to go to school, we're proud of you both and we're a family; we'll stick together."

The other children agreed with Mona.

Madge and Carole hugged their children and their eyes filled with tears. Adolphus was then eight years old and already talking about becoming a doctor.

Carole was in Ethics class one day when Rebekah came into the classroom and sat next to her. Because of the car accident, Rebekah had missed several nights of class.

"Hello, my name is Rebekah Mosley. I wasn't here last week. I was out sick. Were you in class last Monday and Wednesday?" she asked Carole.

"Hi, Rebekah. Yes, I was here last week. You're welcome to see my notes." Rebekah pulled her chair closer to Carole's and began reviewing her notes.

"I don't want to get behind in my classes any more than I already am," said Rebekah. "I've already missed a whole semester. I was in a car accident. Well, I wasn't exactly in an accident; I saved a little boy and I got hurt."

"You saved a little boy?" asked Carole. "That sounds interesting. Tell me about it."

"It's a long story. We'll talk about it sometime," said Rebekah.

"I was studying at the University of Maryland and I had my credits transferred here," said Carole. "I might not be able to keep them all, but I'm okay with that. I need to be at a school where I can get home quickly even in bad weather. My friend works in Washington, D.C. We both have children and one of us is always where we can get home in a hurry in case of an emergency."

"Your friend?" Rebekah asked.

"Look," said Carole, "I might as well be up front with you 'cause I don't like to shock anyone. I'm gay and my friend and I have been in a relationship for several years. Together we have five children. So if you want to walk, now is the time."

Rebekah looked at Carole, extended her hand for a handshake, smiled and said, " Hello, Gay, I'm Rebekah."

They both laughed, and from that moment a friendship developed. They began to study together, and with Carole's help, Rebekah was able to catch up on her studies. When the semester was almost over, Carole and Rebekah had lunch together in the college cafeteria.

"I don't know why I told you about Madge and me when I first met you. We had decided that it's not time to come out of the closet yet. Our children, family, and friends might not understand. Besides, Madge has a good-paying job with a large architectural firm and we need the money. Some employers act like our sexual preference might rub off on them," Carole said.

"That's your call. As far as I'm concerned, you're still 'in the closet.' I know exactly what you're saying. I've been there and done that. Now stop worrying and let's get busy studying for final exams," said Rebekah.

"'Been there and done that?' Does that mean you're gay, too?" asked Carole.

"Let's just say I was confused when I was growing up. I didn't understand the strange feelings that I had for girls. I was interested in boys and girls. I used to have sleep-over parties and I liked the feel and scent of girls. But I also liked to be with boys. I don't know. It was just strange," said Rebekah.

"Perhaps you're bisexual," said Carole.

"Maybe," Rebekah said. "I'm glad that I met you, though. This is the first time I've had this conversation with anyone. It's the first time I've felt comfortable enough to talk about it."

"That's what friends are for," laughed Carole. "You needed a friend, and so did I."

One evening after final exams were over, Rebekah and Carole were sitting in study hall talking, glad the pressure of college was almost over, when Nadine Culpepper walked in. She and Carole were in some of the same classes; however, Nadine was studying for a graduate degree in psychology. Nadine saw Carole and waved to her. Carole beckoned Nadine to join them.

"Hello, to you both," Nadine said.

Carole introduced the two women.

"I know you're glad that final exams are over," said Nadine.

"I sure am," said Carole.

"Me too," Rebekah laughed.

I'm getting a Master's degree in psychology and my last exam just ended. I feel like shouting," said Nadine.

They all laughed.

"I've seen you around campus," said Rebekah. "Have a seat and join us. We're just sitting here running our mouths. I was telling Carole about an organization I'm in. We're always looking for more women to join us."

"What type of organization is it?" Nadine asked.

"It's an organization of women to help other women," said Rebekah.

"Sounds interesting. Tell me more about it," said Nadine.

Rebekah explained that she and some colleagues had started an organization to help women take control of their lives, to provide a better quality of life for their children and for themselves.

"This is perfect," said Nadine. "Some of my colleagues were discussing the same thing last week. Count me in; this is exactly what women need."

The three women sat, talked, and sipped on sodas. Rebekah continued discussing the WOMAN Power Club.

"There are a lot of young women who need help coping with life. Members of the organization have experienced a lot of difficulties in their lives. We believe that we can help a lot of women succeed in life by giving them the benefit of our wisdom and experience. We would love for you to join us. Nadine, you and Carole would be great assets to the organization; and Carole, from what you've told me about Madge, so would she," said Rebekah.

"You don't think your friends would object to a gay couple being members of your organization? You know society isn't ready to accept such a relationship. Having Madge and me in the organization might cause you more harm than good," said Carole.

"Look," said Rebekah, "there are a lot of lesbian and bisexual women in Maryland who could benefit from your life experiences. You could counsel them and provide support. Plus, you can educate others in the straight world. Believe me, I know you have a lot to offer. I know the narrow minds of some people. But it may mean that you might be 'out of the closet.'"

Carole and Nadine liked the idea of joining the WOMAN Power Club. When Carole went home that evening, she explained the organization to Madge who also liked the idea. They discussed what Nadine and Rebekah said about coming out of the closet. They decided to give it some thought.

Madge gave a graduation party for Carole and invited Rebekah, Nadine and members of WOMAN Power. Carole and Madge talked about how blessed they were that God had changed their lives and made them successful people. They wanted to give back to the community and they decided to do that by providing services for WOMAN Power. Rebekah stayed at the party for a while, but she had a lot on her mind, so she went home early.

****

Nadine

Nadine used the pain of her past to help others. While sharing one evening she said, "My family and I were living in Tennessee. My pain started the first time I was abused by my stepfather. I must have been about five years old. I remember kissing him good night and he put his tongue in my mouth. I didn't like that and I didn't like him. I didn't like the way he touched me in my private parts. I didn't like the way he made me touch him.

"'Come and watch Daddy shave,' he used to say to me. And I would stand in the bathroom and watch him. 'Want to see something jump?' he asked me one morning as I watched him shave. I thought it was a game. 'Touch Daddy there.' He pointed to his penis. I touched it and it began to grow. I giggled, I thought it was magic.

"It got hard and he started breathing funny. 'This is our secret,' he said. 'Don't tell your mama.' Then he started wanting to give me a bath and play a game, by tickling me on my vagina. One day when he was bathing me, he took me out of the bathtub to dry me off, and sat me in his lap. His penis was exposed and it got hard as he dried my body. I tried to tell my mother but she wouldn't believe me and punished me for lying.

"The first time he tried to penetrate me, I thought I was dying because of the blood. After that, each time he was in the bathroom I hid in the closet. My mother told my stepfather that I said he touched me in my private parts so he beat me. Lord, did he beat me. He also beat me 'cause I wouldn't watch him shave anymore. He always found an excuse to beat me and my mother didn't protect me.

"I often wondered why the teachers at school didn't question my bruises. Why didn't they ask why my arm was in a cast? How did I get a black eye? Why were my lips busted and bruised? Why did I go to school with strings tied around my shoes when my mother and stepfather could afford to buy me better shoes? Why was I always dirty and hungry at school? We had a bathroom at home, but I wasn't allowed to use it unless I let my stepfather bathe me. I wonder why the neighbors didn't intervene when they heard me screaming at night? This went on for six years.

"When I was eleven years old and in the fifth grade, I made the mistake of trusting one of my teachers. One day at school they showed a film about sexual abuse. When I saw the film, I told my teacher that's what my stepfather was doing to me. My teacher came to our house supposedly to see if what I said was true, but he also told my stepfather what I had said. My teacher said he didn't believe me but he had to check out my story just the same. His visit to our house ended with him and my stepfather sitting in the living room drinking beer and laughing. My stepfather rolled his eyes at me when my teacher wasn't looking, and I knew I was going to be in trouble later.

"When my teacher left, my stepfather tied me to the bedpost

and beat me until my back bled. All the while he was beating me, he kept repeating how he told me that no one would help me and that no one cared about me. After that incident with my teacher, I believed my stepfather and I didn't tell anyone else. If my mother wasn't home when I arrived home from school and my stepfather was there, I hid under the house until my mother came home.

"One day my stepfather found me hiding under the house and made me come into the house with him. He sent my mother to the store. I believe that she knew what he wanted me to do, but she didn't protect me. She just left me to his mercy. I had decided that I would kill myself, and kill him too, if he touched me again. But that time he had another trick. He told me to kiss his penis. 'Lick it like you do a lollipop,' he said."

Nadine tried not to cry as she remembered the horrible experiences.

"If talking about it is too painful for you, sis, don't do it. Let's talk about something else," said Rebekah.

"No, it's okay. I need to talk about it," said Nadine and she continued.

"When I refused, he took my head and pushed it down to his penis. I tried to resist but he was too strong. I opened my mouth and bit him on his penis as hard as I could and wouldn't let go. I had decided that he was going to kill me anyway, but I would die with the satisfaction of knowing that he couldn't hurt any other little girls. I bit him as hard as I could. He screamed and hit me in my head trying to make me let go. But every time he hit me, I chomped down harder. When I finally let go, I ran out of that house and never went back. I knew he would kill me if he caught me, so I just kept on running. When I left, he was rolling around on the floor, holding his crotch and moaning in pain.

"The police found me wandering around in the cold rain wearing a thin, ragged, rain-soaked dress. They put me into the patrol car and took me to the police station. I wouldn't tell them my name, so they sent me to Ms. Huff's house. That's where all the colored children were sent when they didn't have a home, or when their parents didn't want them. At that time it was called the orphanage, today it's called a foster home.

"I lived there until I was seventeen years old, when I graduated from high school. The State required that children attend school, but neither my mother nor stepfather came to the school to see if I was still attending. I guess they were afraid of what I told the police when they found me that night.

"Because of my shabby clothes and because I lived in an orphanage, I was embarrassed when I went to school. The school separated those of us who lived in the orphanage from the regular school children. Their parents didn't want them mixing with poor unwanted kids like me. I wore used clothes that were donated to the orphanage. I pretended that I didn't know where my parents were and they never came looking for me. I graduated from that school and one of my teachers, Miss Stanback, helped me find funds for college tuition. I consoled myself by dreaming of one day becoming somebody important, living in a big white house, having a husband who adored me and two children, a boy and a girl.

"I entered an essay contest and Miss Stanback helped me with editing. I won the contest and the prize money paid for one semester of college. However, I had to find money for my transportation to college, so I got a job washing cars.

"I was the only girl working at the car wash. The only reason I was hired was that Miss Stanback told Mr. Tom, the owner, why I needed the money. He said if he could help me get an education, it was a wise investment. I enrolled at Morgan State College and got a job in the college library to help pay my living expenses, but my classmates kept teasing me about my second-hand clothes, so I dropped out of college. I met a man named Keith and we started dating. When I learned that I was pregnant, Keith and I got married. He said he married me to give the baby a name. Not because he loved me, but he was being a man, he told me one day.

"After our son was born, Keith got locked up. He and one of his buddies tried to rob a store, and they got twenty years for being stupid. I left Memphis, Tennessee and went to New York to get a better job. One of my college friends was from New York and she said jobs were plentiful there. Keith's parents kept the baby until I could afford to support us both. I found a job as a waitress in a restaurant, but I wasn't making enough money to take care of me and my son, so I started prostituting. I sent money home to Keith's parents for the baby and to help pay bills. They never asked where the money came from. They just wanted me to keep sending it.

"My son died of pneumonia when he was six years old, so I went back to Tennessee to bury him and to file for a divorce from Keith. When I went back to New York, I had a room in a boarding house where the landlady ran a brothel. White men looking for Black women came knocking on our door; sometimes we got them drunk and robbed them. Naturally, they wouldn't tell the police; they were too ashamed of being in a whore house. I started doing drugs and prostituted my body for drug money, food, and rent.

"When I found myself lying in the gutter one night and couldn't remember how I got there, I knew it was time to change my life while I still had a life. I also knew that I couldn't do it myself, so I prayed. I hadn't thought about prayer before, but nothing else seemed to work so I figured I didn't have anything to lose. I kept hearing people say, 'Take your burdens to the Lord in prayer,' so I said, ' I'll try Jesus,' and you know what? It worked. I got a job in Woolworth's Five and Dime store and went back to college part-time. It took ten years to earn a Bachelor's degree, but I did graduate."

"Now you know why I wanted you to help me build this organization," said Rebekah. "It was my dream to do just what we're doing, using our life's experiences to help each other and to help others. When I first had lunch with Nadine, I said to her, 'Girl, I can share some stuff with you and we need to reach those women who think they need people like Marty, Mike, Brian, Teddy, Ken, and all those other distractions that I allowed in my life,' and she was eager to help," said Rebekah.

CHAPTER SEVENTEEN
The Last Goodbye

Rebekah thought about her telephone conversation with Breeze. She was amazed at how beautiful and provocative an intelligent conversation could be. She dressed and drove to the bank located across the street from a park. She went inside, mumbling to herself that the line was always long. She stood in line, and when she got to the window the teller said, "You'll have to see one of the people in the back office."

He pointed in the direction of two glass doors with a sign on one of the doors that read, "Please take a number and be seated."

She took a number — number three — and sat to wait her turn. She looked out of the window daydreaming. A little boy about three years old, ran near her, put his face against the window pane and looked outside. He turned to face Rebekah.

"I bet I can count all those people out there," the little boy said, as he pointed to the people in the park across the street.

"I bet you can't count that many," Rebekah teased.

"I betcha I can," he said. "I can even spell my name."

"Durrell, come back over here," a lady in line hollered.

The little boy ran to the lady's side and held her hand. A woman in the office opened the door and said, "Number three."

Rebekah stood up, showed the woman her ticket and entered the door that the woman held opened for her.

"Good morning," the woman said. "I'm Mrs. Marshall. How may I help you?"

"I want to discuss investment opportunities and open an account for my organization," said Rebekah.

The woman pulled out a portfolio and began to discuss different account options with Rebekah. Rebekah learned that the woman's first name was Montana and that she was a member of the Ray of Hope Baptist Church. Learning that they were both members of the same church, they struck up a conversation. As they talked, one of the two glass doors opened, and the little boy stuck his head inside and waved to Montana.

"Hi, Durrell. I'll see you tonight," she said.

The little boy waved to Rebekah. She waved back.

"I see you've met my nephew," said Montana.

"Yeah, he bet me that he could count," laughed Rebekah.

"He's something," Montana said. "He's as smart as a whip to be three years old."

They started talking about Montana's sister, Durrell's mother, and the hard time she was having supporting him on her salary. Rebekah learned that Montana was the host of a radio talk show.

"I see so many young women on their way to destruction," said Rebekah, "and many of them are down the street from our church, hanging on corners and in liquor houses. We started advertising free counseling services at the church. You'd be surprised how many people actually come for help."

"I don't know why we haven't met," Montana said. "I'm in church almost every Sunday, but I've heard about this organization."

"Perhaps it wasn't time for us to meet. I'm convinced that God does everything in His own time and His time is sometimes different from ours," Rebekah said.

"You're right. I've seen Him work," Montana laughed.

Montana told Rebekah that she was a part-time business owner with her partner Cynthia, and they were working on becoming full time.

"How can you do all these things and still have your sanity?" asked Rebekah. "You're a bank clerk, a radio talk show host, and a business owner. Are you married, too? And if you say you also have children, I'm going to call you superwoman," Rebekah laughed.

"I sure am married, to a wonderful man named Bruce," said Montana. "He helps me keep it all together. But we haven't been blessed with children. I guess God says He has something else in store for us."

Rebekah discussed the purpose of the WOMAN Power Club with Montana and the type of account they needed. Rebekah invited

Montana to attend the next meeting and Montana said she would.

****

Friday, when Rebekah returned to the prison, she wore a black dress that had gold buttons up the front and a split in the back. The dress clung to her curvaceous body. She was built like a brick shit-house and she knew it. She also knew that men, especially Breeze, liked to look at her body, and she liked to show it off. She wore a black and grey fedora cocked to the side. She carried a grey handbag, long and sleek. She was bare-legged and her freshly-pedicured feet were stunning in the open-toe grey shoes with a strap around the ankle.

Rebekah swung her hips and wiggled her way down the walkway to the school. Wolf-whistles came from the buildings with windows and from some inmates who were outside in the prison yard. She went to the meeting with the principal of the school that was being conducted inside the prison for inmates. She walked into the building and her eyes searched for Breeze.

"He's near. I can feel him," she whispered to herself as she walked.

She walked into the office and met with Ms. Joyner. They talked about the educational needs of inmates and what programs the school and the Ray of Hope Church could develop together to benefit the inmates. But Rebekah's mind wasn't on the conversation. She was searching for a familiar voice and those deep dark eyes.

After Rebekah and Ms. Joyner had talked for approximately thirty minutes, Rebekah was ready to leave. She ended the conversation by promising to put together a plan and said they would meet again. She was disappointed at not seeing Breeze, but when she and the principal walked out of the office a familiar voice said, "Hello, Ms. Mosley."

Rebekah's heart skipped a beat and her throat got dry. She turned and there stood Breeze, leaning against the doorframe, a toothpick in his mouth, his long braids pulled back into a ponytail and held together with a rubber band. His neatly-trimmed mustache made his lips resemble a rose petal.

"Hello, are you still writing and painting?" she asked, trying to make small talk.

"Yes, ma'am. I'll show them to you Tuesday when you come to teach your class," he grinned.

Rebekah smiled and walked on. She didn't want the principal to suspect a relationship between her and an inmate. Besides, Rebekah had already been rejuvenated by seeing Breeze. She drove home, elated that she had accomplished her mission. She had seen her love and he had seen her.

That night while sitting at home reading, the telephone rang. It was Andy. As soon as she heard his voice she knew something was wrong. He was crying. Rebekah panicked, her heart started racing and a lump came in her throat. When Andy was finally able to speak he said, "Rebekah, we lost Mamie," then he sobbed.

"What do you mean 'lost Mamie?'" she shouted, panic gripping her heart.

"She's dead," he said, then he started crying so hard he couldn't speak anymore.

Rebekah screamed, she stood holding the telephone and screaming. When she could compose herself, she called the other members of WOMAN Power and told them what Andy said. All the members went to Mamie's house to be with Andy. He told them that Mamie had started going to the track at the highschool near their house every evening and had had a heart attack while jogging. She had collapsed on the track and an ambulance took her to the hospital. She never regained consciousness.

"Mamie started exercising the way she did everything else," said Andy. "She should have started slow, and gradually worked up to jogging. She should have gotten a check-up first. But she bought a pair of running shoes and some sweat suits and went to the track."

Mamie's funeral was held at the Ray of Hope Church. Reverend Wendall preached the eulogy. He called Rebekah to the pulpit to speak for WOMAN Power.

"Here before us today lies one of my dearest friends, whom I've known since college. I'm sad because she left this world before me, but she left me with such beautiful memories of times we shared.

I'm proud that she was a part of my life. She was a person who didn't judge others, she accepted everyone as one of God's creations. Mamie was one of the original founders of WOMAN Power. That's a testament to what she thought about people. She was one of the best attorneys in Maryland, and her list of clients who couldn't afford to pay for her services was as long, if not longer, than the list of her paying clients. That was the way she lived her life — helping those who needed help without a thought of 'what's in it for me.' God can dream a bigger dream for us than we can dream for ourselves. Mamie fulfilled God's dream for her on earth, and He promoted her to heaven. She is now with God. Sleep on my beautiful sister. Say 'hello' to my family for me. From the members of WOMAN Power, you'll be forever loved and forever missed. So many women and families owe you so much. Thank you for allowing God to use you during your short stay on earth. And save a seat for me."

Rebekah walked back into the congregation crying and took her seat. All the members of WOMAN Power cried.

After the funeral, all the members of the Club went to the outreach center to fellowship and remember their friend. After Mamie's death, they didn't see much of Andy, but he kept in touch with them through occasional telephone calls and letters.

CHAPTER EIGHTEEN
The Pain of Love

For over two years Rebekah and Breeze couldn't show their affection for each other. They communicated through the spoken word in secret, through the written word, and through limited telephone calls. During those years, Rebekah lived for his letters. They were like food for the hungry, a lifeboat for the drowning, water for the thirsty, and music for her soul.

He was a Pisces, the sign of the fish and he referred to himself as "The Fisherman," and almost all of his love letters to Rebekah began with *Dear Ice Cream."* Rebekah had shown Mamie some of Breeze's letters and Mamie hadn't judged her or called her a "foolish woman." Rebekah had made reference to that when she spoke at Mamie's funeral. The following letters were ones that Rebekah kept dear to her heart.

****

"Dear Ice Cream;

"I've known the loneliness of the long, sad nights that drift on memories. I've known the glorious days of being with you, although there are days when we're not allowed to touch or even dare to show recognition, or acknowledge the presence of each other. But, my love, they can't stop the Fisherman from loving his Ice Cream.

Sometimes, I'll do and say things contrary to my heart's feelings. But try to bear with me. Try to understand that I'm only human and subject to man's imperfections. I want to spend a lifetime with you. Each time I think of you, my heart sings. I think in terms of poetry and I feel like a kid.

These months of loving you have been so special to me. They have been the best times of my life. I feel they're just a sample of what's to come, a sample of the life we'll have together. All my love I give to you freely, without guilt and without shame. You touched my heart and set my soul aflame. Your love has filled my life with so much meaning and tenderness. You've taught me how to live and what it means to be loved without reservations. You have taught me how to live each day in happiness.

Regardless of what happens inside these walls, as long as I know you love me, I can handle anything. Your honesty amazes me. I've built my life on lies, but when I look into your beautiful green eyes, the honesty I see there makes me want to cry.

Your respect I'll always treasure. The sound of your laughter makes me happy. And your love I want forever. I know that forever is a lifetime, but a lifetime is what we'll have. We'll spend a lifetime, living our dreams together, and loving each other with tender care.

Sitting in a prison cell, early in the morning, has a strange effect on me. Thoughts race and run through my head. What causes a person to dream of things out of their grasp? Somewhere along life's road, I lost touch with what is considered real happiness and peace of mind.

Pray, my love, that time does not drag its feet, that it will hurry for our chance to enjoy the beauty of it all. Pray that we grow old together, and when the years have turned our hair to silver, and the days of our youth are left far behind, we'll have memories that we'll treasure in our hearts and minds.

I've watched myself stumble and fall. I've felt myself reach and not touch. I've loved and yet, I hadn't found the ultimate love, until now. I've shared tears with pain, and laughter with joy. Many things I've done, but none has sustained me as your love has. So tell me, my love, are you real or are you just a window of my prison cell?

I pray that the angels walk before you, behind you and on each side of you today, while God watches over you from above. I wish you warm sunshine and Christmas Eve nights.

I reached for the stars tonight as I passed the moon, searching for a moonbeam to bring me to you. I had a fleeting thought of you as I passed Venus. Should you think of me, by all means treat me kindly in your thoughts, and I shall always remain compassionately yours in *heart and body.*

The Fisherman

****

Dear Ice Cream:

I hope your day was a very pleasant one, the kind that has you wishing for others like it. I pray you will never experience in life anything like my days of confinement. I'm well and keeping the memories of you as a day-lifter. Gee, love, my lover, I miss you considerably. I know seeing is believing, but it's hard to understand the whispering of your heart when everything outside of you discusses other things that are also important, maybe not as important, but important nonetheless. Do you understand what I'm trying to say?

I admire and understand certain things about you that, at times have left me puzzled. I've learned much about myself, too. Not everything, but enough to realize what I don't know. I've met a lot of people in my lifetime, but never have I met anyone who will have such a lasting effect on my life as you. I love you.

I looked out the hole of my cell this morning and I whispered to you. I said, "Hurry, my love, the morning sun has yet to reach the hour of noon. Love, do hurry. The birds have had their fill and are now singing. Hurry, love, before the windows of the world greet my day."

I caught a sparrow today. I saw a miracle in a rainbow. I talked to an angel by the garden. I laughed and ran with love over meadows and mountains. I felt and thought about you when loneliness passed by. I watched a sunflower kiss the sun rays, and guess what else? I wrote it all down for you.

Wow! What a wonderful day I spent day-dreaming. I must be high because these dreams can only be the thoughts and imaginations of a confined man.

I feel alone. I don't know why I'm feeling like this. I guess I'm experiencing the humdrum of depression. You don't know how lonely it is being in prison, not sure if you will live until the next day. You may not hear this from many men, but I need constant caressing and love. My ego has been badly bruised and denied for so long. I'm in desperate want and need of your inspiration. Can you understand my pain? Can you understand that I need you? No, I don't think you believe I need you. That doesn't fit your idea of independence.

Forgive me, my love. I don't mean to take my frustrations out on you. I think I'll write tomorrow. Perhaps tomorrow will be nice to the Pisces. You take care and know beyond a shadow of a doubt that you are loved, wanted, and needed by yours truly. You're my friend, my life, my love...aren't you? Just me loving you.

The Fisherman.

****

She loved the way his words made her feel. She wanted to stop working in the prison, but she knew as long as Breeze was there, she would be, too.

For two years, Breeze fantasized about the first time he would hold Rebekah, his Ice Cream, and show her love. Rebekah fantasized about the first time she would be held in his arms without the interference of the prison guards.

It was a sunny spring morning. The birds were singing and the flowers gave a fragrance that intoxicated minds. It was the day Breeze went home to Rebekah. Finally, they could fulfill their dreams of being together. They both knew the time and day he would be released, it was standard prison policy. Rebekah informed her office that she would be out of town for the weekend. She made all the arrangements, getting the hotel where they would stay. It had to be a place with room service. Everything had to be perfect.

When he walked out through the gate, she was there waiting for him. He ran to her car, threw open the door and jumped in. Before she could speak a word, he kissed her long and passionately, trying to put two years of longing into that first real kiss.

"At last, Ice Cream, I can hold you," he whispered as he held her tenderly. At that moment, they didn't care if they were seen embracing. He was now a free man.

They both were as excited as teenage lovers discovering the meaning of love for the first time. Although it was late in the afternoon when he was released, they went to a restaurant and ordered breakfast. Neither was hungry, they were nervous after waiting for two years for that moment. Now that it had come, they were afraid of disappointing each other in their lovemaking. They had talked about love, dreamed about love and read about love. Now it was time to experience it and they were scared.

Without eating, they went to the hotel. Once inside the room, Breeze said, "We finally won, Ice Cream. We beat'em; they can't stop me from touching you, now."

Rebekah was wearing a lightweight, two-piece, baby blue suit with matching shoes. It was the outfit she was wearing when Breeze first saw her. They relaxed for the first time and shared a glass of wine. She was nervous. She walked to the window and looked out, apprehensive about whether or not she could please him. He stood behind her and enfolded his arms around her waist. She could feel him growing hard against her back. She turned to face him and stood on her toes to receive his kiss.

She changed into a sheer negligee and he undressed to nothing. Lying stretched out upon the bed on the chocolate-colored silk sheets she had brought with her, arching slowly under Breeze's body and feeling the effects of his kisses, Rebekah's negligee worked itself up around her waist and her legs started to open naturally. He removed her negligee and positioned her upon the bed with pillows under her back and thighs. He adjusted her position — like Marty had done — so that she could watch him making love to her, and that's when the loving started.

On her eyes he planted warm kisses. From there he explored her ears and neck, pausing to pay tribute to her cute button nose. From her left breast he sent signals to her right breast, telling it that this same treatment would be rendered unto it also, until the nipples were as erect and as full as the honeysuckle from which the bee steals nectar.

He began his downward travel where her navel and tummy awaited his arrival. With his tongue making little circles inside her navel and his two fingers tracing the shape and contours of her vagina, he experienced and enjoyed the steps to paradise.

Once Breeze had set Rebekah's body on fire and her hips started to slowly rotate under his assault of kisses, he opened the petals of her flower and sent his tongue and lips searching for the channel of her being.

"Why don't you place your hands behind my head and guide me where you want me to go?" Breeze whispered.

She obeyed his instructions.

Hearing her softly moaning with pleasure and gasping for air, Breeze realized that it was time for him to penetrate her and carry her to a much greater state of ecstasy and fulfillment. She used her hand to guide his penis into her waiting vagina. He felt a sudden urge to stab forward with his hips, but she restrained his excitement with the pressure of her fingers, and speaking soft words of endearment.

"Don't hurry, baby," she softly whispered. "The time and moment belong to us for as long as we want them. Tonight we don't have to hide or be afraid of being seen. We've waited so long and endured so many sleepless nights wanting each other. Tonight is ours."

As she gently guided him into her and his arms slid under her shoulders, the weight of his body shifted to his hips and her arms enfolded his body while their tongues found each other and told their secrets. He slowly pushed his hips forward and her thighs encircled his back. As Rebekah pulled and Breeze pushed, they built a rhythm all their own. They made love in such a special way that the colors of the rainbow, the stars and moon dimmed by comparison.

She wanted time to stand still as she licked the sweat of lovemaking from his body. His hands were powerful, carving away her limitations.

"You're so beautiful. Rebekah, can't you see the beauty of our love?" he whispered.

No one had ever made love to her the way Breeze did. She felt her box of limitations expanding and her reservations decreasing.

Her body melted like candle wax. He had given her the key to her own liberation.

"My precious love, my Ice Cream, I love you so very much," he whispered. "Please, please, don't ever forget that."

They stayed together the entire weekend, never leaving the room. They ordered breakfast and ate it in bed. When Monday morning came, she went to work and he went to visit his family. He was to meet her at her condominium that night. They made so many promises to each other, they vowed never to be separated from each other.

She rushed through her day at the office and hurried home to wait for Breeze. She waited all night, he never came. After two days passed, he finally called. He said he was living in a halfway house in Washington, D.C., and he wasn't permitted to make or receive telephone calls for the first week of the "adjustment period." That was what the time of transition from the penal institution into the community was called.

Of course, that was a lie, he had really been living with his other woman, the woman who visited him in prison and whom he called from Myron's office. Rebekah had promised a friend that she would visit her at the hospital. Rebekah told Breeze to meet her at the hospital that day.

When she arrived at the hospital, Breeze was already there waiting for her. He looks so damn good, she thought. I can't wait to get him into bed again and make love with him. She forgot about the broken promises and how she had waited for him and he hadn't come. Two years of yearning overshadowed the fact that she wasn't the one with whom he spent his first week at home. She was remembering the love letters she had received, the poems he had written for her, the nights at the prison when they both cried because they couldn't touch each other and their first weekend together when they made love for the first time. Her heart overruled her brain.

Rebekah couldn't concentrate on lifting her sick friend's spirits. She couldn't think of anything except being in bed with Breeze. She cut the visit short. Rebekah's condominium was an hour's drive from the hospital. When she saw Breeze, she didn't want to wait an hour to make love with him.

"Let's stay at that hotel across the street," Breeze said. "I want to hold you, and driving to your house in this traffic will take too long. Besides, we can have breakfast sent to our room and we won't have to get up," he grinned.

They left the hospital and went to the hotel. She couldn't wait to feel his body against hers again. After such a long time yearning for him, one weekend together wasn't enough. When they went into the hotel's office to register, he didn't have any money. Rebekah paid the clerk. They went into the room and Breeze started searching through the dresser drawers.

"What're you looking for?" she asked.

"Sometimes people leave things behind and I want to see what I can find," he said.

Sure enough, in one of the drawers were old clothes left by whoever had previously occupied the room.

"Yeah! I just hit the jackpot. I'm going to take these home to my sisters and their children. They can use these." He was acting like a child who had just unwrapped a present and discovered it was exactly what he wanted.

"Why do you want that junk? Buy something new to give to them," Rebekah said.

"They'll be glad to get anything I give them," he said, and he put the clothes in a pile to take with him.

She didn't want to spoil the moment, especially since they both had waited so long to be together. She figured this was behavior he had learned from being locked up so many years. With time, she hoped he would change.

He grinned and reached for her, "Baby, we made liars out of them all. We won, baby, we won. Tonight we'll collect our trophy, again. I know I have some strange shit about me, baby, but please be patient. I promise that it'll get better. With you, it's like growing up all over again. The behaviors that I used in the past don't work anymore. But like a fool, I'll probably keep trying them anyway, 'cause that's all I know."

She smiled. "I'll give you time, honey. But one thing I'll not tolerate is to be lied to. I've spent enough time and years dealing with lies, liars, and deceit. I don't need those in my life anymore. If I can't have honesty, I'd rather be alone."

"I'll make this promise to you tonight," he said, "I'll never lie to you and our relationship will be built on honesty, trust, loyalty, and love. This is my commitment to you."

With that, she was confident that all was well with their relationship. He began to unbutton her dress. She moved her body slowly against his and unbuttoned his shirt. After they had removed each other's clothes, they began to move slowly toward the bed as if they were one person. He was still kissing her. When they reached the bed, he gently nudged her to lie down. She spread her legs and circled them around his body. He had an erection so hard, his penis throbbed like a palpitating heart. She was breathing hard in anticipation of making love with Breeze, partly because he smelled so good. She told him to take his time. She wanted to savor the moment.

Breeze whispered, "Can you feel the blood pulsating in my dick? Can you tell how much I need to feel your warmness and wetness surrounding me?"

Rebekah whispered "yes" and held him tighter.

He kissed her neck and kissed between her breasts. Her nipples were standing at attention, her belly rising up and down with each sigh. She whispered to him to hurry and enter her. He obeyed her command, and she drifted into paradise. Each push her body made, his was ready to receive.

They made love all through the night, stopping only to savor being able to hold each other and enjoy the privacy for which they had longed. They rested, caressed each other's body, then resumed their dance of love.

When they were exhausted from lovemaking, Rebekah went to the bathroom and closed the door behind her. When Breeze heard the door close, he jumped up from the bed like a wild man, kicked open the bathroom door, and stormed in, his eyes glazed with rage.

"I told you about that shit! What are you trying to hide with this damn door closed?" he yelled.

"Told me about what shit?" she asked. "Can't I have some privacy?"

"You don't need no damn privacy from me! What are you trying to hide? I want you to keep the door open!"

She couldn't use the bathroom with the door open, she needed privacy. She tried not to use the bathroom when he was awake. But her mind wondered what he meant by, "I told you about that shit." She wondered with whom did he have such a conversation. They had never had a conversation about her closing the bathroom door. She was confused and startled by his behavior, storming into the bathroom in anger.

Rebekah tried to focus on the good qualities of the relationship. He could kiss her and send her rocking, touch her body with his warm hands and send her head into a spin. Feeling his warm, hard body made her shiver, and smelling the fragrance of his cologne mixed with the fragrance of fresh soap made her pant with desire. They discovered lovemaking and pleasure together.

"When we chose to love each other, it was because we saw in each other those qualities which we knew we needed to build a life on," Breeze said. "With each passing day, Ice Cream, I thank God for sending you into my life. You are not the first woman I have loved, but you are the last."

Rebekah got up and walked to the window. She stood there, looking at the moon and stars. She turned to Breeze.

"What we have is so rare and unique. If we could bottle it, we would make a fortune," she said. "It's not about sex. It's about two people finding each other among the millions of people on this planet."

Breeze grinned. "Now, what I would like for you to do, Ice Cream, is come back and lie on the bed, close your eyes, relax your body and turn your mind over to me."

"Is this going to be one of your games where we go on a make-believe trip?" she teased.

"I told you that I'd always make you smile," he grinned. "Now sit back and let's take a ride on my super-sonic rocket of thoughts. Buckle your seat belt. Countdown: 10,9,8,7,6,5,4,3,2,1, blastoff! Our destination is the planet of passion. We'll stop and play on the Milky Way. From there, we'll travel to Pluto, and I'll take the ring from around Saturn, shrink it, and place it on your finger. We'll travel together light years away, into another galaxy into a new time and dimension.

"We're now on the planet of passion. Here, I am King and I crown you Queen. I know all before all is known. Now come and follow me, we shall christen our bedroom. I'll bathe your beautiful body in the tub of stars and pick you up with a moonbeam, then I'll dry your body with sunshine and a warm breeze — I'm the Breeze — I'll lay your naked body on a king-sized pillow of clouds with a silver lining and rainbow sheets. I'll tenderly caress each part of your body and place my big dipper into your orbit, and when you and I reach our orgasm, thunderbolts and meteorites will gracefully carry us into another time. We'll exchange greetings with the man in the moon and he'll marvel at the love two earthlings created who were never destined to love, who have defied all odds and found each other among the millions and millions of other searching souls."

As Breeze talked in his low voice, he caressed her body and made love to her. They stayed at the hotel all night. The next morning they called room service and ordered breakfast. At noon they dressed and left.

A few days later, Breeze called Rebekah, as excited as a child discovering presents on Christmas morning. He had rediscovered apple pie a la' mode.

"Apple pie with ice cream on it. They call it pie a la' mode.' You down with that?" he asked.

"Yeah, I'm down with that," she replied, amused at his question. "I thought everyone knew that pie a la' mode is pie topped with ice cream, said Rebekah."

"My mama told me that I need to start being around women who can teach me something 'cause I've been out of touch so long. She said to stop messin' with these young girls who don't know nothing about life. I've spent so many years of my life locked up, caged like an animal, treated like an animal, and thought of as an animal. A simple thing like ice cream on top of a slice of apple pie is news to me. You must think I'm real backwards."

Rebekah thought it was strange that he didn't know that ice cream on pie was pie a la' mode. It wasn't an invention he missed while in prison. She thought he was a big kid, rediscovering the world. "When did you taste it?" asked Rebekah.

"Yesterday. My mama, my niece, and I went over to my aunt's house and she gave us some. Now that's my favorite desert."

"Yesterday?" Rebekah asked in disbelief. "How could you and your mama go to your aunt's house yesterday? When you were in prison, you told me that your mother had died."

Breeze was silent for a moment. Rebekah could hear the air whistling through his teeth, then he let out a sigh. "Let me tell you something, baby. I've been wanting to tell you the truth for a long time. My mama ain't dead. That was a friend of my mama's who died. But she was a very special friend to me. She was almost as old as my mama and she was good to me. I didn't tell you the truth 'cause I didn't think you would understand. Years ago, I left home and went to live with her. She bought me clothes, gave me money, brought me breakfast in bed, but I couldn't love her. She was just a means to an end at the time."

"Did you have sex with her?" Rebekah asked.

"Baby, that was years before I met you. Let's not talk about the past. Let's concentrate on the future, our future together."

"I need to ask you something else," she said and she asked him about his behavior at the hotel when she wanted to close the bathroom door.

"I thought a lot about that too," he said. "I guess my behavior is the result of me being in prison so much and so long. I have to adjust to privacy. In prison there is no such thing as privacy. I'll get better, baby. I promise, please don't give up on me, yet" he said.

But she was beginning to realize that Breeze wasn't all she thought he was. For one thing, she kept catching him in so many lies, yet he had promised her honesty, loyalty, and truth. He obviously had lied about those, too.

Breeze needed a job. With his record, he couldn't find

employment that paid a decent salary, but Rebekah thought he had potential and a great mind. She thought if given a chance, he would change his life. She convinced the firm partners of the law firm where she worked to hire Breeze as a supply clerk. She thought he could learn how to use data processing machines and develop himself for a better job. It also meant that he and Rebekah would see each other every day.

One day, while Rebekah and Breeze were alone in the office, he pulled her to him and kissed her. His warm body aroused her.

"Oh, I want you so much," he said softly.

"Now, baby?" she asked.

"Yes, right now. I can't wait."

"But suppose somebody comes into the office?"

"Lock the door," he said.

They kissed passionately and she lay down on the thick carpeted floor, they made love. At that moment, Rebekah didn't care who walked in. She wanted Breeze as much as he wanted her. After that first time, each time they were alone together in the office, he wanted to make love. At first she was eager. But she began to worry about getting caught and ruining her reputation. When she hesitated, it aggravated him.

After he had worked at the firm for two weeks, Breeze accompanied Rebekah to a conference in Hunt Valley, Maryland. Breeze and Rebekah were sitting in one of the conference rooms listening to the facilitator present her seminar about computers, the wave of the future. Rebekah noticed a woman sitting on stage — one of the panelists — who kept looking at Breeze. Rebekah looked at Breeze and noticed that he was staring at the woman.

A few minutes later Breeze said, "I'll be back. I have to go to the restroom."

As he stood up, Rebekah noticed that he carried a program booklet in front of him the way he had carried papers to conceal his erection from the prison guards. She knew of no reason why he needed to take a program with him to the restroom. She also noticed that the woman sitting on stage was gloating. Rebekah was angry. She felt that the woman was looking like the cat that ate the canary.

When Breeze returned to his seat, she didn't say anything about the woman. The conference recessed and all participants went into the main ballroom where tables were set for lunch. Each table seated ten people; Rebekah and Breeze sat at a table with eight other people. This made their table full, but the woman from the stage came to their table, anyway.

"Is there any room for me here?" she asked while smiling and looking directly at Breeze.

Breeze looked sheepishly at Rebekah, and avoided looking at the woman. He pretended to concentrate on his glass of water and ignored her question.

"No, there's no room for you here. This table is full," Rebekah said adamantly and obviously annoyed with the woman. "I suggest you look for some other place to sit. I also suggest that you look somewhere else for your other needs, too. You won't find the answer here."

Breeze never said a word, neither did the other people at the table. The woman went to another table. After lunch Rebekah was ready to leave. She didn't want to stay for the second half of the conference.

When they first arrived at the conference, Breeze was driving her car and she sat on the passenger side. There weren't any empty parking spaces close to the front entrance of the building. A sign was posted indicating there were additional parking spaces in the rear of the building. Breeze let Rebekah out at the front entrance, then he drove to the back and parked. When Rebekah decided not to stay for the second part of the conference, she and Breeze walked to the car together. As they approached it they noticed a folded piece of paper under the windshield wiper on the driver's side. Breeze unfolded the paper, it was a note. He read it, laughed and put it into his shirt pocket.

"Let me see the note!" demanded Rebekah adamantly.

"No, it wasn't meant for you," he said, still smiling.

"I want to see the note!" she demanded again.

"Why? It wasn't meant for you. It was meant for me," he said, annoyed at her persistence.

"How do you know it was meant for you?" she asked. "It was on my car. How can it be for you?"

When she said that, he took the note from his pocket, threw it to her and said, "Here, take the damn thing if you insist. I don't know what the fuss is about anyway."

As soon as she read the note, she knew what the fuss was about and so did he. The note was written on a piece of paper towel. The words were scrawled in pencil and read, "Don't look and wonder how it is. Call this number and find out." There was a telephone number on the note.

"Who is this from?" asked Rebekah.

"I don't know. Probably somebody who works in this place," he said, pointing toward the center. Rebekah knew exactly what had happened. Just as he had flirted with the woman on stage at the conference, he had probably done the same thing to some woman passing by the car when he was parking it. The woman interpreted his flirtations to mean he wanted to meet her and she left her telephone number.

They drove back to the office in silence. As soon as they arrived at her office, Rebekah called the telephone number. Sure enough, it was a number to the kitchen at the conference center where the woman was employed. The woman said she thought Breeze was staring at her because he wanted to meet her. Rebekah told the woman that it was her car on which the note was left. She also told the woman that Breeze was her husband.

"I don't want no problems," the woman said. "He was flirting with me. You ought to tell him to stop leading people on. You probably need to put a leash on him."

Rebekah hung up the telephone and confronted Breeze about disrespecting her and flirting with other women when he was with her.

"You're too jealous, girl. I'm only having fun. You need to lighten up some," he said.

Two weeks later he accompanied her to another conference at the Lord Baltimore Hotel. During the conference, he kept fidgeting in his seat and acting bored. Finally he stood up and said he was going to the restroom. When he stayed for over an hour, she went to look for him. She found him sitting in the lobby having a conversation with the shoeshine stand operator, a young woman who appeared to be about nineteen or twenty. They were standing close together talking and laughing, too close Rebekah thought.

Rebekah was angry and jealous. She walked to where they were standing. She ignored the woman, deliberately walked between them and said to Breeze, "I'm ready to go."

"Why are you leaving so soon, is the conference over?" he asked, oblivious to her frustration.

"No, it's not over. I'm just ready to go," she said in an agitated tone.

"I thought you wanted to stay until the end," he said, obviously wanting to stay.

The shoeshine-stand operator put her hands on her hips and rolled her eyes at Rebekah. Rebekah ignored her. Rebekah wanted to slap the woman but decided not to create a scene.

"I didn't say that. Perhaps you aren't ready to leave. You can stay if you want to, but I'm leaving with or without you," Rebekah said and turned and headed for the parking garage to get her car.

"Call me later," Breeze said to the shoeshine girl and then followed Rebekah, cursing under his breath. He and Rebekah argued all the way back to the office. Rebekah tried to explain to him how she felt when he flirted with other women, but he didn't see where it was such a big deal. When it came to women, he was like a wild bull. He had been incarcerated so long and so many times that his social skills were underdeveloped. He appeared to not understand anything about committed-relationships. His life had been one of running in and out of jail, stealing what he needed, breaking promises, lying to different women, and playing by his own rules.

The following day, the woman from the shoeshine stand called Rebekah's office. Rebekah answered the phone and immediately recognized her voice. The woman asked to speak to Breeze.

"Your new friend is on the phone," Rebekah said angrily as she handed the phone to him.

He looked amused at her anger and took the receiver from her hands. After talking with the woman for about ten minutes, he hung up, grinning and said, "She wants to get with me. I don't know why she's calling me."

"How did she get this telephone number?" Rebekah asked.

"I gave it to her. She said she needed a friend to talk to sometime," he said.

"How can you be her friend when you just met her? Do you know this is an insult to me? This is my office. You're having your women call you here on my private line? The more I get to know you, the more I don't want to know you. We're drifting apart and we really haven't even begun," she said adamantly.

He frowned. "You're getting all bent out of shape 'cause I gave some broad my telephone number? Girl, you're trippin.' But I'm gonna hang out with you more often. You're always going to places where there are women who want something out of life. That way, I get to meet upscale women." then he laughed and walked away, rubbing his chin as if the thought of different women was a delicious taste in his mouth. His words were like a razor blade cutting into Rebekah's heart, and he appeared not to care about the effect they had on her. She thought that maybe in time, he would change. But now she was beginning to wonder.

A week later, Gladys rented two suites at the Hyatt Regency Hotel and gave herself a birthday party. Rebekah and Breeze attended. They were standing around talking, when one of Gladys' guests walked in. He kissed Gladys on her cheek, handed her the birthday present he held in his hand and announced, "I just rode up on the elevator with some fine women. They said they were also going to a party and got off on the third floor. I started to follow them," he laughed.

When Breeze heard that, he wanted to go to the party downstairs, but he didn't want Rebekah to go with him. "Come on, man. I'll go down there with you," Breeze said to the guest.

"Naw, I was just kidding," said the man. "I don't know them folks down there and I don't like crashing nobody's party. You never know who might think you're cruisin' their woman and start a fight. You can get hurt like that."

"What do you mean you want to go to another party? You

escorted me here. I'm supposed to be your woman. How can you disrespect me like that? What am I supposed to do while you're off chasing another skirt?" Rebekah retorted in anger.

But Breeze didn't seem concerned that she was upset.

"Look, woman! I'm my own man. I can do what I want to do. I don't need your permission to go nowhere. Why do I need you to tag along with me?" he said. He was hostile and walked away from her, leaving her standing alone.

Montana and Bruce were also at the party and overheard Rebekah and Breeze's conversation. Montana walked to where Breeze was standing and said, "I know I'm getting in your business but I don't care. How can you think it's alright for you to leave your woman alone, while you go cruising other women?"

Breeze shook his head. "My woman ain't got nothing to do with me going to another party. I'm a man. I go where I want to go. I don't need her permission."

Breeze looked around the room and saw another one of Gladys' male guest standing against the wall holding a drink in his hand, watching and listening to his conversation with Montana.

"You wanna go downstairs and check out another party?" Breeze asked the man.

"Naw, man, that's some wrong shit you're about to do. I'm staying here where I belong," said the man.

Breeze walked back to where Rebekah was standing. "I'm not going to the party so you can stop sulking," he said.

Rebekah looked at him and walked away. She was already feeling embarrassed. She didn't want to draw anymore attention to their discussion, thinking she would deal with the situation later after they left the party. She realized that the only reason he didn't go to the party was because he couldn't get another man to go with him.

Rebekah was tired of his womanizing. This was the fourth time he had embarrassed her, three strikes were out and she had allowed him four. A shoeshine clerk, the woman on stage at the conference, and the woman working in the kitchen at the conference. Rebekah was beginning to feel that she had meant so much to him when he was locked up because she was different from the women he had known before he met her. But now that he was traveling in her circle, meeting a different caliber of women than he was accustomed to. He was like a kid in a candy store. He didn't know what flavor to sample, so he tried to sample them all.

Rebekah and Breeze stayed at the party for a few more hours but she really didn't enjoy herself. He was taking pictures with the women who were there without male escorts, flirting and having a grand time. As the hours passed and she mingled with her friends, she didn't see Breeze in the room and went looking for him. She found him in the bedroom of the suite, sitting on the bed next to one woman while another woman stood, leaning against the wall, holding a drink in one hand and the three of them were laughing and flirting with each other.

"I have a headache and I'm ready to go," she said to Breeze. She didn't wait for him to reply. She walked out of the bedroom, said her goodbyes to everyone and started for the door, leaving the party. Breeze realized she was serious, swore under his breath, said goodbye to the women, and walked out behind Rebekah.

They rode home in silence. Rebekah was having second thoughts about their relationship. "I'll drop you off. I don't feel like company tonight," she said, faking a headache.

He tried to shmooze things over with her but Rebekah wasn't giving in that time. "You know what? You don't have to drop me off anywhere. I can get out here and I'll be alright," he said angrily.

Rebekah was tired of his mess. She had had enough for that night. She stopped the car. He got out and slammed the door. She didn't bother to ask him where he was going. At that point, she didn't care.

Rebekah went home, threw herself on the bed and cried. She was beginning to doubt her capabilities of finding "Mr. Right." It appeared that all the men she had chosen were Mr. Right Now.

****

A week later, Rebekah learned that Breeze could be dangerous. She read in the paper that a fifteen-year-old Black girl was found dead in an alley in East Baltimore. The girl had been shot once in the head and her body was lying in a pile of garbage. The girl's last name was the same as Breeze's, that's what made Rebekah curious. When Breeze came to Rebekah's house that evening, she asked him if he knew the little girl. He told her that the girl was his niece.

"What happened?" asked Rebekah.

"She left the house about five o'clock that evening and told my sister that she was going to visit her girlfriend. When she hadn't returned home by midnight, my sister got worried and called me. We went looking for her and found her body about three o'clock in the morning, laying in a dark, dirty alley. The word on the street is that one of my rivals — a man by the nickname of Steel Man, — killed her. I think her murder was to get revenge against me," he said in anger.

Rebekah asked him, "Revenge against you, for what?"

"A drug deal that some people in the hood think I had something to do with," Breeze said.

"Did you have anything to do with a 'drug deal?'" she asked.

"No, baby. I told you, I'm through with that shit," he lied.

He was acting nervous, not wanting Rebekah to know the truth. She suspected that he was lying, but her heart didn't want to believe it.

The next day, Rebekah heard on the radio that a young Black man named Tyrone was found dead in the park. He had been tied to a tree and shot in the head. When Breeze called her that evening she mentioned the news she had heard on the radio about the murder. She hoped that she was wrong, but her gut feelings told her that Breeze knew something about the murder. Breeze told her that the dead man was Steel Man's kid brother, Tyrone. Breeze hinted that the reason for Tyrone's death was payback. Rebekah's legal mind wondered how he knew it was payback if he wasn't involved.

During the news broadcast about the murders, the reporters said that the little girl's death and Tyrone's murder were suspected of being connected. The following day, she read in the local paper about the drug war and more killings. She felt uneasy as she began to suspect that Breeze hadn't changed his environment or his hanging-out buddies.

A week later, Breeze asked Rebekah to drive to New York with him to visit his aunt, Kitty. He wanted Rebekah to meet his favorite relative. Rebekah declined to go. She hadn't forgotten how her mother was killed in New York. And she was still thinking about the murders from the prior week.

At the last minute, Breeze decided not to go. Instead his twenty-seven-year-old uncle, Dwayne, Dwayne's girlfriend, Wanda, and two of Breeze's buddies, Bubbie and Slim, drove to New York together. They planned to spend the night at Kitty's apartment and return to Baltimore the following day.

As it turned out, Wanda was the only person from the group who returned to Baltimore alive. Wanda told Breeze about her trip to New York, and what happened to the others who went with her. She said she was upstairs in Kitty's apartment when she heard loud arguing downstairs. Then she heard a loud noise that sounded like a gunshot. She said she was too afraid to go downstairs, so she hid in a closet until everything got quiet. When she went downstairs, she found Dwayne and Kitty sitting in kitchen chairs with their hands tied behind their backs. They were blindfolded, their mouths were taped shut, and each had been shot in the back of the head. Bubbie and Slim were handcuffed to the radiator. Their faces were battered and bloody. They had gaping shotgun wounds in their chests, and rags stuffed in their mouths.

Rebekah thanked God that she hadn't gone to New York. She might have been in that apartment when the killings occurred. When Wanda told Breeze about the shootings, he hinted that someone might have been getting revenge for Tyrone's killing. The police couldn't find the killers in either crime. Rebekah felt that the police attributed the murders to rivalry between drug gangs and therefore, didn't really put forth much effort to solve the cases.

Rebekah's feelings for Breeze were changing more and more each day as she learned about his past, which hadn't changed, and had become his present and seemingly, his future. The last straw was when he left her office with the data processing machine saleswoman.

Rebekah's firm had purchased new equipment for their offices and the staff were being trained in the use of the equipment. One day the saleswoman was in Rebekah's office training Breeze on the use of the machines. Rebekah thought the woman and Breeze were sitting too close together for training but she kept quiet. She didn't want to show her jealousy. The saleswoman went into the restroom and when she returned, the top three buttons on her blouse were unbuttoned exposing her cleavage. The saleswoman constantly found a reason to bend over in front of Breeze, giving him a clear view of her breasts. Rebekah tried to contain herself, she didn't want Breeze to accuse her of being jealous as he had done in the past, like with the shoeshine woman. When the saleswoman put on her coat to leave, Breeze put on his coat, too.

Rebekah put her hands on her hips in defiance and looked at Breeze, and then rolled her eyes at the saleswoman. At that point, she didn't care if he did think she was jealous. She was livid. Breeze tried to avoid Rebekah's glance.

"I'll be back later. I'm going to show her where to buy some weed," he said without looking at Rebekah.

"I thought you were through with all that junk," Rebekah replied in anger.

"I said, I'll be back!" he snapped, and walked out the door with the saleswoman, without so much as a glance over his shoulder at Rebekah, leaving her standing in the office.

Rebekah sat down and began to cry. She felt as if she had been played for a fool, again. As she put her head in her hands and wept, she noticed a brown bag on the floor under the desk where Breeze sat. She pulled it out and found his journal. She remembered once when he had asked her to read it, he had said that he didn't have any secrets from her. But, again, he had said so many things that she was now learning were lies. She held the journal, contemplating whether or not to read it. She wondered if he had made any new entries since the last time she read it. She decided to read it.

To her surprise, there were entries about several sexual encounters with various women. He had written in details how he met the women, the sexual acts in which they engaged, and comments describing the woman.

After she read the journal, she was furious with herself for believing his lies. Because Breeze hadn't entered dates as to when he made the journal entries, she didn't know if the women came before he met her, or during their relationship. But one thing was for sure, that information wasn't in his journal when he had given it to her to read while he was incarcerated. Maybe he had given the journal to Rebekah to read when he was in prison so that if she found it again — like now — she wouldn't be curious about its contents. She'd think she had already read it.

Rebekah was tired of the mental anguish that seemed to always come whenever she was with Breeze. She knew the type of man she wanted and he was not it. She decided that she wasn't going to allow him to make a fool of her any longer. She was too hurt and too humiliated to confront him about the journal entries. She decided to write him a letter and tell him how she felt. She thought if she saw him face-to-face, she might not have the courage to do what her good sense told her needed to be done. She wrote the following letter:

****

"My love,

"I can remember the nights leaving MCI-J, wishing to God that you were leaving with me. As I walked to my car, I could hear your voice in the still of the night calling, 'Ice Cream, I love you.' No one knew who you were talking to, but I knew. Now, I wonder how many times you called out those same words to someone else.

"I remember the first time I saw you, standing behind the glass cage looking at me. I felt someone staring, I turned and there you were. Soon, looking for you became a habit that I didn't want to break. After you won my heart, why did you break it? After reading your letters and poems, I melted like butter on a hot summer day. But after reading your journal, I died inside.

"Maybe you're saying I got what I deserved because I shouldn't have read your personal journal. Perhaps you're right, I did invade your privacy.

Nevertheless, I'm glad I did. Now I know the real you. I

asked God to show me if you were the man for me and he allowed me to find your journal and read it. It's not just the journal entries about which I'm upset, it's a combination of things such as the woman at the conference, the shoeshine woman and other such heartaches inflicted by you on me.

Call it jealousy if you want to, it really doesn't matter to me anymore what you say. I've had enough. I have received the answer to my prayer. Although it wasn't the answer I wanted, it was the one I needed.

Goodbye, my love. May you find your dreams. Something tells me you're going to spend many years searching for that special someone you already had, and lost.

****

Rebekah put the letter into Breeze's journal. When he returned to the office, she handed it to him and said, "You were hired by this firm because of me. You no longer have a job here, because of me. I suggest you find another place to work. I'm curious to see how long you'll stay out of jail. You have so much potential but your mind doesn't seem to be ready to put your past behind you and move on. You still have that thug mentality and I'm no longer willing to accept that."

Breeze tried to protest. "Baby, please let me explain," he said.

"There is nothing to explain. I've heard enough of your lies. Please, don't make this any harder than it already is. Just go," she said, tears streaming down her cheeks.

He realized that trying to apologize was futile. He stood and looked at her. He slowly raised his hand to brush the tears from her cheeks. She stepped back, out of his reach. He stood and looked at her lovingly, perhaps for the last time. At that moment, he realized how much she really meant to him. But it was too late. He turned and walked out the door with the journal in his hand and whispered to himself,

"Damn, how could I have been so careless to let her find this journal? I blew it, big time. I need my ass kicked."

Rebekah decided that she wouldn't be vulnerable to anyone else. She would now focus on her career and if God wanted her to have a man in her life, He would send one her way.

Breeze read Rebekah's letter and called her on the telephone.

"After reading your letter and thinking about you," he said, "I can't say I'll no longer believe in love because I would be denying the blessing of hearts being united. I'll say, though, that I'll no longer take love for granted. But, you have taken away my miracle of being loved by you. Wherever your spirit goes, my spirit shall follow. Forgive me for hurting you. I never knew how much you meant to me until you took your love from me.

"I know that saying I'm sorry, isn't enough, but I *am* sorry. I'm sorry that I didn't keep your love. I'm sorry that I was too foolish to realize how important our relationship was to me. I'm sorry I lied to you. I'm sorry I hurt you. If you can find it in your heart to give me one more chance, I promise that I'll never again have to say, 'I'm sorry' and I'll never again make you sad. So, my dear beloved, send me your love, that I may find peace here on earth once more."

Rebekah had tears in her eyes, and without saying a word, she hung up the telephone.

"You'll never get another chance to make me sad," she whispered.

CHAPTER NINETEEN
Searching For Answers

Rebekah didn't know if she was really in love with Breeze, or in love with the idea of being in love. Breeze was refreshing and fun to be with, like Donnie was. He reminded Rebekah of Donnie in many ways.

Breeze had been out of prison for over a year and hadn't seen Rebekah since she broke up with him eight months earlier. He thought about her many times. Too late he realized that she was the best thing that ever happened to him. His entire family told him that he was a fool for throwing away his future.

Breeze attended a jazz concert at the Coliseum with three of his buddies, Pee Wee, Wiley and Little Man. They were standing outside, admiring the beautiful women entering the Coliseum when Rebekah walked in, wearing a red leather dress — that showed the curves of her body — and a matching long red leather coat trimmed in mink from the collar to the hem and around the sleeves. She was with the mayor, members of the WOMAN Power Club, and other political figures. They had front row seats. Because it was a benefit affair, Trukes and Rosenberg law firm had purchased tickets and part of the proceeds were being donated to WOMAN Power.

"Look at the fine women," Wiley said. "I feel like I done died and gone to heaven. Man, this is what I call class. One day I'm gonna have a woman like one of them, and travel in high society circles. That ain't nuthin' but money and this ain't nuthin' but the truth, fah-real!"

Breeze wasn't looking at all the women. He was trying to find a way to get Rebekah's attention. He pointed to Rebekah and said to his buddies, "See that woman over there in that red leather outfit, she knows me. She used to be my lady."

Wiley laughed. "Yeah, right, a woman like that knows a nigga like you, huh? Like we believe that shit, you wish," he said and kept laughing.

"I'll show you, come on" said Breeze.

They walked over to Rebekah, and Breeze said to her, "Hello, Ice Cream. I've missed you. My friends here don't believe you know me."

Rebekah looked at him as if she were looking straight through him and said, "I'm sorry, sir. You must be mistaken. My name is not 'Ice Cream' and no, I don't know you." She looked away and walked down the aisle to her seat.

Little Man laughed. "I thought you said she knew you. Man, you don't know no woman like that. That's class. She's outta your league."

Breeze and his buddies went inside and sat in the balcony. He could look down to where Rebekah was sitting on the front row. She looked around, searching until she spotted Breeze. Their eyes met for a few seconds and she quickly looked away. Throughout the performance she would glance at him and then look away. Each time she glanced at him, she found him staring at her. When their eyes met the second time, they just stared at each other for what seemed like an eternity to Breeze. Even when she wasn't looking at him, she could feel his eyes burning through her like hot coals. Breeze was remembering and he hoped she was remembering too, the night they had promised that they would never part.

"We'll always be together," she had said that night. "Promise me that we'll always be together as we are tonight."

"I promise you," Breeze had answered. "I'll always love you the way I love you tonight." He had raised himself up to get on top of her as they lay in bed. She held him at arm's length in mid-air, caressing his body with her eyes. He remembered the words she whispered that night, so softly and so long ago: "Precious are the walls that shield you from eyes that are not mine." He shook his head as if to make the memories go away.

When the concert was over and people were leaving, Breeze rushed downstairs trying to see Rebekah before she left. He was standing by the door, waiting for her. As she passed by him, she paused, and without looking at him she whispered, "That's for hurting me. You'll never get another chance," and she walked out of his life for good.

As she walked away, Breeze watched her walk out of his life and this time, he knew it was for good. He had tears in his eyes and he whispered, "Good bye, happiness. I'll always love you, Ice Cream."

As his buddies rushed down the stairs, Breeze quickly wiped his eyes before they could see him cry.

Rebekah never looked back. Breeze's words of endearment had lost their magic. She knew that he didn't know what love was, and back then, neither did she. But she knew what love wasn't.

****

A year later, Rebekah received a call from Breeze's mother. "Hello, may I speak to Rebekah Mosley?" the caller said.

"This is she."

"Miss Mosley, this is Mrs. Fontain, Curtis' mother."

"How are you, Mrs. Fontain? This is a surprise. I never expected to hear from you. How is Curtis doing?"

"That's the reason I'm calling. He died last month from meningitis. I wanted to call you earlier but I couldn't find your telephone number. His death left me so devastated that I couldn't bring myself to go through his personal belongings. But today I started packing up his things and I found one of his bags with some papers in it. On one of the papers was your telephone number. Before he died, he made me promise to call you and give you a message.

He told me to say these exact words: 'I'll always love you, Ice Cream. Please forgive me.' Those were his last words. He said you would understand. Do you know what he meant?"

Rebekah's hand gripped the telephone so hard that her knuckles turned white. She felt as if she wanted to scream but no sound would come from her throat. Tears were falling so fast, she couldn't see.

"Yes, ma'am, I understand," said Rebekah. "Was he at home or had he gone back to jail?"

"No, he hadn't gone back to jail. He was making greeting

cards and had gone back to his art. He had a contract with several places to sell his cards. He used to say he was going to be the person Ice Cream thought he was and then he was going to beg her forgiveness. Do you understand any of that? Do you know who Ice Cream is?"

Rebekah choked back a sob. Her throat was tight. She hesitated before she spoke so her voice wouldn't tremble. "Yes, ma'am, I understand what he meant and yes, I know Ice Cream. Thank you for calling."

Rebekah hung up the telephone and wept for what was, and for what could have been. Breeze was twenty-three years old when he met Rebekah. He was twenty-five when he was released from prison. He was twenty-seven when he died. He never made his thirtieth birthday.

"What a waste," she whispered. "Maybe he really did love me in his own special way. He just couldn't get it together."

****

Rebekah felt that something was missing from her life. She felt like a failure in her personal life, like a success in her professional life, and like she was still searching for answers in her spiritual life. She fell on her knees and prayed.

"Lord, please help me. Please forgive me. I've been a drug addict, a prostitute, a liar, and a whore. I've been with men and women, but I've had enough. Use me, Father, whatever Your will. I can't make it without You. I don't want to make it without You. Please help me."

Then she began to weep.

For hours she lay prostrate on the floor praying. She fell asleep lying on the floor and dreamed about her mother. In Rebekah's dream, Beulah was as beautiful as she was when she was twenty-five years old. Rebekah had seen a picture of Beulah when she visited the house after the funeral.

"Mama, I'm sorry," Rebekah said, tossing and turning while talking in her sleep. "I'm sorry I caused you to die. I'm sorry I was ashamed of you. I'm so sorry. Please forgive me!"

"Baby, I came back to tell you to let go. You've been on a wild journey to nowhere, but now it's over. There's too much work to do. You were not to blame for my death. It was time for me to leave. Don't feel sorry for me, I'm home, "Beulah said in Rebekah's dream.

"Mama, you're beautiful. I want to come with you," Rebekah cried.

In Rebekah's dream, Beulah was standing straight; she had beautiful skin and her raven- black hair rested on her shoulders. She was slender and her green eyes were bright and clear like Rebekah's.

"It's not your time. You'll know what to do when it's time. Listen to Lola. She's a good woman. Use the insurance money and remember our dream to help women. Remember what Williemae went through and help other women like her. God heard your cry. He heard your prayers. He saw your anguish. He knew you needed help before you asked for it, but He needed *you* to know. He wants you to look inside yourself for peace. You have the power to help yourself. I must go now but know that I love you, love yourself, and understand that God loves you best." Then she was gone.

"Mama, Mama!" Rebekah shouted. She hollered so loud, she woke herself up. Then she realized that she had fallen asleep. She didn't know if she had been dreaming or if Beulah was actually sent as an angel in answer to her prayers. Rebekah did know that her dream had been too real. She could swear she smelled lilacs, the fragrance of Beulah's favorite cologne. For the first time in weeks Rebekah slept in peace.

The following day was Sunday. Rebekah dressed and went to church. Before the service started, she went to the altar and knelt to pray. When she finished praying and was getting off her knees, she saw Anita walking down the aisle, coming toward the altar. Rebekah hugged her and told her she wanted to talk to her after service.

The Praise and Worship singers started singing and asked the congregation to join in. Their singing was usually an indication that the service was about to start. As they sang, the ministers of the church took their seats in the pulpit. Rebekah looked at the program and saw that Reverend Berneda was going to preach the sermon.

Reverend Berneda preached about God using ordinary people to do extraordinary things. She talked about how God brings people up from the ashes and uses them to glorify His Kingdom. Rebekah felt as if Reverend Berneda was talking directly to her.

Other WOMAN Power members also attended the service. After service, Rebekah and Anita walked out of church together and went across the street to the ice cream parlor. They went inside, ordered two ice cream cones and sat at a table by the window.

"It seems that you have a lot on your mind, Sis," said Anita.

"I do," said Rebekah. Then she told Anita about her dream.

"Wow, that's heavy," said Anita. "It seems that your mother is trying to tell you something. Isn't this the second time she has visited you in a dream?"

"Yeah, she visited me when I was in the hospital. I think she's trying to help me get prepared to do the work of the Lord," said Rebekah. "I'm thinking about resigning from the law firm to become the full-time director of WOMAN Power. What do you think about that idea? I haven't mentioned it to anyone else. What do you think the other members will say?"

Anita jumped up from her seat and hugged Rebekah. "They will be elated as I am," said Anita. "But resigning from the firm, that's a big decision. You'd be giving up a good salary. Are you sure this is what you want to do? How will you handle your personal expenses? WOMAN Power doesn't have enough money to pay a salary comparable to what you're presently earning."

"I know, but I think it's time that I stop thinking about myself and do what God wants me to do. Mama keeps returning to talk to me in my dreams. She's trying to tell me that it's time for me to follow our dream, hers and mine. I keep hooking up with the wrong men. I keep looking for Mr. Right and all I find is Mr. Wrong, and Mr. Right-Now. Maybe if I stop looking God will send me Mr. Right-on or Mr. Right-for-me when the time is right. Every time I come out of a relationship, I think about Donnie and the mistake I made by not marrying him."

"Stop worrying about the past. You can't change it so learn from your mistakes and move on. That's what you always tell me," said Anita.

"That's good advice," said Rebekah. "So, what you're telling me is that I need to take my own advice, huh?"

"Yeah, that's right," said Anita.

They both laughed.

Rebekah and Anita sat, ate their ice cream and looked out the window. The 9:00 o'clock morning service had ended and they could see the congregation leaving the church. Gladys and Cynthia stopped in the parlor, ordered ice cream, spoke briefly with Anita and Rebekah, then left, promising to talk later on in the week.

"What drives you?" asked Anita. "We really need the services of WOMAN Power but what's motivating you to want to dedicate all of your time to the organization?"

"It's been my dream since I was a little girl," said Rebekah. "My mama and I used to dream about helping other women. Mama's friend, Miss Williemae, lived two doors from us, and was abused by her husband, Mr. Tanner.

"One day when I was a little girl, I saw her being abused by him and I've never forgotten that. Cecelia was a little girl who lived next door to us. She and her family lived between our house and Miss Williemae's house. We were playing in Cecelia's yard one evening when we saw Mr. Tanner beat Miss Williemae. Miss Williemae ran and hid under their house, bleeding from a cut over her eye and from her mouth, and her eyes were swollen.

"We heard her crying and screaming when he beat her. We felt sorry for her 'cause there weren't any organizations to help battered colored women. Mama and I used to lay in the grass under the sky and dream about what we would do when I grew up. We talked about starting an organization to help women. That's how the idea of WOMAN Power was born. But my life is so messed up, I need as much help as the women we're trying to help," said Rebekah.

"You might as well stop talking like that," said Anita. "I believe that everybody has skeletons in their closets. I know I do and so do all WOMAN Power members, including Reverend Berneda."

"I don't think Berneda has ever done anything that she's ashamed of," said Rebekah. "She's such a sweet and God-fearing woman."

"You'd be surprised," said Anita. "We had lunch together last week and I was shocked when she told me that she used to be in the world like we were. You should talk to her about her past. She'll tell you. She's not ashamed of where she came from. She said if God can forgive her, she 'ain't studin' 'bout nobody else.'"

They both laughed.

"That sounds just like her, too," Rebekah said, and laughed again.

"But, seriously, before you make your final decision and even before you talk to Berneda, why don't you talk to God again? He'll answer your prayers. You know that for yourself," said Anita.

They finished their ice cream and got up to leave.

"I have a case to prepare for tomorrow," said Rebekah. "I'd better get home. I'll call Berneda and see if we can meet before I make my final decision about resigning from the law firm."

Rebekah went home and got on her knees. She prayed for guidance, forgiveness, mercy, and directions for her future. Because of her past, Rebekah felt unworthy of doing God's will. But, through Reverend Berneda, He showed her that everyone has baggage. God showed her that even His chosen people who preach and teach His Word have come through many of life's obstacles.

****

Rebekah knew that she needed help before she made such an important decision about resigning from the law firm. She was considering making a major career move and she needed to be careful about what she decided. The following day, she called Berneda.

"I have a major decision to make about my future and I value your advice," said Rebekah.

"I'm honored," said Berneda. "I'll have some free time tomorrow about noon. Why don't you stop by, then? We'll have lunch and talk, girl talk."

The following day Rebekah went to Berneda's house. Berneda had prepared sandwiches and salads for their lunch.

"I'm always honored to have one of my sisters visit me during the day for lunch," said Berneda, "'cause I know how busy y'all are. And when you can take time out of your busy day for me, I feel blessed."

Rebekah laughed. "We, the WOMAN Power members, are blessed to have you as a member. We feel blessed because you have such a sweet spirit."

"The feeling is mutual," said Berneda. "When you called me, I got the feeling that you had something troubling your mind. What can I do to help?"

"I don't know. I'm struggling over a decision of whether or not I'm worthy to direct other women. My past is so sordid," said Rebekah.

"God knows your past, present, and future," said Berneda. "You are where you need to be. I've had some not-so-good situations in my life, but I know that God has forgiven me, and I also know that He doesn't keep a file on my mistakes. He does the same for you. Stop beating up on yourself."

"You may have made some mistakes in your life, but I bet they weren't as horrible as mine. Y'all really don't know about my past," said Rebekah.

"I don't need to know," said Berneda. "I know you're a fine woman, a gifted attorney and a Christian. You have to answer to God for your own actions. You don't owe me or anybody else on earth an explanation about your past. I'm going to share something with you about my past.

"Wendall and I were childhood sweethearts. We got married when we were teenagers and we've been married for thirty-eight years. We've gone through so many battles together that sometimes we both look back and laugh about the hard times. People talk about how to love a colored man, how to treat a colored man, how to marry a colored man. But I think the most important point is how to *stay* married to a colored man. Colored men are beautiful creatures who have been emasculated by white men, and sought after by white women because of the myth of them having large penises. They're thought of as sex machines, aren't trusted by colored women and, in some cases, are disrespected by colored women. Why? Because over the years, colored women have been conditioned not to trust or respect colored men."

"I envy you and Wendall for being together for so many years. When I see a couple with staying power like that, I know that God must have joined y'all together," said Rebekah. "What's the secret of y'all staying together so long?"

Berneda smiled. "A lot of people ask me that question. Wendall and I were in the world before we were called to preach. Honey, we were something else! Wendall used to get so drunk that he'd pass out on the front lawn. I had to drag him into the house before the neighbors saw him. But I did my dirt, too. I wasn't exactly an angel. Wendall isn't all to blame for the turbulent times of our younger years. I didn't do much to help the situation; I did my own thing. When he was in the streets telling other women how good they looked, some man was telling me how good I looked.

"There was one man named Sam, who used to work at the cleaners around the corner from our apartment. I kind of liked old Sam. He was tall, dark, and handsome. I knew Wendall was playing around with other women. I just couldn't catch him. Then I stopped trying." Berneda sighed wistfully, shaking her head at the memory of what used to be.

"Sam kept asking me for a date, and one night I was angry because Wendall had stayed out all night so I agreed to go out with Sam. We went to a motel and as soon as we walked inside, my stomach started hurting. It must have been my nerves, but Sam thought I was lying, and pretending that I had a stomach ache to keep from having sex with him.

"'You can have a stomach ache or any other kind of ache, but I'm going to tear that little old pussy up,' he said.

"I felt cheap. There I was, getting ready to have sex with a man from the cleaners in the neighborhood. I ran out of that motel so fast, honey, he didn't have time to unzip his pants. I always carried enough money with me to get home. I used to call it my 'mad money,' in case I had to pay my own way home. I used my mad money, got a taxi and went home. Needless to say, I changed cleaners."

They both laughed. It was hard for Rebekah to picture Berneda with another man. But just imagining her running and ducking Wendall made Rebekah laugh so hard that tears ran down her cheeks.

"But that was a long time ago," said Berneda when she could finally control herself. "I kept praying that God would change Wendall and me. I learned that you can only change yourself. But I found that if we trust in God, everything will be all right. Someone once asked me what my favorite passage in the Bible is. I said, 'And it came to pass.' The person looked at me as if I were crazy. Then I explained, 'Don't you see? Trouble doesn't come to stay. It, will pass.'

"My mama used to tell me 'Don't prepare your man for another woman.' I didn't know what she meant until Wendall and I had been married for almost five years. She meant when you marry young, sometimes you don't have the patience to weather the storm. A lot of storms will come into your life, but if you just face them together and don't give up so easily — don't abandon the ship at the first sign of trouble — you both will grow into the people you each thought the other person was when you first married.

"When I counsel young women, I tell them to ask themselves 'Would I marry him now, given what or who he has become?' I ask them, 'If you didn't remember the hard knocks and emotional pain that it took for him to become who he is or for you to become who you are, would you marry him now?' That forces them to take a look at their present situation."

Berneda advised young married women who are considering separation from their spouses to, "Look at him. You've had your own problems. If you learn to be who God meant for you to be, you won't have time to worry about what your man is doing or who he's doing it with. If you pursue your own goals and develop yourself, you'll find that happiness lies within yourself. Live your life. Start a career. Get an education. Become independent. I don't mean desert your man. I mean be a part of the team instead of being someone who will accept anything just to be able to say you have a man."

"I needed those words of wisdom," said Rebekah. "I've

made mistakes in relationships thinking that I needed someone else to make me feel worthwhile. Do you think I'm making a mistake by resigning from the law firm?"

"I think you're on the right track," said Berneda. "Just keep trusting in God. He'll show you the way. But I think it's commendable that you want to devote all your time to making the organization work. It sure is needed."

They talked a while longer and Rebekah left feeling more confident and self-assured than she ever had before.

A month passed and Rebekah submitted her letter of resignation to the law firm. It was hard leaving. She had so many fond memories of working there. The law partners of Trukes and Rosenberg gave her a going-away party.

"You haven't gotten rid of me," she laughingly told Rochelle. "I'm in your life forever. In fact, I want you to help me with clerical functions for WOMAN Power."

"That's all you got to do, tell me what you want," said Rochelle. "You and the members have been so good to me, my feelings would have been hurt if you didn't need my services."

Josh Trukes hugged Rebekah and told her that she always had a home and a friend. "If things don't work out for you, you know where to find me. You have one of the finest legal minds I've had the pleasure of working with and the door to this firm is always open to you," he said.

Rebekah often wondered what happened to his wife Candace, but she wouldn't dare ask him about her.

The Sunday after Rebekah resigned from the law firm was Women's Day at the Ray of Hope Baptist Church. Rebekah was the guest speaker and the WOMAN Power members were in attendance. She sat in the pulpit with Reverend Berneda, Cynthia, the Chairwoman of the Women's Day Committee, and other women on the program. The women of WOMAN Power made a $2,000 donation to the church's building fund in Mamie's memory. Reverend Berneda was at the podium praising the women for the work they were doing in the community. She asked the club members to stand. They all stood, smiled and nodded their heads to the congregation as the congregation gave them a standing ovation. Reverend Berneda told the congregation that she too was a member of WOMAN Power and said how proud she was to be associated with such a fine organization. When she introduced Rebekah as the guest speaker, she informed the congregation that Rebekah had made a major career move by leaving a very lucrative position with one of the prominent law firms in Maryland to take the position as Executive Director of the WOMAN Power Club.

As Rebekah stood at the podium prepared to deliver her speech, she received a standing ovation. She made a moving and enthralling speech. She told the congregation that the club was her mother's dream. When she finished speaking the congregation gave her another standing ovation and Rebekah sat down, tears in her eyes.

Reverend Berneda returned to the podium and introduced the other original founder of the organization, Anita. "I'm glad to be the third original member who's here today. Mamie, our fourth original member, one of the founders, and the person who named the organization, has gone to a higher reward. God needed her home. But I know she's with us today in spirit. So, if you will, just wave to her," she said.

And they waved.

****

It had been almost two years since Rebekah resigned from Trukes and Rosenberg. She had remained in contact with the attorneys at the firm and used that relationship to help women who came to WOMAN Power and needed legal advice. The attorneys provided the services *pro bono*.

Rebekah was in the office at the outreach center working on a grant to get funding for WOMAN Power. The board of directors of the outreach center was meeting without Rebekah's knowledge. She was also a member of the board but this night, the meeting was about her. After the meeting had adjourned, the board members went to Rebekah's office.

Rebekah was surprised to see them. "What are y'all still

doing here?" she asked. "I thought I was the only one working late tonight. I see the entire board is here. Was there a meeting that I forgot about?" she asked knowing how busy she had been lately.

"There was a meeting," said Berneda, "But we thought it was best if you didn't attend. You might have tried to talk us out of what we wanted to do."

"This sounds serious," said Rebekah. "Does this mean I'm fired? Should I be looking for another job?"

They all laughed.

"Well, that's what we wanted to talk to you about," said Gladys. "We have unanimously voted to submit your name to the Governor to be included on a list of attorneys from which one name will be selected to fill a judgeship at the District Court of Maryland. That's it! No discussion!" she teased.

Rebekah was overwhelmed. She was speechless. She stared at the board members, not knowing what to say. Her eyes filled with tears.

"I don't know what to say," said Rebekah.

"Say, 'yes,'" said Berneda.

"I've seen a lot of my somedays come true," said Rebekah. "I've said 'someday' I would finish college and I've done that. I said 'someday' I would start an organization for women, and I've done that. Now you're talking about me becoming a judge. I've said that someday I will write a book about my mama," said Rebekah. "I want to write about her life. I'll call it 'Eyes of the Beholder,' because she had such a beautiful spirit. She had an inner beauty and she loved everybody."

"Doesn't the proverb say 'Beauty is in the _eye_ of the beholder,' instead of _eyes_ of the beholder?' asked Berneda.

"You're right," said Rebekah. "But I want to send the message that the definition of beauty is individualized according to the perceptions of many different observers. Therefore, I chose to use the word _eyes._

"Okay, okay, when will you write the book?" asked Berneda.

"I don't know, someday," laughed Rebekah.

They all laughed.

"Do you really want to submit my name? I'm thirty-six years old. Don't you think I'm too young to be a judge?" asked Rebekah. "And what about my past? Y'all know the baggage I carry."

"You are absolutely not too young," said Reverend Berneda. "We need young judges. The defendants are mostly young Negro men and women. They need you. You will be an asset to the bench and certainly to our people. No, young lady, this city needs you and your talent."

"And as far as your past is concerned, who can better understand a situation or circumstances than one who has lived the experience? If God can forgive you, who are we to judge you?" said Gladys.

"Well, if you think I'd make a good candidate for judge, I'll accept the challenge," said Rebekah. She was reluctant to become a candidate, not knowing who would take her place as the leader of WOMAN Power. It was Rebekah's baby and she wanted to ensure that it was well managed.

"You'll make the best judge," said Cynthia.

When Trukes and Rosenberg heard about Rebekah's nomination, they supported her and wrote letters to the Governor.

Six months later, Rebekah was appointed a judge of the District Court. Being a judge at the District Court level allowed her to deal with the community, traffic cases, landlords who wouldn't fix their properties, domestic violence, and first-time offenders.

The WOMAN Power Club elected Anita to take Rebekah's position as Executive Director of the organization and Rebekah was elated.

"I'll still be here to help," said Rebekah, "but I'm so glad they chose you. You've been with me from the beginning of my dream. I feel like I'm leaving my baby in good hands."

They all agreed.

CHAPTER TWENTY
No Easy Road

The WOMAN Power members were proud of the successes of the women they helped over the years. They received referrals from different sources. Many women were referred by community halfway houses and homeless shelters, some were referred by local churches, some women learned about the organization through word-of-mouth, some were referred by community centers.

They were especially proud of Kathleen Brown, a young woman Montana and Rebekah met at a social event at the Lexington Terrace Projects community recreational center. Montana was there to encourage young women who knew how to style hair to become entrepreneurs, return to school, get their cosmetology licenses and start earning money to get out of the projects. Rebekah talked with the women about finishing school.

"I started out just like you," Montana told the crowd of women. "Now my partner and I own our shop and building. They used to call me a 'kitchen hairdresser.' Now those same people who laughed at me when I told them I was going to own my own business one day aren't laughing anymore."

"I was worse off than some of you," said Rebekah. "If I compare your past to mine, you'd probably be shocked at how much I've had to deal with. If my dreams can come true, yours can, too."

Kathleen sat in the audience and listened to Montana and Rebekah. After the meeting, Kathleen asked Montana and Rebekah if she could speak with them privately. Kathleen said she wanted more from life but she felt that her life was already ruined because of her past. Montana and Rebekah gave Kathleen the telephone number of WOMAN Power and told her to call the following day.

"We've all done things we're not proud of. You'll find that no one in WOMAN Power will judge you," said Montana.

"If you think you've got problems, girlfriend, you need to talk to some of our members. See where they used to be and look at where they are now," said Rebekah. "The first step to changing your life is wanting to change."

Kathleen called the center later that week and spoke with Rebekah, who became her mentor. After four years, the women of WOMAN Power went to Kathleen's graduation from the local community college where she had earned an Associate's degree in social work. Kathleen then enrolled in a four-year college.

As Rebekah sat at the Community College of Baltimore watching Kathleen accept her degree, tears of pride rolled down her cheeks. She quickly wiped them away and chuckled to herself. She was remembering when she first met Kathleen and the stories she shared at a club meeting one evening.

****

Kathleen

Kathleen, her husband Rudy and their four children lived in the Lafayette Courts Projects. She used to say she slept around a lot to get even with Rudy for being unfaithful to her, but in fact, she had started sleeping with different men before she and Rudy got married.

Rudy worked for a company that made fertilizer and Kathleen got a job making window shades. They both planned to work, save money and purchase a house. Kathleen had planned to go to college part-time; but the streets took Rudy. He became an alcoholic and a drug addict and couldn't keep a job. Meanwhile, Kathleen was pregnant again and gave up the notion of going to college. She decided that life had dealt her a lemon.

"I decided that I would raise my children the best I could and make every man pay for my misery," she said. Rudy was violent and belligerent when he was drunk, so I didn't bother him when he went out. I just started having affairs with other men, and after a while I began to like it."

One of Kathleen's lovers was her supervisor, Wesley. Kathleen worked as a clerk with the Department of Motor Vehicles

(DMV). A month after she began working there, Wesley started flirting with her. She liked him, too; he was cute, a flashy dresser, and wore his hair long and curly. Wesley had bracelets on his arms, from his wrist halfway to his elbow, and rings on every finger. He was married to a beautiful woman but that didn't stop him from playing around with other women. A lot of the women at the DMV flirted with him, but they said he was stuck up because he never dated any of them. When he asked Kathleen for a date, she was flattered. She told the other women that he asked her out 'cause he only wanted the best.

"I was such a fool in those days," she told Rebekah. "Wesley only wanted a plaything for one night and I didn't have sense enough to know it. We had a date one Christmas Eve. I never should have gone out with him that night. I needed to be at home with my children. But, I cleaned the apartment, baked cookies, and made sure that everything was ready so I could play Santa Claus when I returned home. I knew Rudy wouldn't be home anytime soon. If we had toys that needed to be put together, I always made sure they were assembled three days ahead of time, 'cause when Rudy came home on Christmas Eve in the wee hours of the morning — if he came home at all — he was always drunk.

"That night, I called the babysitter to come over, and when she got there I left to meet Wesley. We met at a bar, had a few drinks, sat and talked a while, then went to a motel.

"Our sexual encounter was a disaster; he couldn't screw," Kathleen said. "He was so vain, he was pathetic. He wouldn't take off his rings and bracelets while we were having sex, and they scratched my skin. His hair was so greasy that he left rings of grease on the pillow case and on my face. When his bracelets scratched me the second time, I said, 'Look, you got to take that shit off.'

"That insulted him. He was already aggravated because he couldn't get hard. I was tired of his limp dick and him scratching me. He thought he was the finest thing walking and I was tired of his false sense of superiority. He was lying on top of me at the time I told him to take that shit off. He rolled off me and said, 'I ain't got to take a damn thing off.'

"I sat straight up and said, 'You're right. You ain't got to take a damn thing off, but you got to stop scratching me, that's for damn sure. I don't know about you, but as far as I'm concerned this shit is over.'

"He lay there looking at me in disbelief. I guess he wasn't accustomed to women talking to him like that. I jumped out of bed and put my clothes on as he still lay there smoking a cigarette. When I was dressed, I said, 'Either take me home or give me taxi fare. You may think you're Mister Cool but when I'm through putting your shit out at work, you'll be too embarrassed to show your face Mister 'It-won't-get-hard.'

"He was furious. 'Here, you call a taxi. I ain't taking you no damn place,' he said, and threw a twenty dollar bill at me. That made me boiling mad!"

"No, you won't treat me like I'm nothing," I said. "You'll take me back to where you got me or I'll fuck up your reputation, Mister Supervisor. You ain't got no business screwing an employee in your department anyway."

"I was pissed! Who in the hell did he think he was?" she said to Rebekah, "I figured he was as big a 'ho as I was. He was just a male 'ho."

"Did he take you back to where he got you?" Nadine asked.

"You damn right he did, and he was speeding all the way," said Kathleen. "If I hadn't been so angry, it would have been comical. He finally met his match. I was time enough for his tired ass. When we reached the bar, I got out of his car and slammed the door. Needless to say, he never spoke to me again. In fact, he requested and was given a transfer from the department where we worked. I guess he didn't know if I had told anybody about our encounter, and he was too embarrassed to work there anymore. Oh, by the way, I kept the twenty dollar bill."

They laughed.

"I'm tellin' you, I was one of the biggest 'ho's in Baltimore. I'm not proud of my past. I'm just glad that I finally got myself together. My hanging out buddies used to call me 'Whoretta' and at the time, I deserved that name. I used to do some crazy shit, but God changed all that. I've had my share and a whole lot of other women's share, too. That's why they nicknamed me Whoretta. That's also why I thought I had already ruined my life until I met Rebekah and Montana. Y'all don't know, but WOMAN Power saved my life. For the first time since I became an adult, I'm looking forward to a bright future, and for the first time, I feel that I can be a role model to my children. If I can get my life together, anybody can. WOMAN Power was a Godsend for me. Being around positive-minded women is powerful."

"We WOMAN Power women sometimes share with each other our past, and honey, we all got some stories to tell. So, don't feel that you're alone. That's called experience and wisdom. That's why you're so qualified to help someone else, 'cause you've been there. And that so-called nickname of yours, what was it? 'Whoretta?' We could all be called that. We just chose to shake it off and keep on truckin."

"Amen, to that," shouted Rebekah.

They laughed.

"God was just merciful," said Kathleen. "When I had those affairs with different men, I was married to Rudy at the time. I'm just glad that God didn't let Rudy find out about my mess."

"Go on, tell me about the next one, 'cause girlfriend, you're something else!'" laughed Nadine.

They all laughed.

"You're going to crack-up on this one," Kathleen said. "I wanna tell y'all 'bout a man I met while I was standing at the bus stop. It was a cold December evening and I was tired. I had been standing on my feet all evening, putting items on a conveyor belt in the catalog department of Montgomery Ward department store. It was a part-time job for the holidays. They always hired a lot of part-time help during the Christmas rush," said Kathleen.

This day, a red and white convertible pulled to the curb where I was standing. The driver wasn't especially good-looking but he was handsome in a rugged sort of way. He pushed the button and the window on the passenger side rolled down. He leaned over to look out the window at me and smiled.

"'Come on, get in, it's cold out there,' he said. ' I'm a good guy. I just think you're too pretty to be waiting for a bus in this cold weather.'

"I hesitated. I was reluctant to get into a car with a stranger unless I was with my buddies. But it *was* cold. It was one of those bitter cold days when you think your nose will freeze off, you're afraid to cry 'cause your tears might freeze. The wind cuts your face like a switch from grandma's hedges. The heat from the car felt good on my skin, so I got in, grateful for the ride and the heat. He said his name was Albert, but his friends called him Stick Man, because he only bought cars with stick shifts.

"I think we're going to be friends, so you can call me Stick," he said.

"Stick drove me home and gave me his telephone number. During the next few weeks, we talked on the telephone several times. We dated a few times and became good friends. One of the gambling houses in South Baltimore was raided by the police, Rudy was in there and got locked up. So I was left to support myself and our four children. I couldn't afford to make payments on the children's bedroom sets so the furniture store repossessed them. I didn't know what to do. I just sat down on the floor in the empty room and cried. Then I called Stick. I was still crying when he answered the telephone. I told him about my furniture being repossessed.

"I don't know what I'm going to do. My children don't have a bed to sleep in. They have to sleep in my bed with me," I said.

"I have a friend who owns a furniture store and he owes me a favor. Maybe I can help. Stop crying; it's not that bad," Stick said.

"Stick worked at a place that sold car tires. He called his friend — a white man — and made a deal with him. Stick would steal tires from the store where he worked and exchange them with the furniture dealer for a set of bunk beds for my children. Stick asked nothing from me other than friendship. After we had been dating for a month, the friendship turned into something else, and we became lovers. But even when we were in bed together, it was as if it was a friend I was having sex with," said Kathleen.

"One night while at Stick's apartment, he and I were in bed making love when suddenly the lights came on. Stick's hard fell like a cake when the oven door is slammed during baking. He jumped up and in the doorway, with her hands on her hips, stood his girlfriend, Valerie.

"What the fuck is going on?" shouted Valerie.

'Oh, shit,' said Stick. "Valerie, you know you ain't got no business busting in my place like that."

"Stick and Valerie started to argue and I started putting on my clothes."

"I ain't finished with you, bitch!" Valerie shouted at me.

"'Look, ho',' I said. "'If you got a beef, I suggest you take it up with him.'" I pointed to Stick, sitting on the side of the bed trying to put on his shorts. 'I'm in his house. I'm his guest. You marched your ass in here uninvited, you got exactly what you deserve. I ain't gonna be too many mo' bitches, either; if you fuck with me, I'm gonna give you more than you're looking for. I'm walking out of here and if you put your hands on me, I'll blow your fuckin' brains out."

"I kept my hands inside my purse like I had a gun. Stick took the hint and helped me with the bluff.

"'Look, Valerie, don't start no shit. She carries a gun and I don't want nobody to get hurt,'" Stick said.

"Valerie looked scared and started for the door. 'I'm getting the fuck outta here. You can have this dry-fuckin' mutha-fucka,' Valerie said. She almost tripped over her own feet running out the door.

"Stick and I laughed.

"'I'm glad you took the hint about the gun bluff, 'cause she was a big bitch. I'd hate to have to fight her," I said.

"'She's rough,' said Stick. 'Come on, let me take you home. She just might be crazy enough to come back.'

"He drove me home and after that night we stopped being lovers, but we remained friends," Kathleen said.

"I had a lot of one-night stands and a lot of them made a fool out of me," said Kathleen. "I'm just glad that I didn't catch a venereal disease."

"When Rudy got out of jail, his thinking about sex and women had changed. He joined a church called United Brethren that didn't believe in women holding positions in the church, and believed that sex was supposed to be for reproduction instead of pleasure. Rudy stopped having sex with me and I felt rejected. I was on the road to self-destruction and having sex with all those men meant nothing to me. I was looking for something, but I didn't know what. I later learned that I was looking for inner peace. I think I've finally found that and my self-respect too. I figure if I can realize my dreams, with all the mess in my life, everyone and anyone can," said Kathleen.

****

Rebekah looked on, smiling, feeling blessed that she had some small part in Kathleen reaching this day. She almost laughed out loud thinking about the crazy times Kathleen had had in her life yet she made it against the odds.

CHAPTER TWENTY-ONE
Overcomers

The WOMAN Power Club members were holding their monthly meeting at Montana's house. She prepared food for the members as was the tradition of the club. Sometimes they held meetings at the outreach center where their office was located. But they often met at each other's home to enjoy home-cooked food. Sometimes their monthly meetings turned into backyard barbecues for the members and their families.

Montana and Cynthia's business had become a thriving enterprise. They renovated the two buildings, put a clothing boutique on the first floor, a hair, skin, and nail salon on the second floor. On the third floor was a health spa offering physical fitness and body massages.

Montana worked at the bank until the business was able to pay her a salary, then she resigned. She was married to Bruce Marshall, a retired police officer who had been injured in the line of duty and now used a wheelchair. Bruce was participating in a drug raid, and one of the people he thought was a victim was actually one of the criminals. He was shot in the back by a twelve-year-old boy who sold drugs for his mother. The bullet pierced Bruce's spine and left him paralyzed from the waist down. He considered himself lucky; the doctors didn't think he would ever be able to move anything but his head. Luckily, he could move his body, but his legs refused to hold his weight. He had always wanted to be in radio, so he went back to school and majored in broadcast communication.

Montana did hair in her kitchen until she went back to cosmetology school and earned a certificate. She went to school at night and worked at the bank during the day. Bruce was an inspiration to her.

Nadine asked Montana how she came to live in Baltimore. "I never hear you talk about your childhood," Nadine said. "I'm not trying to pry. Rebekah has told us a lot about you but I want you to tell us about your fascinating life. I'm just amazed at how well you and Cynthia have done in your business. I know you're an inspiration to other women. Did you have any experience operating a business before you opened your own business?"

Montana and Cynthia both laughed.

"No, it was trial and error for me," said Montana.

"For me, too," laughed Cynthia.

"I'm just blessed that I found a friend and partner like Cynthia. I'm also blessed to have found a group of women like you WOMAN Power members. I've learned so much from all of you. People don't understand what pain is until they've lived it like we have." Montana looked around the room at the women. "I'm glad to have so many sisters who can identify and who care and want to help others as much as we can. Yes, I have a story. Just like all of you, I have baggage in my trunk, too."

She proceeded to talk about her painful past.

****

Montana

When Montana was two years old, her mother died of leukemia, and Montana went to live with her grandmother. For seven years Montana had felt love, nurturing, and the warmth of her grandmother's home. Montana cried when her father came and took her to live with him, her stepmother, and half-sisters when she was barely ten years old.

"Leave her be, Lester," Montana's grandmother pleaded in vain. "She's been living with me for seven years. I've looked after her, sent her to school, been Mama and Daddy to her. Why take her from the only family she's ever known? With her mama gone," she raised her hands to the sky, "God rest her soul, she ain't got nobody but me. Leave her be."

"My wife needs help 'round the house," Montana's father said. "I come to fetch my youngun' so she can help her step-ma."

"She's too little to help anybody; she's still a baby," Montana's grandmother pleaded.

"She ain't no baby. Look at her, she's big enough to work. I said she's coming wid me."

Montana had always had a weight problem. Her size made her look older than she was. He took her meager possessions and Montana left a life of love and went to a life of hell.

"I was taken to be my step-mama's slave. At least that's the way she treated me. She beat me from the time I got there until the time I left. She called me 'fat cow,' 'big fat pig,' 'tub of lard,' and a lot of other names. I was so scared of that big red woman, I used to wet the bed at night, and when I did she made me get the scrub board and wash the bedclothes by hand in the tin tub in the backyard, while my half-sisters watched and laughed at me. My step-mama and my father had three daughters, — Helen, Lula and Millie — my half-sisters. The two younger daughters, Helen and Lula, felt sorry for me. But Millie, the oldest, was mean like her mama."

Montana was almost in tears as she relived the painful memories of her childhood. When she was fourteen years old, her stepmother told her to deliver a package to Mister Sampson at his store and to come straight back home. Montana delivered the package and ran all the way back home so she wouldn't anger her stepmother. But her stepmother couldn't be pleased with anything that Montana did.

"I did like she told me and went straight back home," said Montana. "But she said I took too long. She said she timed me and I hadn't come straight back. She threw me down on the floor and told Helen to get a switch so she could beat me. Helen brought back a small switch trying to protect me. Helen knew I had come straight back home like I was told. She had seen me running across the field, trying to hurry home. My step-mama wouldn't accept Helen's little switch, so she sent Lula to get one. Lula also brought back a small switch.

"When Millie saw that her sisters were trying to protect me, she got a piece of firewood from the stack by the stove and gave it to her mother. My step-mama hit me in my head with the wood and put a deep gash right in the middle of my forehead. That's what that mark is."

Montana pointed to the scar in the middle of her forehead. The club members sympathized with her. They looked at the scar and felt her pain.

"It's not as visible as it used to be. When I was old enough and could afford it, I had plastic surgery to remove the scar. The doctor did the best he could. It was a deep gash and I didn't get medical treatment when the wound was first made. Because I didn't get stitches to close the wound, it was difficult for the plastic surgeon to completely remove the scar.

"It was an ugly, nasty-looking scar," Montana said. "I was self-conscious about it all of my life. I was also self-conscious about my weight. I guess that's why I fell in love with Bruce. He thought I was beautiful regardless of how scarred my face was and he said he loved every ounce of me. I still battle the calories, but I no longer have a weight problem. I now have a weight concern. I watch my weight for health reasons. But I don't get upset because I'm not a size five."

The women laughed, applauded, and nodded their heads in agreement with Montana.

"Before Bruce got hurt, we used to go dancing every weekend. When we met, I was the host of a local radio talk show. Now he's the host of his talk show."

"That's what I wanted to talk to you about, your radio talk show. How did you do that?" Tracy asked. "Rebekah said you used to have your own talk show but she didn't know the details."

"I just wrote a letter to the station manager and told her my idea for a program, although I didn't know the manager was a woman. I just addressed the letter, 'Dear Program Manager,'" said Montana, "and it worked. The manager asked to interview me on her show. I agreed, and after the show was over she said I had a nice voice. Then she asked me about hosting a show."

"Now, that's nerve," said Rebekah.

"No, that's guts," said Tracy.

"And guess what?" said Cynthia, "that was the first time she had ever hosted a radio talk show, no experience; the challenge was there and she took it."

"That's my girl," said Anita, grinning. "Don't let nothing tell you that you can't do something. You can do anything you want to if you want it badly enough."

"You got that right!" said Rebekah.

"How often were you on the air?" asked Tracy.

"Every Monday evening from six to seven," said Montana. "Bruce was one of the regular listeners. He used to call the studio every week to talk to me. He said I had a beautiful, sexy, voice, but because I was fat, I was too embarrassed to give him my home telephone number. I weighed over two hundred pounds and wore a size eighteen dress. I was afraid he wouldn't want me if he saw me. People always said, '...but she has a pretty face.'

One evening he showed up at the radio studio, just as I was getting off the air. He was tall and had just graduated from the Police Academy. He was standing in the doorway smiling. When I walked out and saw him standing there, I knew who he was before he spoke. I had never seen him in person, but I knew who he was. Isn't that strange? You know how sometimes you talk to a guy on the telephone and he sounds so good, his voice is to die for, but when you see him in person, you want to run and hide? Well, this brother was so fine, his voice fit the package." Montana closed her eyes and thought about Bruce. "Ooh-whee, I can see that hunk now."

The women giggled.

"I was devastated when I saw him at the studio. I planned to ignore him and walk past without saying a word. But he touched my arm as I passed and said in a deep bass voice, 'Excuse me, my name is Bruce Marshall. I'm the person who calls you every week.' I extended my hand and introduced myself. I figured, hell, I didn't have anything to lose. He took me to dinner that evening and now, twenty-five years later, we're still having dinner together. He still thinks I'm beautiful. I wasn't ashamed to undress in front of him. He's the one who encouraged me to go back to college and earn a degree. Girl, that man makes me think I can fly.

"With a man as active as my husband, you'd think our lives would have been totaled when the shooting paralyzed him. But he turned that tragedy into an opportunity to pursue other goals. He's organized a singing group and they're fantastic. He's one of the lead singers and that's something he always wanted to do. The group orders their stage outfits from our boutique. I got back my self-confidence through Bruce's love for me and I began to love myself," said Montana.

"Honey, you're not the only one worrying about weight," said Gladys, as she got another bowl of ice cream and cut another slice of chocolate cake.

"Yeah," said Nadine. "We see that diet chocolate cake you're eating. Is this your third or fourth piece? I lost count."

"Just mind your business," Gladys said jokingly.

They all laughed again.

"Y'all be quiet, I want to hear the rest of Montana's story," said Anita. "Go 'head Montana, what happened next?"

Montana continued telling the group her story. "When my step-mama hit me, she didn't care that I was seriously hurt. She pushed me aside, looked at my blood on her hands and told me to go wash up and wash her clothes before she hit me again. I told her to wash her own damn clothes. I was crying so hard and the pain in my head was so intense, I thought I was going to pass out. She had no reason to hit me. I had done as I was told. I told her that was the last time she would hurt me. I left that house and I told her that I never wanted to see her or my father again as long as I lived."

"What did you do about your wound?" asked Nadine. "Wasn't there a hospital where you could have gone?"

"No, where we lived there was no hospital for miles. Besides, who was going to pay the hospital bill? My father didn't care about me. He just wanted me to be a slave to his high-yellow wife and their high-yellow daughters. They used to call me ugly, black, picky-ninny.

"I put cobwebs and soot on my wound, and I ran up the path, into the woods behind the house, up the hill that overlooked our backyard, and I walked the fifteen miles to my aunt Totsie's house. Hunger pangs made my stomach ache and growl, and my head hurt and was bleeding, but I wouldn't turn back. It was night before I finally arrived at her house. I decided that I wasn't going to take any more beatings from my step-mama.

"I got a lot of beatings. Most of the time it was when Millie had done something and blamed me. My step-mama always believed Millie, she never believed me. Each time I had run away from home, I ran to my aunt's house, who lived five miles away and each time my father came and made me return home with him. But that time I was determined that I would never go back again."

When night came and went, and Montana hadn't returned home, her father went looking for her. He found her at her aunt's house and tried to persuade her to return home with him.

"I told him I wasn't going back. I said I wasn't taking no more beatings from that woman. He said I didn't have to. He said my step-mama ranted and raved all night, threatening to leave him if he didn't make me return and if he didn't beat me for running away. But when he saw my wound, he cried and begged my forgiveness. He said he was sorry for the hell they put me through. He didn't know how badly I was being treated until Lula and Helen told him. He gave my aunt Totsie some money to look after me. I might have misjudged him. Anyway, I never saw him again. I don't know what happened to him. So my aunt sent me back to my grandmother's house. I was glad."

The WOMAN Power Club members looked at Montana, then glanced around the room to see the reactions to Montana's painful childhood story.

"That just goes to show us that we all have baggage and that's the image we as a club should project. Each has risen out of the ashes of despair and we are now in positions to help others," said Anita."

"I know I'm glad to have y'all around for me to lean on sometimes when I'm feeling blue. Sometimes life gets heavy for me and I'm glad to know that I have friends like you. We've been around a long time," said Montana.

"Yeah, we're here for each other. That's the beauty of the club," said Rebekah. "But I sure do miss Mamie. I used to call her all the time and talk about my troubles. All of you are my homies, but Mamie was my part-nah. She used to keep me straight. Y'all know how I can screw up sometimes. Mamie used to keep me in check and she never judged me. Plus, I never did get the chance to taste her lemon chicken recipe."

"I know what you mean," said Anita. "Sometimes, I just can't believe she's gone. I pick up the telephone and start to call her, then I remember that she's not there anymore. It's hard."

"Yeah, nobody could enjoy a good joke like my girl, Mamie," said Tracy.

"You mean, nobody could enjoy dirty jokes like you and Mamie," laughed Rebekah.

The other members started laughing in agreement with Rebekah. Some of them had tears in their eyes, thinking about Mamie.

"Come on now," said Montana. "Let's not spoil the meeting. Mamie wouldn't want that. This club was her baby."

"Montana is right. Let's talk about something else," said Rebekah.

"I agree, said Tracy. You know this is the power of WOMAN Power, all of us have problems and mountains in our lives that we have overcome. When we share our pain and realize that we have all struggled, it gives us the impetus to go on. I'm glad we can share and bond with each other. I know that whatever I have experienced or if I'm still experiencing difficulties, I have a place where I can go and talk to another sister who not only understands my pain, but doesn't judge me for the mistakes I've made," said Gladys."

"That's exactly the reason we were formed," said Rebekah. They exchanged stories and jokes until the meeting adjourned.

****

Gladys
Rebekah shared with the women how she had explained her dream of WOMAN Power to Gladys and it didn't take any persuasion for Gladys to grab the vision. At the next meeting, Gladys shared her story with the women.

"After listening to my sister, Nadine at the last meeting, I'm glad there are women out here such as the women in WOMAN Power.

I have baggage in my past just like everybody else, and I think my baggage is special just like everybody else does," said Gladys.

"I keep thinking that I'm the only one with all the junk in my past, but God is showing me that everyone has a cross to bear," said Rebekah.

Gladys talked about how she became a high school principal. She also discussed her mixed marriage. She said she and her husband still dealt with racial slurs from both races.

"When I met Walter, I was dating a colored man. Walter was in law school at the University of Baltimore and I met him at a jazz show on campus. We went to church together on our first date," Gladys said. "After we started dating, I didn't want to see anyone else. When we first started dating, colored women accepted us as a couple and treated Walter quite pleasantly. However, white women shunned us both. Walter and I lived together for two years before we got married. He loves the color of my skin. He says it looks like velvet and he calls me his chocolate candy.

"When we first started living together, each week we listed the bills we owed and I paid them with our combined salaries. From the money left over after bills, we each took personal spending money and put the rest into a joint savings account. The colored men on his job asked him why he let his woman handle the money in the family. He said, 'cause she buys whatever I need.'

"Each morning before I leave for work, he tells me that he loves me. When he takes a shower and the bathroom mirror is steamed up, he writes the words 'I love you,' on the mirror. We disagree with each other sometimes, but we haven't had any violent arguments. We've been married for thirty-five years and we've never gone to bed angry with each other. I'm his world and he's mine. When we were younger, some of his buddies tried to entice him to hang out with them. He refused and told them that he had everything he wanted and needed at home.

"Colored men used to get upset with me when they learned that I was dating a white man. They asked me, 'How could you sell us out?' I told them that I wasn't selling them out. I fell in love. I wasn't in love with a white man; I was in love with Walter, a man who was white. Colored men don't like to see a colored woman with a white man. I know it sounds strange, but his white male friends accepted me quicker than my colored male friends accepted him. They used to call us the 'zebra couple.'"

Gladys held out her arms so Rebekah could see.

"Look at me," she said. "My skin is dark. I wear my hair in a natural style. I have a big nose and I look like an African. There's no mistaking me for anything other than who I am. I don't pretend to be anything else. I'm proud of my African heritage and Walter respects that. When his white buddies ask him about me he says, 'I didn't fall in love with a Negro woman. I fell in love with Gladys.'

"Walter goes to a colored barber to get his hair cut. Most of our friends are colored. He likes to go to colored nightclubs with me, and he loves soul food. We've raised two beautiful children who are both professionals and doing well. Our children will probably have trouble with some people because they're mixed race, but there will always be someone who'll start trouble. That's the nature of people. But I don't mind, neither does Walter. We've been together so long, we believe that God put us together."

"Thanks for sharing," said Rebekah. We all have learned from you. I know you sure did help me when I first started teaching in the prison. I messed up with my private life, but that wasn't your fault."

"No, you were just hardheaded," kidded Tracy. "It's time to eat folks," she shouted and everyone decided to join her in the kitchen.

CHAPTER TWENTY-TWO
Anniversary Celebration

It was the tenth year anniversary of the WOMAN Power Club. The years passed quickly and Rebekah became a fine judge, dedicating her life to helping the underprivileged community and women. She hoped her dedication to helping others made up for her years of self-destruction.

She wanted to get to the restaurant early to make sure everything was perfect for the celebration activities. She pulled in front of the LaPierre Restaurant, parked her car, looked in the rearview mirror, and made sure her lipstick wasn't smeared from nervously moistening her lips while thinking about her trip to Mobile, Alabama. She stepped out of the car, smoothed her skirt, handed her car keys to the valet, and walked up the ramp, into the lobby, and to the registration desk.

"Please direct me to the room where the WOMAN Power Club is holding its reception this evening," she said to the woman behind the desk.

"Certainly, go down that hallway and the first room to your right is the Ambassador Room. It's being held in there," said the woman. Rebekah thanked her and walked in the direction she had pointed. She entered the beautifully decorated private room overlooking the Chesapeake Bay and saw that she was the first to arrive. She counted the chairs, making sure there were enough.

"We must have enough chairs. This reception is so special," she whispered to herself. She looked out the window at the spectacular view of the Bay.

The maitre d' entered the dining area.

"Good evening, ma'am," he said. "I am Andre, the maitre d'. Is everything to madam's satisfaction?"

He clasped his hands in front of him and slightly lowered his head, bowing from the waist.

"Everything is beautiful, Andre. Thanks for your help."

"You are quite welcome, ma'am. It is my pleasure. If you or your guests need anything, please do not hesitate to let Andre know," he said and continued to instruct the waiters and food servers as they entered the room.

Five tables were pulled together for the WOMAN Power Club members and their guests. Rebekah smiled and looked around the room at the pink and green table cloths with red and white flowers in white vases adorning the tables. Members of the club belonged to different sororities, some were Alpha Kappa Alpha (AKA) sorors and some were Delta sorors. AKA colors are pink and green and the logo is the ivy leaf — Rebekah was an AKA, Mamie was a Delta. The Delta's colors are red and white and their logo is an elephant with the trunk pointed upward. Rebekah grew ivy in pots inside her home, and she had a beautiful collection of over five hundred elephants in her home and office. Her friends often teased her calling her a "frustrated Delta."

Rebekah touched the picture of Mamie that stood in a chair at one of the tables. "We miss you, Mamie," she whispered and wiped the tears from her eyes. "No, not today. I will not grieve today. Today will be a happy time," she said defiantly, half to herself and half out loud.

****

It was a beautiful Thursday evening in Baltimore. The sun was shining, a gentle breeze blowing, and not a cloud in the sky. All the members of WOMAN Power had gone through many obstacles in their lives. Because of the problems they encountered along the way to becoming successful in their chosen fields, they sometimes thought they would never survive. When they made it through the hard times, they looked back and wondered, how.

Rebekah thought, "When did I become my mother? When did I become someone to whom young adults say 'back in your day?'" But here she was, waiting for that noisy group of friends who stood bonded together over the years. She couldn't believe it — ten years of laughing together, crying together, with each other, for each other, and watching their families and themselves mature. Ten years of sharing secrets with good friends, sharing grief, sorrow, births, deaths, marriages, graduations, promotions, career changes, accomplishments, and just being there for each other.

They had watched each other's children grow from infants to become parents themselves. They had watched some members become grandmothers. They had attended each other's weddings and christenings. They had gone to each other's homes for backyard cookouts and pool parties. It was ten years of memories, of good times and difficult times. Even now, members of the WOMAN Power Club got together and shared a laugh about the good times the years brought to each of them.

They were a unique group of successful, independent women who had prospered against the odds. They were a diverse group of friends from different races and different ethnic backgrounds, coming together for a common cause, and not deterred by their differences. Instead, they chose to celebrate and magnify their sameness.

In ten years, Rebekah hadn't missed an annual celebration of the club. As one of the founders, she was also on the event planning committee. She was proud of how the organization had grown. She was also pleased that such a diverse group of women could work as a team for years to develop one common goal.

After Rebekah had been at the restaurant for about half an hour, Tracy walked in with her husband, David.

"Hello, honey," Tracy said as she hugged Rebekah. "I see we beat the others here. I just knew that Mama Anita would be the first one here, putting her final approval on everything."

They both laughed.

"Hi, David," Rebekah said as she hugged him. "Tracy sure keeps you looking good," she teased.

"Hello, Beautiful," said David hugging Rebekah. "I'm a big boy now. I can dress myself, thank you very much!" he said laughingly.

"Yeah, but I still select your clothes," kidded Tracy and gently nudged him with her elbow.

Over the next half hour the other members and their spouses began to arrive. Anita and her husband, Muhammad; Nadine and her husband, Stephen; Gladys and her husband Walter; Cynthia and her husband Marvin all arrived about the same time. Madge and Carole looked fabulous. Carole was now an attorney — tall, slender, fair-skinned and with reddish hair worn in a slick cut. Madge was now an engineer.

Each woman had taken a different route to this point in her life. That was why they had come together as a support group — offering the value of their wisdom, experience, finances, any other means they could muster — to help women realize that they didn't have to be products of their environment. Members of WOMAN Power often counseled other women who were suffering from low self-esteem, reminding them that they were important, created by God, and the measure of their success was not limited by anyone or anything other than themselves.

All the members of the club were older now, and much wiser. They certainly had some skeletons in their closets. But the message they came together to give to women is that it's not how you fall, but how you get up that matters. They never thought they would still be together after ten years. Each had cried many nights, hurt for many years, yet they also had a lot of laughter and sunshine in their lives.

They were proud of their record of community service. They had opened the doors of opportunity for hundreds of young women. Many young women, influenced and encouraged by members of the WOMAN Power Club, had become professionals in many fields, from business to education, medicine to law, entertainment to social work.

Rebekah didn't have time to stay for the entire celebration, she had a plane to catch. Her bags were in the trunk of her car, packed. She planned to leave the celebration early and go to the airport to fly to Mobile, Alabama, to attend a dedication ceremony in her mother's honor. She felt sad, thinking about Mamie and was depressed because she had to leave the celebration early. She was upset because she couldn't get Pete Waldon to change the dedication date, and she was apprehensive about returning to Mobile in the first place.

Some members brought guests with them. Rebekah had

Andre and his crew bring in more chairs and set up additional tables. She was glad they had chosen the room that allowed them to increase their count.

As each member and her spouse arrived, they greeted each other. The waiters and waitresses served the appetizers and beverages. After they finished toasting the occasion and congratulating each other on the organization's ten-year history of outstanding service, they acknowledged the successes of some of the women they met over the years. Reverend Berneda stood up and tapped a spoon against her drinking glass to get everyone's attention.

"Attention everyone, please take your seats. We want to go on with the program. We didn't prepare a formal program; we wanted this occasion to be fun and full of ten years of memories. Someone please turn off the lights," she said.

The room went dim and Reverend Berneda told Pastor Wendall to turn on the projector. There, on the screen, were pictures of the club members at various functions. One was a picture of the women in Gladys' backyard at one of her famous barbecues. Walter always swore that he could cook better than Montana's husband, Bruce. There were pictures of Mamie trying to roller skate, pictures of the women and their families, and pictures of the original four founders of WOMAN Power: Rebekah, Anita, Mamie, and Berneda. There were pictures of Rebekah being sworn in as a sitting judge of the District Court, with Lola assisting Rebekah with her robe. Lola had returned to Baltimore to attend Rebekah's swearing in ceremony. There were pictures of Bruce and his group, singing at affairs.

When they finished showing pictures, the lights were turned back on. They all applauded the films and shouted for Rebekah to make a speech. "A speech? No one told me to be prepared to speak. I helped coordinate this event and no one said anything about me speaking," she protested.

"Well, we're telling you now, Your Honor. As the founder of this magnificent organization, we'd be mighty proud to hear from you," teased Gladys.

Everyone applauded.

"That's right," they shouted, "mighty proud." The room grew

quiet as Rebekah stood to speak.

"I still say, no one told me 'bout speaking," she pretended to pout as she continued, "I am indeed honored that all of you caught my dream and now, ten years later, we're still celebrating the realization of that dream. I wish Mamie and my mother could be with us today, but I'm sure they're looking down on us from heaven. I'm proud of all of you, my sisters and brothers and we owe the men our gratitude, without their support, we women have made it to this day in this organization. You women remember the nights we were down at the center until after midnight, working with a hard-headed sister, trying to get her to take control of her life, or working on fundraising events. The men would prepare dinner for the children, get them bathed and into bed 'cause they knew that you women would be late getting home. Plus, when our funds ran low during the lean years, the men chipped in and helped us pay our office rent. They have always been supportive of us. "Just being with positive-minded sisters made me grow into the woman who God meant me to be. I no longer regret yesterday because yesterday contributed to who I am today. I thank God for the pain, for now I understand suffering. I thank Him for rain because every once in a while, I need to be refreshed and energized. God has been good to us all and we're blessed to have each other. I'm sorry that I must leave early tonight but y'all know that my heart will be with you and my mind will be on you. Thank you so much, I love you and God Bless you all!"

The crowd gave her a standing ovation and all the women had tears in their eyes. After Rebekah finished speaking, she joined in a toast to Mamie's memory, hugged everybody, said her goodbyes and left for the airport.

A half hour later, while everyone was socializing, Gladys asked, "Why did Rebekah leave so early? She said her plane doesn't leave until 12:45 a.m., it's just 9:30 p.m. and it only takes twenty minutes to get to the airport from here."

"When I talked to her last night, she was depressed, but she tried to pretend that she wasn't. She was determined not to miss this celebration. She was apprehensive about going back to Mobile. Trying to confront the white part of her life is taking a toll on her. I offered to go to Mobile with her, but she said she'd be all right," said Anita.

Tracy and Anita exchanged glances.

"Get the car keys, Tracy. You said Rebekah sounded depressed last night, and that sounds like trouble to me. We'll be right back," Anita said to the group. "Hold the fort until we return. I think our sister needs to feel the comfort of friends. Don't leave before we get back. Give us about an hour. We've rented this room until eleven o'clock, we'll be back before then, and even if we're not, as many years as we've been coming here, they'd better not try to throw us out. Besides, it's a Thursday night. Who else is going to rent this room tonight? Come on Tracy," Anita said.

"Where're they going?" asked Bruce.

"They're going to the airport to cheer up Rebekah. She's dealing with some personal issues. We can't send our sister away feeling depressed," said Montana.

****

Rebekah sat alone in the airport in Baltimore, waiting for her plane to Alabama. Tracy and Anita walked inside looking for her.

"This is a huge place," said Tracy."

She and Anita went to the woman at the ticket counter.

"From what gate is the plane to Mobile, Alabama leaving?" Tracy asked.

The woman looked on her data screen and said, "Gate seven," and pointed straight ahead. "Go through those double doors. But you have to go through the metal detectors and scanners first," she said.

Anita and Tracy walked to the entrance of the passengers' waiting area, put their pocket books on the conveyor belt, took the keys from their pockets, laid them on the belt, walked through the metal detectors, picked up their belongings from the belt, and headed toward gate seven.

"There it is," said Anita, pointing to a sign that read, "Gate 7."

"I'm glad, 'cause my feet are killing me. If I'd known we'd

be running through an airport tonight, I'd have worn more comfortable shoes. The distance to gate seven seems like seven miles," complained Tracy.

"Stop complaining; remember, we're here to cheer up Rebekah," said Anita.

"I ain't complaining, I just said my feet hurt. You know they always hurt," said Tracy as she hobbled along trying to walk as if her feet didn't hurt, hoping no one would notice.

Anita tried hard not to laugh. She turned her head and giggled.

Tracy rolled her eyes at Anita, "Poot you," she said and waved her hand as if to shoo Anita away.

"There she is!" said Anita, pointing to where Rebekah sat, staring into space.

They quietly tiptoed behind her and Anita said, "Penny for your thoughts."

Rebekah jumped, startled at the sound of Anita's voice. The three women laughed. Rebekah stood up they hugged each other, greeting each other as sisters.

"What are you doing here?" asked Rebekah, obviously pleased to see Anita and Tracy.

"Well, you looked kind of down when you left the restaurant and we just wanted to let you know that you're not alone. We're here for you, all of us. We're sisters, remember?" said Tracy. "Besides, Mama Anita said you needed some sisterly love; so when you left the celebration early, we decided, I mean, Mama Anita decided, to bring the cheering squad to you."

"'Mama Anita?' I beg your pardon," said Anita in mock indignation as she laughed and put her hands on her hips.

They all laughed.

"I'm glad y'all did come," said Rebekah.

"You hear that?" said Anita. "'Y'all did come,' if that ain't a countrified saying, I don't know what is. I told you she was country," she turned to Tracy and laughed.

Rebekah laughed, too.

"That's what we want to see, you laughing and looking

happy," said Anita.

"I was feeling down in the dumps, sitting here feeling sorry for myself and wishing I had a sister to talk to. I know that all of you are my sisters, but sometimes I get lonely for a biological sister who can share my family's problems. But you guys cared enough to leave the reception and come all the way out here just to be with me. I'm blessed," said Rebekah.

"You're darn tootin' you're blessed. Rebie baby, you know you're my girl," said Tracy as she put her arms around Rebekah and hugged her.

"You know you're my ace-boon-coon," said Anita.

"I'm your ace, but watch that 'coon' shit," joked Rebekah.

They all laughed.

The three women sat and talked a few moments. When they were satisfied that Rebekah would be alright, Anita and Tracy left to go back to the restaurant, promising to see Rebekah when she returned from Mobile.

****

While Anita and Tracy were at the airport with Rebekah, the crowd at the LaPierre Restaurant went on with the celebration. The husbands of the WOMAN Power members were bursting with a secret. They were dying to tell the women, but Walter, Gladys' husband, convinced them to wait until Tracy and Anita returned.

Although they were having a grand time remembering the past and enjoying how they had grown through the hard times, the memories turned bittersweet when they looked at the two empty chairs of Rebekah and Mamie. Mamie's death forced them to face their own mortality.

"Well," said Montana as she lifted her glass, "here's to you, Rebekah. May you find your happiness. And here's to you Mamie, may you be pleasing God and may you be pleased with what we have done with your dream."

The mood of the group turned somber as they toasted their two friends. But the women wanted to enjoy their celebration. Montana could always tell good jokes, so she decided to liven up the group. She told a joke about a salesman who stuttered. The women stopped focusing on the two empty chairs and began to laugh at her jokes.

As they laughed and enjoyed the celebration, Reverend Berneda's stomach started hurting from laughing so hard. Nadine laughed until she cried and her mascara ran down her face, leaving tracks in her makeup. Montana laughed at Gladys because, as usual, Gladys was trying to act sophisticated, but the rest of the crowd wouldn't let her. They all were getting tipsy on the champagne the waiter kept pouring into their glasses.

After Mamie's death, her husband, Andy, had maintained contact with the club members. Minutes after Rebekah left for the airport, Andy arrived at the restaurant. Reverend Berneda saw him before the others did. She squealed with joy, "Andy! There's Andy everybody! Hi, Andy, I'm so glad to see you," said Berneda getting up to hug Andy.

He hugged Berneda, waved to everybody, shook the hands of some of the men, gave some a brotherly hug. "Hey, everybody, y'all ladies still look good," he said. "I received a flyer about WOMAN Power's tenth anniversary celebration and y'all know I had to come. If I didn't, Mamie's spirit would've visited me tonight and worried me to death."

"You're right, 'cause this was her baby," said Berneda.

They all laughed.

He looked around the room and said, "Where's Rebekah? This is her baby, too. I know she's here unless she's sick," said Andy.

"You just missed her," said Montana.

"Why did she leave so soon?" asked Andy.

"She's going to Alabama to officiate at a dedication in her mother's honor. You know she's a judge now," said Montana.

"I heard. It's been on the news. Mamie would be so proud," said Andy.

"Tracy and Anita went to the airport to cheer her up. They'll be returning soon," said Montana.

"Cheer her up? What's that about?" Andy asked, obviously

concerned about Rebekah.

"It's a long story," said Montana.

The waitress brought in a cake with the words "Happy Anniversary" and all the members' names, including Mamie's, were written on it. Andy looked sad when he saw the cake. They thought he was probably thinking about Mamie. He and Mamie had met in law school, had fallen in love and married. They never had any children.

Then a voice said, "Hello, I hope I'm not too late. I got stuck in traffic." To the men seated with their mouths open, the woman said, "I'm Dakota; Dakota Dane."

"I forgot to tell everybody that my husband's new law partner was going to join us," said Gladys. "Everybody, this is Dakota. She just moved to Baltimore."

"Hello," Dakota said again. "I've heard a lot of good things about the WOMAN Power Club. I'm glad to meet you at last."

Andy turned around, startled by the young woman's voice. It was the sweetest voice he had heard in years. To him, it sounded like soft wind blowing through musical wind chimes. It was Mamie's voice.

Gladys laughed at the expression on Andy's face. "I knew you'd react like that when you heard her voice. As soon as I met her and heard her speak, I told her she sounded just like one of my best friends whom we lost a couple of years ago. It's uncanny," she said, then she introduced her to Andy. "Dakota, this is my friend, Andy."

Andy extended his hand, "Hello, friend," he said. "God sent an angel. That's what I'll call you, Angel."

"Ooh, watch out, Andy is moving fast," teased Reverend Wendall. "I think Andy has more than friendship on his mind."

The group laughed and began to tease the blushing Andy.

"Well," said Gladys, pleased with herself, "I think we're going to have a good time tonight."

"Now wait a minute. Don't I have a part in this? I'm new in Baltimore. I don't know anyone here. Andy, do you have references?" Dakota teased.

"Ooh, I think the lady is saying watch out!" kidded Bruce.

"It's okay, I can handle it," said Andy and the men started giving thumbs up and laughing.

Dakota was thirty-eight years old, five feet five inches tall, weighed 110 pounds, and had dark eyes. She was an attractive woman with her shoulder length hair was pulled back from her face.

****

Tracy and Anita returned from the airport. They hugged Andy, glad to see him.

"How's Rebekah?" asked Gladys. Did you tell her some dirty jokes to liven her up?"

"We wanted to, but she wasn't in the mood," kidded Anita. "She's feeling down in the dumps. She didn't want to leave the celebration early and she doesn't want to go to Alabama alone after so many years, especially after the way things happened with her mother's death, but she's a trooper. She'll be all right."

"Hey, Andy!" said Tracy. "I'm glad to see you." she looked at Dakota and said, "Is this your new lady friend?"

"This is Dakota, Walter's new law partner," said Gladys.

"Hello, Tracy," said Dakota extending her had to shake Tracy's hand, "Nice to meet you."

They made small talk and when Tracy got Gladys alone she said, "You never said anything about Walter going into private practice with a partner, especially with such an attractive partner."

"I know, girl, it took me by surprise too. Walter and I usually talk things over before either of us makes a decision that will affect us both. But this time, he just announced this decision to me, and I must say, I'm pissed!"

"There's no need for worrying," said Tracy, trying to cheer up her friend. "You know Walter loves you and would never do anything to hurt you."

"I'm not worried, I'm just concerned. Oh well, we'll address this later. Right now I want to enjoy myself."

Gladys didn't want to admit that she was worried about Walter's unusual behavior. Why hadn't he discussed his plans with her as he had done over the years? She shook her head to erase the thought from her mind, forced a smile and joined the festivities. In the meantime, Walter looked at Gladys, knowing that she was aggravated with him. He hugged her in an attempt to reassure her of his love.

"Okay, it's time to let the cat out of the bag," Walter whispered to Bruce.

Bruce lightly tapped his drinking glass with his spoon to get everyone's attention. When they got quiet and, with a smirk on his face, he said, "We men have a surprise for you women. I could hardly keep the secret. Had I told my wife she would've let the cat out the bag, I was determined that this would be a surprise. So I didn't tell anyone except the men. We were waiting for Anita and Tracy to return from the airport before we told the secret, and it's been killing me to keep it."

The women started talking at once, teasing Bruce about his comments.

"Are you saying that men are the only ones who can keep a secret?" asked Gladys. "Are you saying that women can't keep a secret? I beg your pardon," she jokingly said.

"Uh-oh," said Anita's husband, Muhammad, grinning. "I think you've started something, brother. You got this all to yourself."

"Will you all please be quiet? I want to know what the secret is," said Anita, anxious to hear.

"Me too, what's the secret?" said Berneda.

"The secret is, we'll be leaving tomorrow, flying to Mobile, Alabama, to be there when Rebekah dedicates the burn center to her mother. I'm not saying that women can't keep a secret," Bruce laughed, "All I'm saying is that we didn't want Rebekah to know about it, so we men made all the arrangements. Mr. Goldstein is helping with the expenses."

The women started screaming, talking all at once, asking questions, hugging each other.

Stewart Goldstein still felt that his family owed Rebekah a debt they could never repay.

"Stewart read the article in the News American paper about the WOMAN Power Club's tenth year celebration. He wanted to make the celebration special, so he contacted me at the radio station. I contacted Rebekah's secretary, Rochelle. She contacted Lola Jackson. Lola contacted Pete Waldon. Hotel reservations have already been made and here are the airplane tickets," said Bruce as he proudly held up the tickets.

The women started laughing, crying, cheering, and hugging each other. They pretended to be angry because the men kept a secret from them, but they were too thrilled to really be angry. Instead of feeling sadness because Mamie was dead and Rebekah wasn't there, they were excited about going to Mobile and surprising Rebekah. She had always boasted that no one could keep anything from her. They were enjoying the thought of surprising her.

"Are you serious? You mean we're actually going to Alabama?" said Cynthia, excited about the thought but still a little apprehensive about believing it.

"Yes," said Marvin. "We are going to Mobile tomorrow. That's why we asked you to schedule the celebration on a Thursday night this year. We need to leave early tomorrow, the dedication ceremony in Mobile is Saturday."

"I don't believe you kept a secret," Nadine said to her husband Stephen. She pointed her finger at him and said, "This man can't keep a cold," then she laughed.

"Maybe not," said Stephen. "But I kept this secret." He laughed and hugged Nadine, who was pouting, pretending to be angry.

The men winked at each other. They had another surprise for the women but they weren't about to tell that one, yet.

"Are you going to Alabama, too?" Dakota asked Andy.

"No, I think I'll pass this time. I'd probably be a wet blanket anyway. I'd start missing Mamie and thinking about her and make everybody miserable. Are you going?"

"No, I'm going to stay here and hold the fort until Walter returns," said Dakota. "I've never met Rebekah but I've heard good things about her. Since I'm new in Baltimore and Walter and I will be operating our own law practice, I'm going to stay here, try to learn more about Maryland Law, and get adjusted to this new partnership."

"That's good," said Andy. "That means you'll be in town so maybe we can have dinner together some night. That is, if you're not already spoken for. And I can't see how someone as beautiful as you are not spoken for."

"No, I'm not spoken for," said Dakota. "I always wanted to go into private practice but I was afraid to take the risk. I worked as a law clerk for a federal judge for a year after I graduated from Howard University's Law School. Then I took the bar exam, passed that, worked in criminal law for about five years, and taught at Howard's law school for a few years. Walter is a friend of the judge for whom I used to work and he introduced us. Walter and I talked. I wanted to move to Maryland and the rest is history. What about you?"

"I'm a judge at the Circuit Court," he said. "My wife, Mamie, was also an attorney. It's incredible how much you remind me of her."

She laughed. "Just remember, my name is Dakota, not Mamie."

Noting that Andy and Dakota were engaged in a conversation that seemed to exclude the others, Gladys said, "Hey, you two. We want to be included in your conversation, too."

"Yeah, that's right," said Bruce. "What's going on? Are you smitten already, Andy? But I can't say that I blame you."

"I want to talk about how our trusted husbands kept a secret from us," said Tracy.

"Yeah, that's right," said Gladys.

"No, I want to talk about our trip," said Anita. "If we're planning on leaving tomorrow, I think we should be at home packing now."

"Let's hurry, finish our meal, go home and prepare for tomorrow. Oh, I just remembered. I can't go to Mobile. I have a wedding to perform tomorrow," said Berneda.

"We have a buyers' conference planned for tomorrow. We can't go either," Cynthia said to Montana.

"That's right," Montana said as she thought about the conference. "We can't go."

It was as if a light bulb had suddenly gone on in their head. In their merriment, they both had forgotten about the conference.

"You know what, we all have business affairs we need to

wrap up before we can leave. This is a rather short notice. As much as I would like to go, we can't just drop everything and leave," said Reverend Berneda.

"Yes, you can," said Reverend Wendall. "We men have taken care of everything. Berneda, the wedding will be handled by an associate pastor. The buyers' conference will be attended by Dakota. Montana and Cynthia, all the legal information you'll need to handle your new contract will be compiled by Dakota and will be available when you return. Everything is all settled."

"Wait a minute, the conference will be covered by Dakota?" said Cynthia, surprised.

"Yes," said Dakota. "I knew I wasn't going to Alabama. When Marvin and Walter were talking on the telephone trying to figure out how you could get away for a few days, I volunteered to help."

Cynthia got up from the table, went to where Dakota was sitting and hugged her. "This woman is going to be a great asset to WOMAN Power, I love her already," said Cynthia excited about the possibility of leaving her business for a few days of pleasure in the company of her friends.

"If everything is taken care of, I think we should take Anita's advice and go home and pack. We'll meet at the airport tomorrow morning. The plane leaves at 7 A.M.. We'll meet at 6:30. That'll give us time to check our luggage without being rushed," said Nadine.

They all agreed, finished eating and left for home.

CHAPTER TWENTY-THREE
Home Again

Rebekah's plane arrived at the Baltimore Washington International Airport. Tracy and Anita had left the airport and gone back to WOMAN Power's tenth anniversary celebration at the LaPierre Restaurant. Rebekah got on the plane, settled in the first-class section, and looked out the window. Her eyes filled with tears. How strange it seemed to return home without her mother there to meet her. It would never again be home for her, Rebekah thought. It was just the place where she was born forty-one years ago.

Rebekah had been confused about her race. She felt that she really didn't have a race. But, now she knew who she was. She was sorry it took so many years, so many tears, and so much pain to find out. Those were Rebekah's thoughts as she traveled back home, back to where it all began, back to Alabama, back to her roots.

As she sat daydreaming, Rebekah reflected on her life. She thought about the many roles she had played in life and the image she portrayed in different situations. In some circles they called her a bitch. Some people called her a lady. Some considered her a strong woman. Some people called her a friend. She had even been called a sweetheart and lover. Some people have called her boss, colleague, businesswoman, attorney, judge, and scholar. Regardless of what she had been called, there was no denying that each role she'd played had been a class act. But no one had called her wife or mother. Perhaps those titles would come, perhaps not. "I wonder what the future holds for me," she whispered to herself.

Rebekah wondered if any of her high school friends would be at the dedication. She whispered, "Imagine me, Rebekah Mosley, returning to Mobile, Alabama for the dedication of a hospital burn center in memory of the most beautiful woman who ever lived — my mother. And I never knew how beautiful she was until she was dead."

Rebekah thought about her mother and the last time she saw

her alive. She thought about the expression on Beulah's face when she denied knowing her. Judas, that's what I am, a Judas," she said angrily as she slipped into a pity-party-guilt-trip, got melancholy and started to shed tears.

The aisle seat next to her was empty. She was glad, she didn't want company. The flight attendant noticed Rebekah crying and asked, "Are you all right, ma'am? Can I do anything for you?"

Rebekah smiled, tears in her eyes. "No, I'm all right. I was just reminiscing. Thank you for asking," she said.

"If you need anything, just push that button," the attendant said and pointed to the call button. She smiled and walked away.

Rebekah turned her attention toward her thoughts. She could always get lost in her thoughts and often put them on paper. She thought to herself, "Perhaps that was one of Breeze's charms, he had great penmanship and creativeness." She looked out the window at the soft, fluffy clouds. She thought about the years gone by and the pain and happiness they had brought. She thought back to her childhood and remembered her mother, Beulah, and how much Beulah had loved her. Rebekah couldn't stop the tears, so she just let them flow. She closed her eyes.

Rebekah would have to change planes in Atlanta, Georgia. The flight from Baltimore to Atlanta would take an hour and thirty minutes. She would have a four hour layover in Atlanta. Rebekah took some old photographs from her purse. One was a picture of Donnie and her when they were in college, when they first met and were so much in love with each other. It had been over twenty years since she'd last seen him.

"Gosh, we made a beautiful couple. I should never have let him get away," she whispered as she gently ran her fingers over the pictures, caressing them with each touch, remembering the beautiful times gone by. For a moment, the thoughts of Donnie filled her mind. She thought about the way he loved her, so pure and honest — the promises they made — he had kept his, she had broken hers. "I wonder how life treated him," she said, tears falling into her lap.

The other picture was of a four-year-old Rebekah standing beside Beulah in their living room in Mobile. They were standing beside the Christmas tree where Rebekah was showing Beulah the doll Santa Claus had brought. Beulah had scrubbed office floors for two weeks to pay for that doll and when Rebekah saw it Christmas morning, she screamed with joy. When Beulah saw how happy Rebekah was, she thought that scrubbing floors to pay for the doll was all worthwhile.

"Mama, I'm sorry," Rebekah said softly, as she let her mind wander to Beulah's death.

****

Amy had kept in contact with Rebekah after Beulah's death. She had sent Rebekah copies of the investment portfolio showing how she and Pete had invested Beulah's insurance money. In one letter Amy said, "You'd be proud to know that your father is a judge. He took the oath yesterday at the State's Capital. He's Chief Justice of the State of Alabama."

Rebekah could feel Amy's pride in each word she read. Rebekah was proud of her father, too. She had sent him a congratulatory card. Rebekah thought it was ironic that she didn't want anything to do with her white father but she was following in his footsteps without even trying.

Now, she was on her way to Alabama, back to her roots. It had been over twenty years since she left. While she waited in Atlanta, she could think of nothing else but the dedication and how Mobile people would react to her. When the plane landed at the airport in Alabama, Rebekah was hesitant to get out of her seat. The flight attendant announced that everyone must deplane. Rebekah still didn't move. When all the passengers had left the plane, the flight attendant noticed that Rebekah was still sitting in her seat and she went to see if she could be of assistance.

"Are you sure you're all right, ma'am?" the attendant asked.

"Yes, I'm fine. I was thinking of a similar flight many years ago. Thank you for your concern."

"No problem, ma'am," the attendant said. "Let me help you with your luggage."

The flight attendant retrieved Rebekah's carry-on luggage from the overhead compartment and headed toward the door. Rebekah followed; her eyes red from crying.

"Watch your step, be careful as you leave, and enjoy your stay in Mobile," the attendant said.

Rebekah thanked the attendant, took her luggage, and left the plane. She walked through the long tunnel that led into the airport. There had been some changes since she was last in Mobile. The airport wasn't in the same location.

She wondered what she was supposed to call Pete. She certainly couldn't call him Daddy. She smiled as she thought about the gossip and the shocked faces of the citizens of Mobile when they learned that Judge Peter Waldon was the father of a Negro daughter.

Rebekah walked through the airport, admiring the shops and the newness of the five-year-old airport. Signs along the way guided her to the lower level where the baggage claim area was located. Passengers who left the plane before she did had already claimed their luggage. Rebekah's luggage was still riding around on the conveyer belt. When it came back around, she took it off, got a cart, put her luggage on it and pushed the cart and luggage outside to get a taxi. The night air was crisp and fresh, just as she remembered.

"Can I get you a taxi, ma'am?" the airport attendant asked.

"Yes, please," Rebekah answered.

Just as Rebekah said, "Yes," she saw a white man dressed in a chauffeur's uniform holding a sign with her name on it. Puzzled, she went to the man and said, "I'm Rebekah Mosley."

"Yes, ma'am. Right this way, please. The car is waiting for you. I'll get your luggage," the man said.

"Waiting for me? Where are we going?" asked Rebekah.

"I have instructions to take you wherever you wish to go, ma'am," but your reservations are with the Tivoli Hotel. Rebekah smiled. Wherever I wish to go, she mused.

The Tivoli was a new hotel in Mobile. Before she left Baltimore, Rebekah had received a call from Rene Green, the woman who coordinated the dedication ceremony. Rebekah was apprehensive about returning to Mobile. She thought coming back home would be too emotionally painful for her. The day after Rebekah received the telephone call from Rene Green, she also received a call from Pete asking her if she was coming to Mobile for the dedication. Rebekah hesitated before giving him her answer. Finally, after thinking about the great tribute it would be to her mother's memory, and to the Black community of Mobile, Alabama, she decided to return.

"When you return, Amy and I will be delighted if you stay with us. After all, I am your father," he had said.

"I'll think about it and let you know," Rebekah said.

But she didn't let him know. After all the years, Rebekah was still uncomfortable with the thought of Pete being her father. She realized that not knowing he was her father wasn't his fault. He hadn't known either. Still, it would take some time for her to become accustomed to recognizing him as her father. She also didn't tell him that she, too, was a judge.

When Rebekah hadn't agreed to stay with Amy and Pete, he interpreted her silence to mean no. He didn't mention it again.

"Take me to the hotel, please," she said to the driver.

"Yes, ma'am. The Tivoli Hotel is the newest and the finest in town. You made an excellent choice."

Rebekah didn't tell him that her father had made reservations for her. The driver took Rebekah's luggage from the cart and guided her toward a long, black limousine waiting at the curb. He held the door open for her to get in. As she entered, she smiled, thinking of the years Beulah spent scrubbing floors at the Panmora Ritz Hotel. As she remembered Beulah's last ride through Mobile to the cemetery in a limousine, tears rolled down her cheeks.

The driver looked in the rearview mirror and saw Rebekah crying. "Is there anything I can do, ma'am?" he asked.

"No, I'm just tired. I'll be all right after I get a few hours rest." It was early Friday morning. Rebekah had been traveling all night. The dedication ceremony wasn't until the next day, Saturday. She would have plenty of time to rest and do some sightseeing before she was expected at the dedication.

The limousine pulled into the driveway of the Tivoli Hotel. When Rebekah lived in Mobile, the Panmora Ritz was the best hotel in

Mobile. But the new Tivoli Hotel was by far the most impressive.

"Wow, things sho' done changed." Rebekah giggled as she remembered how Beulah used to mimic how white folks thought Southern colored folks were supposed to talk.

The limousine driver told Rebekah he would return to take her anywhere she wanted to go, or he would wait for her if she wanted to go someplace immediately. She decided she just wanted to have some time to herself.

Everything was so beautiful in the hotel: the elegance of the furniture in the lobby, the paintings on the walls, the thick carpeting on the floor, the marble steps leading into the lobby, and crystal chandeliers. She thought she recognized the area where the hotel stood but it had been so long ago. The bellhop took her luggage to the front desk. After she completed checking in, the front desk clerk gave Rebekah a room key and beckoned for the concierge to assist her with her luggage.

"Take Miss Mosley's luggage to the penthouse," said the desk clerk.

The concierge summoned a bellhop and gave him instructions where to take Rebekah's luggage. Rebekah followed the bellhop. When they got to the penthouse suite, with windows that opened onto a balcony overlooking the bay, she was sure she had seen that view before. Without unpacking her luggage, she ran to the elevator and went downstairs. She walked around the hotel grounds and looked at the scenery. Sure enough, it was the hill where she and her mother used to lie on the grass under the stars.

Rebekah sat on the grass and reminisced. She and Beulah used to come to that hill, lie in the grass under the magnolia tree, listen to the birds singing, and talk about their dreams. Beulah dreamed that Rebekah would someday become a fine, respectable, intelligent, educated woman, driving around in big, chauffeur-driven fancy cars. Beulah would laugh and hug Rebekah. Rebekah would giggle, get up and prance around like she said she would do when she graduated from college. Beulah planned to be right there waiting for Rebekah, encouraging her as always. It was at times like this that they had discussed someday starting an organization to help troubled women.

Rebekah picked up a handful of sand, let it fall slowly through her fingers and began to weep.

"Nothing means anything to me anymore, Mama. Not without you here to share it with me. I'm the loneliest person in the world. I'm a success professionally, but I've made such a mess of my personal life," she whispered.

After all those years, she still grieved. She walked slowly back to the hotel, went to her two-bedroom suite and lay across the bed without taking off her clothes. Each bedroom had its own private bath, a fireplace in the master bedroom, a piano stood in the living room and a television set was in each room. The bedrooms overlooked the living room. There was a kitchen and a dining room; it was indeed a beautiful suite.

Rebekah walked to the French doors that opened onto the balcony. She stood on the balcony, sadly looking out across the hills of yellow daisies. She buried her face in her hands and wept. The hotel, the most luxurious in all of Alabama, was built on the spot where Beulah used to come to think, to be alone with her God and her daughter. When they built the hotel, they mercifully spared the tree that hung over the banks.

Rebekah looked across the parking lot at the field of daisies where she played, running from her dog, Peggy. Unable to sleep, she went back outside, walked across the parking lot and through the neatly cut grass and hills of yellow daisies.

She returned to the hotel and walked through the lobby, heading back to her suite. She passed newsstands with her picture on the front of the local newspapers. She hadn't noticed the newspapers when she was out looking around the hotel the first time. Local talk show hosts and radio and television personalities were focusing on the return of a famous "hometown girl who had become a prominent judge."

"Well, I guess the whole city knows I'm a judge. It won't be a surprise to my father after all," she whispered to herself.

She hadn't seen the new hospital. She didn't know where it was located. She figured the hospital would be a small building on the South Side, where it served mostly colored people. Nevertheless, she was going to make them sit up and take notice of her because she was representing Beulah Mosley.

Pete Waldon and Stewart Goldstein had donated money, helped to raise additional funds, helped to get government grants and built one of the finest burn centers in the country. Lola was instrumental in helping Stewart and Pete get together. They worked on the project for over a year without Rebekah's knowledge. When Rebekah left Mobile over twenty years ago, she vowed never to return; therefore, they had to be innovative to get her there for the dedication. After Beulah's funeral, Pete and Donnie developed a friendship and kept in contact with each other over the years. After college, Donnie went to medical school and became a plastic surgeon, a burn specialist. After spending years working in Africa, he returned to Mobile, Alabama, to help poor people, especially Blacks, get the medical treatment that wasn't available to them. He had been so moved by the turnout of people at Beulah's funeral, he had made a vow that he would someday return, and he kept his promise.

Pete wrote to Donnie about his dream of a burn center with all modern technology — the best that money could buy. He told Donnie he couldn't think of any doctor in the world more capable of being the medical director of the center than he. Donnie didn't hesitate to take Pete's offer. He had never stopped loving Rebekah and he had never married. Tamara often teased him, saying he was such a good doctor because he was married to his work. He dated several women over the years and almost got married once. But he didn't think he was ready to be a husband to another woman when he still dreamed of Rebekah. He believed that she was meant to be his wife, but he had almost given up hope of ever seeing her again. Through Tamara, he was informed of Rebekah's accomplishments over the years. When she walked across stage and received her law degree, he was there, sitting in the audience. He had never let her know that he was there. When she was handed her degree, he whispered, "Congratulations, baby. I love you," and he walked out of the auditorium.

Rebekah called room service and ordered a bowl of soup and a tuna salad sandwich. When the food was delivered, she paid the young man. When she had eaten, she took a hot bath and tried to sleep.

CHAPTER TWENTY-FOUR
The Best Is Yet To Come

The following morning, Rebekah had breakfast sent to her room. She couldn't understand why she wasn't able to contact Pete or Amy. She tried to call some of her high school friends but their numbers were changed or they had moved. She called Baltimore to speak with someone from WOMAN Power and couldn't reach anyone. "I guess everyone is out having a good time," Rebekah whispered, feeling sorry for herself.

She dressed in a three-piece, white and gold suit with matching shoes and bag. The front desk had called her suite to let her know the limousine had arrived. When she walked through the hotel lobby to the limousine, people turned to look at her as she passed by. She felt beautiful and she looked fabulous.

"Yeah, this is Beulah Mosley's daughter," she whispered, feeling proud.

Rebekah was nervous. The limousine drove out of the parking lot of the Tivoli Hotel, along the riverbank, doubled back, drove over the hill, through a winding road of daisies, and across the field of daisies that separated the Tivoli Hotel from the burn center. The driver had been instructed to drive so that his passenger wouldn't know how close the hospital was to the hotel. All of that was to be a surprise to Rebekah, and it was. The window shades in the limousine were supposed to remain closed until they reached their destination.

Rebekah remarked to the driver about the shades being closed. She said she wanted to look out the window at the scenery. The driver told her the window shades were stuck and they needed to be repaired. He said he had reported the broken shades to the limousine company. After they had been riding for approximately fifteen minutes, and the driver was confident that he had confused Rebekah about the distance of the dedication site from the Tivoli Hotel, he released the button and the shades opened. The driver acted surprised.

"Oh, ma'am, I finally got the shades to work. I apologize for the inconvenience," he said.

"A nice car like this and the window shades don't work," muttered Rebekah. But she wasn't going to let anything spoil her day.

When the limousine drove up the path to the burn center, she saw the hospital and gasped for breath. It was beautiful, with white columns, trees and flowers everywhere. The driver stopped in front of the building, she got out and stood looking at the magnificent building. She couldn't believe her eyes. Tears rolled down her cheeks. A crowd of people had already gathered and was waiting for her as if she were a celebrity. Flashbulbs started popping when someone recognized her.

"There she is! I saw her picture in the paper," someone shouted.

Standing in front of the crowd was Pete Waldon, whom she hadn't seen in over twenty years. He was still handsome with mixed grey hair.

"Hello, daughter," Pete said, tears glistening in his eyes. He walked toward Rebekah with outstretched arms, "You sure do favor your ol' man. You look fantastic!"

Rebekah hugged him. "Hello, yourself. You look fantastic, too," she said. "I've made so many mistakes. Some I can't erase, like lost years. But I'll spend the rest of my life trying. I'm sorry for not keeping in touch with you and Amy." Rebekah couldn't explain it but the moment she saw Pete, she felt homesick and was glad to be back in Mobile.

Pete hugged her and whispered, "Welcome home. We've all made mistakes, honey. We'll talk later. I'm so proud of you, Your Honor."

She grinned and said, "Thank *you*, Your Honor."

They both laughed.

He extended his arm for her to hold as he escorted her into the building. Through a crowd of cheering people and reporters they walked into the packed auditorium. The sound of Mobile's Bethel Baptist Church's choir reverberated off the walls. Reverend Berneda was standing on the stage. Beside her stood Sister Vickie, who sang at Beulah's funeral. Beside Vickie stood Reverend Ashford, a little older with more grey hair but still a handsome man. Beside him stood Amy Waldon, and Stewart Goldstein, and Lola stood on the end. When Rebekah saw them all on stage, she covered her mouth with her hands to stifle screams of joy, shock, and surprise. Tears rolled down her cheeks.

"I don't believe this," she said over and over as she walked down the aisle to the stage, arm-in-arm with Pete.

Pete assisted Rebekah as she mounted the steps to the stage. The crowd stood and cheered. She looked into the audience of smiling faces and was flabbergasted to see that the first two rows were filled with members of WOMAN Power, their spouses, and some women who had been helped by WOMAN Power. Rebekah gasped in disbelief.

Some of Rebekah's high school classmates, Beulah's friends, politicians, government officials, the media and practically the entire city were celebrating a great citizen of Mobile, Beulah Margaret Mosley, and most of them were at the dedication. The Governor had declared it "Beulah Margaret Mosley Day."

Rebekah took her seat and tried unsuccessfully to stop the tears. As speaker after speaker talked about how Beulah had touched their lives, Rebekah realized that she wasn't attending a dedication ceremony, she was attending a testimony to Beulah's life and she was so proud to be Beulah's daughter, she could hardly breathe.

Amy Waldon told the crowd how proud she was of her stepdaughter, Rebekah.

"I couldn't be more proud of her than if she were my own daughter. I know tongues will wag with gossip, but I'm asking Rebekah to stay in Mobile and manage the legal operations of this center," Amy said.

Before Rebekah could answer, a voice from the back of the auditorium said, "I'd like her to stay and help me manage my life."

Rebekah looked in the audience and saw Donnie walking down the aisle toward the stage. He was as tall and as handsome as ever. His hair was grey around the temples, but that made him look distinguished.

Rebekah was crying so hard she had completely ruined her makeup.

Amy smiled and said, "Rebekah, I'd like to introduce you to the director of the Beulah Margaret Mosley Burn Center, Doctor Donnie Albert Crawford."

"Donnie," she whispered, "Oh, Donnie."

Rebekah met him as he approached the steps leading onto the stage. She stood at the top of the steps and waited for him to ascend. As he walked closer to her, she looked into eyes she hadn't seen in over twenty years. They stood, staring at each other, not daring to speak, not knowing what to say, although they each had rehearsed that moment hundreds of times in their minds.

"Donnie, how long has it been?" she asked, tears running down her cheeks.

"A lifetime of years, and I've cried every one of'em. My heart has never stopped aching for you," he said, his voice trembling with emotion.

At that moment, Rebekah regretted the years she had wasted looking for what she already had.

"After all these years," said Rebekah. "You still look good."

"You look better," he said.

He tenderly embraced her, kissing away the tears on each cheek, and the years melted. The audience cheered, applauded, and some cried. Donnie held her as he tried to fight back his tears, but he couldn't control them.

"What are you doing here?" she asked.

"I'm following my love," he said. "A needle is no good without thread. I need you in my life; you are my thread." He held her face in his hands ever so gently and looked deeply into her eyes. "If you cannot live in my world, I'll live in yours. As long as we're together. I love you and I just found you again. I can't let you go. Not again. Not ever," he said.

People in the audience were standing, cheering Rebekah and Donnie. Donnie escorted Rebekah to where she had been sitting. Someone had placed an empty chair for him beside hers. The audience was still cheering.

Stewart Goldstein went to the podium, turned to Rebekah and said, "You wouldn't accept any money for giving my family and me back our most precious gift, our grandson. So we tried to figure out what we could do to show our appreciation, not only for your act of heroism, but because you did it without expecting anything in return, and because you dedicated your life to helping others without accepting money for your work. I know you could have earned an extremely lucrative salary in private practice but you chose to help other women free of charge. You are truly big in my sight."

Then he proceeded to tell the audience how Rebekah had saved his grandson's life at the risk of her own.

His grandson, now in his teens, took the microphone and directed his words to Rebekah. "You're my guardian angel. Thank you for saving my life." He hugged her and presented her with a basket of red and yellow roses. "Yellow is for friendship and red is for love," he said and the audience cheered and applauded.

Rebekah accepted the roses, tears streaming down her cheeks. She embraced him and kissed him on his cheek.

Someone in the audience shouted, "She's a chip off the block. Beulah would have done the same thing. I couldn't get her to accept any money either."

It was Mr. Camphor, a white man now in his eighties, whose family owned almost everything in the Asheville section of Mobile that the Waldons didn't own. He was standing and leaning on a cane, his hair as white as snow.

"My Martha was sick one year, and for three nights straight, Beulah stayed up all night nursing her through the fever. Beulah would then leave my house, go and scrub floors at the Panmora Ritz Hotel, leave there, go to the Waldon's house, cook and clean for them while running back and forth to her own house to check on Rebekah. Yet not one time did I hear her complain, and God knows the woman had to be tired. When Martha's fever broke three days later, I tried to pay Beulah, but she wouldn't accept any money. She said, 'God will pay me when I get to Glory. Just speak to me and my daughter when you pass us on the streets.'

"All Beulah wanted was respect for herself and Rebekah. So, Rebekah, I have in my hands the deed to the Panmora Ritz Hotel. Whatever you want to do with it, it's yours. Your mama earned it years ago." He handed her the deed and the audience cheered.

Rebekah nearly collapsed with joy, clapping her hands in excitement. She knew exactly what she would do with the hotel. For years she had heard Beulah talk about the need for a home for old people where they could live independently with care and dignity. Plus they need an organization such as WOMAN Power to help women..

"I'm going to turn it into a residential complex and women's center like my mother wanted. It will become the Beulah-Beatrice Mosley Senior Residential Complex and Women's Center, named after my two mothers," Rebekah told the audience.

Lola walked to the podium, took the microphone and turned to half face Rebekah.

"I'm willing to move to Mobile and be the director of the residential center, if you don't have anyone else in mind. It has been my dream all my life. I wish I could have met Beulah. You were blessed to be her daughter," Lola said.

Tears fell from Rebekah's eyes. Lola put her arms around her and hugged her.

"Yes!" Rebekah said when she could control her emotions. "We want you to be the director and engineer the renovations."

The audience cheered, Rebekah was still crying, and Lola helped her to her seat.

Mr. Camphor shouted from the audience, "I have something else to say."

Pete motioned for him to come on stage. He went to the steps leading to the stage and Pete assisted him up the steps. Mr. Camphor went to the podium and talked into the microphone.

"I rather suspected you would turn the hotel into a residential facility for senior citizens, and use some of the space for a women's center." said Mr. Camphor. "For years that's what Beulah said was needed in this town, so I took the liberty of contacting a construction company. They'll be contacting you to provide consulting services on the renovation of the project. I just wanted to personally present you with these documents and to give you the hug I wish I could give to Beulah."

He embraced Rebekah and Pete assisted him back down the steps to his seat. Mr. Camphor took a handkerchief from his pocket and wiped his eyes.

Pete Waldon went to the podium and said into the microphone. "We have another surprise for this magnificent group of women of WOMAN Power. In this world of separations, negative behaviors, crime, violence, and discrimination, when you see a group of people come together as one body to help all people, it's like a breath of fresh air. When I heard of the work this organization has been doing for over ten years to help other women, my heart filled with pride and joy. I'm proud to say I know them."

"I want to tell you a little story about the women of WOMAN Power," he said to the audience. "They help young women overcome personal barriers by giving their time, talent, and money. During the past ten years, they have helped hundreds of women of all races and from all walks of life, to get their lives back together and go on to become successes in various fields. Many of the women they helped were single parents, some were on welfare, some were using drugs, some were homeless, some were living a life of despair contemplating suicide, and some were prostitutes. The WOMAN Power women have helped these women realize that they are somebody, are worthwhile humans, and that they can achieve success. The women of WOMAN Power are positive role models for children and adults.

"One woman, Carrie McCray, said she was on a fast track to destruction when she heard about WOMAN Power. She was using drugs, drinking alcohol, and often ended up in homeless shelters after she used her rent money to buy drugs. When her children were taken from her and put into orphanages, she tried to commit suicide. Someone referred her to WOMAN Power and now her children are back with her. Her son, who kept going in and out of jail, started going to school and eventually graduated with honors. He's now a sophomore in college and plans to become an attorney. Carrie and her four children are here today to say how much they love all of you fantastic women. Carrie, will you and your family please stand?" said Pete.

An elegantly dressed woman stood and waved her hand to the crowd. Her children stood beside her and also waved. The audience gave them a standing ovation.

"There are other women here from Maryland who came to show their love and respect for Rebekah. Will those ladies please stand?" said Pete.

Lillian, Rose, Rochelle, and Kathleen stood and waved to the audience, tears streaming down their cheeks. The women of WOMAN Power also got misty-eyed, they were pleasantly surprised. "In fact, there are over fifty women in the audience who were helped by the women of WOMAN Power. Will those ladies please stand?" Pete said. Three rows of women and children stood. The audience gave them a standing ovation. All the women of WOMAN Power were in tears.

Bruce had formed a singing group, called Happidaze, with two friends, Rose, and himself. For over six months they had practiced in Bruce's basement.

They sang "You'll Never Walk Alone," with Rose and Bruce as lead singers and the audience cheered. Then they sang another of Beulah's favorites, "Amazing Grace," and dedicated it to Rebekah.

"You are terrific. You have a great future ahead of you," Pete said to the group.

"But, we're not finished yet. We have two more surprises. I love this. I love to give pleasant surprises," Pete said to the audience.

The audience laughed.

"I want to know about the two more surprises but I don't know if I can handle anymore," Rebekah said jokingly.

"Oh, yes, you can," Pete said. He turned to look at her without taking his mouth from the microphone. "First, I would like for you to start a similar organization, like WOMAN Power, here in Mobile. Second, we tried to come up with a way to show you the Goldstein's family's gratitude. We've been talking with the husbands of the WOMAN Power members and with a young, bright, attorney named Dakota Dane, who was hired by Stewart Goldstein. When the outreach center wasn't available or couldn't accommodate the number of people who registered for your seminars and workshops, you've had to rent additional space. Sometimes you've had to turn people away because there wasn't enough room for counseling sessions. Well, we're going to help you with that problem. Money has been placed in a trust fund to help you locate a suitable place to carry on your much needed work."

The women gasped, hugged each other and cried. Gladys now understood why Walter hadn't mentioned that he was considering going into private practice with another attorney. She playfully punched him in his side. He laughed and grabbed his side, pretending to be in pain.

"Why didn't you tell me?" whispered Gladys, pretending to be angry. "That's why Dakota was there. She was in on the surprise all along. I thought all kinds of things."

Walter smiled and shook his head. "How could I tell you without spoiling the surprise? I was determined that for once in my life, I would be able to say to you, 'Gotcha.'" He laughed and hugged her. "Anyway, I kind of liked the idea that after all these years, you still get jealous. You're cute when you're jealous."

"I wasn't jealous," Gladys kidded, trying to act indignant, "I was just concerned."

"Yeah, right, I saw the fire in your eyes. But, baby, as long as I live, there will never be anyone for me but you." He lovingly touched her nose with one finger. She giggled and rested her head on his shoulder.

The women of WOMAN Power hadn't counted on being surprised themselves. They thought they were traveling to Alabama to surprise Rebekah. It was indeed a blessed day.

"I have a surprise for the husbands of these fantastic women," said Pete. "We want you to start a male component of WOMAN Power. I'm sure if you need guidelines, the women will be glad to teach you."

"We sure will!" Montana shouted.

The audience laughed.

The men shook each other's hand. The women laughed and

hugged each other. They never dreamed that people had been watching their progress with the women they helped.

Pete turned to the Governor and said to the audience, "Governor Kohler, Governor of the Great State of Alabama, has something to say, so without further ado, I would like to introduce to some of you and present to most of you, Governor Fitzpatrick K. Kohler."

The audience applauded and the Governor went to the podium.

"I've been sitting here listening to person after person speak the praises of Beulah Mosley. I didn't have the pleasure of meeting her and that's my loss. I hope Rebekah will consider staying in Mobile and organizing a WOMAN Power Club in Alabama and be the Administrator of the burn center. We sure can use her legal mind. Whatever my office can do to help, all you have to do is let us know. I know you're a judge now and that's a prestigious position, but I think you have a higher calling. Besides, you can become a judge later if that's what you still want," said the Governor.

The crowd cheered, shouted, whistled, applauded, and gave Rebekah another standing ovation. The Governor hugged Rebekah and so did Pete, Lola, Amy, and Donnie.

Pete Waldon called Reverend Ashford to the podium to make a few remarks.

"This is a great day," said Reverend Ashford. " A great day to honor a great lady. I just want to say a few words about Beulah. I was privileged to have met and known her. Although her stay on earth wasn't as long as some of us would have liked it to be, she touched more lives in her brief years than some of us will touch in a lifetime. Because of Beulah, a burn center has been built here in the section of Mobile called Asheville. Because of Beulah, we have the best staff in the country to operate the burn center. Because of Beulah, Mobile is getting a new senior residential complex. Because of Beulah, that too will be operated by the best minds in the country. Because of Beulah, new friendships have developed. Because of Beulah, Mobile will become famous. Because of Beulah, thousands of lives will be improved. Because of Beulah, white folks and Negroes have come together for this great occasion."

He turned to face Rebekah, taking great efforts not to take his voice from the microphone.

"Rebekah, because of your mother, Beulah, Mobile is getting one of the best legal minds in the country as one of its new judges. Because of Beulah, all these blessings are here. I'd say she did her job well. Beulah said that she didn't want her death to be called a funeral, but a celebration of life. So don't mourn Beulah's death, celebrate her life and the legacy she left. God calls his flock home when it's time. It was your mother's time. You were left to carry on her work. You can't fill Beulah's shoes; they're not your size. Wear your own shoes and leave a trail."

Rebekah hugged Reverend Ashford and waved to the crowd as they cheered and gave another standing ovation.

"You look like your mother did before the fire. She was a pretty woman and so are you," said Amy as she hugged Rebekah.

Lola returned to the podium.

"I'm proud of this lady, called Rebekah," Lola said. "I feel as if I've found a four-leaf clover among a field of weeds. She has never disappointed me from the time I met her. She has gifts that she hasn't discovered yet. God has used her in a mighty way. She has done her family proud."

Lola turned to look at Rebekah.

"You don't have to be ashamed, or feel guilty about anything in your past. Everyone in this auditorium has skeletons in their closets. Some of them have so many skeletons that they're afraid to open the closet door, so many bones will fall out," said Lola.

The audience laughed and agreed with her, some shouting, "That's right!"

"So, go on with the work that God has for you to do," Lola continued. "Let Him use you to minister to others. You have come full circle. This place, this town, this community, amongst these people, is where you started and where God has brought you back. This is where you belong."

Lola extended her hand, inviting Rebekah to join her at the podium. Rebekah went to the podium, hugged Lola, while Donnie looked lovingly at her.

Rebekah saw Tamara sitting in the audience, holding a sign that read, "You're still my best friend."

With tears rolling down her cheeks, Rebekah blew Tamara a kiss. Tamara blew Rebekah a kiss back.

"Friends, family, colleagues," Rebekah began, her voice quivering with emotion. "I don't know what to say. This is indeed a surprise and a blessing. I had no idea this massive celebration was planned. I thought I would come to Mobile, dedicate a small building to Mama, and take the next plane out to Baltimore. Now I'm hearing that if I return to Baltimore, it will be to settle all my business ties, pack up my belongings, and return home to Mobile."

The audience applauded and shouted, "Welcome home! Welcome home!"

"I'm proud to call this place home. Members of my family are buried here." She turned to face Pete and Amy Waldon, "and members of my family still live here."

Amy waved at Rebekah. Pete stood and cupped his hands over his mouth and shouted to the audience, "That's right!"

The audience cheered.

She turned to look at Donnie and saw the love in his eyes. She felt the love of her father and the respect of her stepmother. She looked into the audience and saw respect and pride on the faces of women and men whom she proudly called friends, realizing they had traveled many miles and left many projects undone to be with her in this place at this time. It was as if a light had gone on in her head; she realized how blessed she really was.

"We're all so blessed," she said to the audience. She turned to the people sharing the stage with her and let her eyes move across each face. She stopped when she looked into Donnie's eyes and, with a trembling voice, said, "I'm blessed." She turned back to the audience and said, "I'm so honored that you took the time to spend this day with me to honor my mama. I know that it took a great deal of coordination to pull this event together, and to have present in the audience women who have succeeded against the odds, is spectacular. A simple 'thank you' sounds inadequate, but I do thank you all from the bottom of my heart. To my sisters whom WOMAN Power helped,

I'm so glad that you're not wasting time enjoying self-imposed pity parties. That's a lesson I had to learn the hard way.

"I was happy here in Mobile," Rebekah continued. "But I didn't know what happiness was until I lost it. Now, it's time to continue my mother's work. For so many people to come to honor a poor Negro woman from Alabama lets me know that she was one of the richest women I've ever known. She was rich with friends and love. For all of you to spend an entire day honoring my mother lets me know how blessed I am to be her daughter. I know that she's in Heaven smiling down on us, and I promise that for the rest of my life, I will remember the love that I feel from you today. I dedicate this center in the memory of the most beautiful woman I've ever had the privilege of knowing, to my mother, Beulah Margaret Mosley."

She cracked a bottle of nonalcoholic apple cider into a basin that had been provided for the dedication.

"I'm so touched by the love you continue to show for my mother. It seems that love doesn't know color, it just is. I was blessed to inherit an insurance policy from my mother. For personal reasons I refused to accept the money; it was invested for me by my father and stepmother. I think now is the time to use the money. I'm going to donate a portion of it to help the men form an organization like WOMAN Power. There are a lot of men who need help. I met some of them when I taught in prison."

The crowd applauded Rebekah for her generosity. Pete hugged Rebekah then walked to a table with a cloth draped over it and removed the cloth to expose a bust of Beulah with the following words etched on it: "Beauty is in the eye of the beholder."

"When we look upon the face of Beulah Margaret Mosley," Pete said, "We, the citizens of Mobile, behold beauty beyond comparison, the beauty of love, the beauty of truth, the beauty of righteousness, the beauty of forgiveness, and the beauty of godliness. Behold, the beauty of humankind. I hereby dedicate to Mobile, Alabama, this bust of a woman of beauty."

The audience gave the unveiling a standing ovation.

Pete said to the audience, "You've been giving so many standing ovations this morning, you might as well have stood during the entire ceremony."

Everyone laughed.

After the ceremony, Amy told the crowd that refreshments would be served in the dining room.

Everyone wanted to shake Rebekah's hand, to touch her. Someone asked her if she was going to stay in Mobile.

She looked at Pete and said, "I think so, if it's what my father wants."

He slowly walked to her and said, "Please, will you repeat what you just said."

Rebekah smiled, tears in her eyes. "If my father wants me to stay, I'll stay."

Tears filled Pete's eyes. He embraced his daughter. "Your father very much wants you to stay. Thank you. You've made me the happiest man in the world." In the microphone he said, "My daughter's father wants her to stay."

The audience laughed and applauded.

Rebekah learned that Stewart Goldstein had contacted Bruce, who contacted Lola, who contacted Pete. Together they raised money to help build the center. Mobile, especially the residents of Asheville, really put out a spread for the guests: fried chicken, steaks, baked ham, barbecued ribs, collard greens, cabbage, potato salad, macaroni and cheese, cole slaw, pickled peaches, pickled beets, sweet potato pies, apple pies, chocolate cakes, coconut cakes, candied yams, and hot homemade breads. The WOMAN Power women and their spouses had reserved seats in the dining room.

When Montana saw all the food she whistled. "Buffet style, yeah, I can get with that! This means I can go back and fill my plate as many times as I want to. I'm going to enjoy this Southern cooking." She laughed, looked at Bruce and said, "I don't want to hear a word about calories. I'll worry about that when we get back to Baltimore."

Bruce was already sampling the food.

"Don't bother me woman, can't you see I'm busy?" he teased. "Plus, there's more bounce to the ounce."

They both laughed.

When they had all eaten as much as they could, they walked

outside to enjoy the scenery. "You know, we make a great team," Reverend Wendall Barnes said to the husbands of the WOMAN Power women. "Since we've been challenged to open a men's center, we should talk about getting organized legally when we get back home."

The excitement mounted as they discussed the possibilities of a women's and men's center. The wives liked the idea of working with their husbands.

"We may need to discuss this more," said Madge. "Carole and I won't have a man representing us. Perhaps we need to talk about that."

"Yes, you do have a man representing you and Carole," said Reverend Wendall. "We all represent each other. We're a team. And as far as anything else goes, I won't ask you about your private, personal life if you don't ask me about mine."

Madge laughed, "That's a deal!"

"You know, we're celebrating but if you think about it, we're losing Rebekah. She'll be moving away from Baltimore and away from us," said Anita.

"It just means that we now have a friend in Mobile to visit," said Reverend Berneda.

Donnie put his arms around Rebekah and asked her to go for a walk with him.

"Ah, to be able to hold you again, to touch you again, to smell the fragrance of your perfume again, to be with you again," he said. "God has truly blessed me! I'd know your voice anywhere and I hear it everywhere — in the wind, in the rustle of the leaves on the trees. As the day turns into night, I hear your voice each time I sit still and listen to the silence. I hear you softly whisper in my ear 'I love you,' like you used to do when you were mine. I know today has held a lot of surprises and a lot of pressure for you. I just want to show you a little strip of land I bought where we can build our dream house."

He showed her a picture of beautiful green property about five miles up the shore, where Beulah's house once stood.

"Donnie, this can't be. This is where my mother and I used to live. She used to sit under that tree over there and spread her apron in her lap." Rebekah pointed to a giant oak tree, the same tree in the picture. "I laid my head in her lap, looked up at the stars and we pretended there were spaceships landing over the hill. We said one day we would get on the spaceships and travel all over the universe. We talked about one day opening a center to help women. Mama used to say that we would operate the center together. When we both got sleepy, we walked back home humming a tune that we made up as we walked. There are many beautiful things about my mother that I took for granted when she was alive. Mama carved our initials on that tree. I bet they're still there."

She ran to the tree. Sure enough, the initials B.M.M. and R. J.M. were on the tree. They stood for Beulah Margaret Mosley and Rebekah Jeanette Mosley.

"How did you know about this property?" she asked.

"Pete Waldon is a great resource person," Donnie said. "You have a lot of people in your corner. I told him that I wanted to live in Mobile in a place by the water and he did the rest."

Rebekah looked at Donnie, "I've never known a love as sweet as the love we shared," she said. "I've looked for it in so many wrong places."

"But now you're home," said Donnie.

"Yes, I'm finally home," Rebekah softly said with tears in her eyes, "and everything is so beautiful."

She looked at the water.

"Yes, 'beautiful,'" Donnie said, looking at her.

Realizing what he meant, Rebekah smiled and said, "No, silly, not me. I mean the water, the sand, this celebration, these people, everything is just beautiful!"

"So are you," said Donnie. "I fell in love with you over twenty years ago and nothing has changed. I never found anyone who could take your place in my heart. I don't care about the past years. We can't change them. I just care about our future and I want to spend my future with you."

"Donnie, you don't know what kind of life I've lived. I'm not the sweet little girl you met in college. There are some things you should know about me. I ...."

Donnie gently put his finger on her lips to silence her.

"Are you married?" he asked.

"No, but ...."

"Shh, are you in love with someone else?"

"No, but ...."

"Shh, do you still love me?"

"Yes, but ...."

He kissed her before she could say anything else.

"Then I don't need to know anything else, except, will you marry me?" he asked.

"Mama always said if I had a decision to make, the water was a place to relax and reflect on my answer. It's a beautiful day for a walk. I'm glad I don't have to walk alone."

"You never will again," said Donnie. "Rose sang that song especially for us."

"Well, let's have a soda and talk about it," Rebekah said as she held his hand, and rested her head on his shoulder.

They walked in the sand in their bare feet, toward a little stand that sold beverages and snowballs.

The leaves in the bushes rattled as the spirits of Beatrice and Beulah danced away, holding hands and humming.

"Hot dog! I didn't think they'd ever get back together. You think she's too old to get pregnant? Who's turn is it to be born and return to earth, mine or yours? I think I want to be a boy this time. Maybe we can come back as twins again. Hurry and get pregnant Rebekah, we're waiting," said the spirits of Beulah and Beatrice. But of course, Donnie and Rebekah couldn't hear them, or could they?

At the same time, Rebekah felt a gust of warm air engulf her body as if she had just walked inside a sauna. She thought she heard her mother's voice say, "Welcome home, baby girl. We've been waiting for you."

Rebekah stopped, looked puzzled and saw no one except Donnie and herself.

"Is anything wrong?" Donnie asked.

"Did you hear something," asked Rebekah.

"No, but are you sure you're okay, is anything wrong?" he asked again.

"Nah," she said. "Just my imagination playing tricks on me. Now about that cold soda."

"You didn't answer my question, will you marry me?" asked Donnie.

Somewhere in the past, Rebekah had read the following words, and as she and Donnie walked, her mind reflected on them: "Grow old with me, the best is yet to be, the last of life, for which the first was made."

"I'm still in love for the first time in my life," said Donnie.

"I'm in love for the last time," said Rebekah, "and the answer is 'yes' for always."

1.   Rebekah, the main character, (Donnie, Marty, Mike, Teddy Bear, Brian, Ken, Breeze).

2.   Mamie, an attorney and her husband Andy, also an attorney.

3.   Reverend Berneda and her husband Wendall, pastors of Ray of Hope Baptist Church.

4.   Nadine, a psychologist and her husband Stephen, an entrepreneur.

5.   Gladys, a high school principal and a Black woman married to Walter, a white man and an attorney.

6.   Montana, a white woman and an entrepreneur, married to Bruce, a white man and an ex-policeman.

7.   Anita, married to Muhammad, a Muslim and, an entrepreneur.

8.   Tracy and her husband David.

9.   Cynthia, an entrepreneur and, a white woman, married to Marvin, an accountant, and a Black man.

10.   Madge, an engineer, and her partner, Carole, an attorney, both are lesbians.

11.   Lola, is Rebekah's friend and mentor.

12.   Nicole, is Rebekah's friend from college with whom Rebekah moved to Boston.

The Founders of WOMAN Power

Rebekah
Anita
Mamie
Berneda

ORDER FORM
BeuMar PUBLISHING
The BeuMar Building
12 W. Montgomery Street
Baltimore, MD 21230
(410) 727-1558

"EYES OF THE BEHOLDER"	$18.00
Sales Tax 5%	$ 90
Shipping/Handling	$ 3.20
TOTAL	$22.10

PURCHASER INFORMATION

Name: _____

Reg, #: _____
     (Applies if incarcerated)
Address: _____

_____

City: _____ State: _____

Zip Code: _____

e-mail address _____

Quantity? _____

Credit Card # _____

_____ Exp. _____

For orders being shipped directly to prisons, $5.00 will be deducted from the sale price of the books.

"Eyes of the Beholder"	$13.00
Sales Tax 5%	$ .65
Shipping/Handling	$ 3.20
TOTAL	**$16.85**

Visa, MasterCard and Checks accepted
Also, to schedule book signings, appearances, lectures or
seminars by Barbara Robinson call (410) 727-1558
or e-mail barbara@selfpride.com

ORDER FORM
BeuMar PUBLISHING
The BeuMar Building
12 W. Montgomery Street
Baltimore, MD 21230
(410) 727-1558

"EYES OF THE BEHOLDER"	$18.00
Sales Tax 5%	$ 90
Shipping/Handling	$ 3.20
TOTAL	$22.10

PURCHASER INFORMATION

Name: _____

Reg, #: _____
(Applies if incarcerated)

Address: _____

_____

City: _____ State: _____

Zip Code: _____

e-mail address _____

Quantity? _____

Credit Card # _____

_____ Exp. _____

For orders being shipped directly to prisons, $5.00 will be deducted from the sale price of the books.

"Eyes of the Beholder"	$13.00
Sales Tax 5%	$ .65
Shipping/Handling	$ 3.20
TOTAL	**$16.85**

**Visa, MasterCard and Checks accepted
Also, to schedule book signings, appearances, lectures or seminars by Barbara Robinson call (410) 727-1558
or e-mail barbara@selfpride.com**